D0773294

GONE TOMORROW

▲

ALSO BY THE SAME AUTHOR

Eddie and the Cruisers

Biggest Elvis

Season for War

MacArthur's Ghost

The Day That I Die

Final Evan

The Edge of Paradise

Alma Mater

GONE TOMORROW

▲

P. F. KLUGE

THE OVERLOOK PRESS
Woodstock & New York

This edition first published in the United States in 2008 by
The Overlook Press, Peter Mayer Publishers, Inc.
Woodstock & New York

WOODSTOCK:
One Overlook Drive
Woodstock, NY 12498
www.overlookpress.com
[for individual orders, bulk and special sales, contact our Woodstock office]

NEW YORK:
141 Wooster Street
New York, NY 10012

Cataloging-in-Publication Data is available from the Library of Congress

Book design and type formatting by Bernard Schleifer
Manufactured in the United States of America
ISBN 978-1-59020-090-2
10 9 8 7 6 5 4 3 2 1

Every morning in Gambier, Ohio
I have coffee with friends.
This story is for them.

INTRODUCTION

▲

GEORGE CANARIS IS THE FIRST FACULTY MEMBER OF THIS college in half a century whose death merited an obituary in the *New York Times*. He was our best-known professor, one of those outsized characters who arrives in an obscure place and makes it his own. "A writer, a critic, a professor, a campus legend and a national figure, the very embodiment of the liberal arts," the *Times* obituary said. And a mystery. He was the author of two well-received novels and a book of essays, all published more than thirty years ago. Taken together, they were the beginnings of an impressive shelf to which, in all his years here in Ohio, he added nothing. "Compared to Faulkner and Dos Passos at the start of his career," the *Times* observed, "in the end he resembled Harper Lee."

To some of us on campus, that last remark seemed harsh and condescending: the what-have-you-done-for-me-lately school of criticism, unfair to George Canaris and to Harper Lee. They were both authors—one could add J.D. Salinger to the list—who left readers wanting more and whose accomplishments, even as they recede, remain fresh and new and magic. Of how many writers can this be said? Also, there was always a chance that something more would be coming from a small town in Alabama, a remote New England farm, a small college on a hill in central Ohio. There was that hope, tantalizing, like a phone call from an unlisted number. In Canaris' case, there were specific grounds for hope, his references to a novel underway, something major, years in the writing. He called it "The Beast." But, as time went by, inevitably, there was speculation that the book was a myth, a lie, a joke. Every passing year made skeptics more confident. But never certain.

At about 6 a.m., Monday, June 5, 2005, George Canaris awakened, made himself a cup of coffee and sat in a chair on the porch of his home, located at the base of the college hill, along the banks of a river that slowly winds its way towards union with the Mohican, the Walhonding, the Muskingum, the Ohio, the Mississippi. The place had belonged to Hiram Wright, another legendary professor, who died a few years before. Wearing a white, short-sleeved shirt, a pair of khaki pants and lightweight shoes, he set out on his morning walk. Spring takes its time coming to this part of Ohio. So does summer. It can snow in April here and roof-rattling hail sprays out of July thunderstorms. But this Saturday, we all later agreed, was the first day of summer: the smell of plowed fields and first-cut grass, the river flushed by rains, its banks covered with ferns and May apples and early wild flowers, dame's rocket and white trillium. It was a morning that promised more than a day, it promised a season, the only season we could really count on: summer. It's hard not to picture Canaris in a good mood, walking into an early fog that the sun would chase away by breakfast time.

With age, Canaris' walks had gotten shorter, just two or three miles, near the end. But he walked almost every day and once, in the alumni magazine, he conjectured how many miles he had covered: take, say, 300 days a year times an average—probably low—of six miles and multiply it by 35 years. That was twice around the world, almost. "An accomplishment or a reproach?" he wondered. "Never mind. It is the path I chose. My path."

His death was a hit-and-run accident. Canaris had walked out onto the road that ran by his house, turned onto the highway that leads to the bottom of the college hill, then turned right, on to a road that crosses the river and leads to a walking trail running from Mount Vernon to Danville. He never made it to the trail. Something came out of the fog, crashed into him and vanished. Canaris was hurled off the road, into a gravel parking lot near the river. A jogger found him there. Hit and run. Case closed. Granted, any untimely death in a small place generates gossip. When the small place is a college, the gossip becomes theory and the theories compete. Was it suicide? Murder? Or . . . disappointingly . . . an accident? And, in Canaris' case, all this conjecture reflected what people felt about Canaris' brilliant truncated career: they had to have more than they had, to know more than they knew.

▲

We do funerals nicely here, elegies and memorials, "celebrations of life," we call them, whether it's a ninety year old math professor in a nursing home or an unlucky student drunkenly falling into a snow bank or tumbling down an elevator shaft. We grieve sweetly and well.

I sat way in the back, wondering—the way everyone wonders—what they'd say about me when the time came. I arrived six years ago with a wife who was the provost of the college and with no job, no real job, of my own, just a few courses they threw my way as a courtesy to my wife. But, after an unforgivable first year, I found I liked the place, liked it more than my wife did. So now I had a job—visiting assistant professor in the English department—and no wife. It occurred to me, just then, that Canaris may have made room for me, that movement at one end of the tenure-track line would create an opening at the other end. That, I admitted, would please me. It wasn't what I came here wanting but it's what I wanted now. That "visiting professor" title became more grating every year.

One by one, at the front of the chapel, people talked about Carnaris, his charm, his modesty, his insight and erudition. But after a while, their testimonies cloyed. When people mourn, they mourn for themselves and there was something self-serving about these elegies, a jockeying for position in the deceased's esteem. I picture the man I'd known, though only slightly. Dispensing with the kind of novelistic portraiture that drives me crazy—"the suggestion of a Roman nose, flanked by off-mauve eyes slightly too close together,"—I can be concise. Think of a tall, shambling man, awkward but energetic and sharp-eyed. Impeccably polite. Yet you could sense a mix of moods and humors in him, public brightness, private darkness. Familiar and well-advertised as he was, no one could be sure they knew him.

"Excuse me," I heard someone say. I'd stopped attending to the ceremony, beyond guessing how much longer it would continue. A peculiar thing about college ceremonies: like elementary school arithmetic, like high school civics, like every lecture I've ever attended, you never lose your sense of time passing, the slow movement of hands on the clock. But that "excuse me" caught my attention, and the sight of an old man steadying himself as he arose to speak.

"My name is Erwin Kirsch," he said, pausing to catch his breath. "I shall introduce myself: I am George Canaris' oldest friend. My parents, like his, were among the German exiles who made their way to California, to work in Hollywood in the years before World War II. Canaris' father was a camera man, mine a screen writer. George and I grew up together near Santa Monica. Later I became his editor, who saw his three books into print. And I take pride that those books have never gone out of print. *Out On the Coast*, that wonderful novel about the Hollywood studio system in its prime, seen through a prism of humor and pain, has not been matched to this day. And *Here, Today*, recounting an exile's return to the ruined and rebuilding Germany of the 1950's is a search into the past, a search for meaning in history, all contained in the account of a three week visit to Berlin in 1954. And finally his collection of essays, *Friends Of My Youth*, which, some of you may recall, has a chapter about me . . ."

He had us now, the old man: all of us were straining to hear what this soft-voiced dapper gentleman might tell us about the professor we celebrated and advertised and never really knew. Kirsch was Jewish, and that was interesting as well. There were plenty smart people on campus, but none had quite that mixture of cockiness, neurosis and something resembling wisdom.

"Our friendship survived his fame," Kirsch continued and I thought it was great to have him here in the college chapel surrounded by dark wood and stained glass windows. "Fame and its aftermath. For years we met in the summer, and during your inexplicably protracted winter vacation, we traveled together to strenuous places. To Europe . . . which was one kind of strenuous, to Burma, Bangkok, Paraguay, which was also strenuous. Europe, though was always hardest. And Germany hardest of all . . ." Another pause, "Excuse me. I have only a little more to say . . ."

He stood quietly, as if he were reviewing what he had in mind. I looked at the others who had spoken, former students galore, some older faculty, the college provost and president. Did I detect some nervousness? A slight discomfiture, a fear of knowledge that was earlier, possibly better, than what they had?

"We talked about this place," Kirsch said, "where I come now to say goodbye to him. Though I prefer *auf wiedersehen*—see you again. May I confess that it puzzled me? That I never understood why he came here, this man who had the talent and ability and, frankly, enough money to go anywhere. Upon this point, I pressed him. All the world before him and . . . forgive me . . . he chose *Ohio*?"

That was comical, in a rueful way. Kirsch was like a Saul Bellow character, maybe like Bellow himself, wise man and wise guy, part ideas and angst, part street-smart hustle. And well dressed, a blue blazer, light blue shirt, yellow silk tie, sharp gray summer-weight slacks. The shoes escaped me, but loafers soft as bedroom slippers would have been my guess. I noticed that the nails on his pew-gripping fingers were manicured and polished.

"He loved this place," Kirsch said with a sigh. "Bafflingly. He thought he was fortunate to be here. I never could so much as dent that conviction. He said he was lucky and even . . . he used the word . . . 'blessed.' I had my doubts. It's incalculable, how much more we might have had from him, if he had made another choice. We'll never know. But know this . . ." He raised himself up a little, a bantam tenor straining for a high note. "You were fortunate to have him. You were the lucky ones. You were blessed . . ."

▲

This is Canaris' book not mine and the goal of this unavoidably long introduction is to let me get out of the way, make room for a better writer. But bear with me here. The evening after Canaris' memorial service I heard the unwelcome sound of a knock on my apartment door. Before my divorce I'd lived in style, in the provost's house, a handsome place which my wife made the college remodel: the maintenance guys still kid me about the phone she had them install above the bathtub faucets. When she left, I moved into a nondescript bungalow well away from the tours the college gives prospective students. I didn't entertain much but that evening I wasn't alone. I'd gotten to know Billy Hoover a few years ago. He was a campus cop and he drove me home from a college reception where I'd had too much to drink. He asked me to turn over my car keys. I liked the way he handled himself that night, which was way better than I handled myself in those days. We were friends now. On this night, we sat in comfortable silence, comparing things that were for sale, and the girls who were selling them, on two competing television shopping channels.

"Got a minute?" Willard Thrush asked from the doorway. "A little more than a minute, actually."

"At your disposal," I said, gesturing into a room that had a t.v., a couch, a writing table and Billy Hoover drinking a Honey Brown ale. Willard Thrush was a college development officer, a money-raiser. He was also a campus insider, a local wit and, at least half of the faculty would say, a major nuisance.

"Hey, Billy," Willard said. He acted tickled to find Billy there and there were some people who'd say that's just what it was, an act . . . a salesman's act. But the truth was Willard liked running into, rubbing up against people. "A stranger," he liked to say, "is just a person I haven't honked-off yet." His kiss-my-ass-attitude towards important donors and self-important faculty was famous.

"We need to talk," he said to me. Billy took the cue.

"I should be moving along," Billy said, a little reluctantly, his eyes on the t.v., where a pouty model lifted her dress so that another pouty model could apply liquid instant tan to a shapely but pale leg. Even Thrush got interested.

"How far up . . ." He stopped and shrugged.

"They do Brazilian waxing right here in town," Billy said.

"What's that?"

"They go right into the rain forest," Billy answered.

"God," Thrush replied.

"I'll go now," Billy said.

"Could you stay? You need to be here for this. I was going to call you."

"You still can." I saw what Billy was thinking: if you wanted me to be here, why *didn't* you call me?

"Give me a break, Billy," Willard said. "And . . . you . . ." He nodded my way. "Turn off the instant tans. We know how the story ends. Everybody has great sex." The t.v. was off. "Okay. George Canaris. How well did you . . . both of you . . . know him. Billy?

"I saw him around . . . walking the way he did . . ."

"Talk to him?"

"Sure. He was easy enough to talk to."

"About what?"

"Same things everybody talks about. We need rain and the deer are eating up our gardens and is it true that an Olive Garden restaurant is going in at the shopping center and how much did so and so sell their house for and how many years do you think the President will last . . ."

"Anything else?"

"He knew who I was. My name and where I lived and how I finished up my degree a couple of years ago. I liked that."

"Okay. How about you Mark? You must have known him, being in the English department . . ."

"Canaris was a sweet man, a gentleman, like everybody hopes to find in college. He was the one person in the department you could count on for a discussion of books and ideas. There's all this chat about who should we hire, who shouldn't we have hired, whether semester courses are better than full-year, how can we be expected to be scholars and teachers and community resources all at once. But these aren't conversations. These are cages that we walk around in . . ."

"Whoa, Buster . . ." Willard said, raising his hand.

"Not Canaris. You'd come across him in line at the post office. 'The snow is melting on *The Magic Mountain*,' he'd announce. 'It isn't what it used to be. It may be Heinrich's turn.' Well, that was the Mann brothers, Thomas and Heinrich, and I could follow. But another time it was Gwyn Griffin. Who ever heard of him? Or her? "The world is on the edge of forgetting him," Canaris says. "He wrote a great novel about World War II. *An Operational Necessity*." Well, I read it and he was right. He always had something he wanted me to read. We never had a drink or shared a meal but we were on some kind of wave length. But I never was inside his house . . ."

"That's exactly why I'm here," Willard said. He reached into his pants pocket and pulled out a set of keys he tossed me. "We'd like you to go into his house. Do a kind of inventory. Not the furniture or appliances, we'll take care of that. Your concern is papers . . . manuscripts . . . book manuscripts . . ."

"You mean . . . *the* book?"

"Could be," he answered, shrugging, "but I doubt it. My

guess is, someone writes a book, they'll do anything to get it in print. They'll sell it to anyone. And if anyone doesn't buy it, they'll give it away. Doubt if you'll find much. Still . . ."

"Where'd you get the keys?" Billy asked. "That house doesn't belong to us."

"Does now," Thrush said. "Canaris willed it to us a few years ago. The 'residue' of his estate. The usual conditions. He can stay there till he dies, gets a charitable tax break in the meantime. Know what we call it when someone like that dies?"

"No . . ."

"A realized bequest. Nice phrase, huh. Book title? Get right on it Mark, Time's a-wasting . . ."

Get right on it. That was Willard, honking me off. My own writing had slowed down, the last few years, I admit. Some of the promises I'd made to myself—and made aloud in the presence of others—hadn't been kept. There was something about this place, in the air and water, that overtook our keenest ambitions and our cuttingest edge.

"I'm just wondering," I said. "There was that fellow at the funeral. His friend from Los Angeles. His editor. Wouldn't he be the one to go through Canaris' papers? He seemed interested . . ."

"Our friend Mr. Kirsch," Willard acknowledged. "Interested? More than interested. Hungry. He came to me after the memorial service, wanted me to take him into the house. And he pointed out that he has an option to see the next manuscript . . . even if we've had six U.S. presidents since Canaris' last book."

"Well then . . ."

"Seems like old George took a couple hefty advances on that big book. Really snookered them, I guess. Anyway, I told him we'd be in touch, if we found anything. Then he asked, was there was anyone here able to *judge* what might be found. Got a little snooty. He's worldly, we're a bunch of dumb goobers . . ."

"Okay. So . . . why me?"

"You weren't my choice, Mark," he said. "You were his . . ."

"Canaris?"

"He named you his literary executor."

▲

After Thrush and Billy left, I sat there, at the mercy of a memory that had just now found me, an encounter with Canaris, waiting for a teller at the village bank. It turned out he never used an ATM in his life and after that he was off on something he thought I needed to read, another recommendation. "She gets read in high school," he said—before he mentioned the author's name—"but it's the wrong book at the wrong time and for the wrong reasons. And what a hash the critics have made of her! Was she a manly woman? A lesbian? A celibate? On and on. Trans-sexual, asexual, pan-sexual, uni-sexual, heterosexual? Absurd." Then he named the book, like someone opening an envelope at an awards show. "What a fine, heart-felt, beautiful novel. *The Professor's House*. Willa Cather. Read it."

▲

The house was a professor's house alright. You had it all: the river, the woods across the river and, some corn and soy fields leading up to the college hill, where a church steeple and dormitory tower poked through the oaks and pines, like submarine conning towers breaking the surface of the sea. We'd pulled into the driveway and I had my hand on the car door. The house was waiting, empty. We had the keys to enter and we had business inside. Still there was something about going into a dead man's place. Lingering presence, permanent absence, something like that.

"I don't like this," Billy said. "I mean I'll do it and all . . . but . . ."

"Don't like what?"

"The way houses outlive us. Creepy."

Everything was, as they say, just as he left it: the coffee cup on the table, the breakfast dishes in the sink, the dripping shower and the unmade bed, the laundry in the corner. Billy and I were here for a specific purpose: to search the house for manuscripts and seal it. But we did what we hoped someone might do for us. We straightened up, as if company were coming. We wiped the counter, washed the dishes, put out the garbage, tossed some shit-stained underwear into a laundry bag, doing a dead man a favor.

'Hey, Billy," I said when we were about done. "If something happens to me, I get run-over by the Frito-Lay delivery truck, say, I want you to be the one who goes into my house."

"Consider it done," he said. "You've got one less thing to worry about." He headed outside to check the windows and the back door, leaving me alone to do the job I was there for. It was one big room, actually, a bed and a dresser on the side near the river, a kitchen and dining table in back and a sofa and television on the other side of the room. Another table sat close to the front door, right behind a window, with a single chair tucked underneath, desk blotter and a cupful of ball point pens and at one side, a manual typewriter, Underwood Standard that smelled of oil and ink. When I touched it, it moved briskly and happily, like it welcomed my touch. All of the walls had bookshelves. There was no basement, no attic, no closet or compartments, just one room to search. I got up, carrying a clipboard I'd brought along, and began my work.

Canaris' books went on forever, history, fiction, some poetry, about what I expected. I guess there's a case for culling books periodically, thinning out the ones we'll never read again. Like me, Canaris was forced to buy new copies of the books he taught, because publishers changed the pagination from one edition to the next and, God knows, you had to be on the same page as your students or your class turned into a game of hide-and-go-seek . . . make it hide-and-go-sleep, with five students playing and twenty nodding off. So you'd read a book a dozen times, but never the same book. Along came new editions with reading guides for discussion groups: was King Lear a little too proud? If so, was it a father's pride or a king's? Is there anyone in your family like King Lear? There were papers tucked in some volumes, but they were syllabi, lecture notes, after-class reflections about what needed to be stressed or clarified in the next class. I knew the genre well and there was nothing in it for a literary executor.

I sat back down, heard Billy screwing and hammering away at the windows. Then he looked in and announced he was on a hardware store run: the back door needed a new lock. I had the place to myself then. The spookiness was gone now and I felt that I was visiting—paying my respects—to someone whose presence lingered. There's no way of knowing where life will take us, where death will find us. This bungalow on an Ohio river was far from the Hollywood he'd captured in his first novel or the shamed Germany of his second. But I could sense the pleasure he took in this place. And I could picture him in this easy chair. Maybe he wrote, maybe he didn't. But he must have considered the distances in his life, and the connections.

Next I headed to a green army-surplus-looking three drawer file cabinet near his writing table. The first drawer, a series of upright manila folders inside, was college contracts, medical records, checking account statements, home repair invoices, tax returns. I couldn't resist the tax returns. Pure nosiness on my part, I admit. The college paid Canaris $80,000 a per year, which was plenty for a single man with no particular vices that I knew of, living in a part of Ohio where you could crack a $100 bill and walk around most of the week. The books he'd written were hanging in there. *The Friends Of My Youth*, the runt of this small litter had been republished in a $50 "Collector's Edition" by a boutique publisher. Still, it earned $2,000 a year. And the two novels chunked in $10,000 each.

The middle drawer was richer: a half dozen photo albums, going back to the middle Europe his parents had fled, with sharply focused black and white scenes of family picnics, boulevard walks, mountain chalets. California came next. Early Polaroids, fading into sepia. It was interesting. The black-and-white photos were like new. They claimed their place. Remember this, they sternly insisted. The California snaps didn't last like that. They faded: that was then, this is now, now you see us, now you don't. There was no album for Ohio.

A drawer of files, a couple of scrapbooks: enough material, along with his books, his table and typewriter, for a shrine, a little museum. Indeed, the whole house might be a memorial to George Canaris, a kind of Walden pond cabin in Ohio. "But Thoreau wrote about that pond!" I could hear Willard Thrush right now. "What did our tiger Canaris do in his shack? What would the memorial be for? Or to? Coasting? Hey, that's a greatly overcrowded occupation around here already."

Now I moved to the third drawer, the bottom, where hard-boiled detectives keep pistols and hard-boiled editors keep whiskey bottles and hard-boiled reporters keep novel manuscripts. Canaris kept—or left—nothing. The drawer was empty. That stopped me. You had two drawers filled to overflowing: you had to yank them open. And one right below with nothing more than dust, a broken rubber band and a couple of paper-clips. Empty? Or emptied out? I went out to the front porch and came down the driveway, where Billy Hoover was parking behind Canaris' black Jeep Cherokee.

"Find anything yet?"

"No. If there's something in there, it might be tucked away someplace . . ."

"Could be there's nothing to find," Billy said.

"Sure. But then, why would he name me as literary executor?"

"Maybe he wanted you to find nothing. That's a discovery, alright. Maybe that was his personal message to you. Quit while you're ahead . . ."

"Sure. But I'm not ahead."

▲

Canaris' campus office was near but not in the English department, in an auxiliary building called Sharp Hall. It had been a faculty residence, back in the day. God knows, the bridge that was played, the drinking, the gossip, all of it on a campus that had been even smaller, even more of a company town than today's place. It must have been isolated and intense, back then. As the College grew, the maintenance crews converted bedrooms and parlors into offices and classrooms. A rough and ready makeover which meant that you went up the steps of a servant's entrance in to Canaris' office, which had once been a pantry. George Canaris: Stribling Professor of English. His name was on the door, trailed by his e-mail address, office hours and phone number. On the top step, just barely under the eaves, I found a box of papers from a fall semester class, graded and corrected by Canaris. Canaris' comments were detailed, forbearing, critical but encouraging, that mix of good cop/bad cop we offer here. He wrote in ink, a fountain pen from the looks of it, and there were about a dozen students who'd left without bothering to pick up his last written words to them. Little shits.

The office was all business, I saw right away, everything course-related. The file cabinet had grading sheets going back for years, end-of -year student evaluations. I winced at those. We grade students, and, at upwards of $120 thousand per diploma, they get to grade us back. Sometimes they're generous, often too generous, but there were always a couple who hated you. I had mine and—I saw at a glance—Canaris had his. For now, I didn't want to read this stuff: it was like going into his medicine cabinet.

College calendars, course catalogues, blue books, phone books: his estate. No paintings, no music, no photos, no personal touches of any kind. Sample textbooks—anthologies, mostly —were stacked in the corner, waiting for a book buyer to visit. Publishers ripped off students, professors ripped off publishers, re-selling free samples at half price.

"That's cash," Billy said, gesturing at the pile. "Five bucks, eight bucks a copy times . . . what . . . .a dozen books . . ."

"Let's go," I said. "There's nothing hiding here . . ."

Billy nodded and we returned to the college van. I half

expected him to drop me at home: tomorrow I'd go down on my hands and knees and search every inch of Canaris' house and that would be it. But Billy headed back there now. I didn't protest. I liked Canaris' place more than I liked my own.

"Give me ten minutes," Billy said, heading inside. I decided to loaf around outside. Inside, I'd be searching, outside I'd be thinking. I found the Professor's rocking chair, from which Canaris had looked out into the woods, across the river. It must have been interesting, the way it went from a putrid trickle in the summer to a torrent in spring, and the way the high water washed away the soil and eighty year old sycamores lost their grip on the river bank and toppled into the water. I got up, walked across the lawn, down to the river's edge. There were steps going down to the water, leading to stones, just below the surface, heading across. I slipped off my shoes and socks and stepped into the river. If Canaris had walked across here that last morning he'd be alive now, he'd have avoided the road. I couldn't help wondering about him. All day long, I'd been touching things that he had touched, his books, his clothing. I'd sat in his chairs, flushed his toilet, wondered what he had in mind for me. Or himself. It was easy to understand his coming here. A couple of years at a small, likeable college never hurt. But why had he stayed, letting time turn a world class author into a local character? And when I speculated about Canaris, I speculated about myself. I wasn't close to him, nowhere near it, yet I'd come here as a writer. And the years since then had complicated things, dealing with students, with colleagues, with an institution that nickel-and-dimed you to death with chores you couldn't refuse. Was what happened to Canaris happening to me? And, if so, was it such a bad thing?

"Come in here," Billy shouted from the porch. "I found something."

What he found was what was left behind in Canaris' refrigerator. He'd been gone a week, so there was no bread or fruit we could eat. We settled for the professor's Gorgonzola cheese, kalamata olives, prosciutto, pickles, rye crackers, Bavarian wheat beer, all arranged on the table. It felt odd, dining on what came out of a dead man's larder. But Billy was so buoyant and he carried me along, talking about what it was like growing up along the river, fishing and inner-tubing and getting stuck in an honest-to-god patch of quicksand a few miles downstream from where we sat. He told me about a trestle bridge that had a serious swimming hole right below it and a rope hanging down so that you could swing out over the water, Tarzan-style. Billy went deep around here.

"I made coffee," he announced, filling a couple of cups he'd pulled out of the cupboard. He brought out some chocolates and some dates and then, by god, a bottle of grappa that might have been left behind by Hiram Wright.

"Well thanks," I said, raising my glass. "Here's to the man who lived here."

"Amen," Billy said. "But I got something for you, Professor."

"Like a dinosaur frozen in ice . . ." he said. He pulled out a plastic bag, walked over and handed it to me. I saw a pile of pages inside. "On one condition, professor," he said. "You read it first, okay by me. I read it second. No matter what's in it. Deal?"

"Deal."

"Okay," he said. "Let's have dessert."

▲

That night, I read George Canaris' book. Holding those pages, which he had typed on a machine I'd touched, only deepened the sense of communion I'd had all day, sifting through his books and clothing, eating his cheese and olives, drinking his beer and whiskey. I'd been chosen to play a certain role, that was clear now. What it was, why I was chosen, I couldn't say. But Canaris had seen something in me—ambition, discontent, talent—that made him reach out. It's a quality some professors have—only the great ones and not all of them—that they see into you, they see the person that you're going to become, a person you might not even recognize. No wonder, then, that I didn't go home that night. I stayed at Canaris' place out on the porch, in his rocker, until the sun disappeared behind the hill. Then I went inside and sat in his chair. Later I stretched out on his bed, always reading. Sometimes I stepped outside, walked down to the river, glanced at the movement of a not quite full moon across the sky. Call it silly, but if there's something to hearing Wagner in Bayreuth or Puccini in Milan, there was something about reading Canaris' manuscript in his home. A couple times I pissed on the grass and it was lovely.

In the last hour of darkness I finished the manuscript—untitled—that Canaris had left behind for me. I was exhilarated, spending a night with a book, dusk to dawn. I did it often when I was a student. After that life got in the way, jobs and chores and other people. Blackmail, all of it. I watched closely, with the moon still shining, until I noticed a slight lightening in the darkness to the east, out beyond the college. It was tricky because there were college buildings, a new science quad, where the lights were on all the time. People complained that the nights weren't what they used to be, the darkness wasn't absolute, the moon and stars had been subtracted from. Still, dawn came, and it was hard not to feel that I had the world to myself out here.

▲

Some things you need to know. George Canaris was born to an ethnic German father, Max Canaris, and a Jewish-German mother, Emma Stern, in 1938 in Karlsbad, a famous thermal spa in what was then—and is now—Czech territory. Then, however, it was part of the Sudentenland, a German enclave which—as a result of the Munich agreement—was soon to be incorporated into Hitler's Reich. The turmoil associated with that annexation and the events of Kristallnacht in November 1938 made the infant Canaris a refugee from a place he never knew. His parents escaped via Lisbon to Mexico and proceeded from there to Los

Angeles where Max Canaris found work as a cameraman and also—the irony is obvious—as a bit player, the bad German in a dozen war movies. His unpublished (and unfinished) memoir was entitled: We Have Ways of Making You Talk.

The family lived in Santa Monica, later in Pacific Palisades, near Thomas Mann. But where Mann remained engaged with his homeland, the elder Canaris appears to have thrived in Hollywood, never looking back. He loved the Los Angeles of the forties, the orange groves, the empty beaches, clear skies. Also, he prospered in a cheerful, robust, cynical studio-dominated Hollywood. The anxiety and depression that plagued so many exiles escaped him. Young Canaris attended public elementary and high schools and then graduated, with a degree in English and Comparative Literature from UCLA. His senior thesis was on Carl Zuckmayer, a friend of the family and a frequent guest at his parents' Sunday afternoon cake and coffee parties.

Out of college, young Canaris worked as a studio publicist—"flack." He was charming, polished and—up to a certain point—well-connected, a sought-after escort and confidante. He was also—and this must be stressed: secretive. "I had," he told an interviewer later, "some hidden compartments." Published in 1965, *Out On The Coast* came as a surprise to everyone who knew him. It was a Hollywood novel, it was *the* Hollywood novel. F. Scott Fitzgerald was a spent writer when he came to town. Nathanael West worked for a minor studio. More deeply involved than other writers, then or since, Canaris brought a participant's enthusiasm and an exile's perspective to his writing. In *Here, Today*, which came along five years later, he offered a more tightly focused and mordant volume. It sold well, but slightly less well than *Out On the Coast*. However, that negligible dip in sales was accompanied by a heightened critical reputation, an assurance that the first book wasn't a one-shot wonder. *Here, Today* was different in theme and tone from its turbulent, character-rich predecessor. "I am . . . we should all be . . . grateful to be living, and reading, while Canaris is writing," said the Washington Post reviewer.

In 1972, not long after he was hired by a small college in Ohio, he released a collection of essays called *The Friends Of My Youth*. The writing was remarkable, the material fascinating, but no one knew what to make of it. It had the appearance of non-fiction, even autobiography, for the people who appeared in it were, many of them, visitors at his parents' home: Peter Lorre, Arnold Schönberg, Kurt Weill, Bertolt Brecht, and Erich Maria Remarque. But he took liberties with these real life figures and crossed and recrossed the line between fiction and non-fiction, in a time when that line was more of a barrier than it is today. One piece—the best —-is almost entirely fictional. That is "Gerron in Karlsbad," one of the loveliest things Canaris ever wrote, and it would haunt him for the rest of his life. Its subtitle: *Scene From A Novel to Come.*

Canaris presents Kurt Gerron, a real-life Berlin Jew, a cabaret artist, actor ("The Threepenny Opera"), film star ("The Blue Angel") who travels from exile in Holland to perform in a Karlsbad cabaret sometime in the late 30's, around when Canaris was born. In Karlsbad, he reprises his Weimer Berlin routines, dances, wisecracks. The good old days return. It's a sad, wonderful scene, a last night in a lost world, a comic's sassy swan song. But what follows is miraculous. After the performance, after midnight, Gerron—a huge man, a 300-pounder, the very caricature of the overweight, money-bags Jew—walks alone through the spa town, along the banks of the Tepla, past coffee shops and restaurants, past the casinos, the monuments, the Grand Hotel Pupp, the Richmond, past memorials to Goethe, Schiller, Beethoven. He wanders past gazebos and gardens. It's as if he knows his doom, knows that this lonely promenade is his last walk. Another writer would have him thinking of Hitler, Nazis. There'd be swastikas on shop windows, some Hitler Jugend might come trooping down the street, or the sounds of the Horst Wessel song would come pounding out of a crowded beer hall. There would be incidents, coincidences, all sorts of clumsy foreshadowing. Gerron just keeps walking, past the steaming river, the colonnaded fountains, past a few late night drinkers, ancient people at the springs of youth and health. They are old and frail. He walks by, their eyes meet, sharing doom. Then bit by bit, he disappears into a cloud of steam, mist, fog that swallows him, except that we hear his voice—rolling "r's" the Berliner way—singing "Mack the Knife." We know what awaits him: arrest, starvation, imprisonment. All that is there, between the lines of this loving, unforced inventory, this magic walk, so nonchalant, so meaningful. The work of a writer's writer. Gerron's death at Auschwitz waiting for him in the fog, his huge body turned into ashes and smoke, it's there too, in the lines, between the lines. "The raw ingredients of a novel, a great novel," a critic said.

▲

The manuscript Billy pulled out of the freezer isn't "The Beast." This is not the book Canaris promised years ago in his Gerron essay. This is something altogether different and hard to define. Memoir or fantasy or practical joke? The book is printed precisely as I found it. Nothing has been changed, nothing cut, nor has anything been added, outside this introduction and the afterword.

What was left for me to decide was the title. In this, any credit or blame is mine. I could offer a clever essay about the candidate titles that came to me. For the record, the runner-up was, with a grateful nod to Dylan Thomas, *That Good Night*. It would have served nicely. In the end I turned back to *Here, Today* and realized there was an implied and fitting title for Canaris' last book : *Gone Tomorrow*.

One thing more. Canaris' book stands alone and requires nothing more from me. But in the months that followed my first reading, there were further discoveries bearing on events and characters who appear in *Gone Tomorrow*. At first I resisted the idea, but I was eventually persuaded that an afterword was needed. After such a lengthy introduction, I do not mean to presume too much; if readers choose to halt at Canaris' last line, they owe no apology to me. Still, like Canaris, like other writers, I hope that what matters to me will matter to others.

Mark May

I. NOW: JUNE, 2005

THERE WAS AN ENVELOPE TUCKED UNDER MY FRONT DOOR when I returned from California. At first, I thought it might have been left by a former student driving through town, regretting that he'd missed the chance to satisfy my curiosity about his or her progress through life. And of course they'd want to hear about what I was up to, what I was reading or "might" be writing. But the envelope was from the college administration in the person of the provost: John Alfano.

> Dear George,
>
> I know you travel in the summer and no one in your department knows your whereabouts. You also have no answering machine at home. You're an inspiration to all of us, really! Still, I have news, which I will attempt to persuade you is good news. In any case, talk we must, ASAP. Call for an appointment. Late afternoon is best. The thoughtful time of day. Besides, I always enjoy our (too rare, these days) meetings.
>
> —John

I read the letter while I was still standing in the doorway, my luggage at my side. Now, without unpacking, with barely a glance around my home, I took a seat on the front porch and tried to guess what was headed in my direction. It might be something good, I gamely told myself: a chair in my name, endowed by grateful students, a new building named after me. But I could feel anxiety settling into my body, a tension in my legs, a queasiness in my stomach. Something bad in the neighborhood. "Sooner or later, they come to get you," my father told me on his deathbed. Was he talking about the Nazis who drove him out of Europe, holding me in his arms? Or the genial, sun-tanned Los Angeles oncologists who sentenced him to death? Sooner or later they come for you.

Provost Alfano—John—is the officer of the college who contends with faculty hiring, tenuring, promotion, sabbaticals, release time and so forth. We'd met when he was a student here, a philosophy major who minored in English and took two courses from me. Once you've had that teacher-student relationship, you never lose it. That's not an unmixed blessing. John was a good, not great, student. What he lacked in inspiration, he made up for in tenacity. When I thought of his student days it was his father and mother I remembered, in the same way that, though you may forget this or that long-ago girlfriend, you sometimes remember, forever, their parents.

His father ran a dry-cleaning store on Staten Island, his mother worked at a travel agency. John was the first in his family to go to college and the kind of college he chose, liberal arts and midwestern, must have worried them. At his commencement, with his diploma in hand, he led them over to me. These meetings can be awkward, like introductions at a wedding, strained happy banter with people you'll never see again. Yet it mattered to parents to see the person who captured control of their son's life, which they had lost. The elder Alfano was a toughie, a bit of a Soprano, with no particular deference to Academe. As soon as we met, he dispatched his son to the table, where lemonade was being poured at the front of a long line.

"I want to thank you for . . . looking after him here," he said. "He talks about you all the time."

"We've wanted to meet you," his mother added.

"Not easy, Professor. I run a business that shows no mercy . . ."

"I understand . . ."

"So, like I say, thanks for everything you did. But . . . uh . . . what is it exactly?"

"What?"

"What you did. Or put it another way, what is John supposed to do? I look in the classifieds, professor, there's nothing for philosophers . . ."

"He's off to graduate school, I think."

"That just postpones the question, Professor. It doesn't answer it. And please, don't give me that line about how the liberal arts set you up to do anything on account of you educated 'the whole man.' Let's skip that part . . ."

"Consider it skipped," I said. The senior Alfano sounded cocky, but when I looked at them the no-nonsense father, the fretting mother, I saw that they were hurting. Across the lawn I saw John moving slowly our way, balancing four glasses of lemonade, concentrating on not slipping. One glass, however, lurched over the side of his tray, then another. He rejoined the back of the line and that bought us some more time.

"I guess we can forget a career as a waiter," Alfano said.

"He's going to be alright," I told him. "I've seen my share now. Students who'll be in graduate school until they're forty. I've seen students who'll settle for jobs and never be happy. Not him. Your son is going to be alright."

"Well, what kind of work . . ."

"I bet that he has a permanent job five years from now and is making more than $50,000 a year in ten. I'll bet you the cost of his education."

"The whole thing?"

"No. The cost of my courses. Two semesters, one unit, 1/16th of the whole . . . $15,000 let's say."

"Hey . . ." Alfano turned to his wife, looking for guidance. "You're a piece of work."

"It's a money-back guarantee. Deal?"

"I could be dead . . ."

"Now you have something to live for. Think of it as a win-win situation. Your son enjoys success or you win a trip around the world for your wife and for yourself—or for her next husband."

"What's this about?" the younger Alfano asked when he returned with four lemonades. His father and I were shaking hands on our bet.

"Money in the bank," his father said.

▲

John Alfano jumped out of his chair and came around his desk to shake my hand. He called me "professor." He dressed crisply, in executive, not professorial style. He was a man of affairs now and he acted as if he were sandbagged by work, the world was too much with him. He also communicated a kind of . . . what to call it? . . . arrogance, maybe. Having left the faculty to become a provost, he couldn't help thinking that he was chosen from among his peers because he was better than they were. An occupational hazard for teachers who become administrators.

"How long's it been since we talked, Professor, really talked?" he asked. "We see each other around, this ceremony, that reception. We wave when our cars pass. But talk . . ."

"You're busy, John," I conceded. "I understand that. Lots of claims on your time. Problems. I go my way. I make no problems. I don't need much attending to, at this stage."

"How's life down on the river? I've never even been inside your house."

"The place suits me fine. And you're welcome to drop by anytime. Unannounced. I think you know that."

"Thanks. That means a lot to me . . ." He stopped and then drummed his fingers on the table. To my surprise, he seemed as nervous as I was. "There's someone else who's coming," he said. He did not offer who it was and I decided not to ask.

"I sometimes wonder how you like your job," I said. He sighed, grateful for the chance to offer a speech that we both knew by heart. John had turned out to be the solid professor I'd foreseen. Solid professor, minimal scholar and adroit campus politician. Attend the college, teach at the college, run the college, that was the ladder he climbed, shrewdly, suavely, even good humoredly, provided he was the one making the joke. His hair was trimmed, his shoes polished. He thought he'd risen and he had. He'd also succumbed. He'd become as good a teacher and as much of a scholar as he'd ever be. He'd reached his limit and teeing up Plato every year for the rest of his life didn't appeal. Being a provost enabled him to judge, tweak, admonish his erstwhile colleagues and, in some cases, betters. He reviewed their dossiers, their salaries. On some occasions—and this was one of them - he could confide how he missed the classroom, the mano-a-mano with undergraduates. He could joke about grade inflation, act like he was still one of us. But not for long. His view was broader, deeper. He kept secrets. And pleaded for understanding.

"Knock, knock . . ." There was Willard Thrush, beaming and jocular as usual. What on earth was he doing here? Thrush was the college's development officer, its money hound. An intimate of trustees and wealthy alums. "No matter how tainted the money is, it 'taint enough," he sometimes quipped. Had someone wealthy mentioned me in their will?

"I asked Willard to join us," Alfano said.

"Fine. Why?"

"Yeah," Willard seconded. "What did *I* do?"

"Let's just proceed ," Alfano said. Something was up. There was no way Thrush would come to a meeting without asking what it concerned. The joviality was an act.

"George . . ." Alfano began. "You read my note to you . . ."

"Of course I read it." This was getting stranger by the minute. "You said . . . with some urgency . . . that we needed to talk. You alluded to good news . . ."

"I said I *hoped* it was good news. That you would take it as such . . ."

It was going to be bad. I knew that now. They hoped I liked what was coming but feared that I would not. They'd prefer that I like it. But either way, it didn't matter.

"And let me just add that what we're putting on the table here is something you can say yes or no to, George. There's no mandatory retirement age here . . ."

His voice trailed off. He'd dropped the bomb and watched for my reaction. Something bad was rounding into view. Something I could—in theory—say no to but I wasn't supposed to. Something I could—should—pretend to like.

"You've been here since 1970," Alfano proceeded. "Tenured almost on arrival. There wasn't much to worry about, was there?"

"No," I said. "Not then. But now, your faintly litigious review of things that are known to all of us . . . that generates some concern, I admit. For whose benefit, John, is this walk down memory lane?"

"A few years after you came you were awarded the Stribling Chair," Alfano said. He didn't respond to my question. "Before that you'd won a teaching award, had your salary nicely increased . . . and, though your teaching load had been projected to increase from two courses a year to five, it remained light."

"Shee . . . it," Willard Thrush said with a sigh.

"What's that, Willard?"

"I don't get it. Never have, never will. You identify someone as a wonderful teacher . . ." He threw a mock-military salute my way. "You give him . . . or her . . . a raise and a chair to sit in and then you say, hey, you're so good we don't want you to teach so much. What's wrong with this picture?"

"I'd like to stay on track here," Alfano continued. Now I sensed that Willard's presence here was not the provost's choice. But then, why was he here at all?

"You'd published two books, great books . . . I mean that,

Professor . . . before you came and one more, well-reviewed, right after your arrival. After that, your record of publication slackened . . ."

"Slackened?" Thrush asked. "That's like saying the population of carrier pigeons slackened . . ."

"But your reputation grew. As an author, yes, but also as a professor, a vital part of this community. Your name is linked to this place. Generations of students attest . . ."

"Is this being recorded?" I asked. By now I had heard about enough: a long series of whereas clauses that only delayed the inevitable: be it resolved.

"Why no," Alfano answered. "Why on earth did you ask?"

"Because it sounds so for-the-record, John. Once again, I'm pretty well acquainted with the course of my career. And, what's more, I trust you to give a fair account of it . . ."

"Thanks," he said, looking up at me. "I mean that."

"Fine," I said. "Then get to it . . . whatever it is . . ."

"It's about continuing and refining a relationship that we value highly. Your relationship with this college."

"If you value it . . . thank you very much . . . why change it?"

"Alright then," Alfano said. And that's all he said for a while. He studied the surface of his desk, glanced out the window. We had come to the heart of the matter. "It's about the need for an injection and of energy and talent in this place, from an author who is involved in today's culture, today's literary market place. Who is at the beginning of a major career and not . . ."

"Yes?" He was hoping that I'd supply the next few words. I left it for him. It was a dirty job, right, and somebody had to do it.

"At—or past—the end of one."

"I see. Well, who do you have in mind?"

"I can't say. We're still negotiating. I don't mind telling you that it hasn't been easy. It's about money. And housing. And transportation. And secretarial assistance. Plus, this person wants to make sure there's plenty time to write. No committee assignments, no students to advise. The list goes on . . ."

"Jesus Christ on a Cross!" Thrush exclaimed. "Everything but an unlisted phone number." He ran his hands over his face, rubbed his nose, as if trying to wipe something off of it: a trademark gesture of his, when there was bullshit in the air.

"There's also a request—non-negotiable—for an endowed chair," Alfano said. "That means the Stribling Chair. Your chair, Professor . . ."

"I see . . ."

"We need the money that's budgeted for you and the chair you hold. There's no way around it. Even if we had the money for a new endowed Chair—two or three million—the other departments would scream about yet another endowed chair in the English department. I hate having this conversation, George. But that's what it comes to . . ."

"Is all this a fait accompli?" I asked.

"Just about. What's needed is the newcomer's consent. And yours . . ."

The newcomer's consent: I noticed that Alfano hadn't indicated my replacement's gender. Was Joyce Carol Oates headed our way? Or maybe Toni Morrison?

"I have a question, before I agree. In your message you said there was good news . . ."

"Yes . . . but it . . . has to follow your agreement . . ."

"The agreement," I said. "Well, then . . . I agree." I saw Thrush's head disappear behind his hands again. What kind of simpleton was I, not asking for time, for a year's salary, for a call to my lawyer?

"I never go where I'm not asked," I said. "And I never stay where I'm not wanted. That's how I was raised. My parents' lesson to me. They learned it in Europe." This was for Alfano, casting him as a persecutor. I saw him flinch. But he stayed quiet.

"So what's the good news? Have we gotten to that part yet?"

"Hold on," Alfano said. He reached for his phone, pushed a button. Down the hall, in the president's office, I could hear a phone ring. "We're ready," Alfano said.

We sat quiet then, just waiting. I thought of the five reactions to death: denial, anger, bargaining, depression, acceptance. I'd gotten to acceptance in record time.

"Good afternoon." There, in the doorway, was our president, Robin Tracy. "So nice to see you," she said, beeming at me in a way that suggested I was someone special. "I think," she ventured, "that a hug might be in order."

"Well, then," I said, rising out of the chair. "Here is my body, broken for you." And the twentieth president—the second female president—hugged me. "Thank you so much," she whispered in my ear. And then, where other women in other years might have said "for a lovely evening," she said: "for understanding." Then she released me.

"No hug for me?" Thrush said.

"When your time comes," President Tracy responded.

"Oh. You mean I have to get the axe? For a hug?"

"That would work."

"You might have to wait," Thrush warned. He'd outlasted three or four presidents already and, in a couple cases, he was reputed to be the one the Trustees sent to tell a president that it was time to go.

"My job this afternoon is to tell you the good news," President Tracy said. "I know it's difficult for you to agree to resign, and on such short notice."

Resign. The word surprised me. When I heard it. I panicked. Like the word cancer, coming for the first time out of the doctor's mouth. Resign. Is that what I'd agreed to do? My eyes found John. Resign? Now I saw it: a resignation was voluntary. Something I did. A firing was something they did. When I flinched the President cast a worried look at Alfano: she'd been assured that everything was ready, the condemned man strapped onto the gurney, the first syringe in his veins. He nodded for her to proceed.

"This college will never let go of you, Professor Canaris, I guarantee you that . . . I won't permit it, the students—thirty years of them—won't permit it. Or the trustees. We're going to keep you incredibly busy. Everyone agrees . . ."

"Oh," I couldn't resist, "I'm sure there are a few people around who wouldn't much mind seeing the last of me . . ."

"Well, we all have a few of those," the President conceded. "Now, after you resign, there'll be an announcement. The people in College Relations have been working on something. We hope to announce the new Stribling Chair shortly. The year that's coming . . . your last . . . will also be your successor's first, at least in the second semester. And what a time! A celebration of writing, or writing at this college, and of you! We'd like you to go on the alumni trail too, a kind of valedictory tour, the obvious stops and some that we'll leave up to you."

"Anywhere?"

"Well, as long as it's in the U.S.A.," she responded, laughing. "We'll want you to deliver the baccalaureate address on graduation weekend."

"I want the commencement address," I said, with all of the firmness I could muster. When it came to small things, I was merciless. Baccalaureate was a lightly attended preliminary ceremony on the Friday of graduation weekend. The big deal was on Saturday, when students received their diplomas.

"Oh . . ." the president was rattled. "We had that in mind for your replacement . . ."

"My replacement will wait. Give my replacement the baccalaureate address. I'm the commencement speaker."

"Very well then," she said, a certain grimness suggesting that things hadn't gone by script. She was there to be forbearing, generous, and I was not responding properly. I was pushing it.

"We'd like to reduce your teaching by one course. You'll teach in the first semester. Not the second. And, I know you've signed your contract for next year but we'll have to adjust your compensation . . ."

"Your replacement indicates a preference for the fiction writing seminar," Alfano said. "That leaves you the American Novel since 1950."

"Thanks, I'll keep the writing seminar," I replied. 'Let whoever it is read a few books before arriving." I was being contrary. One more round with Bellow, Updike, Roth, Morrison and the rest or one more with students fictionalizing their grandparents' death, their first love, the existential bleakness of dormitory life: who cared? But I took the writing seminar because that's what my replacement wanted. Let him wait a little, I thought. Time was on his side.

"I haven't complained, have I, about the suddenness of all this?" I asked. "About the so-called resignation? About having a contract I signed reneged on and a salary you'd agreed to preemptively cut. So: next year's writing class is mine. Was there anything else?"

"We also . . ." The president was less chipper now; she just wanted to get to the end of her list of things to say. ". . . would like to announce a fund-raising initiative in your honor. We hadn't decided what would be best . . ."

"You'll need my permission for that," I said, "as long as I'm alive . . ."

"Of course. Well, that's all I have. I want to thank you . . ."

With that she got out of her chair. "There's a phone call I have to make . . ." I didn't ask who she was calling. She stepped towards me, contemplating a farewell hug, settling for a handshake and left the room. Then John Alfano got up, ready to end the conversation.

"We'll send you some papers in a day or two, Professor. Any questions, I'll be here for you." Now it was his turn to wonder how to end this meeting. He extended his hand, smiling gratefully. I shook his hand, I turned and left. A treacly saying came to mind as I stepped out the door: *today is the first day of the rest of your life*. At the moment, it seemed profound.

▲

"Hey, I've been looking for you." Willard Thrush found me twenty minutes later, sitting on a bench in the college cemetery. A cliche, I admit, but as I tell my writing classes, cliches become that way for good reasons: they are true. Alas, they are still cliches. So there I sat in a burying ground that went back close to two centuries. I knew a fair number of the recent arrivals, professors and their wives, students who'd died young. And I would know more of them. The dead keep showing up. Another cliche. And the graveyard is full of indispensable men. A third.

"Profound thoughts come to mind, professor?" Thrush said, parking himself beside me. From inside his windbreaker he produced a metal flask that some old grads carry with them to college football games, fortifying themselves against another embarrassment. He offered it to me and I took a drink. He did the same.

"See over there, next to that mausoleum?" he asked. "That empty space? That's where I'll be spending eternity. Bought it for fifty bucks. Price has gone up since then. And, what an investment! Since they required cremation, you can put two people where one used to go. Like a stock split. Some nights, walking the dog after supper, I come over here and take a piss. Now that you know . . . feel free. Owner's permission."

"How kind of you," I replied. Thrush was an abrasive fellow. But he had a companionable side, alright. At an increasingly transient place, Thrush was a fixture, entirely at home. Attached, like a tick to a collie.

"Why were you at that meeting, Mr. Thrush?"

"Orders," he said. "From President Tracy, but maybe some trustees got in the act before her. There was concern it might get unpleasant. And she doesn't like unpleasant. Me, I lap it up."

"Was it unpleasant?"

"A day at the beach!" he laughed. "You were easy. I don't mind tell you that I counted about six lawsuits you could bring against the college, three or four of them slam dunks. And, win, lose, draw, what a hell of a flap you could make. The Chronicle of Higher Education? They'd be all over the place. And that would only be the beginning. The newspapers would pick up on it, the book review sections, the op-ed pages. And after that, some of the t.v. guys. And National Public Radio."

"Did I disappoint?"

"No way! It was one for the books! I saw a professor earning . . . what . . . eighty thousand a year . . . turned into a substitute teacher. I saw an endowed chair turned into a stool sample! Jesus . . . I need another drink."

"Me first."

We sat together quietly for a while. He was better company than he knew. I would not have wanted to spend these first hours alone. Part of me had seen something like this coming, coming for years. But it still shocked me, when it came.

"Can I ask you a question, George? Not that it's any of my business . . ."

"Go ahead."

"It's no more than everyone else has been wondering for years. Too scared to ask though. . . . What ever happened to you? You just stopped."

"Who says I stopped?"

"Stopped publishing, anyway. Maybe you've been writing all along, that's what people say, that's what you've encouraged them to think, this Beast thing, which is either a major masterpiece or Harvey, the Invisible Rabbit."

"Well, everything's invisible, until it's written down."

"Invisible to all of us, until it's published. Listen, George, I came looking for you because I've always liked you. I rag on faculty all the time. For the sabbaticals they get and don't do anything on. A year off on salary and no one checks up on what they did. Or their pre-tenure sabbaticals that they get right after they arrive and the terminal sabbaticals they get when they're already half-dead. And tenure itself. It's easier to get clap off a toilet seat than miss getting tenured around here."

"I get the thrust of what you're saying Willard . . ."

"The way they act around here, like Ohio was a cruel joke someone pulled on them. Like they're in the witness protection program, this amusing little college in this goober state. What a joke! But funny only for a while. Then they go sour. But you never did that, any of that."

"That's true . . ."

"And I hate to see you get screwed, George . . ."

"But you were there . . ."

"To make sure you got screwed. That's right. Still, that was business. This next is fun. Let me look over those papers they want you to sign. There's some things they can give you that they didn't offer. Full salary for this year, that's for openers."

"But I'm down to one course . . ."

"That's their doing. They'll piss and moan. Bullshit, abject bullshit. They'll find the money alright. You should be able to keep your office too. Send those papers over. And your letter of resignation. Keep it short. 'I resign as per our conversation of what, June 29, at your request, and on the following conditions, mutually agreed to.' Then list everything that occurs to you . . ."

"Which ones?"

"Anything. All of them. Salary, office. The alumni trips, don't forget. Commencement speech . . . Just send it over to me. I'll take care of it."

"Isn't that a conflict of interest? I wouldn't want to put you in an untenable position . . ."

"It's alright," he said. "Plenty tenable. Now, back to the original question. Why'd you stop? Why no more books from you? Round figures. Let's say 250 days a year . . . I'm giving you time off. Let's say what . . . four pages a day. Three? Two . . . Okay, George, *one* page a day. Keep the arithmetic simple. 30 years times 250 pages. That's 7,500 pages. About five novels . . ."

"It's one. Really."

"Listen, this isn't my business. Tell me to shut up right now and I will . . ."

I didn't. I'd been asked that question before, the same question again and again. Sometimes it came as an insult or a charge of betrayal, sometimes as an expression of concern. Thrush wasn't like that. He was only curious.

"Like I said, I just wonder what happened to you. Even if you came up with something, anything . . . something that smart guys were disappointed in, you'd've gotten it published easy. Am I right?"

"Oh certainly." There had been years, although not recent years, when Erwin forwarded all sorts of offers and inquiries, some with handsome figures enclosed. Whether my book was good or not didn't matter. To them.

"Everything can't be a service ace," Thrush said. "Might be a sack of shit. Still, at least you'd be in the game. And . . . my last point, professor. What they did to you in there this afternoon . . . they wouldn't have done . . ."

After he finished, I nodded. Maybe he took it as understanding, maybe agreement. I told him thanks. And offered no more. Still there was a nice mood in the cemetery just then, with early evening breezes kicking up and the sun heading into the woods across the river.

"I love these long days," he said. "Did you play baseball when you were a kid. Is that something you did?"

"Of course," I said. "I wasn't any good, but I played."

"Nights like this we went out after supper . . . this was back in Indiana . . . and we all went down to this crappy field in back of a grade school and the two best guys took turns picking players out of the pack. I'll bet you were the last one picked. That's what made you a writer, probably."

"Sometimes, there was someone worse."

"Yeah? What was her name? Anyway, we decided who got to bat first the old way, grabbing the bat at the middle and going hand to hand, so the last one to get a grip went first. Wonder if they still do that. It'd be a good way of making decisions around here, which department gets to hire somebody, that kind of thing. Then we played and first we lost the sun and then we lost the sunset except for the last glow in the sky, like what's out there now. And we kept at it, this gang of homework-avoiding jerk offs. When it got so dark that you could only see the damn ball when it was hit up against the sky, ground balls didn't count, line drives either. Couldn't see the bases, couldn't hardly see the pitcher, just that ball going up against the orange and the purple . . ."

We sat there, in the very setting he described. There might have been kids playing just that way, somewhere nearby, but now that I thought about it, I realized I'd never seen such a thing. Only brightly lit little league parks, with bleachers full of urgent parents.

"God that was fun . . . Waiting for flyballs coming up out of the dark, into the sky, back down to where you were standing in the dark . . ."

"Sound's good," I said. Now it was almost dark.

"That's the kind of game you should be playing, professor. And I don't mean with a baseball bat. Know what I mean?"

▲

The next morning made me remember why I had come to this place and why I'd stayed. After the usual springtime, rainy, chilly and reluctant, we'd had a dry early summer, the ground baked like adobe, the river turning into a puddle. But a storm rolled in during the night, awakening me, and I lay in my bed, listening to the rain drumming off my roof, coursing into gutters, watering the world, and it came to me like a message from above, wrapped in lightening and thunder, that said *live*, *live*, *live*. And when I awoke, everything was glistening, the grass, the leaves, which made little showers whenever the wind blew, water spraying the way it comes off dogs shaking themselves after a swim in the river. The air was heavy, almost tropical, with that simultaneous sense of growth and rot. I sat out on the porch as I always do, savoring my house and the world around it. That was when I decided to keep this account of my last year. No worries about plot, meaning, moral. I'd take things as they come to me, memories and discoveries. Like a kid after supper trying to make a catch against a darkening sky.

II. THEN: AUGUST, 1970

▲

MEXICAN FANS WERE PISSING INTO OVERFLOWING BEER cups on the night that changed my life forever. They were apologetic about it, that stream of urine trickling down from the upper tiers of seats at the Olympic Auditorium around 10 p.m. August 7, 1970. My friend Erwin, my editor, had come from New York to visit his failing mother and his most important client. And we were seated in the front row of a balcony that overlooked a boxing ring. In high school, this was our secret pleasure: we never dreamed of telling our parents. How American, how Hollywood it felt, how noir! The smoke, the beer, the smell of rest rooms, locker rooms, concession stands, what was there not to love? The way the security force patted us down for bottles and weapons when we came in from the street! We know the name of the matchmaker, Aileen Eaton, the ring announcer, Jimmy Lennon, the managers. We knew the demi-celebrities. And the boxers. Decades later I see them—forgotten now, even the best of them—Lopez, Ramos, Chacon, Navarro, Baltazar, Pintor and Pineda—and I remain grateful for a certain kind of night that I would never have again. Granted, the boxing was sometimes boring: elbows, clinches, missed punches. We devised what we called Erwin's Law: that there would never be an honest film about boxing until film makers were compelled to include a three minute round that was indecisive, clumsy, boring, no clear winner or loser. Tonight's bad fight presented a flashy black fighter with not much heart, Cassius Johnson and a cheerful, stolid Mexican punching bag named Cipriano Hernandez, who ate punches like popcorn and—his claim to fame—had never been knocked down. This tedious contest gave Edwin an opening.

"Do you have an idea for your next book?"

"Of course."

"We don't need to see much. A sample chapter, a bit of an outline. Maybe not that much. A description, no different from a book jacket blurb. A teaser. And a title. That would be appreciated."

"And a deadline."

"A melodramatic term," Erwin said. "Call it a tentative delivery date."

"Not this time," I said. "I don't want to make a promise I can't keep. Not even a paragraph."

"George, is there something wrong?" He was a refined man and he'd heard something in my voice. I shook my head and feigned interest in the talent-free melee down below. A cup of beer—at least I thought it was beer—went sailing out of the balcony and onto the canvas.

"Let me make things clear, George," Erwin said. "Just listen. No answer required. You are in position to receive a large advance on your next book, now. Emphasis: now. The longer you wait, the less you get. Perhaps you don't need the money. Fine. But take it anyway. Put it someplace. For there will be less money next year and much less, five years from now."

I waited in silence, eyes on the ring, waiting for the main event. No reply required, he'd said. But I couldn't resist.

"What if it's ten years?" I asked. "Or twenty?" With that Erwin put his head in his hands, rocked back and forth, as if in mourning.

"Isn't it odd?" I asked. "We sit here . . . and talk about publishers and contracts . . ."

"Alright," he said. He backed off, a little hurt, but what I'd said had nothing to do with him. It was about my absolute conviction that not one of the fighters, not one of the fans had the slightest interest in the next book I gave the world. There were lots of smart people who'd find that deplorable, an indictment of a culture's failure to read. But it was equally an indictment of literature for not reaching out to the people around me. There was more. I *did* have a book in mind—The Beast—and no idea whatever if I could bring it off, or how long it would take. It pleased me to be at the Olympic Auditorium among a crowd of people who weren't waiting to hear from me.

"You complain about the things I bring you," Erwin said. "This or that offer. You'll never know what I keep from you. Appearances, interviews, job offers . . ."

"A job offer? As in work?" I wasn't looking for a job. But I was the son of immigrants. Yes, it had amused me for years, being listed as a "foreign-born author," when I'd been wheeled in a baby carriage to the end of the Santa Monica pier. Yet something foreign was in me. I was not such an American success story that I would not be interested in a job offer. Someone must have thought highly of me! Someone deserved, at least, my thanks.

"So tell me about it," I said. But by now the crowd had keyed itself up. Sometimes they were wrong but tonight didn't feel that way. Mando Ramos, a handsome Chicano who'd won and lost the lightweight title by the time he was 22 was on a comeback and he was to face Ultiminio "Sugar" Ramos, one of—possibly the last of—the pre-Castro Cuban professionals. The Cuban, too, was a former lightweight champion. So it was Cuban versus Mexican, age versus youth, innocence against experience and I could feel it, that pre-fight tension in my legs and hands, something I have felt since then before classes, but nothing close to what I felt back then.

"Well," Erwin pressed on, "there's an agent who has a connection with some college in Ohio. *Rural* Ohio, George. The place seems to have a literary reputation of sorts. They publish a quarterly. Anyway, they asked him to ask me to sound you out . . ."

What came next was perfect. Before I could respond, the fighters came down the steps, into the arena, their trainers and cut men behind them, carrying buckets, towels slung over their shoulders. The arena roared: it almost levitated. Our conversation died. This, gloriously, wasn't about us. It was Ramos vs. Ramos.

That night, Mando Ramos was a thin, handsome, youth. Fame came early to him, and defeat—he'd been knocked out—and now he was out to reclaim the title. He had whipcord arms, lightly muscled, that generated surprising power. He was a fighter of speed and angles. And one thing more: he still believed that time was on his side. His opponent, Sugar Ramos, could harbor no such illusions. He'd been fighting when Mando was nine years old and, in any contest between youth and age, you know that youth will prevail. Eventually. Maybe not tonight, though. Sugar was stocky, shorter, an easy target perhaps. But there was something about him: a darkness not only of skin but of fate. He'd won the championship from Davey Moore, who died after a tenth-round knockout.

In recalling what happened that night, I grant that maybe you had to be there. Here, writing has an advantage: books are there for you, whenever they are opened. Memories shift and change. Yet Ramos vs. Ramos was a night unlike any other. I would not care to see a film, not that one exists. I content myself with memories, dodgy and tantalizing as they are, memories of Mando moving, shifting, slashing punches and Sugar answering advancing and with the slightest move of his head and shoulders, avoiding the worst of Mando's shots. There was a back and forth in every round, tidal shifts, questions and answers that involved their heads and hearts, a fight that was impossible to score, that was so mixed and fast that I could not tell—would not have wished to tell—winner from loser. I can still see them, just after the fight ended, in the seconds before coins and paper money rained into the ring and they were forced to shelter in the corners, where their seconds held towels overhead to protect them. I see them leaning against each other, exhausted, the taller Mando with his head back, gasping, as though coming up from underwater, the shorter Sugar resting his head on his opponent's chest, both of them knowing—I hope—that together they'd made something great, that they would never equal. How I wished, oh how I wished, that writing were like that!

"Ever been to Ohio?" I asked Erwin. It was the first we'd spoken, since the decision: the younger Ramos was judged the winner. We'd just come out of that last tunnel in Santa Monica, beyond which the Pacific Ocean announces itself.

"No reason to go," he said.

"This college . . ." I'd forgotten the name already and didn't bother asking now. "How long do they want me for. Six months? A year?"

"Actually . . . forever," Erwin said. "They are offering what is called tenure . . ."

"What's that?"

"Employment for life . . ."

"You must be joking."

"Normally, it's awarded after six years of diligent service. *You* would be considered for it at the end of your first year."

"How odd . . ."

We drove north on the Pacific Coast Highway, then turned uphill into Pacific Palisades. The air was cleaner here, pine and grass and salt were in it. Flowers, too. But not oranges, not the way my father remembered them, back when the San Fernando Valley was a citrus orchard. My mother had just died: my father preceded her by a few years, and my home had a for-sale in front. I was deciding what to keep, to sell, to give away. It had not occurred to me to keep the house but I had no idea where my next home would be.

"Erwin, you know what?" I said. "I believe I would like to talk to those people in Ohio. What was the name of that little college?"

III. NOW: AUGUST, 2005

▲

WE MET ALMOST EVERY MORNING AT 8 IN A CAMPUS coffee shop, Harvey Leichter from History, Derrick Madison from English. We were a trio of old timers, curmudgeons, *alte cockers*. Someday we were going to publish a magazine for old farts: retro recipes for meatloaf and for tapioca, debates on colonoscopy versus sigmoidoscopy, Florida or Arizona: Life's Last Choice, pop quizzes which only ancients could pass: name the four principle actors of t.v.'s Singer Four Star Playhouse. And, for local purposes, there were lists, campus lists: the top ten all-boring people, the ten craziest, the ten most likely to leave. All this happened at the same table, a corner place with a commanding view of the college, the sidewalk and the street. Seen from the outside, we were a cabal, passing judgment on everything. We might have been dangerous, if we ever agreed.

"Nice weather," I said, as I entered. "Reading and writing. Walking . . ."

"That's it?" Leichter asked. He leaned forward. "George, come on. You got?"

"I got nothing," I said. A lie of course. But to simply come out with an account of Friday's massacre would mean preemptively trumping what Harvey—and surely Derrick—had already discovered. So I lobbed the ball across the net, to the other side of the court. "You got?" I asked.

"I heard," Harvey said, suddenly downcast. I knew better than to ask what he had or how he had found out. Secrets are currency, to be spent. Sources are sacred. "Did you see it coming?"

"Did I see it coming?" I asked aloud. I sounded like a student stalling for time, pretending he was choosing among a number of dazzling responses. We all knew that trick. "Maybe not," I finally responded. "Maybe forever."

"He knew it was coming," Derrick said. "The way we all do."

"They're going to have to carry me out," Harvey said. There's no mandatory retirement age. Period. It's up to me."

"You wait," Derrick said. "You'll look at your taxes, your social security, you'll see that it costs you money to work. You love it that much? Then they'll dangle a sabbatical in front of you, a year off with pay and as far as the scholarly research requirement, hey, they can live with anything you give them . . ."

The more he spoke, the more I suspected that Derrick knew a lot about my case. Derrick was a politician, cheerfully and shrewdly so. Everyone knew it and that was the problem, he couldn't help intimating his connections with higher-ups. An endearing fault, in a way. They had come to him of course: he was the chair of the English department. They had asked him about me, after they decided or even before. How would I take it? What would it take? Would I bargain, would I make a fuss? And he had told them. And perhaps they'd already been back to him, to tell him how right he'd been.

"So . . ." Harvey said, "How are you?" His eyes met mine. The way he looked at me, it's as if I'd gotten the worst possible news from my doctor, with words like "malignant" and "inoperable." "How are you?" A hundred mornings, at least, we'd talked about how long we'd teach, how we'd retire, about professors who had left with more to give, about professors who'd stuck around with nothing left. We checked the list of announced retirements, seeing whose turn it was to walk the plank in May. That's how we thought of it, that awful moment in commencement ceremonies. After the honorary degrees had been conferred on outsiders, celebrities and donors, it was time for local heroes who stood up to be eulogized, to have a sash placed around their shoulders, to face an audience that applauded, then turn to the faculty who arose out of their folding chairs for a standing ovation. They were not invited to speak: there were four hundred students waiting to traipse across the stage and be handed their diplomas. So they nodded, bowed, waved and shuffled off. Mute, at the end. Walking the plank. How was I, Harvey had asked. I shrugged.

"Did *you* know?" Harvey asked Derrick.

"I can't say," Derrick responded. "All I can say is, whoever they're getting it better be someone good."

"Thank you," I said.

"*Thank you*?" Harvey snapped. "That's it? That's all? I wish you would stop being so gallant, George. You wrote a couple good books that people still read of their own free will, outside of classrooms. And you've been a good professor. And this crew . . . these guys we've got running the place now . . ."

"And girls," Derrick corrected.

"And girls . . . Let me just put this on the table. If they had the chance to hire Jennifer Lopez to teach Spanish here, I bet they'd go for it."

"No way!" Derrick said.

"Bet?"

"They'd want her for Women's Studies, American Studies . . ."

"Drama? Film studies . . ."

"Actually, Harvey, it's a wonderful idea." I said. I was reminded why I could not imagine my mornings without these two fellows.

"I'd take her course anytime . . ." Derrick volunteered.

"You wouldn't get a passing grade . . ." Harvey said.

"The gentleman's C . . ." I said.

"Fair enough," Derrick responded. And with that, we bantered as usual for a while. But something felt different. Something had changed forever, the players and the game. There'd been the three of us for years at this morning ritual, turning to the obituaries to see who hadn't "made it through the night." We thought of it as an elevator, with, say, an ancient senator, an overdosed rock star, a dictator in exile, a football placekicker sharing the trip upstairs. It was something we did every day that was sad and funny and now . . . over.

▲

I found Professor Jefferson Overstreet in a rocker at the Valley Vista Home where he'd resided, ever since he'd rear-ended an Amish wagon on the main street of our village as a group of high school seniors took a campus tour. The Amish were fine, the horse was okay, a hundred dollars of baskets and pies were a write off and not one of the prospective students ever returned to town. The sheriff was unimpressed by his explanation that he'd been reading the New York Times while driving.

"You missed my birthday," he said. Jefferson Overstreet had ruled the political science department when I came to college in 1970: a growling but gentlemanly conservative, he'd been one of the last of that magisterial club that included, among its classroom weapons, the students' fear of failure. He was a conservative, but he welcomed Marxists and despised neo-cons when they took control. His conservatism was classic, prudent, secular, erudite. Opportunists were not his friends.

"Here," I said, extending my gift, a bottle of Asbach Uralt brandy. "Happy birthday. Where do you want me to put it?"

"In my mouth. Or do I call the nurse for that?" Alcohol wasn't permitted here and he often asked me to tuck a bottle in back of a closet or in the lower drawer of a bed table. This time he sent me to his room, where I would find two small glasses on his dresser.

The assisted living premises where Jefferson had landed was better than average. His wing was for the sane and (mostly) continent. "The assisted dying wing," he called it.

The doors were open, all down the hall, and I took a more than passing interest. I was no better, no smarter than Overstreet and there was no reason why I might not land here myself someday. The rooms were a gallery of last resting places, final scenes, pictures—snapshots —— that might be captioned: *the last time I saw my grandfather, my mother, my husband, my wife.* I glimpsed family pictures, plastic flowers, bird-feeding stations positioned outside windows and televisions, always televisions, always on, that technicolor glow from even the darkest room. Overstreet's place was different. It had the mark of a professor, a table with letters, magazines and such, books and clothing in the corners. On the walls were black and white cityscapes of New York and Chicago in the forties and fifties, smoke drifting out of manholes, blurry taxi cabs on neon nightclub streets, passenger liners passing up the Narrows to Westside terminals, women in furs, men in hats. It was as though his faculty office had shrunk with him. A bottle instead of a bar, books by the dozens not the thousands, a wardrobe that was confined to a tiny closet. Did he still own a raincoat? Sturdy walking shoes for February slush and mud? That dark, pin-striped three-piece suit, was it waiting somewhere for his funeral?

I found the cups on his night table, next to a copy of *Farewell, My Lovely*. Back out on the porch, he asked me to stand in front of him, blocking the sight of him pouring brandy. He handed me my cup, raised his own.

"So they got you," he said.

"What?"

"The secretary in the office here prints out campus e-mails for me. Nature walks and new courses, lost dogs and somebody needs a ride to the airport. And the College's most famous professor calls it a career. That *is* what you call it, isn't it?"

"Can I see it?" I asked. "I didn't think they would act so

quickly . . ." He reached into a folder that was in his lap and handed me a printout.

"They thought you might change your mind."

We used to joke, we old timers, about the college's valedictory e-mails for departing employees. Everyone was precious, valuable, indispensable, everyone would be sorely missed. Burn-out, dementia, sexual predation: the circumstances didn't matter. Whether they were headed for Leavenworth or Al-Anon, we always blew a farewell kiss. Now, my turn had come. "Writer, professor, legend," President Tracy maintained. "A special person, unforgettable for his grace, his wit, his patient tutelage of generations of college writers." What a challenge it would be to replace me, Provost Alfano said, to do justice to the legacy I'd left behind. He'd known me when he was a student, known me as a faculty colleague, as a life-long friend. Fond memories of my landmark books. It was hard, they said, to imagine American literature without them. All in all, it was the college's great fortune that it had attracted me and a miracle that I'd stayed so long. President Tracy closed the show. The coming year, she promised, would be a celebration of my sojourn at the college. There'd be seminars on my books. I'd visit alumni groups, coast to coast, be heard from during graduation weekend.

"The Ministry of Disinformation," Overstreet said. "Did you interfere with a female student? Rob a convenience store?"

"They have someone they want very badly. I don't know who. Someone expensive, someone demanding. Someone who wants an endowed chair waiting on arrival, empty and warm."

"I wonder who. They're really fussing over you, George. They must be worried about something."

"In some ways, they've been generous," I allowed. "In some ways." But, I realized even as they spoke, the announcement was deceptive. It made no connection between my resignation . . . which had been requested . . . and someone else's arrival. They weren't lying but they weren't telling the truth. They were uprooting me to put someone else in my place. Owners of football teams sacked quarterbacks more straightforwardly.

"George?" Overstreet's voice broke in on me. "You there?"

"I drifted off . . ."

"Drifted off? Then you should get put on the list for Valley Vista. I'll recommend you. Would you believe it? There are people lining up to come here. A hot-bed hotel wouldn't be as popular . . ."

'That's what I wanted to talk to you about."

"It's splendid! Hawaiian night one week, casino night the next, Dixieland and jazz and church choirs on weekends. Pet therapy in the afternoons . . ." He raised his hands, where among age marks and purple blotches I could see the imprint of a canine's canines. "I flunked pet therapy!" Overstreet chortled. "But listen, I have a question for you . . . I'm wondering if you know who did you in?"

"No one in particular . . ." I said. "I just thought that this big reputation came along and they needed to make room . . ."

"Oh, George," Overstreet said, running his fingers through his hair, shaking his head. "Do you really believe that? George, you're walking around with a knife between your shoulder blades. Couldn't you at least consider the possibility that someone put it there?"

"Yes. But it's not the question I came to ask."

"Okay then. Your question, old friend, is *quo vadis*. Am I right? What should you do, stay or go? Linger at the scene of former glory and recent humiliation, stay close to a dwindling circle of old friends, on the margins of an institution which remembers you less each year. Or go off . . . what was it Tennyson said? . . . 'to seek a newer world.' Come as a stranger to a strange place. Settle into that place, a last place finish if ever there were one . . ."

He stopped, nodded, as if satisfied with the somewhat orotund speech he'd just unloaded on me. Then he raised his glass. "Prosit. To you," he said. "How old are you?"

"Sixty-eight."

"In good health?"

"As far as I know. Right now."

"That's a *yes* answer. Anyone in the neighborhood who needs you?"

"Only . . . people like you . . ."

"I don't come into this," he said, waving me off. "Is there anyone you could not bear to leave? For instance . . . someone you sleep with?"

"No."

"At least you didn't add 'as far as I know.' Last question. I don't want to break the campus wide code-of-silence about your literary output in the last quarter century or so. But is there anything in this place that is necessary for you to work? Or to *escape* from work."

"No and no again." I hated to hear myself say that. I loved my patterns at the college. I knew where the sun came over the college ridge and you could tell the season of the year, down to the month, from the place where it broke through the trees. I traced the phases of the moon, how it floated in the crook of a sycamore across the river from my house, bright as a searchlight when it was full, like a silver crescent nail clipping when it waned. But the sun and the moon—and The Beast—would follow me anywhere.

"Then for Christ's sake, get out. I mean it, George. I mean right now. Forget this recent gilding, gelding, embalming. Whatever. Get out."

"But you stayed . . ."

"Until it was too late to go. You picture yourself around campus, a senior counselor, an elderly statesman. But it doesn't happen. You're either all the way in or all the way out. Hang around for lectures, Phi Beta Kappa initiations, ceremonies, it doesn't matter. Four years and there's not a student in town who knows you."

He sat there, sipping brandy, mulling things over. He

reminded me of something you see in the biographies of famous men, those books that have a cluster of pictures on glossy paper tucked somewhere in the middle. There's always that last photo: the hero at the edge of death. LBJ on the ranch, smoking away, waiting for his heart attack, Mark Twain on the verandah in Elmira, Elvis jeweled and medicated, Nietzsche in the last stages of paresis, mad and sad. The last picture. That was Overstreet today.

"Alright then," I conceded. He was getting tired and, as luck would have it, an attendant came with a cart loaded with trays of food. One had Overstreet's name on it. She slid it out and cheerfully lifted the lid.

"Well, professor, we've got breaded veal cutlet, broccoli and cheese, rice pilaf, jello with mandarin slices and Amish apple pie for dessert."

"Jesus Christ," Overstreet said. "Put it in my room."

"We're not declining our meal again, are we?"

"We're only postponing the pleasure." She had her doubts but she backed away.

"Thank God for flush toilets," Overstreet said. "Get out of here, George."

I shook his hand, then I backed away, off the porch and along the sidewalk, past a mulched bed of tulips directly below where he was sitting. We were bad at saying goodbye. Both of us.

"George . . ." He was back from the porch, behind the railing. I could hear him but not see him. He couldn't see me. We were voices, at the end.

"Understand, George," he said, "that I'll miss you."

"I feel the same way about you," I said. I'm not sure we'd have spoken this way if we were eye-to-eye.

"Fine. But it's no reason to stay."

IV. THEN: AUGUST, 1970

▲

LIKE AN IMMIGRANT CARRYING A SINGLE SUITCASE OFF THE Ellis Island ferry, I stepped into my life's next chapter, into a dingy, moldy, stuffy apartment in a student dormitory. The carpets had been much spilled on, the sofa tortured by cigarettes. But the provost had left a cheerful note inside. He assumed that I'd be exhausted after my long trip; he explained that the linens and dishes and such, pillows and blankets and toilet paper were all his, no rush about returning. All but the toilet paper: that was a gift outright. He'd put some food in the refrigerator, half a chicken, some macaroni salad, wheat thins and silver-foiled triangles of Gruyere and a six-pack of the same cheap beer my father had put out to kill slugs when they invaded our garden. There was instant coffee, too.

I opened the back door of my apartment and stepped into the hall that ran the length of the dormitory, still summer-empty. Dimly lit, the hall was waxed and sanitized, the bathrooms polished. The doors to the rooms were open: one by one, I looked inside at desks and cots and sliding door closets, at walls that had been pockmarked by nails and thumbtacks and gobs of glue. The place was eerie, in its emptiness and silence. I stepped outside the front of my apartment, my private entrance. Mine was the only lighted room in the dorm. An Adirondack chair waited for me across the lawn and I placed myself in it, wondering what I had gotten myself into, taking a job I'd never done in a place I'd never been. Nothing stirred, the air wasn't budging. A dog barked somewhere and, a little nearer, I heard the screech of a bird in the woods, every now and then the sound of a truck bombing along the highway at the foot of the hill. If this was a mistake, I promised myself, I would correct it quickly.

▲

A knock on the door awakened me from a deep sleep, sent me groping for a towel to wrap around my mid-section. I'd planned to walk the campus at dawn, to reconnoiter the campus. Now, though, it was midmorning.

"I'm Felix Cather," my visitor said. "The college provost. Welcome to Ohio!"

"Yes, sir," I said. "Thanks."

"Are you tired?"

"I'm fine. Give me five minutes."

I took a fast shower, brushed my teeth, stepped into the same pants I wore on the plane and a new shirt and a pair of socks and walked out to where Cather awaited me in the Adirondack. Provost Cather was a slight, polite Mr. Chips in a pre-wrinkled summer suit. His voice was gentle, his manner effete, his eyes shrewd. He might have been one of those men who turned out to be gay, if it weren't such a fuss. I sensed good manners and old money.

"We have a bit of work to do," he said. "But first, let's walk."

There's not a step we took that morning that I have not covered a thousand times since then, from the former seminary, down the mile-long path that links one part of the campus with the other, through the tiny village—post office, market, restaurant of sorts, barbershop—past dormitories and classrooms and the college cemetery where Cather would arrive a few years later.

It was strange. It was, in the old-fashioned sense of the word—queer. A handsome, somewhat down at the heels college in a place that might as well have been named Winesburg. What was I doing here—last night's perplexity—yielded to a larger question: what was *anyone* doing here, what was the college itself doing here? I had gone to UCLA, one among thousands of students on a campus, in a pricey neighborhood near Beverly Hills. UCLA was a place that had no reason to notice me. This, I sensed, was a place that watched you from the day you arrived and remembered you, long after you were gone.

In an odd way, it was beautiful, raggedly beautiful. That came through from the start, gravel paths lined by ancient trees, rickety wood and stone buildings, a medieval castle of a dining common with stained glass windows offering tableaux from the works of famous English-speaking authors, surrounded by lawns—maybe they were playing fields-and-gardens. And all this on a hill. A strange, strange place. Cather kept apologizing for it, every step we took: the list of things that weren't here was endless, restaurants, night life, bakeries, foreign films, theater, clothing stores, shoe stores, shoe-repair stores, spices, good coffee. Did I know how to cook? Had I lived alone before? Did I enjoy village life? It was if he were making book on me on how long I'd last, a week, a semester, a year before I went a.w.o.l. It was hoped I'd be happy. But nothing to bet on.

After an hour's walk, Cather guided me to the administration building, Stribling Hall, named after a celebrated poet-critic-editor, a courtly southerner. I prided myself on knowing the name.

"A building named after a writer," I said. "A headquarters building. That's remarkable. It says a lot. How long has Stribling been gone?"

"As of yesterday, he was still alive."

"Oh . . ."

"You'll meet him this evening, I expect." That night, it turned out, was the "opening dinner" of the college year. Faculty and administrators and spouses would be there and all newcomers would be introduced.

Cather's office was on Stribling Hall's second floor, down the hall from the president who was "working at home" this morning. This was the first time I heard that wonderful phrase: *working at home*. We took half an hour to discuss office space, office hours. I would give a fiction writing seminar in the first semester and a lecture course on literature. Together we cobbled together something called "American Nobelists: Sinclair Lewis, Pearl Buck, John Steinbeck, Ernest Hemingway, William Faulkner." Luckily, Bellow and Morrison were in the future then.

"That's fine," I said, wincing at the amount of reading—not just brushing up and re-reading, I mean first time reading.—I had let myself in for.

"We'll announce it tomorrow, campus wide."

"It's so last minute," I said. "Do you think anyone will come?"

"Mr. Canaris," Cather said. "You're famous . . ."

▲

The faculty dinner was at 6 pm and I sauntered in at half past, when cocktail time was history and everyone in town but me was seated, contemplating a grapefruit-walnut-lettuce salad that had awaited them since mid-afternoon. Felix Cather waved at me, like a crewman guiding a shot-up wing-and-a-prayer fighter onto the deck of a heaving air craft carrier and I made my way across to the hall, past people who were looking at me, at least that's the way I felt. This was not the land of fashionably late arrivals. Here, dinner dishes were washed, dried and put away before dark.

"I'm sorry," I said, when I took my seat at the last unoccupied place-setting in sight.

"No problem at all," Cather said. He pointed out the other guests, President Lindt and his wife Jennifer. The president had that polite, slightly ineffectual southern gentleman air that never quite made it out of the decade. Later, I heard people say that he didn't have a mean bone in his body. It wasn't meant as a compliment. His wife was all fluttery politeness: she couldn't wait to host a dinner for me. The others at the table were senior professors, Harry Stribling and his wife Birdie, Hiram Wright, unaccompanied and nicely sherried up, and Jefferson Overstreet and his wife Martha. We shook hands, then I poured myself a glass of white wine and caught up with my salad.

The women carried the conversation: how they'd spent the summer, what was it like in Maine, gardens and children. The men concentrated on their food, chicken with what looked like mushroom soup splattered on top, broccoli and carrots as sides, menacing slabs of apple pie. Wright, Stribling, Overstreet: these were the college's marquee professors. Until he arose an hour later, saying what a pleasure it had been to meet me, Harry Stribling said nothing. He was almost deaf, I later learned, and I ought to take it as an honor that he'd shown up at all. Overstreet and Wright eventually engaged and the topic was co-education: the college had recently admitted its first class of women.

"Do you have any problem with women?" Overstreet asked me. "In front of you, in the classroom?"

"I hope not. I've never taught before. My problems could come from any direction . . ."

"Never taught? Anywhere?" This was from Wright.

"No place. Ever."

"Any relation to that German spy-master-admiral?" he asked.

"Wilhelm Canaris," I said. "A cousin of my father's. They met when they were children."

"Interesting fellow. Unlucky, too. The Nazis hanged him, no?"

"Just before the end of the war."

"Where this started," Overstreet resumed, "was about women in this college. My point was that their coming here was market-dictated. There weren't enough males interested in attending an all-male liberal arts college in Ohio. A regrettable thing, I think . . . And to claim . . . with only slightly less hyperbole than accompanied the invention of penicillin, that we were being brave and virtuous is nonsense. We did what was necessary . . ."

"Survival is a virtue, then, isn't it, Jefferson?" the president gently ventured.

"Certainly. And the survival of the college for 150 years without women might be something of an accomplishment as well. No need to apologize for being what we were . . ."

"Thank you," President Lindt said, getting up and heading for the rostrum. It took longer than it should have for the place to quiet down: once professors started talking it was important to them that they finished. After some clinking of glasses and dirty looks, President Lindt proceeded with the very speech that featured a riff on the word *fair* as in *fair* sex, *fair* play, *fair* deal and . . . hah hah! . . . *fare* well. Overstreet shook his head sadly. "What bilge!"

Provost Cather popped up next. He asked that when a new teacher's name was called, he or she advance—with spouse—to the podium to shake hands and be acknowledged by new colleagues, friends and neighbors. Then it began, department by department, introduction of the new hire, the spouse, their undergraduate college and graduate school, their area of interest. It must have been awkward: it's changed since then. There are more women professors, more gay partners; the rookies no longer walk across the floor to shake an administration hand. Instead they stand at their table and offer a genial, half-mocking wave. Then it was solemn. Now it is ironic. Solemnity has its limit, it invites derision. But irony is corrosive, it never ends. Never. I wonder if we ever again award an honorary degree to a commencement speaker who does not begin by deprecating the importance of such speeches as he or she is about to deliver. That night, the place still took things seriously.

"So much for our introductions," Provost Cather said. "But President Lindt has a few words more."

The audience whispered a groan. There's no other way to put it. They were a captive audience, ready to be set free. Did the President sense their discomfort. Was he oblivious? Hurt? Or—this is my wish—secretly delighted?

"A few weeks ago," he began, "someone suggested that we take a gamble. The mission of a great college, or city, or nation is that it welcomes talent. Wherever it finds it. Even in California. Even in Hollywood . . ."

There was an honest ripple of applause at this flash of wit. I could see the President's heart leap: this was a first for him.

"In greeting our new colleagues, we welcome talent. In receiving our new class . . . men . . . **and** women . . . we welcome talent. A few weeks ago we asked George Canaris if he might be interested in a stay at our college. And . . . amazingly, joyfully . . . we welcome him tonight. We welcome talent. *Professor* Canaris?"

Now it was my turn to stand. *How* are you supposed to look . . . *where* are you supposed to look . . . when you're presented in this way? I couldn't clown, I couldn't sit there, savoring the occasion, praise for my two brilliant novels, my bright reputation, the prospect of great things to come. So I glanced at Hiram Wright, gave him a little shrug and a weak smile which, to my surprise he returned.

▲

What startled me that night, and ever since, was how quickly the place emptied, once people were free to go. A few people came over to introduce themselves and fuss over me. I sensed some unpublished manuscripts headed my way. Soon only food service employees remained, clearing tables. But at my table, Hiram Wright remained, slowly hefting himself out of his chair as I approached.

"Come with me, please," he commanded. And I followed him out of the hall, up the steps, out into the village, where he eventually found a bench on the path that ran through the center of town. He sighed when he sat down, resting his hands on a malacca cane that he stabbed into the gravel. A crutch or a weapon.

"I've read and liked your books," he said. "Do you mean to write more of them?"

"Yes," I said, a little startled that he would even ask. "Of course."

"Then I have some advice for you. But only if you want it."

"Please."

"I've seen people come here. I don't say 'people like you' because everyone is different. Or so they insist. Never mind that. Everyone who comes here has a certain talent and a certain ambition. Sometimes the ambition is consistent with the talent, sometimes not. Talent can exceed ambition, ambition—often—exceeds talent. Your talent and ambition are outsize, I grant. Unprecedented, perhaps . . ."

"That's very kind," I said. "But I can't sit here thinking that I'm the first of my kind to come here."

"You're not," Wright said. "Trust me. But you're unusual. A back door hire, presidentially blessed, gift-wrapped, formally introduced. Some people resent you already, take my word for it. In the corridors of the English department, there is talk . . ."

He stopped just then, inviting me to look around a one-block village that I felt I already knew by heart, a movie set more than a college. The college had been around for 150 years but it felt accidental, like it might be gone in the morning. *Brigadoon.* Wright read my mind.

"Canaris, this is a place that eats careers, ambitions, talent. It will destroy you if you let it. Not maliciously. Fondly, smilingly, appreciatively. It will flow into every crevice of your life, occupy every vacuum, claim every moment of rest and silence, if you let it, and it will change you into someone you don't recognize. Understand? You've arrived at a place that swallows careers . . ."

"Did it swallow your career?"

"It did not," he said. "I've done about everything I wanted to do, so far, in research and writing. And I'm not done yet. I have managed to play a certain role in the life of the college as well . . . But you have no idea how this place will come at you. Headaches, problems, issues. Letters of recommendation, reports, committees, invitations, lectures. All delivered with respect, flattery, affection, appealing to your heart, your art, your character, your stomach, ego, id, libido . . . Well, maybe not that, not the libido. You may like it. You may **love** it. But the world won't know you and you won't recognize yourself. And you will not have done whatever you came here to do."

He stopped for breath. He'd put a lot of himself into that last paragraph. There were people who loved me but few who'd worked as hard on anything they said to me as Hiram Wright.

"I'm almost done," he said. "Write and say no to other things. Write . . ." He leaned forward. I could smell tobacco that saturated his suit, and liquor on his breath, and the smell of sweat. His hand touched mine as if he were passing a black spot, like that ancient pirate, Old Blind Pew, at the start of *Treasure Island*, a passing black spot. "It's tempting to be nice, in a nice place. But niceness is a greatly overrated quality. Ruinous to a writer."

"Forget nice," I said with a nod. And now we were done. We both sat back. Whatever else that scene we'd just played was, it was also faintly ridiculous. He laughed at me, at himself, glanced at his watch.

"Well, I sense a penchant for niceness in you . . ." he said.

"I hope you caught it in time . . ."

"That would be . . . ." I caught myself, just in time, I thought. But he knew the word I didn't say.

"Nice?" he asked. "I hope not."

▲

Back in the freshman dorm, I walk right over towards the closet, reach for an antique suitcase, dark wicker with leather straps and handles, that my parents took with them when they fled the Sudentenland in 1938. I picture them, me in my mother's arms, my father holding that suitcase, checking into a Lisbon hotel, boarding a freighter for Vera Cruz. I miss the knowledge of those years, of my parents before I knew them, that lost world in which I was born. To have been alert for those first two years, I'd gladly trade two of the years I have left. We were both just baggage, crossing the Atlantic, the suitcase and I. The leather is scuffed and dried, the lock cannot be counted on to close and so I'd looped a belt around the suitcase and buckled it near the handles. Great hotels left their labels on the suitcase, the Vienna Imperial, the Adlon in Berlin, the Grand Hotel Pupp in my birthplace, Karlsbad, all sit there like stamps on an ancient letter.

I carry the suitcase over to the kitchen table where it seems out of place on a linoleum surface, neighboring a bottle of catsup and a lime-colored artificial sponge. I undo the belt and peek inside. Manuscripts are like tombstones: they don't change, no matter how long you've been away from them. The Beast is there, story outlines, character sketches, time-lines, fragmentary scenes, reading notes. How it scares me, this project, from the very beginning. I've written two fine books straightforwardly, notes, first drafts, revisions as appropriate. It wasn't easy but it was orderly. And I've beaten any deadline I've ever been given, from other people or myself. From the start, The Beast shrugs off deadlines. Death is the only deadline it acknowledges.

"Welcome to Ohio," I say.

▲

The weather, I noticed, came from the west. Clouds crossed over the river and impaled themselves on the steeples of our college hill that night, rain poured onto the grassy quadrangle, cool air punched its way into my stuffy bedroom, puddling the window sills next to my bed. I awoke and savored it. In Los Angeles, rain was an interloper, timidly spattering freeways or brutally washing hillsides off cliffs, but never quite at home. In Ohio, rain was family. I went back to sleep, listening to the rain and I awakened in late morning. To chaos. In the parking lot, at the far end of the dorm, horns were beeping, doors and trunks slamming. People were racing and shouting up and down the dormitory hall and someone was hammering on the wall in the room next to mine. And a moment later, hammering on my door. I slipped into a bathrobe and looked outside.

"You the super here?"

I squinted into muggy late summer morning and an irate middle aged man in khaki pants and an alligator-pocketed tee-shirt. Behind him a youngster stood in madras shorts, penny loafers—no socks—and a short sleeved white shirt that he hadn't tucked into his belt.

"Super . . . what?" I asked. This drew look of impatience. The college was costly, the students elite, the parents entitled to good service.

"Super-in-tendent," the man pronounced, slowly, long-sufferingly. "We need a dolly."

"I'm not a super-in-tendent," I replaced. "And I have no idea where you go for a dolly."

He stared at me. I'd sounded rude, not as rude as he, but the college staff weren't supposed to be rude at all.

"Actually, I'm a professor here," I told him. And added a line which I'd been wanting to use for years. "I'm a stranger here myself. I'm George Canaris."

"Holy shit," muttered the incoming freshman. He knew my name.

"Over there . . ." I glimpsed a college truck pulling in. "They can help you."

I reentered my apartment, nodding to The Beast. The apartment's toaster had died. I stepped outside to see if I could find a decent breakfast somewhere. When I returned—from the dining hall—the dorm was bedlam, a family safari, parents and children turned into porters, carrying bags of clothing, sports equipment and stereos down the hall. It was a life-changing moment, a rite of passage, the end of one kind of family life and the beginning of something else. These boys had spent eighteen years at home. Add it all up, the time that remained and what would it come to? Little more than the summer that was ending now. So it was poignant. Also ugly. *Where did you put my tapes? You're not wearing that, are you? My lacrosse stick, I can't find it.* Fine, farewell sentiments melted into heat and irritation. *We've got to get home tomorrow, Kevin . . . We'll be driving all night at this rate* . . . There were two dozen rooms up and down the ground floor, another two dozen above, and in every one of them a drama was taking place, roommates' families who wanted to be as helpful and congenial as possible, laughing and smiling, trading stories, but not so friendly that they could not sever relations instantly and forever if their offspring hated each other, parting with words like "dickhead" and "asshole" hanging in the air. Oh, it was lovely how they radiated good will, while bracing themselves against future shit-storms. And I was part of it.

▲

At last the parking lot was emptying. I took a chair outside and watched people drive away, with heartfelt hugs and tightlipped anger, yawning boredom and old-fashioned love. They pulled out of their parking lot, their left or right turn signals waving goodbye and I saw their kids walk away thoughtfully, fighting a tear perhaps. Then, in a matter of seconds, a certain spring came to their steps. Sadness was shrugged off, families atomizing, homes emptying. It was time to party.

I called out for pizza that night, which I accompanied with some California wine. I ate and drank sparingly: I felt the nearness of The Beast, spread out over the other half of the table, like a guest who'd declined to eat but was willing to keep me company as I yielded to my weakness. When I finished I put my glass and plate in the sink and pulled The Beast towards me, moving towards the end of what I'd written. I was in the Sudetenland in 1938, in Karlsbad. I had my father to thank for that. Or blame.

Was it the drugs that he was treated with? The cancer that soon killed him? What made my father so talkative in his last days? Was it a last surge of life or the imminence of death? Max Canaris was the least nostalgic, the least wounded, the least political of all the emigres who fled from Holocaust to Hollywood. No wonder the others liked to visit him. The ill are always drawn to the healthy, to a comical, garrulous man not given to brooding or—it had seemed to me—deep thought. But on his deathbed, he found a new voice, more Jewish, more German, also more European, filled with melancholy and irony and loss. That was the voice he saved for me. He rambled, he repeated, he wandered in and out of dreams. Something had burst. The past flowed through him, just when he was on the brink of joining it.

On the morning of the day we left Karlsbad forever, my father took me for a walk around Karlsbad. He did the walking; I was in his arms. In the pre-dawn, he stepped out into a place that had gotten dangerous, whispering to me as he walked, pointing out the drinking fountains, the grand and small hotels, whispering his memories. Then it was uphill, past the ashes of the synagogue. He took me up some steps, way above the river, to where the town ended and the forest began. "Gogol stayed here," he whispered as we passed one nondescript apartment building. "Brahms here," he said. "Neighbors, a century apart." Then, behind the Grand Hotel Pupp we entered the surrounding forest, a mixture of maple, beech and pine. He had the forest memorized, all the trails and benches and chapels, the great and famous promenades. This was the Europe of Turgenev, Beethoven, Goethe, this was where they had walked. We looked through the perfect forest, down to the towers and turrets of the great hotels, the red-tiled and slate roofs of shops and houses, the river itself, exhaling hot steam, good for digestive, circulatory, pulmonary, nervous problems, complaints of body and mind. But what Europe had that morning in 1938 was terminal.

I was six weeks old. This was the time—that resented time—before I had a memory. But, from his deathbed, my father gave me his account of that morning, over and over again. I could recite it from memory, match it to the photographs and postcard albums that I found at home, the books I later located in libraries. The walk was for his benefit as much as mine. He believed—and so do I now—that something was imprinted in me then that waited for years to declare itself. Now it confronted me. This was my time to write. I was a stranger in a sparsely furnished room in a small town. No phone, no woman, no television and only one course to teach. I stepped away from the table to open the window, admit the evening breezes that would comfort me as I worked. That was a mistake.

Outside, they were playing frisbee and volleyball, students clustered together, chatting, shouting, mixing, making the most of their first night at college. What, what on earth could I have expected? That they would file silently into the library? God, they were noisy. It wasn't conversation, though it may have begun that way, and it was not singing though I heard scraps of songs. It was a continuous series of ejaculations, hoots of laughter. Now, up and down the dorm, music streamed from open windows, the dormitory was a jukebox, each room but mine was button, and all buttons had been pushed at the same time.

I turned away, closed the window, but once I heard the music I couldn't ignore it, it came through the windows, the ceiling, the walls. And there was a commotion inside, out in the dormitory hall. When I opened the back door of the apartment, a hockey puck came flying by. I stepped out into the hall—"time out," some muttered apologies—and walked to the far end, wondering if I'd made the worst mistake of my life. When I opened the door that led out onto the parking lot, some kids passed by, carrying a couple of cases of Milwaukee's cheapest beer. They thanked me for opening the door. "You're welcome," I said, before I could think better of it.

"Hey, Professor Canaris, sir," one of the beer-men said. His name tag identified him as Avery CARSON. "I'm sorry about this morning . . ."

Now I remembered him: the boy whose father had treated me like a janitor. Super-in-tend-ent.

"Honest mistake," I said.

"I read your book. The Hollywood one."

"Well, fine."

"I didn't know you were a professor here." Now his companions were listening. Some of them. Others looked away. Down the hall I saw some women going into one of the rooms.

"I didn't know I was a professor here either," I said. "It was a last-minute decision."

"But why are you here?" asked another freshman, tagged Larry LEVIN.

"In this college?"

"Well, that too. But I mean here . . . this dormitory."

"It was short notice. I may look for a place later on. We'll see. I may look *fast* . . . '

They nodded. They could understand that alright.

" . . . then again, I may stick around."

"Uh . . ." Carter looked around. "Want a beer?"

"I shouldn't," I said. I supposed it would be unwise to be drinking with freshmen on their first night here.

"Take a couple to your room," he said, tearing open the cardboard and hoisting out some cans. "For the road." The Beast was on the table, jilted. This partner for life, this project that meant more to me than anything in the world. I went to bed wondering, as I listened to howls and giggles, thumps and slides—whether I would last out the semester.

V. NOW: AUGUST, 2005

▲

WHAT I HAVE DONE THESE FIRST DAYS AFTER MY "RESIGnation" is spend hour after hour, sorting through my books. It makes no sense. I don't plan to move. There's no more reason to sort through my library than there was last week or last year. But still—as after a death in the family—there's the urge to do *something*. Books stay around if we let them. They survive one move after another, they sit on shelves for decades, reminding us not so much of how much we have read as how much we have forgotten, an uneven contest between reading and memory which might well end with someone surrounded by all the world's books yet incapable of summoning up his own name.

Alphabetical order. That has been the rule, and not much of a rule at that: it implies no sense of judgment or value, no way of telling what I read last week from what I immersed myself in during childhood. Wallace Stevens is next to Robert Louis Stevenson, Ring Lardner snuggles next to D.H. Lawrence, Charles Dickens spine-to-spine with Emily Dickinson. There are writers I revered, writers whose whole careers I admired so much that I would not allow myself to throw away their least worthy novel, i.e., *The Beautiful and The Damned. One of Ours*, *Pierre or the Ambiguities*. They're part of such grand journeys that even missteps and dead ends were interesting. *Arrow of Gold* and *Kingsblood Royal*, *A Fable* and *A Son At The Front*. But then, what about lesser authors whose best work matched what the greats produced? Should I throw out *Heaven's My Destination* and keep *The Reivers*, or *Ravelstein*?

I ponder all the night, into the morning. Should I discard books that I would never re-read? I could work my way down the shelf, throwing out everything I'd never pick up again. What about the works of Waldo Frank, James Branch Cabell, Joseph Hergesheimer? I could live forever without touching those books again. Toni Morrison's *Tar Baby.* I could give them to the library now, in the spirit of taking a dog to the pound.

Now the problem: there many, many good—even great—books that I'd never re-read. In the few years remaining would I follow out the life of *Studs Lonigan*? Travel to *Winesburg, Ohio*? Climb *The Magical Mountain*? Determine if *Man's Fate* was still persuasive or *Christ* (still) *Stopped At Eboli*? What an odd place my bookshelves are, odd as life, a mix of unmixable authors which reminds of those paintings on the walls of Barnes and Noble bookstores, James Joyce, Virginia Woolf, Hemingway and Poe and Faulkner sitting around a café, literature's equivalent of hillbilly heaven, just hanging out. My very first shelf goes from Chinua Achebe to Henry Adams to George Ade and to Eric Ambler, Sherwood Anderson and Leonid Andreyev, with Jane Austen waiting, a few inches away. All they have in common is my hand, my eyes, my life. The serviceable Russell Banks' *Continental Drift* keeps company with Hamilton Basso and his almost forgotten *View From Pompey's Head*. Across the room, trailing 18 inches of William Faulkner was Irvin Faust's monologue, riff, elegy *Willie Remembers*. Something told me I would reach first for *Willie* if the house were burning. And, just to the other side, there were two dead Farrells, James G. of *The Singapore Grip* and James T. of *Studs Lonigan*. They are both old friends of mine, both dead, both badly neglected. We spent some days and nights together a long time ago, meant a lot to each back in the day and drifted apart, no hard feelings, but there's something that always remains. There'd better be or it didn't make sense, any of it, the whole reading and writing game.

"Are you alright, George?" Louise Becker was standing in the doorway. "You're laughing, you must be okay."

"I am laughing, yes, but I am not okay. Definitely not. I cannot count the ways in which I am not okay."

"Who did this? You want me to call security?"

"I did it to myself," I said. "Just wait out on the porch. I'll work my way to you." And I did, toeing the books to the left and right and making a path between them. Louise Becker was the English Department secretary when I arrived, the only person in the department who regarded me without suspicion. She chose amusement instead. The wife of a long-haul truck driver, she'd sent two girls to college here, after the discount for faculty kids was extended to all employees, secretarial and maintenance. She smoked, she drank, she laughed and swore. She fended off reporters for years, the ones who wondered what-ever-happened-to-Canaris. I was ill, she said, I was out of town, I was in a cabin or a lighthouse somewhere, typing away. Often it worked but we had at least one huge failure when a reporter did a short story about *not* finding me, with lots of quotes from faculty and students and a devilishly clever photo which caught me in an academic procession, one of a dozen professors in cap, sash, and gown. CAN YOU FIND THE FAMOUS WRITER? it asked.

When I came out to the porch, I pulled her out of the rocker and embraced her.

"I downloaded your e-mail," she said, handing me a bulging manila folder. "Just the important stuff. The nature walks and swimming pool schedule I spared you. And here's your post office mail. You haven't picked it up for a couple of days . . ."

"I've been busy . . ."

"Playing hopscotch in your library?"

"Speaking of scotch . . . Go get what you want. A Manhattan for me." This was our little ceremony: I was a hopeless bartender and she knew what she wanted. And what I needed.

"Oh, George . . ." She almost lost it then. "What they did to you . . ." I saw her eyes get teary.

"Drink first," I said. "Cry later." She nodded and went out into the kitchen, to make drinks for us. I sat outside, studying the river. I was staying, I knew that now. What had happened to me was an insult, an insult gutlessly wrapped in solicitude. But really, how many more years did I have, anyway? Maybe it was a gift, what they'd done.

"A what?" Louise asked, handing me a Manhattan in what amounted to a goblet.

I must have said *gift* aloud. Talking to myself: an old man's habit.

"A gift is what I got the other day . . . Don't we all have to retire eventually."

"Jesus, George. They canned you . . ."

"It's time to think things over . . ."

"Bullshit. You taught one course a semester, sometimes two. Plenty time to think. And those books on the floor. You call that thinking . . ."

"Warm-up exercises. They're all going back onto the shelves. I couldn't discard any of them. Not one. It's only a reprieve. The next person who comes along will take no prisoners . . ."

I meant that the person who would follow me into this place, before much longer. The books I'd spared today wouldn't stand much of a chance. I was talking about something that would happen—had to happen—after I died and that started Louise crying again. "Tell me," I asked. "Do you have anything like that? In your life? That you can't bear to part with?"

She took a deep drink of scotch. Her husband had died of emphysema a few years ago. Wretched death. She'd seen her children leave here, those bedroom-eyed beauties who'd slid through college, working no harder than they had to. Now they were in Columbus. She'd sold the farm and moved into a condo that faced a golf course. That wasn't my choice for her but she told me it would cut down on overnights from her daughters, sons-in-law and grandchildren. The daughters were alternating, a kind of tag-team pregnancy, my turn, your turn, an unbroken chain of maternity.

"Yeah, sure," she said. "It's not losing Carl. Or the girls. I could handle that. Selling the farm? Easy. I never even drive past the place. I'm not that kind of sentimental . . ."

"You just have different sentiments."

"There you go," she said, pointing an index finger and pulling it, like the trigger on a gun. "Bingo. Nice save . . ."

"So answer my question . . ."

"It's you old guys, believe it or not. The cranks. I wouldn't want to lose Jefferson Overstreet. And Harry Stribling. And I still miss that mean old Hiram Wright. And two or three others. You . . ."

"Well. Want to help me put my books back on the shelves? Alphabetically?"

"No," she said. Another swallow. A cigarette. "Why didn't you ever let go of The Beast, George? They talk about you . . . it sounds like a fraud. Not just never finished . . . never *begun*. A big nothing."

"You know better," I said.

"Never finished! I typed it to the end the first time when I was . . . what . . . twenty-five? And three or four times after that. It was finished. You finished it, George, over and over. I can't help wondering, couldn't you have let it go? Sent it out into the world, a third of it, a half of it, prequel, sequel, whatever and saved yourself all this grief?"

"You may be right," I allowed. "You still have all the versions. Including the most recent. In a safe place, no?"

"Yes. And that scares me too. What if something happens to you. Or me? You think those discs will mean anything to my kids?"

"A little longer, Louise," I said. "Promise me. Just hold on."

▲

I reached into the folder Louise left behind, like reaching into a grab bag that contained toys, chocolates, cookie and—in this batch—a rattlesnake. There were letters from students I'd had thirty years ago, my very first class, and some who'd been out of college for a couple of years. God, I loved the way lives passed through this place, the students who lived here in four years and went out into the world and remembered me. Their letters reminded me of that moment in *Goodbye, Mr. Chips* when a career's worth of students parade past the dying professor, shouting out their names, fixed forever in his memory, the youngsters he knew. My popularity was assured—that was certain—and if this were an election, I'd win in a landslide. But what did an election mean, against an assassin?

I always fear bad news when I work through a pile of mail and it almost never comes. But I saw this brown envelope with no return address, my name and post office box in block letters, my town and state. A post-marked Columbus, Ohio. I opened it with misgiving, warning myself against opening it at all.

Canaris

So they've retired you. It's about time. You were the worst professor I've ever had. Arrogant, lazy and cruel. I've never forgotten you but I'll bet you've forgotten me. Never mind. I'll be taking care of you. And soon. I want you to feel the pain I've been in all these years. All the pain. Coming at you, soon, a reunion with me. I'm the last face you'll ever see. Count on it,

Beast

▲

"I have a question," I announced the following morning, when I showed up for coffee as usual. My friends were surprised to see me.

"We've been missing you," Harvey said. "With just him and me, it's not the same."

"But the good news is we get to talk about you," Derrick said. "Say anything we like."

"You do that anyway . . . when I'm around . . ."

"You're looking alright," Harvey said. "Are you?"

"A little shaky," I said. "Louise brought over my mail. All sorts of nice things . . . thanks, good luck, goodbye. We touch a lot of lives, in this small place."

"Mr. Chips," Derrick said, but only half in jest. We all want to be loved.

Harvey nodded, busying himself with a sausage and eggs breakfast. "This free range organic pork tastes like corkboard," he said.

"Listen, gents," I said. "We know a lot of students like us. Some more than others. And some, we have to grant, do not like us. But do you have students who *hate* you?"

"They dissemble pretty well," Derrick said. "But sure . . . you sense it at reunions, sometimes. Around the beer tent, late at night. The way some of them look at you. Like they've . . . I don't know . . . outgrown you. One beer away from telling you what they really think of you, what they've been saving for years. You want to back off before that happens."

"What I got yesterday is different. It looks like a ransom note: brown envelope, block letters, no signature. Lots of hate. And a threat . . . on my life."

What followed was a moment like Harvey, Derrick and I had never had before, we three wise guys. Oh, we thought we were demanding, we cherished our put-downs. We talked about our tough-guy moments like locker room athletes bragging about their performances in bed, how long, how hard, how often. But our victims never came back at us, not like this.

"Okay, George," said Derrick. "This is bullshit. A mind game, mean as hell, but harmless."

"Right," Harvey seconded. "Look at it this way. We evaluate them all the day. Good grades, bad grades. Personal comments that get taken . . . personally."

"And these days," added Derrick, "a B-minus is an insult. Forget about it."

▲

"Would you believe," Willard Thrush said, "that I've heard from a half-dozen students who want to donate money in your name?"

"To me?"

"Not quite . . ."

"Who are they?"

"Johnny Redding, Mary Cantonelli, William Eichberger, wait a minute. He flipped through a pile of papers. "Avery Carson, Larry Levin and Charles Stuckey. Some of them, we were cultivating for other projects. Stuckey especially. Now they want to honor you. You wouldn't be interested in attaching your name to a swimming pool, would you?"

"No, thank you . . ."

"How about a dormitory wing for vegans?"

"No?"

"Smoke free? Recovering drinkers? Blacks? Hillel? Nudists? Buddhists? Gay-lesbian-transgendered-bisexual-queer and questioning . . ."

"Questioning maybe. Really, I don't mean to be difficult. Why not hire someone who'll teach students? A professor. Another writer, even . . ."

"Oh, loosen up, George, that's so 1960's. Hire a professor! Kid me some more! How about a new game room? Or a diet disorder counselor . . ."

"I'll have to think about all of this," I said.

"A new press box down at the football field . . ."

"No . . ."

"After midnight alcohol-free social programming in the dorms. The state grant we got is running out and you know how the kids get in the wee hours . . ."

"Isn't sleep an option?" I asked. "Willard this isn't why I came by."

"No, wait, I've got it. There's a proposal to give all the students laptops that they can use in class. It's the pedagogy of the future, Professor Canaris . . ."

"Remember, Willard, when you told me that part of the fun in being here was honking people off?"

"Who do you want to get?" He was up out of his chair, ready to play. "Is it a faculty member?"

"Come along," I said. "I need a witness."

▲

Jeremy Collinsworth worked in that twilight zone called alumni affairs, in which the college reaches out to its graduates with calendars, e-mails, brochures, invitations, phonathons, reunions, all based on the premise that the people who've passed through here remember and care. It's the department of memories and money, an intriguing place. But its current head, a graduate of 1980 was no friend of mine: in his first months here, he'd called me "a fossil." That was before he realized it would get back to me: things always get back, around here.

"Hello, professor." He looked up from his computer. "And Mr. Thrush. In the bargain." He turned to me. "You're going to be in the news this year. All sorts of plans, all through the years. We're very excited."

"So am I," I said. "There was one aspect of this next year that I wanted to take up with you. Preliminarily, of course."

"Happy to oblige," he said, turning from computer to desk where he picked up a yellow legal pad and a ballpoint pen. The oldest trick of all: feigning interest, flattering someone by taking notes. President Tracy and Provost Alfano did the same thing.

"My visits to alumni groups around the country . . . I'm looking forward to them . . ."

"And lots of people are looking forward to seeing you. Of

course we have to coordinate your appearances with those of other people we're sending out. The president, for instance, she's always in demand . . ."

"And has a few more years in which to sate that demand," I countered. "This, you understand, is my swan song. And the president invited me to pick where I wanted to go."

"Well, then," he said, pen poised.

"I've considered who is out there—the students I've kept in touch with . . . and I am putting in for New York, Chicago, Los Angeles," I watched him flinch. If it were up to him, I'd get Columbus, Cleveland, Philadelphia, and, possibly, Boston.

"Is that all?" he asked, incredulously.

"Yes."

"I'm not sure we can do that. I'll have to check."

"I repeat: the president invited me to take my choice. No foreign travel of course. But . . . Willard . . . help me out here? What were her words exactly?"

"Anywhere the American flag flies," Willard said, snapping a salute.

"That includes all the places I've mentioned," I said. "And Hawaii."

"You want the college to send you to *Hawaii*."

"Aloha," Thrush chimed.

"So let's do New York and Chicago in the first semester, Los Angeles and Hawaii in the second. I"ll send you some dates that work for me."

"You understand, I'll have to confirm this."

"Fine. Confirm."

In a minute we were outside. We walked a few steps, until we couldn't be seen from Collinsworth's office.

"Now," said Thrush. "You really honked him off."

"Coming from you, Willard," I said, "that's high praise. Do you think they'll renege? On Hawaii?"

"I can give you a list of graduates and donor prospects there, don't worry. If I were you, I'd've pushed the envelope a little . . ."

"Past Hawaii?"

"Hell, yeah. There's Guam. There's the Commonwealth of the Northern Marianas and hey . . . American Samoa! Send you out to Pago Pago. The football team would be grateful . . ."

▲

At home alone, late afternoon. Pole-axed by the heavy end-of-summer heat, I took a deep nap. When I half awoke, it was as though I'd fallen down a well. I didn't want to leave or move. Regaining consciousness, moving my legs and arms, turning my head from one side to the other, I slowly crawled into daylight. Maybe when you died, you just didn't have the energy to climb out that hole, up that wall. I remembered what a poet I hadn't thought about in twenty years said happened when you died. It was like one of those radios or early televisions, the ones that had tubes inside. You turned them off, the sound was gone, the picture winkled out, but inside the console the tubes still glowed, dimming slowly, like a fire inside a cave. Something stuck around a while, aura, spirit, memory, something lingered. I liked that image and regretted it was one of those things that today's students wouldn't get, tubes of glass and filament. That was too bad. All the things they didn't get. It wasn't the darkness in front that frightened me, death and non-being. It was the darkness behind, the sense of lamposts going out behind me, darkening the roads I'd traveled.

Now I was awake and, in a minute, I remembered my hate mail. That made me grateful for the minute I'd had, before I remembered.

Earlier, I had gone to my office and picked up my grade books, thirty five years of them. Now I reviewed them. Blue covers, lined paper, a line at the top to identify the course, the semester, the year, room for thirty two names down the left hand side, room on the right for notes and grades and numbers. Quizzes, attendance, essays and stories. Class participation earned bonus points. If you said nothing—if you were Emily Dickinson, say—

you could still receive an A. But you had to be Emily Dickinson to do that.

I glanced at the A's out of curiosity, the C's and D's and rare F's—an endangered species—out of necessity. Among them I might find the one who had sworn to return here. The kids in writing classes were easy to recall, to picture, at least: a workshop format seminar was like a series of dinner parties, fourteen of them, with thirteen student writers around a table, cooking, eating, excreting manuscripts. Character revealed itself and talent, anger, humor. It was writing and in writing you never had it made, I warned them. Everyone would have good and bad nights. I'd have good and bad nights myself. I walked a tightrope, between encouraging them to write and warning them of the odds against success, artistic and commercial. Some nights I fell off the tightrope, one way or another. I tried to keep things good-humored but humor is tricky, irony is trickier and no doubt I'd said some hurtful, scathing things.

The literature courses seemed less likely to produce a suspect. I stood before two dozen students, who took notes on what I said, my take on recent and contemporary American novelists, tired, overweight champions, lean, noisy contenders. I wasn't invariably brilliant, that was certain, but I was never dull or lazy. Like every other professor I was caught in a no-win game: too much lecturing and not enough class discussions. Or the reverse. I moved too quickly through the books or too slowly. My comments on papers were shrewd or they were harsh. One or the other, never both. The students were flattered to be sitting in front of a well-regarded author or were disappointed and found me over-rated. My grading was fair or I played favorites. But there was nothing I did, nothing that I could remember doing that would generate hate.

Then I had it. Not a solution but an approach to one. *I couldn't remember anyone who would come back to haunt me.* Wasn't that the same as saying the poison-pen person would come from the ranks of those students I didn't remember? It wouldn't be the promising hotshot whose career hadn't clicked, who calculated that it was only a matter of time until he or she surpassed me, turning me into a footnote in his or her biography. It would be one of those forgotten others.

Where did this leave me? It was late at night now, one a.m. As happened sometimes, a car was parked at the end of my driveway, lights off. Teenagers on a date. The river drew them, I guess, and the lonely road. Did kids still "pet" and "neck" as I once had? To judge from the thinly-fictionalized narratives that landed on my seminar table, they hooked up casually. Oral sex was just an ice-breaker, a way of getting to know you, getting to know all about you.

The one who hated me, he—or she—would come to me on a night like this. I could picture it. A car in the driveway, footsteps on the porch. Or someone would be waiting for me inside. On the porch, maybe. It didn't matter how our reunion was staged. There would have to be talk. Dialogue required. *Do you remember me?* I would look hard at what I was seeing, imagining a younger face, subtracting time, disappointment, hate. And I would fail. *You don't remember me?* I might be given a name and it would mean nothing. That would make it worse. I might already be bleeding, on the floor. But I'd keep talking. Not to stall, not to avoid anything because, suddenly, the topic of the night—memory—had gotten interesting. Memory was a major theme of all my work, a moral imperative, almost. To be remembered, I would say, you have to be memorable. That's a fact, sad but true. There you have it. The outrage would build, my fate was sealed, but never mind, there was more to say. Think of it this way, I'd resume. In the course of college, four courses per semester, two semesters per year, four years in all, *you* have sixteen professors to remember. But a professor has at least forty kids each semester—that's probably low—and eighty for a year and three hundred twenty, minimum for four years and . . . whoever you are, I'm going into my thirty-sixth year here so you do the math, we're talking thousands of faces, bozo, and a thousand hand-crafted perjurious letters of recommendation that are required to keep your ass off welfare or get it back on some other lucky campus and tens of thousands of student papers from people who are mystified by apostrophes, for Christ's sake, remember those do you? Remember your prose???

God knows, I was having fun and it was easy to picture my sinister correspondent, my night visitor rushing out of the room, down the porch steps, into the car and down River Road, gone forever. But I had a feeling that when the time came, comedy wasn't in the cards. There'd be something. A gun or a tire iron. Or maybe one of those stylish shopping bags from the college bookstore, sturdy shiny plastic with the college seal on it and a drawstring that would tighten around my constricting throat. Whoever it was I'd forgotten would make sure, this time, that I remembered.

I gave it up, put aside the blue books, stepped outside onto the porch, the way I always did before retiring, for a last look at the river, the trees, clouds rolling southwest to northeast across the night sky. The car was still there. On the banks of the river or inside, on the back seat, someone was having quite a night. But as I turned inside, the car's headlights snapped on, high beams caught me where I stood, like a deer on a highway, a racoon up a tree. Something was thrown out of the window on the driver's side, landing softly on the grass. Then the car was on the road, its tail lights fading, red lights blinking past fields of gold lightning bugs. I stepped out onto the grass, already drenched with dew, expecting to find a pizza carton, some underwear, maybe a brassiere. There in the grass, muddy tire tracks on the corner, were copies of my first two novels, with tears and gouges on the back cover, where my author photo had been.

VI. THEN: SEPTEMBER, 1970

▲

MY STUDENTS WERE WAITING FOR ME, SITTING IN SILENCE around a long table. I'll never forget them, so sullen and hushed that they reminded me—I later told them—of a New Year's Eve party on Death Row. In the same way that people assume an opera singer can handle folk music or a four-star chef can preside over a short-order grill, it is assumed that a writer can teach writing. I wasn't so sure that night.

That first class! They thought I was on drugs, wired, talking fast, gesturing nervously. I didn't register my points patiently, didn't give them time to laugh at the jokes I cracked. And, after half an hour, I'd come to the end of everything I'd planned to say: item by item, I'd sailed through it all, name, office hours, attendance policy, all the housekeeping stuff, followed by some talk about grading, class participation, how we'd move from exercises to vignettes to short stories, first, second, final drafts. And then I was done. I asked for questions, looking up and down the dumb-struck table. I prayed for questions! No one spoke, it was awful. No questions. Or rather, silent questions: what were they doing there? What was I doing there? And how on earth were we going to get through fourteen three-hour seminars together, from this late summer sweatbox evening to December's frozen ground and cement-colored sky?

I sat there and the silence compounded, deepened. Later I learned that almost all opening classes were truncated. Typically, the professor described the course, passed out a syllabus and everybody walked out pretending that vacation wasn't quite over yet. I just sat there till one of the students—it was sly Mary Cantonelli—finally spoke. She was Italian, Catholic, from New Jersey.

"So, Professor Canaris . . . what's up with you?"

"I was wondering the same thing," I admitted. "What are we all doing here?"

"Well, then," Mary said, "what are we going to do?" She was destined to turn in three incredibly foul-mouthed wised-up accounts of rites of passage in an x-rated Jersey City parochial school. "It's like, you show me yours, I'll show you mine."

"Okay," I studied the table and realized that everyone knew more about the rules of this game, as it was played in this place, than I did. "You first."

"No can do," Mary answered back. Like that, she had taken charge. A grown-up. "You first. You're the published author. The professor. We're just . . . you know . . . students."

"Okay, fair enough." I began with where I was as a writer when I was in college, my early sense of material and craft. What I'd been reading. What I'd been trying to write. I laughed about an early Hollywood story—never published, never to be published—called "Patio of Widows," set at the swimming pool of the Beverly Hills Hotel. I shared my conviction that at their age—and for a long time to come—the reading that they did was as important as the writing, that the two were inseparable. This came as news to some of them. I talked about what the people I'd read meant, how I carried them around in me, fellow strategists of the blank page. I remembered a time when I had a lot to learn. And—since I was facing a project that scared me, my next novel—it was easy to convince them that there were always a lot to learn.

What a mixed bag they turned out to be, as they gradually

revealed themselves. Sassy Mary Cantonelli, Allan, who was hooked on fantasy heroes rescuing mutant half-human, half-wolverine creatures from laboratories and Cynthia, whose grandmother's death triggered a family dispute over a collection of Hummel figures, and Jared who had burnt-out accounts of a summer job at a dog pound, and Lorrie who'd had a near-miss love affair with an Italian boyfriend and Myra, an allegorist who pictured racial conflict as a war on a burning log between red and black ants, and Eddie, a mafia story, Judith, a road trip across America: "We drove into Indianapolis at the buttcrack of dawn." And Charles Stuckey. Charles told us he didn't believe in talking about anything before it was written. "That's amateur night," he said, clearly signaling that we were amateur and he was not. His eyes never left me that whole night.

At ten p.m. we walked across to the village tavern where we stayed until midnight. They were, I now see, not that different from the dozens of seminars that were in my future. The kids I met that night, ranging from shy diarist to raging sex machine, from angry child to—Stuckey, of course—the self-designated voice of his generation, all came at me again and again. And their stories were stories that I would see forever. My dysfunctional family, my summer job, my summer love affair. Those were the big three. And there was that bellwether opening, a story that began with someone awakening in a strange bed, with a huge hangover, trying to reconstruct the events of the night before, which involved love, lust, disillusionment and vandalism. Most common errors: misuse of quotation marks and total perplexity about apostrophes. Oh, my future was in front of me that night. And it all started with Mary Cantonelli looking at me across a vapor-locked seminar table. "So, Professor Canaris, what's up with you?"

That one line, it now seems, might have been the difference between leaving after one semester and staying for more than thirty years. All credit, all blame go to Mary Cantonelli.

▲

At the start, much was made of me. There were photographers all the time, college publicity types and magazine staffers, in class, watching my teaching, following me across the campus, back to the dormitory, down to football games. The dorm kids got very jaded, posing around me with glasses raised, their feet on a dying beer keg, looking like Hemingway and friends on safari, celebrating a dead elephant.

"What on earth is happening to you out there?" Erwin asked, after he'd glimpsed the media blitz. Erwin had taken on the voice of my dead parents, and their role. "Drinking beer with students at an obscure midwest college."

"Not so obscure," I said. "Harry Stribling's still here. Right on campus..

"Do I know his work?"

"He's a poet . . ."

"Well then . . ." A pause. Erwin was too polite to dismiss poetry altogether, but Eliot and Auden were the end of it. He was a publisher, after all. "Are you singing Heidelberg songs while you drink? Do they have duels out there?"

"They combine the drinking and the dueling . . . beer drinking contests. It's ingenious. No scars. Some terrible hangovers. And . . . on Sunday mornings . . . you don't want to step into the student bathrooms . . ."

"Listen, George." Erwin had heard more than enough. "Am I your oldest friend?"

"So far," I said, a nonsense answer which he ignored. Outside my room, autumn was at its most playful. Students lounged in Adirondack chairs with books in their laps, lay on the grass with books pillowed under their heads. A pity that, though love could be conveyed through lips and finger tips, books required reading.

"Listen," Erwin said. "We need that next novel . . . And soon. People still ask about you, but not like before. 'What ever happened to Canaris?' That's how the conversations begin. And end."

"What about *The Friends of My Youth*?" I asked. I'd sent most of the essays to him; many, in fact, had been printed in magazines. The last one—the one that scared me—was a Karlsbad piece. That was on its way.

"An intermezzo," Erwin said. "Fine as far as it goes. But I am talking about your big novel. Have you taken your first step. There? Among your beer-drinking students. In your . . ." he almost gagged on the word . . . "dormitory. Do you shower with them, by the way?"

"I have my own bathroom," I said.

"And . . ."

"I am sending you a piece of the next book. For inclusion among the essays. It's a taste of what the novel will be. A kind of promissory note . . ."

"The start of it . . ."

"The heart of it."

"Well then . . ."

"Erwin," I said, in what was the first of a hundred warnings. "I don't know where it will end. Or when . . ."

That time, at least, he believed me.

▲

September, October: as autumn rolled along, some colleagues and sharp-eyed students waited for my sex life to declare itself, its quality and quantity. Was I a homosexual? If so, I would not be the first. Was I a predator? Upon students? Faculty wives? Or did I have other interests that didn't bear going into?

All of this ended, and new rounds of conjecture began, on "Homecoming Weekend" in October. Even if I hadn't made special arrangements, I'd have been caught up in Homecoming. It was one of those weekends when time stopped. Graduates of other years returned to campus. To look at the schedule of events, it was about dining and drinking and watching yet another crushing football defeat. But there was something else going on: the past connecting to the present. My past—my future too, I hoped—was there as well. Natalie Taylor had appeared in her first feature film, "Sunny and Blue." She was famous too, enough to make her known everywhere as "the girl who got away." I'd handled the location press for "Sunny and Blue." We'd connected there, in the temporary intimacy of a movie location. To our surprise it lasted. She was smart: it's tempting to say smarter than she looked. But wrong. She looked smart, and beautiful too.

And there she was, at the very end of a parade of gallumphing Buckeyes, looking around worriedly, like the kid a stewardess leads off a plane and also, like the stewardess leading the kid. She'd dressed to disguise herself—she was well known, right then—in sunglasses, kerchief, blue jeans, suede jacket: the I'm-not-from-California-look. When she saw me, she was in my arms. Then we did what we'd agreed we'd do, we just looked at each other, stared greedily. We were entitled to that, we'd decided on the phone. And more.

"Is there customs and immigration?" she asked. "Any inoculations I should've had?"

I shook my head. Around her, I realized, people were starting to notice. But this was Ohio. Instead of "There's Natalie Taylor!" it was "That one over there looks just like that girl in 'Sunny and Blue.'"

"It's still America," I told her as we collected her baggage and made our way to the used Mustang I'd bought a few weeks before. But I couldn't have been moved if she'd flown to New Guinea. Mail Pouch chewing tobacco signs on falling down barns, dusty roads past fields of stubbled corn, trestle bridges, white clapboard cross-road towns, it was easy to make the ride to the college feel like a voyage into the past. And I loved the way Natalie responded to it, wondering what lives were lived in these places, what happened to the bright kid, the handsomest boy, the most beautiful girl. Was there a James Dean in the neighborhood? A Jean Seberg?

"It draws you in, doesn't it?" she said.

"If it doesn't repel you instantly . . . if you don't turn and run on day one," I said. "Yes. It draws you in. I never pictured myself in a place like this. Every morning I wake up here, I surprise myself."

"Is it a pleasant surprise?" she asked. That stopped me. I was still a newcomer, far from making up my mind about the college, but I had to admit, I wanted her to like what was waiting for her down the road.

"Yes . . . so far. A pleasant surprise."

Then, as now, the Ohio countryside had lots of abandoned places, farms that had gone over to brush and saplings, houses that people swapped for trailers, rusting farm equipment and falling-down buildings. There were churches and farmhouses that no one came to anymore, boarded up buildings that used to be stores and post offices. It hurt, seeing front porches sagging, holes in slate roofs, windows broken.

"Hey, George," said Natalie. "You chose the back roads, didn't you?" she asked. "On purpose."

"Okay, you've got me. I drove every bit of it a couple days ago. Rehearsing for you."

"George . . ." She drew close to me, this beautiful girl who was certain to have more than fifteen minutes of fame. A stayer and a keeper, that was Natalie. And at a place I could still find, though the road is paved and the old trestle bridge has been replaced by a nondescript concrete span, she kissed me. To this day, I cannot pass that spot without thinking of Natalie Taylor. Maybe these things don't matter. But I hope they do.

"I chose the *scenic* route," I said, just as we passed a mud pit where some pigs were rutting. She laughed, we both did. She remained on my side, her hand on my leg, my arm over her shoulder and we stayed that way until a hill rose up out of the cornfields and I pointed to a dormitory tower thrusting through the trees.

"That's it?"

"Yes. It's like an island." We took the road that curved up a hill and led into the little one block village.

"A small island," she said. "Why put a college here?"

"To protect young men from the vices and distractions of large cities . . ."

"How'd it work out?" she asked. "Not too well I hope . . ."

"There's something to be said for locating yourself in a tiny distant place and concentrating on books for four years . . . books that you'd never read on your own . . . answering questions that might not occur otherwise . . ."

I parked across from the Post Office. I thought that would be a good place to introduce her to one of my small, daily pleasures. She took my hand and we walked up the steps, into the lobby. At one point, just where you turned into the banks of mail boxes, layers of linoleum had worn off the floor, exposing bare boards underneath.

"There's something about that worn-out spot that pleases me," I told Natalie. "Daily pleasures. Small. That's the kind of pleasure I have here. But they add up."

"Am I . . ." she began. "It's not a sensitive point . . ."

"My first visitor? Yes. My first choice too."

When we crossed the lobby, I walked over to a table where—another pleasing routine—I sorted through all my mail, tossing junk into a waste paper container. At the college, most of the mail was junk. Sometimes all. Today I threw out everything. It felt good; as if the world couldn't touch me. I noticed a line at the clerk's window. And there, among half a dozen students, was the super-serious writer, Charles Stuckey, his eyes riveted on me and on Natalie, whom he'd recognized. Behind him there were four students and a pair of faculty wives, also staring. The only person who did *not* recognize Natalie was the one who greeted us.

"Good afternoon, Professor Canaris!" President Lindt called out. I hadn't seen him at the Post Office before: his wife usually picked up the mail. But this was Homecoming Weekend and he liked to appear in public, folksy and comfortable as the stage manager in *Our Town*.

"Hello, Mr. President," I said. We were meant to chat. I guided Natalie towards him; she gamely complied.

"Mr. President, this is Natalie Taylor." They shook hands; the president beamed. He had eyes.

"How nice to see you. Did you come for Homecoming?"

"Well, I'm glad it's Homecoming," Natalie replied. "But the main thing was George . . . I mean Professor Canaris . . ."

"Then it's your first trip here . . ."

"Yes . . ."

"Where did you come from?" I had a feeling, just then, that the students standing nearby would transmit every word that was said all over campus. The President asking Natalie Taylor *where she came from*. But, actually, the quoted line was a few beats away.

"From California . . ."

"San Francisco?"

"Los Angeles."

"Are you . . . .you wouldn't be an actress?"

"Well, yes I would . . . I mean . . . I am . . . an actress."

"My, my." He was actually at a loss. He didn't want to ask what kind of actress, what "might" he have seen her in, because he didn't go to the movies. "Well then. We have a fine drama department here . . ." His voice trailed off. "Professor Canaris . . . perhaps you could arrange a meeting . . ."

"I'll see what I can do," I said.

With that he nodded and backed away, a sweet, lazy polite man whose goals in life, as I learned, were to do no harm, avoid irreversible decisions and work as little as possible. After he retired, I thought of him kindly, when I thought of him at all.

Even while we were standing there, the news of Natalie's arrival reached all corners of the campus. When we walked towards my dormitory door, a cluster of students were sitting on the grass, picnicking about twenty feet from my apartment windows, waving cheerfully as we approached.

"Do you mind if we say hello?" I asked.

"Not a bit," she said. "Only, George . . . not for long."

So there came the moment that was famous, that echoed through the years, that I still hear about on reunion weekends. When the students in that class—well into middle-age by now—come back to campus, they remember that time when Natalie Taylor sat . . . parked her ass, by golly . . . on the grass and chatted with them on a long-lost golden morning when they were all young.

▲

That weekend we took our place at the Homecoming football game, less a contest than a pastoral ceremony, with fields and farms rolling away in the distance and the teams moving up and down the field in front of us, the home team scoring a single fourth quarter touch down which was construed as a moral victory. We sat with Jeff Overstreet and Felix Cather and we talked about films. We took breakfast in the college commons, drank beer outside a fraternity lodge. At night, the dormitory boys stood out in the parking lot to discourage visitors: there'd been townies cruising up and down the streets all day, they said. We drove around the countryside. It was emptier then, before subdivisions arrived, farmers selling off their frontage property, cutting cornfields into parking lots for trailers and manufactured homes. There were more unpaved roads, more trestle bridges and the nights were darker, the stars brighter and more numerous than now. I know, it's an old man's complaint; it just happens to be true.

People behaved well. It was easy to feel shipwrecked here, but there was good conversation on this island, more of it then than now, and certainly more time to enjoy it. And there were interesting people, a small community of them. Almost every department had a star, a name, someone whose work was followed outside of Ohio and whose presence here—like mine—was meant to suggest the possibility of a first-rate college in a remote location. Possibility, not reality. The college was poor, founded by clerics who believed that virtue was its own reward and fund-raising beneath its dignity. After you got past the faculty stars—Stribling, Overstreet, Wright and the rest, there were dozens of professors who would never be famous. Yet they were content to stay and the college was inclined to keep them because they were congenial, forgiving, loyal. They were closer to prep-school instructors than university professors, closer to their students than to their supposed colleagues across America. Their published scholarship was slight but they could teach. They're gone now, most of them. They weren't driven away, expelled from paradise. But when they retired, they were replaced by a different kind of professor, outward looking, upwardly mobile, restless and transient. When I came, the old timers were still in their prime. They welcomed me, they could be counted on for talk and it was always local, always about the college. They could be counted on for early drinks and midnight drives and end of semester "good-God-they're-gone!" parties. I wonder if they sensed that I would be counted as one of them, someday.

The college was new to me and newer to Natalie and we explored it together. Every time I take a walk, I pass places Natalie and I found, a hillside with a clearing at the top, an abandoned orchard, a place along the river, well above it, out of reach of floods, an alcove of sycamores and fern. This is where we had our talk. This is where she asked me what I was writing, a question that I was to be asked for the rest of my life. That time with Natalie, that was the one time I answered.

"I've just finished a collection of essays . . ."

"Not a novel . . ." She sounded disappointed.

"I had to write it, before I forgot the people who went into it. Time robs you, it'll rob you of the color of your dead mother's eyes. It takes everything. You remember photos of people, not the people themselves . . . So I had to get this down . . ."

She was a thoughtful woman. I can still see her, kicking her feet through the leaves, her hands on her knees, giving my memory speech her full attention.

"You don't forget much, do you?"

"No. There are keepers, things that stay with you. But *you* don't stay around forever. So all the more reason to write. The things that pass, the things that stay, they all need to be written . . ."

"And that's why this . . . essay book . . ."

"Mostly . . ." She didn't press me. She backed off and waited, while I remembered people I'd known, people who'd known me when I was young, sitting in my house on Sundays, squinting at cameras, basking in California sun and survivors' guilt, escapees and refugees. Every Sunday. Never all of them, of course. You had to be careful. Brecht and Mann, never on the same Sunday. But Schönberg and Peter Lorre and Marlene Dietrich, Sternberg and Von Stroheim, Carl Zuckmayer and Conrad Veidt, so many Onkels and Tantes to me. I told her about them and it was easy. She'd heard it before and some of them she'd even met.

"So it's not a novel," I said. "But it's got the beginning of one. And that's how it'll be presented. *Kurt Gerron in Karlsbad: Scenes From a Novel To Come*. And it's about someone I never met . . ."

"Gerron? Is that the name? Kurt?"

"I heard about him from Peter Lorre . . ." I began. On drugs, they said, but still dapper and immensely talented, Lorre sat on our patio, recalling his old friend Kurt Gerron, a Jewish actor, massive and massively talented, who had helped Lorre escape from Germany. Later, Lorre tried to arrange something in Hollywood, but Gerron was difficult. He insisted on a first-class ticket to Hollywood. Later, he'd have taken a ticket in steerage. But he was arrested, sent to Theresienstadt, then Auschwitz.

"I heard he went down on his knees to the camp commandant, when he was ordered onto the transport in Auschwitz," Lorre said. "Pleading for his life. He'd directed a propaganda film for the Nazis, they'd promised to spare him." While Lorre spoke, he smoked, holding his cigarette at the same upright, roguish angle I'd seen in his publicity photos, that I saw when he was Joel Cairo in "Casablanca." Movie stars don't smoke that way anymore. They hardly smoke at all. But this time, whether it was drugs or age or something he was feeling, his hands shook.

"I've also heard," he said, "that when he boarded the train, he swept his overcoat around him, theatrically, like a cape. His final exit. At Auschwitz he told Mengele he was sick. '*Ich kann nicht mehr arbeiten* . . ." Lorre shrugged.

"And that's what you're working on?" Natalie asked.

"Just part of it. I did some homework. I collected still pictures of Gerron. An enormous man, six feet, 300 pounds. Jackie Gleason. I saw some movies that he directed—in the Babelsberg studios in Berlin, till they kicked him out, then in Holland, till they arrested him. Over and over, I watched him in 'The Blue Angel,' with Marlene Dietrich and Emil Jannings. They were great. He was greater. And I listened to him, too, singing The Moritat from the first production of 'The Threepenny Opera.' He was Tiger Brown . . ."

"The Moritat?"

"'Mack the Knife.' It didn't originate with Bobby Darin . . ." That earned me a look which said back off. "Sorry. I also saw his last film. Also famous. Scraps are all that exist, at least all that's been found so far . . ."

I paused and stopped, the way you do, when you're about to launch into a story that, though it's true, is hard to believe, hard to accept. Harder to tell.

"Theresienstadt was a Jewish camp. They had a puppet self-government. Sometimes the Nazis called it 'Bad Theresienstadt' as if it were a spa. It was where they put the Jews who they weren't quite ready to murder. Yet. The assimilated, the cultured, the prominent. The loyal, even. War heroes. There was a lot of talent in Theresienstadt, painting, music, theater. Heartbreaking. They were all on short rations, sick, starving . . . but there was a kind of cultural life. Gerron started a comedy troupe, Kurt Gerron's Carousel, it was called . . . Can you imagine?"

"It's hard. Keep talking, George . . ."

"It's so sad. And cruel. And complicated. Anyway, late in the war—mid 1944—someone in Berlin decides to make a film showing this model camp in which Jews relax, loaf, while German manhood takes on the world. And by now it's clear, the world is winning. The Russians were coming. They had a radio in camp, they knew that time was on their side, if they had enough of it. Anyway, Gerron was ordered to direct that damned film. Which he did. Made himself a pariah to some people. Sell-out, Quisling, etc. Let's face it, he had no choice. And . . . come on, that movie wasn't going to fool anyone. And every day he worked was another day alive . . . and not just for him."

"What's it like. What you saw of it?"

"They called it, unofficially, 'The Fuhrer Gives The Jews A City.' You believe it? What bits I've seen . . . happy Jews sitting at café tables. Having a rousing time at a soccer game. Watering vegetables on the edge of a river, walking through garden plots with sprinkling cans. At times, it looks a little like those early black and white newsreels that came out of Israel a few years later. Muscular, sun-tanned, pioneering Zionists . . ."

"So your book is about Gerron?"

"Not so fast," I warned. "We're almost there. Yes, it's about Gerron. But it's about me. It hits me right at home . . . and it's the home I never saw. It turns out, sometime in the mid-1930's, after he fled from Germany, he went back to his old trade. Cabaret. Songs, skits, patter, wisecracks, all very Weimar. And one of the places he performed was Karlsbad. My parents' place. Where I was born . . ."

I stopped because I didn't know what came next. How odd it was, sitting in this American place, feeling the tug of a lost world, to contemplate Theresienstadt and Karlsbad and Auschwitz, trapped and locked away in my mind, like leaves in the ice of a frozen lake.

"I don't know where it leads, Natalie. I've got this sketch, this vignette of a man I never knew that I'm sending to Erwin . . . it's good."

"Maybe it's just what it is," she offered. Shrewd. "You've got a heartwarming vignette, a little jewel. That's the beginning and end of it."

"Could be," I granted. "But it doesn't feel that way. It feels endless."

"A lifetime of work?"

"Yes."

"And you think you'll get it done here. Faster than any place else? Better?

That stopped me. It was a moment that came back to me for years, comes back still, the young and celebrated Canaris, confiding in a woman he loved. I now know she suspected that what attracted me to the College was not only the chance to write. It was also the chance not to write, opportunities and diversions that were appealing and without end.

"George, you went to UCLA. In four years, how many football games did you attend?"

"None."

"Yet here, you while away an afternoon, watching a losing team in a minor league . . . lose again."

"And your question is . . ." I was trying to recover. "I walk to the game with you. I sit among friends. I know some of the players . . . some of their parents also . . . and did you notice the cornfields beyond? The way hills roll away? The way the sun shifts over the field towards the end of the game?"

"Okay," she said. She stretched, luxuriantly, and shook her hair, one side to the other, and stretched out on the ground, my belly was her pillow.

"That's it. Just . . . 'okay'?" She nodded from down below, closed her eyes, and for a moment, I guessed she might be going to sleep. I loved that, the trust and comfort of it. Some students walked by, going along the trail. Maybe they saw us, maybe they didn't. (They did, I later learned.) I listened to the river, the gear-shifting trucks on the highway, the skittering of chipmunks around fallen logs. Small animals, but incredibly noisy. I looked at Natalie. She was sleeping. And that was the greatest intimacy, closer than sex. I didn't move, not wanting to break the spell. Then, all of a sudden, her eyes were open and upon me.

"Why here?" she asked, immediately taking up where we had left off. "Really . . ."

"I couldn't imagine doing this back in Los Angeles . . . so surrounded. And distracted. I might write another book there. But not this one . . ."

"But . . . here? No girlfriends, no food. Is there even a movie theater? And I saw where you live, I almost cried. Or laughed. I forget which . . ."

"The dormitory is temporary. The movies I'll see some other place. The restaurants . . . hopeless."

"And the women? Temporary like the dormitory? Postponable, like the movies. Or hopeless, like the restaurants?"

"I was hoping that you'd help us out in that department."

"Department? Department of women? That'll have to be a one-woman department."

"May I visit you in L.A.? On location?"

"You better."

"And . . ." This next question might be going a bridge too far. She might be good for one autumn visit to this place. But more? After the novelty wore off? And she was so in demand! A second trip was most unlikely.

"I wonder about you professor," she said. "I wonder about myself, when I'm with you. Whether we might add up to something. Maybe I could help you look for a place. And move you in to it. God knows, you need help and a new shower curtain!"

She was coming back! I rejoiced, and an entire dormitory of students would rejoice, and the admissions department also.

"If you want a better arrangement, something permanent . . ." I took a deep breath. "A long term commitment that lasts forever . . ."

She braced herself, a little touched, a lot more appalled; in my experience, women prematurely escalated a relationship, not men. She regarded me, not wanting to hurt me, to lose what we already had. But I hadn't finished yet.

"Natalie," I continued. "I mean something that lasts! Call the drama department about a job. We have a very fine drama department . . ."

▲

When it was time to go, the kids were out in the parking lot, waiting to say goodbye. She passed through them cheerfully, remembered some of their names and appreciated that there hadn't been a single request for an autograph all weekend. But they wanted, they'd decided, a photograph. So we gathered together, about fifty of us, Natalie in the center, ranks of beaming students to the sides. They behaved well: no silly faces, hand gestures, no passing of cameras, just one local photographer—a professional —firing off a single roll of film and capturing a moment that I can now verify, they would remember forever. As would I.

▲

You might be famous, but that won't save a seminar. Trust me on this. Or, if you don't, go to one of those notorious web sites where students evaluate their professors. Is he hard? Is he entertaining? Is it worth it? Is the professor smart, likeable, sexy? Click on any famous university, find the name of any professor—a National Book Award winner, a certified important poet, a warrior against cancer and see what the students think. Nothing saves you.

By November, my seminar's initial camaraderie was starting to fray. The initial pump-priming exercises—dialogue between two people on a blind date, for instance, were history. They were fun, like charades, but now we were in the deep end of the pool, making fiction, writing and revising short stories. Privately, I disliked short stories; if I hadn't before I started teaching, I did now. The whole genre was lost to me forever; to think about them at all was like contemplating a meal that was all appetizers. I don't mean caviar and shrimp, I mean piggies-in-a-blanket, squares of American, cheddar and Monterey Jack cheese that looked more like bathroom tiles than food.

This was rough going, with rivalries and feuds and hurt feelings, spats and angry silence. Mary Cantonelli thought that Stuckey wrote beautifully but didn't have much to say and Stuckey thought she was a "feminist pornographer." One kid thought another's account of Grandma's last Thanksgiving was a Hallmark card. A dyslexia story was labeled an after-school special. On and on. And they looked to me—famous Canaris—for a thumbs up or a thumbs down and when that didn't come, they looked for an ending, an escape, because this was hell, being trapped in an overheated seminar room with other people, the table littered with manuscripts that ranged from the annoying to the screwed up to the heartfelt-but-hapless.

My habit, then, was to find a country road to walk on, an hour before seminar. The best of autumn was past. Only the oaks retained their leaves, all the other trees were skeletons. Then again, I noticed that white-barked sycamores stood out more: in a gray and brown landscape, their white bark ruled. I always felt edgy before seminar, I still do, but never more than during that first year. Three hours of seminar seemed preposterous. I reviewed what I knew of the feuds and alliances that had formed, the talents and limitations that had been revealed. My knowledge was incomplete. It always is. Mary Cantonelli and Charles Stuckey might be sleeping together. Who knew? Stuckey was a problem though. He might be the most talented in the bunch, but not as talented as he would need to be and not as tough. He slipped easily into the first-person voice, sending thinly disguised versions of himself out into story-land, but his other characters were cardboard. Except for the feisty Cantonelli, the others were scared to criticize him. Another writer produced a teasing, patience-testing fan dance about sexual identify, another used madness as an excuse for any action, however improbable. "Don't you see?! She's crazy!" Fantasy and allegory, sermon and poetry were always somewhere in the neighborhood, along with the conviction that beautiful prose was the most important thing. I tried to tell them, God I tried: the story was the thing. No one ever read a book because it was beautifully written. You had to perpetrate a story. And then, the stories came: movie and television-derived knock-offs. It was hell.

Tonight they were out in front of the building, all of them. As I neared, I expected them to file into the seminar room ahead of me; it was a small courtesy, but necessary, that the professor be the last one through the door. Tonight they didn't budge. Obviously, even insolently, they watched me come down the sidewalk. Was I about to be confronted by an uprising of some kind?

"Professor Canaris," Mary Cantonelli said. "Haven't you heard?" She was crying. They were all grim and Stuckey was studying me as if I were something he'd eventually want to describe.

"She's dead. Your Natalie. It was in the news. A car crash in the desert. And she wasn't even the one who was driving . . ."

Don't say anything, I told myself; anyway, there was nothing to say. I turned away, about faced, and looked across the campus. What do I do now? Time for crying later, time for mourning, time to discover how my life had changed. Friend, lover, confidante. Natalie. Do I go back to the dorm? *She'll* be waiting for me there. Do I take a thoughtful walk? Another one? No crying. Crying was theater. Memory was another matter. I chose memory. I pivoted and faced the kids and, there came a moment that people would talk about.

"Time we started," I said. "We're late . . ."

VII. NOW: SEPTEMBER, 2005

▲

On August's last Tuesday, early in the afternoon, I slipped on the same academic robe I wore when I arrived and walked across to where my colleagues gathered, just as they gathered thirty five years before, for the convocation ceremony that would mark the beginning of my last year. Now I was entitled to a place at the end of the line, among the graybeards. There were just four professors who'd been teaching longer than I had. As I joined them, I remembered something from the Tarzan comics: the magic valley of Paul-ul-Don, where elephants went to die. A tusk-littered place. The other oldsters were all Phd.'s, caparisoned in the colors of places that awarded them their long-ago doctorates: maroons and blues, pinks and yellows. I was still in a choir boy's basic black.

Freshman parents passed by, photographing as they went, and then four and a half hundred teenagers paraded into college life. But not into mine. This was the first class that I'd have nothing to do with, the vanguard of the college that would carry on without me. Grinning and goofy, solemn and straight-faced, they passed me by. Now it was our turn to march, through the ranks of junior faculty. This is when I started feeling self conscious.

Our walk curved into the crowd of visitors, through ranks of folding chairs and up onto the stage, where padded chairs awaited the president, provost and dean of students. Seniority had moved me to the row right behind them. Before long, the speeches began. Familiar refrains after so many years: this day marked a beginning, it marked an ending, this was a college that was challenging yet understanding, a place that forgave and rewarded, that combined rigor with compassion, this was a faculty that featured dedicated scholars, passionate instructors and best new friends. No point in parsing what administrators said: it was like putting jellyfish in an x-ray machine.

"... if George Canaris will please stand." Whoops! President Tracy was facing me, beaming as she often did on such occasions, as if all speeches and ceremonies, all awards and degrees, made the world happier.

"After almost thirty-five years at this college," she began, "Professor Canaris has elected to retire. He will stand here, once again, nine months from now, at graduation. Unless you incoming students accomplish four years work in one—which is not beyond your abilities, our admissions people say—you will not be here to witness Professor Canaris' farewell. We want you to know what George Canaris has meant . . . and means . . . to this college.

Now she gestured towards me, inviting the audience to take me in. I felt a thousand eyes upon me. For a moment, I considered simulating sleep or sunstroke: I would let my chin sink towards my chest, my slumbering body tilt to one side, then slowly slide onto the chair, then off the chair and onto the stage. I was a good soldier, though. I sat and listened.

"George Canaris came to this college and he stayed, not for one year but for thirty-five, a great writer, a great teacher. He was not the first writer to come here and, as I'll be demonstrating shortly . . . not the last. But this is his moment. So I ask all of you, to acknowledge all that he has meant and been."

Now I stood and I heard the applause start to roll towards me, waves of it from all sides, from the president and provost who had asked me to end my career, from the freshmen I would never teach and—more shallowly—from the faculty behind me. To end it, I nodded, I bowed. And I sat.

"We've had a problem here," President Tracy continued. "How to replace George Canaris. No . . . wait . . . there is no replacing him. Our goal is to sustain the tradition that Professor Canaris represents . . . to renew it and enlarge it. And I'm happy to tell you, just as we were lucky once, we have been lucky again. I would like now to introduce the writer who will be our next Stribling Professor . . ."

She paused, she smiled a moment. Cunning stagecraft. She even turned to me. "This won't be easy," she said, a personal, confidential aside that echoed off the walls. "Ladies and gentlemen," she said. "Without further delay . . . without introducing someone who needs no introduction. Please welcome . . ."

A frozen moment, deeper and more intense than the so-long-it's-been-good-to-know-you I'd gotten. I was an hors d'oeuvre. Now the main course. Joyce Carol Oates? William T. Vollmann? Oh, God, not David Eggers or David Foster Wallace! Doorstopper writers, every one of them, the kind of writers who never left you asking for more. The very opposite of me: I never gave more. And always left them asking.

"John Henry Mallon!" the president called out. The audience gasped. This was a name they recognized, the king of the doorstoppers, a generational icon, a rock-star. The students whooped and high-fived, this was someone famous and a real dude besides. I'd had a dozen students who'd come during office hours asking what I'd thought of his massive novel, GAMESHOW. I hadn't read a word of his work and even the kids who declared him their leader eventually confessed they hadn't quite got to the last page. Somehow, this love affair between Mallon and the kids didn't entail climax.

Whatever else they said, everyone agreed that Mallon was clever. His book was a family saga set in West Virginia and San Francisco, with each of its many sections named after and recalling classic television contests: Queen For A Day, for instance, was about a businessman's gay dalliance, the Price Is Right described an election campaign. And so on: You Asked For It, Let's Make A Deal, the $64,000 Question, Survivor, Do You Want To Be a Millionaire? There was no end to Mallon's invention. Jeopardy, You Bet Your Life, What's My Line? And now his fans were cheering for him as he stepped out of the audience, down the aisle, towards the stage. With him, the applause was based on enthusiasm, not reverence, and it kept growing as he approached. There was no counting the number of faculty enemies he'd already made.

On stage, he waved to the audience, even pumped his fist a little, as if what was happening was a triumph for all of them, the kids taking charge. Then he hugged the president. He was a burly shaggy, lumberjack type and the petite president, last seen smiling, vanished in his embrace. Facing the faculty he bowed a little. Now he walked towards me. I arose to meet him. He stared at me, searching for anger and found none. His eyes were smart.

"Welcome," I said. Should I perform for him the service Hiram Wright had done for me? Congratulate him on his arrival at the little college that swallows careers?

"I've read your books," he said. "Great."

"I've lifted yours," I responded. "Heavy."

▲

Nothing is so fine as a nap after a college ceremony, unless it's a nap *during* a college ceremony. There's something about the ritual and the rhetoric, the humidity in the air, the heaviness of the robe that just sets you up for a siesta. At home, soon as my head hit the pillow I was asleep, deep into a pole-axed slumber. Once I arose, I puttered around the house, knowing that The Beast was around somewhere. I couldn't bear it, not today. I hopped into my car and drove to the English department's start-of-the-year picnic, at Derrick Madison's place. From his porch, the smoke of a Weber grill blew my way as if saying, "It's okay, we're only having hamburgers."

On paper, I was the senior member of the English department and, for a few months more, the holder of an endowed chair named for Harry Stribling. Yet I kept my distance from my colleagues and they from me. It had started with my hiring and, though none of the people at Derrick's had been around back then, patterns had been established that became precedents. I was a writer, not a professor, not a Phd. That made me suspect at the beginning of my career, bogus at the end. There'd been pleasant moments but they happened by accident. You'd run into someone at the post office or in line at the supermarket and you'd end up spending an hour. You got a glimpse, then, of someone's inner life. But mostly, it was about vacations and sabbaticals, the latest subdivision defacing the countryside, the newest franchise restaurant that might be coming to town: just lately, people were praying for Chipotle. And, yes, sometimes we got around to books, the statements we made about books were about ourselves, credos, self-assertions. "You've got to read this" wasn't a gift, it was a bullying order.

"There goes next summer's free-reading,"Indira Kumar sighed, as I came in. She taught post-colonial courses with titles like "(Queen) Victoria's Secret."

"Excuse me," said Istvan Mihaly—(Popular Culture, Noir Novels, and the History of the Short Story.) "Has this man taught *where*?" They were talking about Mallon.

"I don't know," Derrick said. "I haven't seen his resumé."

"Why bother?"That was Sandy van Straatan. (Women Poets, Women in Fiction.) "Can anyone here picture John Alfano asking Mallon for his references. Do you think they even care whether he's any good in a classroom?"

"I'm sorry, Derrick," Hannah Farrington ("Writing and Rewriting Gender") said. "But this should not have happened. They just unload him on us. As if we should all stand around and be grateful."

"He might be a genius," Derrick said.

"Is he a Phd.? An MFA? Did he go to college anywhere?"

"He's a huge addition. He might turn out to be a major attraction."

"Or another fraud who'll come and never leave."

"I'll bet he's quite good," I said. "I remember the reviews of GAMESHOW. They weren't silly or voguish. I remember thinking I should read this sometime. And maybe I will. Not that I have to. I'll be gone." Everything I said was fair, even generous. But, I have to admit there was more. "*Or another fraud who'll come and never leave*." Farrington's comment wasn't just about Mallon. It was about me.

"We have procedures," Farrington resumed, taking that impersonal principled tone which academics take when pressured. "We agree on what we need, which goes into a job description, which is advertised. We read applications, conduct interviews, invite . . ."

"We're all familiar with how we hire," Madden said.

"Almost all," Hannah Farrington. Now there was no doubt about it: she looked at me. I'd never served on a search.

"Listen," Derrick said. "Procedures are fine. But sometimes, somebody comes along, you have to hire opportunistically . . ."

"Great. And get another opportunist."

"What are you saying, then? Was Harry Stribling an opportunist? He came in via back channels. And George Canaris. *They* attract the students you teach. *You* didn't. They may not have conventional resumés, but you have to give them the benefit of the doubt . . ."

"Well, then, put me down as a doubter." Another nod my way. "Sorry, George . . . It needs saying I guess. I don't know what the deal was when you came here, but you've become . . . well, a kind of a joke."

I stood there, dumbstruck. Emphasis on dumb. I waited for someone—for anyone—to intervene. And waited, through a long silence that had been a long time coming. It was as though I'd been the last one let in on a secret: some people detested me.

"It's time for me to leave," I said.

"You've got that right." I hear someone say from behind me.

▲

I pull into my driveway. I rush to the edge of the porch and piss luxuriantly, go to the kitchen and pull two beers out of the refrigerator, one in each hand. With no more ceremony than a mechanic dumping a quart of Quaker State into a clunker that's started burning oil, I drain the first beer, crunch the can in my hand and take the second with me to my easy chair. I snap on the t.v. and turn to Black Entertainment Network where incredible women lounge around cracking up at filthy jokes. It's good to be there for a while, for the second beer, but not for long.

I step out onto the porch and into my rocking chair. By now I have a glass of cognac and some food, anything, a bag of potato chips, a piece of chicken, an open can of uncooked corn-beef hash. Eating this way, this late, will ruin my sleep. It's always that way after a seminar. And tonight, even more so. At the end of my driveway, I notice something that wasn't there half an hour ago, at least I did not see it when I turned into the driveway. A shape, a shadow. I walk towards it, where it stands right along the road. And see that someone has planed a sign on my property. HOUSE FOR SALE, it says. BY OWNER.

VIII. THEN: DECEMBER, 1970–APRIL 1971

▲

Natalie died a few days before Thanksgiving. In less than a month, Christmas vacation was upon me. I could have left town, to grieve in a warm climate. But I didn't budge. I just watched the campus empty. Our handful of stores kept shorter hours, the restaurant closed altogether, the Post Office had mail sorted and out in boxes by ten in the morning. Back in the dormitory, room and halls were littered with pizza boxes and sweat socks: it was as though a neutron bomb had vaporized the students and spared me. When I arrived in summer, I'd been shipwrecked. Now, at Christmas, I was marooned.

My companion was The Beast. What had started as a family story, from the end of the first World War to the beginning of World War II was moving backward in time, into the Hapsburg era, Karlsbad's glory days. And forward, through the war, the expulsion of the Sudeten Germans, the decades of communist control. The book got deeper and longer, the more I worked on it. What started with a father taking an infant son on an early morning walk, what included a doomed cabaret actor's midnight stroll through town now encompassed half a century of European history and irony. The Beast was endless. I couldn't help remembering what Natalie had suggested. Maybe my work was already done. I had the Gerron vignette. It was a gem. Why not leave it at that?

I began in mid-afternoon, working on the middle of the book, my parent's lives. Some of this was written, the rest was in range. I worked into the evening, while my neighbors up and down the street—the ones who lived in normal homes, with normal lives—ate and watched television. Then their windows turned dark, their Christmas trees as well, and I was in true night, working backward, working forward, knowing that every page I wrote added more pages I would have to write. The Beast grew as I fed it, grew and grew hungrier. In the last—and darkest—hours before dawn, light-headed I tried out new scenes, Marx, Brahms, Goethe, Schiller, Turgenev, Mozart and Freud and Hitler. And Konrad Henlein, the Sudeten German leader who'd opened his veins in a Pilsen jail cell to avoid a trial and death sentence from the postwar Czechs. Wonderful impromptu scenes, coming in for landings on my desk, new characters waiting for life.

But after three weeks, I was waiting for the students to refill the dorm. Like a kid waiting for company to call, I neatened up my apartment. I cleaned up for students! Amazing! I'd been living like a student. I was shaggy, unshaved, nocturnal and when my dresser was empty, I sorted through my laundry bag for a change of clothing. Now, like the well behaved wunderkind who watched for the Manns, the Ruhmanns, the Veidts to come up our crushed-coral California driveway, all that culture, all those opinions, I now waited for the first station wagon to show up in the parking lot.

▲

No one prepared me for the second semester. Nothing could have. What had been green and blossoming in summer—a camp or a country club—was now gray and penal. The sun was weak, the days were short, the ground was muddy. The faculty were overworked, the students sullen. And people were sick, not all of them all the time but some of them, always, so that in a classroom, the sniffling, barking, honking, coughing were consistent, as if we were in a stadium where a ball goes bounding from row to row, only here it was a ball of phlegm and mucus, coming out of one red-eyed, sleep-deprived student after another.

It wasn't just the season. In my first semester I'd been contending with writers, a self-selected group. A workshop seminar. It was about writing, their writing; the table was covered with it. Now I was professing books to a larger group, who'd enrolled because it might be interesting, or I was famous, or they needed a course, and mine was scheduled for early afternoon, when they might manage to put in an appearance. American Nobelists. I chose Pearl Buck's *The Good Earth* to begin with, and after one or two sessions, I knew I had my work cut out for me, getting them to read, getting them to care, getting them to care about the right things. There were more pure lecturers in the college back then: the current style, sitting in a circle, chatting on a first-name basis, asking students what they made of this or that passage was a few years off. So I lectured. The Buck novel was a period piece, but worth knowing. And so was the author, her adventures, her conviction, her faith. Also, the way her great good fortune—the Nobel Prize—turned bad, with literati identifying it—and her—as the worst choice ever made, a joke, an accident.

I worked hard on my lecturing, attended to the text, its assumptions, accomplishments and shortcomings. It wasn't a great book but there were things to say about it and about the nation that loved it. Nobody skipped class, no one slept and when I thought over what I'd said, I gave myself good grades. But there were a few small warnings. At least once during every class, usually towards the end, I opened up for questions. And what came back was how many pages they'd have to read for next time or was I going to pass out a list of suggested topics for their first paper. Nothing interesting. It got worse. After class, I saw someone had left behind a notebook. I retrieved it, called the student from my office, left a message, not to worry about the notebook. But I couldn't resist snooping. And how it cost me! It wasn't the doodled cartoons, the list of things to do, the stick figures of Chinese peasants, so much as the notes themselves, a simplistic summary, an unintentional parody of what I'd said But all this was prologue warm-up, summary side-line tosses, compared to what happened when their papers came in.

Oh, they were impressive, neatly typed and substantial looking. Until I sat down to read. Then substance evaporated, subverted by wide margins, and as many space-filling quotations from *The Good Earth* as they felt they could get away with. And in every case, what they quoted was a passage I'd cited in class. There was no evidence that they'd discovered anything on their own. Then, there was the writing style: flat, passive-voiced, detached, almost disembodied. A paucity of proofreading, apostrophes a conundrum, misspellings and missed meanings. Confusion of author and central character, moralizing and editorializing mixed into shameless plot summary in the fashion of a high school book report or, worse yet, a grammar school show-and-tell period. Misplaced modifying clauses: "Walking to the fields, it started raining." Countless errors. Careless: it's a word you use casually, describing trivial mistakes, but those small things—careless things—were profoundly depressing. They made careless mistakes. That meant—there was no escaping it—they didn't care.

▲

"Can we talk in confidence?" I asked. In my office sat Charles Stuckey and Mary Cantonelli, who'd been in last semester's writing seminar. They'd enrolled in American Nobelists and their papers were among the few decent ones I'd gotten.

"Absolutely," Mary said. "I can't wait." With Mary, every sentence had some sexual innuendo.

"These papers . . . they're awful, most of them. What they write, how they write, all of it. There's almost nothing good . . ."

"Are they *all* bad?" asked Stuckey, putting first things first. He wanted to make sure his paper had escaped my condemnation.

"Of course not," I said. "But a lot of them are. They mix a little bit of what I said . . . garbled . . . and a lot of what I pointed out in the book. I couldn't help wondering . . . are they . . ." It seemed outrageous when I said it. " . . . doing the reading?"

"Bingo," Mary said. Her usual mannerism, holding her right hand as if it were a pistol, pointing it in my direction and pulling the trigger.

"It's a novel," I protested. "It's *The Good Earth*. It's not an econ text, for God's sake. I don't get it. If they're going to take my course like that . . . why take it at all?"

"You like your students, Professor Canaris?" Stuckey asked.

"Yes," I said. "Though this feels like the end of the honeymoon."

"Do you think the students like you?"

"Yes, I suppose so. Across the trenches . . . as it were."

"*As it were* . . ." He glanced over at Mary, smiled a rare smile. "I've never heard that phrase before. Aloud. Didn't that go out with 'gentle reader,' etc. etc.?"

"Jesus, Charles," Mary Cantonelli complained. "Professor Canaris is in pain here."

"It's getting more painful," I agreed. Stuckey was talented, he was tenacious and he thought the world was waiting for him, on his terms, editors and publishers and movies. But this wasn't about lessons for him. It was lessons for me.

"I like your lectures," he allowed. "Although Pearl Buck . . ." His voice trailed off. He tracked reputations, Fitzgerald up, Hemingway down, Dos Passos further down, Wright up, and Pearl Buck, down and out, off the see-saw and out of the playground completely. They didn't even teach her back in high school, where some writers, like Steinbeck, had found a second home. What did Charles Stuckey have to learn from Pearl Buck? Not to accept a Nobel Prize prematurely?

"The lectures are fine," Mary burst out. "I could listen to you talk about books all day. And night."

"Thanks," I said. Did she tease because she knew I was a safe target? That I'd never cross the line with a student? Or did that make me more inviting?

"Alright," Stuckey said. "What I'd do if I were you is give pop quizzes every week, unannounced. Some little question that, if they've read the book, they know the answer. You'll lose some of them. Hey, they're English majors at an elite college and you . . . you're famous. You wouldn't stoop to that, would you? It's beneath everybody's dignity. An insult. But that's the ticket . . ."

"Okay," I said. I felt insulted, as though I were back in grammar school, with hall passes and blackboards and lockers slamming up and down the hall.

"There's something else that will get their attention. It's how you grade them. Around here, B-minus is bad news. I'd come in with C's."

"They'll hate me."

"At least they'll be hating someone famous. Personally, I don't care about grades. The only grade that matters is the one I give myself . . ."

"Oh, give me a break," Mary said. "Ever give yourself less than an A?"

"A-minus, maybe . . ."

"Mr. Integrity . . ."

"Consider the competition . . ."

"Alright, you two," I said.

"Bottom line," Stuckey said. "Grade hard. And do it all semester."

"He's right about that," Mary added. "Lots of professors come in with low grades on the first papers. They say all sorts of clever nasty things. 'Look at me, I'm no pushover, I've got standards, I'm a tough guy.' Lasts about a month, tops."

"Point taken," I said. I knew an A paper when I saw one. Well-written, well-argued. Alive. And I knew what was stillborn, half-hearted. Careless. I kept rolling the word around. Carefree. Careless. Uncaring.

"Do that all semester," Stuckey repeated, getting out of his chair. "You'll be famous all over again."

"Thanks," I said.

"Glad to help . . ." he said. He glanced over at Mary. "You coming?"

"I think I'll hang out a while."

"I've got to write. You know?"

"Write on."

Stuckey left us alone and the tension drained out of the office, all that sweaty-palmed ambition. I pulled out a desk drawer and put my feet on it, stretching out. Mary lit a cigarette and we were quiet together. A huge winter sunset across the river marked—almost redeemed—a day that was otherwise not worth having. So Mary and I relaxed. This was the second time she'd rescued me.

"What'll I do when you're not around, Mary? When you graduate?"

"Take me to Europe?"

"That'd be nice."

"Why wait that long?"

"For Europe?"

"No, Professor. For me."

I took her in and couldn't help feeling grateful. Mary was 21 and legal, as far as the State of Ohio went. But, by the norms of the college, she was fatal. Too bad. Some students her age were adults, even ancients. Others were kids. Mary was well into a long, fine prime.

"I'd have to resign," I said. 'I'd have to leave this place . . ."

"So leave. I'm leaving . . ."

"I plan to stay. For some time. And . . . if something happened here . . . don't tell me no one will know."

"If a professor falls in a forest, with no one around, did it happen? If no one saw it . . ."

"It would be nice . . ."

"*Way* better than nice." She sensed me weakening and she had every reason for it. The day was fading, the office getting darker. Anyone who found us there, just sitting, would have guessed that something was up.

"It would be nice to meet up with you, down the road," I granted.

"How far down the road? Your place or mine?"

"I wasn't talking about distance. I was talking about time."

"Oh. That. Let me just say, I think we could click, you know that?"

"Could I be a little jealous? Are you sleeping with Charles Stuckey?"

"Stuckey never sleeps, Professor."

"Oh . . ."

"But when he comes, he yelps."

"*Yelps?*"

"Yelps. Not like a bark. More like a puppy sound. I'm pretty sure it's not my fault."

"Well, he does have problems finishing his stories. Climax problems. Common enough. I suppose writing is like love that way. Or flying. Most problems are at take-off or landing."

"Could I just say something? I really am . . ." She stopped, searching for a word, not finding it, beginning again. "I liked your Natalie. I'm sorry you can't be together. But there's more. It's what my father told me when this jerk I dated in high school broke my heart . . ."

"Was he the principal? Or just a teacher?"

"A student. From Jersey City. I kid you not, I was a wreck, my life was over, I'd join a nunnery or the Peace Corps. Maybe the Coast Guard. And my dad says, never kid yourself, there's just one. There's more. As long as you live. I sure hope he was right. For your sake."

"Thanks. So do I." I got up and she arose as well. While I groped on my desk for my keys, she waited at the door. When I approached, she blocked it.

"Come here, Professor," she said. "Just a minute." And she drew me in towards her, expertly, delicately, confidently. Greyhound's slogan came to me unbidden: *Leave the driving to us.* We kissed, only for an instant. She kept her word. But I could feel her straining, drawing me in, so that when we parted I was sorry.

"See you down the road, Professor," she said.

▲

That two week vacation we had in March was called "spring break," even though six weeks of frost, cold drizzle, mud and slush remained ahead. The students fled, to Florida, the garden-variety debauch, also—with parents—to the Caribbean and Mexico. This time, I fled too. I said I was returning to Los Angeles, which people were happy to hear. I'd been through a lot this first year, everyone knew, love and death and too much time on my own. I needed to get out, they thought. How right they were.

I went to Los Angeles, that was true. The airport, anyway. And Honolulu. Another airport. My destination was a place where I knew no one and no one knew me. A place where English was spoken and pleasure was cheap. A place I could plunge into with impunity, leave without regret and nothing—not a whisper—would follow me home.

This isn't an episode I'm proud of, ten carnal days in the Del Pilar Street nightclub/red-light district a few blocks in from Manila Bay. I could hear my mother calling out to me, as she had after more boyish misdeeds, "You should be ashamed of yourself." Though her words were stern, there was always forgiveness in her eyes. I hope for that forgiveness, when I think of Manila. Maybe I'd try to tell her Manila was like Karlsbad, a cure, a rejuvenation, only in Manila you drank San Miguel beer, the pavilions and colonnades of Karlsbad were replaced by a murderer's row of nightclubs, a wilderness of neon, with satay sellers, shoeshine boys, flower vendors, shills and touts of all sorts up and down a street that was choked by belching jeepneys and taxis where the meters were always broken, and that instead of Lehar operetta tunes, the sound track was rock-and-roll. A technicolor world, a film noir landscape, and me. And the women. Would it be fair to say I had them? Or they had me? I had foreseen sex that would be splendid, varied, and anonymous and I was two-thirds right. They were splendid. I went from bar to bar, I had sex for breakfast, lunch and dinner, up and down del Pilar Street and ever since then, and for all the time that's coming, the sight of straight black hair cascading over a woman's back, a woman glancing at me, over her shoulder, calmly, thoughtfully . . . that will be Manila. Splendid and varied. But not anonymous. The women of del Pilar lacked the hard-edged, starved and drugged character one associates with the oldest profession. At times, they were hardly professional at all. It was like a Warner Brothers movie, sometimes Mickey Rooney and Judy Garland and a circle of pig-tailed friends deciding, on the spur of the moment, hey, let's make us a b-girl bar. We'll find a mirror and a few tables, any old jukebox, a place with a few rooms in back, and bingo, we'll have a party. Granted, this is a confession that I would have nothing extenuate. Guilty as charged. But along with darker currents, there was a strain of Catholic romanticism on Del Pilar Street. The women were searching for something better than what they'd left behind in hopeless villages and dead-end barrios. They were no Madames Butterfly. They were closer, I guess, to Miss Saigon. But the old dream lived in them, lived on that notorious street, so dreary and tarnished by day, so gaudy and musical at night. They were smart, some of them, they were talkative, good humored and even brave. In the end, if there's forgiveness I hope we all receive it. But if there's only so much to go around, let them be forgiven first. As for that case of gonorrhea that announced itself on the day of my departure, that gonorrhea which became a polite "non-specific urinary infection" by the time it was quickly resolved back in Ohio, it was a small price to pay. I returned to campus, ready to begin my life again. I resumed lecturing on Nobelist novelists, administering pop quizzes, grading harshly. The boys in the dorm—my eyes and ears—told me the word out: I was "hard" but "maybe worth it." But only if you were willing to risk getting a B minus.

IX. NOW: NOVEMBER, 2005

▲

I HELPED TRUDY KENT, MY COLLEGE ESCORT, CARRY HER alumni handouts into the functions room the college had rented at the University Club in Manhattan, my first stop on the alumni circuit. A maid ran a vacuum cleaner over a bland carpet; otherwise, the place was empty. Two hours remained before my first valedictory. Trudy had to be on hand for the earliest arrivals. I helped her unpack her wares—college newspapers, admissions brochures, college pens and pennants. Then I checked out the podium where I'd speak. Empty, the room was enormous. Inconceivable that tonight's attendance would more than dent it. What an impertinence, that this little Ohio college aspired to capture Manhattan's interest! Might as well set up a lemonade stand on Fifth Avenue. Suddenly, it felt tremendously sad, this little college, this farewell tour.

On Fifth Avenue, I headed north, towards the park. Usually when I came back to New York, New York came back to me, all its directness and audacity. There'd be energy in my walk that would've drawn comment back in Ohio: what's up with him? And an edge in my talk, that would have offended on campus. But this time was different, slow, thoughtful—Gerron in Karlsbad. I passed the Plaza, the Plaza fountain, then the baseball fields, the Great Meadow. Was there anywhere in New York that someone hadn't written about. Filmed? That was what drew me to the city and that was what sent me away: nothing in New York was only, or always, yours.

I took a bench on the park's literary walk, where authors' statues stood in the largest surviving grove of elm trees in America. It made sense: dead authors, nearly extinct shade trees and me, once a promising author, tonight's retiring professor. A melancholy landscape, yet I savored installing myself in it. Then it was time to make my way back to the hotel. Trudy would have panicked by now. But I lingered for a while. "Verweile, doch, du bist so schon." Goethe's Faust said it to a woman: "Linger a while, you're so beautiful." I applied it to this October moment, enjoying it as it slipped away. It would have pleased me if the rest of my last year would be something like this.

▲

"You've got a hundred people in there!" Trudy exclaimed.

"For me?" There had been a time one hundred people wouldn't have surprised me, but that was years ago. My expectations had diminished since then. And I'd heard all sorts of road stories: some crowded, jovial nights, some pathetic mousey occasions that almost no one came to.

"There's college parents and a couple of trustees and, god professor, all those students. And a reporter."

"Where from?"

"Here, I guess . . . ."

"What publication?"

"He didn't say." She sensed, I suppose, that she'd dropped a stitch. "Sorry. I guess . . . we're a little late. Do you want a drink first?"

"I'll want a drink afterwards. Suppose we begin . . ."

"Great. I've got some announcements first. Then I'll say a little about you. I didn't prepare a big . . ."

"Short and sweet will do. I'm not getting an award am I?"

That gave her pause: a Welcome Wagon lady hesitating before ringing a doorbell. I regretted what I said.

"Anything is just fine," I said, in the same way I responded when someone back at the college asked me to dinner, proudly announcing "We're only having hamburgers."

I sat in the back row, listened while Trudy began. She was thrilled she said, at the big turnout for what promised to be an extra-special occasion. There followed a miscellany of upbeat news. Our entering class was unusually talented and carefully selected. We were, according to some poll or other—not that hateful U.S. News and World Report ranking—one of the ten "hottest" liberal arts colleges in the land. The microphone squeaked and Trudy fidgeted with it. Speeches weren't her style. The football team had won a game or two—thank God for Oberlin and tiny Hiram—and the new jillion dollar super gym was approaching completion. I glanced around the room, the so-called function room, studied the backs of people's heads, some inclining into whispers, others sitting politely, even attentively. Did people still care, after they left, about how the football team was coming along?

"Now for tonight's special guest," Trudy continue. "You may have heard that this is Professor Canaris' last year of teaching. President Tracy insisted it was high time to thank him for everything. 'As far as I'm concerned,' she told me just the other day, 'this is the Year of Canaris.' He'll be the baccalaureate speaker at graduation this year. There'll be articles about him in the alumni bulletin, and a conference on his work. And I'm sure, in fund raising, the College will want to do something in his . . . uh . . . memory."

Trudy flushed. It was sweet, she'd said *memory*. But it was too late for her to correct herself.

"Did he die?" someone shouted. These alumni gatherings could be raucous, because that was the style we'd imparted to our students. But Trudy recovered nicely.

"We'll see about that," Trudy said. "Professor Canaris? Where are you?"

"Here," I said and, as heads turned, I made my way forward, tables on my left and right. I hugged Trudy and turned to face the audience.

"I'm still alive," I said. "And for the record, I will *not* be the baccalaureate speaker. I'll be giving the commencement address . . ."

I hadn't wanted to correct Trudy. It might have been an innocent mistake. Or a calculated effort to roll back, in front of an audience of witnesses, the promise they'd made.

"Bear with me a moment," I said. And with that, I executed a slow panning shot of the people in front of me. Like a corpse in a coffin, sitting up and opening his eyes at his own funeral, I took them in. Sometimes the name and faces came together—my God, there was Charles Stuckey, in the front row, and Larry Levin, and a dozen others I vaguely recognized, among many others I did not.

"That's why I came," I said after a moment of unashamed staring. "Whether you need to see me, well, that's for you to say. But I needed to look your way again. Be advised for every face I knew, there are two that are dimly familiar, and two more I don't know at all, all smiling at me, asking to be remembered. Recognizing a face and form, greatly changed, is difficult as remembering a name, and I'm too far away to read your name tags. In my way. A professor who recognizes every student would be suspect, a memory act in a carnival show, a maitre d' whose quick recall earns bigger tips. But there is something more, in this room tonight, not a name or face but what I felt when I knew I'd be seeing you, what I feel when I see you now."

I had not prepared what I was going to say. I was winging it. And that felt right. What occurred to me was a paradox: that even as good writing and its inevitable counterpart, good reading became more marginal, those of us who read and wrote believed in it more passionately. When fiction was central—when even a U.S. president might read a novel—you could take and leave books, as you liked. When it became endangered, when the very act of writing was like sticking a message in a bottle and tossing it into the ocean, then reading, too, was a matter of life and death. We were a club, all of us, a freemasonry, and an underground. And life was lively underground, with code-words, pass-words, smuggled messages, recognitions. But it was still underground. Dark and wet and sunlight deprived, more tomb than womb. Monthly reading groups gathered for monthly seances, waiting for voices from the other side. How, anyone would have to wonder, had it come to this? Could we count on one, just one publisher to reject the next Jacqueline Susanne, if *The Valley of the Dolls* landed on their desk? But all this was familiar. What about writers themselves? Question number one: how many novels did we know that confronted the major issues of our time? The civil rights movement, its shifting alliances, its heroes and charlatans? What about the anti-war movement of the 70's? The greed-is-good-stockmarket of the eighties? Was there a novel worth reading about a presidential election? Or a president? What had we been writing about, all this time? Oh, there might be exceptions, a handful. But where was the energy, the confidence, the hubris that aspired to—and I was going to use a phrase that had become nothing but ironic—the Great American Novel? It receded away from us, like the green light at the end of Gatsby's pier. And we smirked about it, as if great novels were a phrase we were going through when we were young and foolish, aiming to take on the world.

Now I rested a moment. What I'd said was alright, I supposed, but as I studied the crowd I sensed they were waiting for something more than my view of the cultural climate. Something more. They liked seeing me again, hearing my voice one last time. I took them back to college. But they wanted more. They wanted to hear about me.

"Enough of this," I said. "I suppose I'm cranky. I'm using the fact that I've been around forever to say what I want. It's not tenure, by the way, that's the greatest guarantee of free speech. It's old age! I didn't come here to campaign for anything. Only to say goodbye. And to thank you."

I had guessed right. I could see it. A quickening of interest, a heightened attentiveness.

"You know my story. Some of it, that is. I came to the college in 1970. A one-year arrangement at most. And there were times during that year—which some of you shared with me—when that year felt like forever. But forever is what it came to be. I stayed. And I stayed because of—among other things—you. Always you. Other things came and went. But students kept on coming to college and some of them found their way to me . . ."

Now we were all on memory lane. I reprised war stories: comic moments, embarrassments, howlingly lame student excuses. Blunders from brilliant students, lucky strokes from less than average kids. At the end of it all—now that it turned out my career was ending—what I felt was gratitude. Gratitude for what? For time to write. That had been the plan, at the start. But other things came into it. The teaching, the gossip, the students who had mattered—my biographer might say—far more than they should have. But it was they, not my biographer, who faced me now.

"I know how you looked to me back then," I said, "though I may be slow to know you now. But now that this long run is ending, I wonder—too late, maybe—how I looked to you. What it meant, our little time together, what I meant. Whether, frankly, it was worth it. A few of you have become writers. Others are publishers, librarians, teachers. And some have gone into trades and careers, from law to wine, to stocks and bonds. How do you measure your success and failure. Does reading have any part of it? Writing? I hope that your encounters with me have traveled with you since then. I hope that your writing is sharper, livelier, more persuasive, your sense of scene, your appraisal of atmosphere, your ear for your language, your eye for character. And, even if you never wrote another word, I hope that you saw your life as a story among stories, that you sought out its underlying patterns and meanings, measuring your own story against others, that your life was larger, your sense of time deeper and that you felt less lonely in the world. Anyway, that . . . as I shuffle off is my wish for you . . ."

I nodded and backed off from the podium and a round of applause came out of the audience, lasting until Trudy took the podium. She thanked me for an evening she was sure no one would ever forget. Then she asked if I'd be willing to answer any questions and, though I nodded, I expected that after a decent interval there'd be a rush towards the cash bar, which I would lead.

"I go first!" I saw an old man pull himself out of his chair. No former student, that was for sure. "You remember me?"

Dutifully, I studied him, certain that in a moment I'd apologize as nicely as I could. And then: a minor miracle. Against that tide of forgetting, those thousands of collapsed synapses, I knew him.

"Hello, Mr. Alfano. How are you?"

"Come over here, professor." He commanded and I obeyed. When I stood next to him, he turned and addressed the audience. "When John went to college, me and his mom worried ourselves sick. But Professor Canaris and some other professors took care of him. My boy did okay. Better than okay. And we still worried. Could you blame us? He majored in *philosophy*! Okay? I rest my case. I figured, after we supported him for a few more years of graduate school, he'd be living at home full time. And I said as much to Professor Canaris. He told me not to worry. And he put his money where his mouth was. He bet $15 grand that John would make it. And so . . ." He grabbed my hand, reached into a coat pocket with his other hand, placed an envelope I could tell had a thick wad of currency within.

"I pay cash."

"I can't take this," I protested.

"Who says?" he glanced around. "What do you think folks? Should I poll the jury?"

It was hopeless. I took the envelope, while the audience cheered, and I embraced old Alfano. He had a lot to be proud of in his son. And I had much to answer for. "Thanks again," he whispered, his lips at my ear. "If you lost the bet," he said, "I'd've come after you . . ."

The questions, when they came, were easy, at least at first. How had the college changed? How did today's students compare with those of other years? What about the faculty, were they like the professors they remembered? What about the future of increasingly expensive liberal arts colleges in today's world? In all my years, I'd never been deeply involved in the college's operations, the hiring searches, the budgets, the endless self studies, assessment and evaluations that stirred up everything and settled nothing. I was at a distance but maybe that gave me perspective. So, for what it was worth, I had this much to offer: there were two tectonic plates rubbing and grinding away beneath our handsome campus. There was the imperative to challenge, shape, test and discipline. That had always been there. But there was the wish to attract, comfort, accommodate and make happy. The hard versus the happy. They clashed, always had, always would. A necessary tension, maybe. But in recent years happy was winning, two times out of three. It showed up in our buildings, our budget, our brochures. So be it. Was it good news? I had my doubts. When I looked ahead, I worried. But when I looked back I felt gratitude. I hoped those who followed me would feel the same way.

"It's Larry Levin." Enormous, white-bearded. "I was there when you moved into our freshman dorm. As a matter of fact, I gave you your first beer . . ."

"A debt," I hinted, glancing at the bar, "I am anxious to repay . . ."

"I'm just wondering about all those lives you touched . . . all the students . . . and how you compare that with the lives that you touched through your books. *Out On the Coast* and the other two."

"Well, Larry, the audience for the books was larger from the start and it keeps growing. So the books have the edge that way.

And my list of students stops, it's been decided, a few months from now. So paper wins, on paper. But that's not the end of the discussion, is it? That's because I can't imagine not knowing you, not knowing all the students who came into range at college. Granted, I meet people who've read my books. But it's almost always awkward. From both sides. That wasn't the case with the students. That was . . . often . . . joy."

"So how do you regard yourself . . . rate yourself is what I mean . . . as a professor? As a writer?"

"Okay, I have an opinion about my books. But the rating, as you call it, is for readers to do. On the whole, I think I've gotten a fair shake. As for teaching . . . that's harder. Once again, I defer. To the students this time. I wasn't great, every day, that's for sure. But I think I was pretty good when I started. And I got better. Thanks to the students, I might add."

"There's something I've got to say," Larry continued. He turned towards the audience, seated behind his place in the first row. "Something about Professor Canaris. It started when I came back for my fifth reunion. I was a busy guy back then, settling up a practice, paying off med school, about to marry my first wife. I liked to read, sure, but I'm not so in touch with the world of books, know what I mean? So I ask Professor what should I read, because I'm not gambling on Cormac MacCarthy or Don DeLillo, no way. And he says he'll handle it. And every year, Christmas, I get a list of good writing he's come across. Some people I never heard of. And he warns me off some big names. And that was the start of it. Thanks, Professor. Keep 'em coming . . ."

"I got that list too!" someone shouts out. Several others raise their voices also. They make a racket, laughing and pointing.

"I'm caught!" I say. "I confess."

"Well, keep it up, professor," Larry resumed. And thanks for talking me out of transferring to a place that had more girls, and Jews, and nightlife. Don't know how you did it . . . but thanks. Lots of people have things to thank you for."

"You're welcome, Larry." I replied. "But . . . not everyone feels as you do. I have to point that out. It's never unanimous."I paused, just to make sure what I was about to do felt right. And it did. I was calling someone out. Throwing down a gauntlet. This was a decisive moment. But I never really made a decision. This farewell year had its dark side. Why pretend otherwise? Why not acknowledge the nightmare side of a walk down memory lane?

"Let's face it, there are always some kids who don't like you, your style, your grades, your comments in class and on their papers. And they don't like what they discover about themselves in front of you. In writing seminars, there are students who've been encouraged to think that they're God's gift. Their high school teachers told them that everything they did was marvelous. But the college professor isn't so sure. They try. How they try! But sometimes, trying harder doesn't get you where you want to be. So they're hurt and angry. And they stay that way for a long time. One in particular . . . one . . . I don't know the name of . . ."

I had them now, and no wonder. I was right at the edge of a cliff. I could still back away, shrug, say you win some, you lose some. And let it go at that.

"I had a letter," I said, "just the other day." I took them through it: the look and feel of it, the hate distilled. "No one succeeds with every student. And the more you succeed, the more attention you should pay to your failures. That is the reason—the only reason—I mention this tonight."

I realized now, that this was gripping. Poor Trudy, I thought, sitting next to a table covered with pennants and brochures. Were there any prospective students, full-fare parents in the house?

"There's more. I live, these last years, on a quiet road along the river that we all sing about, in college songs. An isolated bungalow that I love, downhill from a college I care for, even though my employment is ending. I've had evidence that someone has been on my property. A car parked in my driveway. A realtor's for sale sign planted in my yard . . ."

"My God, professor . . ." It was Trudy, dear Trudy. "What are you going to do?"

"Nothing," I replied. "I'm not moving. Changing. Running? I'd be easy to catch. These may just be—practical jokes. But I've shared these with you tonight because I want this story to end. I want whoever it is to know I am ready for him. Or her."

Now, now I thought was surely the ending. Impossible that anyone would follow with another question.

"Professor." I saw a slight, well-dressed fellow, with glasses, thinning blonde hair, and a bemused expression on his face. 'I'm Alva Morse," he said and as soon as that came out, there was a stirring, people turning to see someone that they had heard of and I hadn't. "Tonight," he continued, "I'm the guest of Charles Stuckey." More staring. Stuckey sat right beside him, eyes fixed on me; we might have been back in seminar. He hadn't become a famous writer but he was famous, alright, as one of the few publishers—Sonny Mehta came to mind—whose name was in the papers, talking about the state of the industry, the direction of the culture, the future of "the book." He heralded the latest hot author and dismissed the franchise player who'd gone stale: kissing up and kissing off.

"I noticed, Professor, when you talk about your retirement, you suggest that it wasn't your decision." Now he studied a notebook that was in his hand and I know I was in the presence of a reporter. "You say 'it turns out' and 'it's been decided' your career is ending. You refer to the whole thing as a 'replacement.' Anyone would have to ask, was this your decision? Or someone else?"

"Someone else's," I said, without hesitation. God knows what he'll write, I thought. But I couldn't flack for the college, couldn't lie, and I was not the kind to say "no comment."

"You don't have to talk about this," Trudy intervened. "This is a college gathering."

"I can't imagine a better audience." I told her. "Was there something else, Mr. Morse?"

"Just one question," he said. "And thank you for your patience. And candor." He nodded at Trudy. "Thank you, all. To be clear, I'll put my question bluntly. So that you can answer in kind. But bluntness doesn't mean disrespect. I think you know that, Professor. But I want clarity. To you and from you."

"Understood. Fire away."

"You know the question. Why haven't you published anything in thirty years?"

"Fair question. I'd venture to any that there isn't a person in the room who hasn't wondered. Myself included. Short answer: around the time I began teaching, I started something. The famous 'Beast.' For many reasons—mainly because of discoveries I made while I was writing, the book has been shaped and reshaped in response. It has turned out to be my life's major work."

"So . . . it exists?"

"I know many people have their doubts. It's become a joke, in some quarters. Not to me."

"We'll see it? When?"

"Not so long. You won't have to wait as long as you've waited already."

"A safe answer. And shrewd."

"You're welcome. Thanks for asking."

▲

"I'm a prick, Professor," Charles Stuckey said, after almost everyone else had left. "It's been a long time and it's my fault."

"Mine too," I said.

"Thanks . . . but no. It's the student who's supposed to take the first step. We both know it."

We both knew. Students had to decide who they wanted to keep in their lives after they graduated. At colleges our contacts with them had been required and prescribed. Once they graduated our power melted away. They were free to check back in with us. Or not.

"Well, I'm glad to see you now," I offered.

"We're supposed to have dinner together."

"Were we?"

"Oh my God, Professor," Trudy said. "I forgot to tell you. Mr. Stuckey called us last week."

"No worry. I'd love to have dinner."

"Hey, I've got to go," Alva Morse said. "I'm under the gun. Thanks for your talk."

"Was it any good?"

"Very . . ." He turned to Charles Stuckey, brushed his cheek with a kiss. "Later, sweets."

▲

"I've wondered about you," he said.

We had walked a dozen blocks from Fifth Avenue, turned onto 43rd Street and entered the Century Club, a nest for publishers, and well published authors, art and power, where I once would have been recognized but now Stuckey was the one who made the entrance into the upstairs dining room, where his favorite table was set. We ordered food and drinks. Out on the street we'd chatted about the meeting that had just ended. Now, we faced each other. He was well turned out, successful, poised. He still had that judgmental stare, though.

"And I've wondered about you," I returned. A moment of silence. He must be devastating in meetings, I thought, waiting for his silence to weigh on whoever was across from him, some poor writer desperate for judgment on a manuscript. He was using that silence now. "You haven't been back to campus," I finally said. He'd won the silent game. "If you have, I guess I missed you."

"No," he said, dismissing the idea of an Ohio homecoming as something for football players and fraternity boys. "I haven't been within a hundred miles of the place."

"You've done well. You must be on their radar screen. Willard Thrush and company. They must have solicited you."

"All the time. And I've had a few . . . what . . . externs? Kids trailing me around to find out how publishing works." Another smile and wave. "They should be in no rush to find out."

"Have you kept in touch with any of your classmates? The ones in the writing seminar, say?"

"No."

"Well." I had begun to feel that I was working a little too hard. In an odd way it resembled those occasions when I acceded to a request from the admissions department. The college sales force asked me to chat with a prospective student who might be willing to become a great writer. Sometimes it was fun. But now and then you'd face a sullen, tired-of-it-all kid dragged from campus to campus by parents who were more interested in learning than their offspring was. They sat there, uninquisitive, unread, while I struggled to light a match on a bar of wet soap.

"Listen, Charles," I said. "I'm tired and I want to drink more than one drink and have a good meal with someone I've thought about and who, as has been stipulated, has wondered about me. You invited me. I'm your guest. Fine. Now what I remember of you is writing a wonderful letter of recommendation to the Iowa Writing School. I also made some phone calls on your behalf. Then I was sent a short note to the effect that you'd dropped out. Correct me if I'm wrong, the politics of the place concerned you . . ."

He nodded and smiled, as if the memory were quaint.

"I believe I recycled my letter of recommendation to a publishing institute somewhere. And that's the last I heard of you . . . or from you . . . until your name started showing up in print. What else? Willard Thrush told me you'd called, just recently, after the axe fell, wondering about doing something in my name. And, though I've been slow all my life in figuring out who was sleeping with who . . . and this includes some of my own partners . . . nonetheless, I saw the reporter buss you on the cheek in front of me tonight and I gather you might be leaving the lights on for him later on."

Just then, wine appeared and a plate of oysters which were going to be followed, in my case by a veal shank, creamed spinach, and crisp fried potatoes.

"Perfect timing!" I said. "I'm old. I'm done talking. I want to hear from you. You'll get no questions from me. I shall not interrogate. You'll get attentiveness, curiosity, and understanding. Now, would you pass the rolls and butter. And pour . . . or have someone else pour . . . the wine?"

▲

Looking back, I cannot decide whether Charles Stuckey spoke the way he did because he hadn't seen me for so long or because he suspected he might never see me again. At first, though, we ate. I "ate my plate," as my mother used to command. As for Charles, he barely touched his salad. He talked. He talked like a man in a confessional. But what was his sin?

He'd been put on earth to be a writer and I was the first writer he met. I fascinated him, he loved me, he hated me, he'd read everything I'd ever written. He even stalked me, my comings and goings. He knew when I left town, when I returned, what music came out of my dormitory window and when I switched off the lights at night. Had I known? Yet in four years, he'd been in my office just once, with Mary Cantonelli, when American Nobelists was going badly. Nor had we ever had any of those impromptu bondings which the college advertised. And for sure, he'd never had the meal-at-the-professor's house which students regarded as their ultimate small college entitlement.

"You knew, Professor," he said. "You knew before I did."

"Knew what?" I wondered.

"That I'd never be a writer."

It was a lesson he had to go to Iowa to learn, that there were other writers, lots of them as talented as he, dedicated. That didn't mean he couldn't have made it. The bookstores were full of work from much lesser lights. And some of the writers he deemed more talented had . . . guess what? . . . disappeared into teaching, philosophy, web-design. (Of those classmates, he kept track.) He could have made it, alright, and as I looked over a dessert menu and opting for a cognac, I agreed. For a moment I thought we were about to embark on an archetypal literary conversation, sharing our picks for a list all writers keep: the lucky, the over-rated, the unworthy. With wine and time, I could see us confiding. He would whisper "Morrison," looking around to make sure no one was listening. "De Lillo," I would whisper back. But Stuckey had other things to confide.

"When I left Iowa," he said, "I knew it wasn't for me. Work a couple years on a manuscript that some ex-English major with attitude slips in a tote bag to take along on the shuttle to the Hamptons. I didn't want to put my life, my income, my self-esteem at the mercy of lightweights. I couldn't bear it, the half-assedness of it. It just wasn't a grown-up way to live."

With that, he reached into his jacket and handed to me the letter of recommendation that had gotten him into Iowa. I'd written hundreds of letters over the years. Some were studies in faint praise. A student was "diligent" and "attended class faithfully" and "seemed interested" in the material. Some were middling: "a work in progress," "deserves consideration," "will cause no problems." Others were all-out endorsements: "You will thank me for this letter," "one of the two or three best" in a class, in years, in memory. Stuckey's letter, I saw at a glance, was in this category.

"I have no complaints," he said, "about this letter."

"How could you? It got you into Iowa."

"So it did. But there was something in it, a phrase you used. 'Charles Stuckey is among the best writers I've encountered here. And, when it comes to critical assessment of other students' writing, he stands alone. I know better than to forecast the success of anybody's writing. But of Charles' future in the world of books, I have no doubt . . . ' "

"Well, it sounds like me writing about you, alright."

"No, no. Don't you see? You saw it! You predicted it! I was a good writer . . . and a better critic. You knew that I'd wind up in publishing, you knew it when I was back in frigging college. I wasn't the next Joyce or Faulkner. I was going to be the guy who packs some other guy's manuscript in a tote when I take the shuttle to a time-share Hamptons . . ."

"And that's what you became?"

"Not anymore. Those guys with manuscripts in tote bags? They work for me. Point is, you knew me, before I knew myself. Now, let me ask you, have you met your replacement?"

"Just a handshake. On stage. More of a photo-op than a conversation."

"John Henry Mallon is ours now," Stuckey said. "His next book. That's between us. It hasn't been announced yet."

"Congratulations. Signed, sealed, and . . . delivered?"

"Far from it. Mallon serves no wine before its time."

"That could be a recipe for vinegar . . ." I said. "Have you read *GAMESHOW*?"

"Terrific stuff. Mind-boggling."

"Not so mind boggling you finished, though," I suggested.

"I was on board all the way, though. Until I got off."

"I have a theory about big books . . ."

"Having written one yourself?"

"Yes."

"Good. You know, I'm courting you professor. This is a business meal, tax deductible."

"You want me to blurb Mallon's next opus?"

"That's an idea. But what I had in mind was he could write an introduction to your next book. One heavyweight saluting each other. As it were."

"*As it were*." That was the phrase he'd mocked, so long ago. But he didn't react, now.

"Or maybe . . . you'd introduce each other . . ."

"Surely we can't both . . ."

"Nobody keeps track. Happens all the time, believe me. We'll work it out."

"What you propose . . . whatever it turns out to be . . . in regard to me, is it for reasons of business? Or friendship? Does that come into it at all?"

"Business or friendship, that's the choice? I'd say both. But there's something else. Maybe it trumps the other two."

"Yes?"

"Curiosity. About you, professor. You're what I wasn't. You wrote some terrific books and you could've kept churning them out and some of them would have been better and some would have been worse, you'd fail, you'd come back, go away, return triumphant. Like Cher. And you . . . you got into this Beast thing. No teasing excerpts, every few years, to remind the world that something big was coming. No interviews about your work in progress. No guest spots at writers' conferences, no profiles, no up-close-and-personal essays on where you live and what you live for. You just kept doing what you were doing. You didn't even do the hermit I-want-to-be-alone thing. You showed up for work every year and when the place took you for granted that was okay and when they axed you for Mallon, well . . . so what? I want to see your book, professor . . ."

"Is it that you want to see the book? You didn't say read . . . you said *see*. Is it that you want me revealed as a genius? Or a fraud?"

"I'll settle for any answer I can get. I have a theory about you. I hope it's wrong. It's that you've put so much into this thing, for so long. Another guy writes a book people don't like, he had a bad outing, an off-day. They don't like *your* book, it's a misspent life. And my guess is you don't want to hear it. You want to . . ."

"Die first?"

"You control the book. You're the king when they pages are blank. After that it's up for grabs. Will they be fair? Generous? Merciless? Who knows? Beyond control. You're personally stoic and gallant. All that European stuff. But when it comes to this, you don't want to risk being around."

"It's a good book," I said. "Very good."

"Show me, professor. I don't want to wait until you die."

"It might not be such a long wait."

"Don't go there, please. We could make some magic."

"We'll see." I nodded. I shook his hand, thanked him. "We'll see . . ."

▲

The next morning, I was famous. "The Other Canaris," headlined Alva Morse's article on the front page of the N.Y. Times arts section. I was the mystery man of American letters, tucked away at an Ohio college, toiling on a great novel that might not exist and I'd recently been cashiered by people who'd lost hope in me, replaced by the redoubtable Mallon. The article was accurate in every detail. I was not misquoted. Even the descriptions of me, tall, arrogant, elegant and shy, approachable but elusive were in-bounds. *Haunted*, that's the word that struck me. As in haunted by a novel, haunted by a mad student, haunted by a promise unfulfilled. He quoted students' accounts of my classes. He found a number of people who talked—not for attribution—about The Beast. "One of the great and lonely voyages of American—no, world literature," said one publisher. Stuckey? "If . . . big if . . . it exists, I suspect it has problems beyond solving," said another. Morse called President Tracy, who seemed to have been caught off-guard. "All good things come to an end," she philosophized. It was a substantial piece, filled with telling reflections about teaching and writing, about teaching writing, about early success and long silence. As a public relations coup, it would earn me a reputation for cleverness that I didn't deserve. The credit went to Alva Morse and to the man who'd brought him to the party, Charles Stuckey. I was on Stuckey's radar screen now. Whether as a destination or a target, I didn't know.

I thought about all this as I sat next to Trudy on a flight to

Chicago, watching Pennsylvania slide away below. I wondered what I often wonder when I travel in this country, whether it's Pennsylvania from the air or, on the ground, the subdivisions around Columbus. What is there in these places, to make people miss them, make them ache to return? Someone might do a map of America, printed in different colors, according to a place's ability to generate homesickness. Red for *Look Homeward, Angel*, white for "*We gotta get out of here*."

"Professor Canaris?" Trudy had been quietly fidgeting. She'd been almost mute on the way to the airport. Had I slighted her somehow? Had she wanted to be included in my dinner with Charles Stuckey? "They called this morning. From the college. Jeremy Collinsworth, President Tracy, Willard Thrush, Provost Alfano . . . a conference call."

"What did they want?"

"They asked if you'd said what it said in the newspaper and I said yes, pretty much."

"That's correct. So?"

"I guess they're worried what people will think. They were talking about damage control. Then they talked awhile among themselves. Like I wasn't even on the line. They talked about cancelling tonight in Chicago. 'Nipping it in the bud.' They decided they better not. 'Why get in a pissing contest with a skunk?'"

"Who said that?"

"I can't say. It wasn't the President."

"Alright. Was that all?"

"They said I should ask you to please be careful. Think of the college. Everybody loves the college. We're all on the same team."

"Is that so?"

"It's what they said."

▲

A few moments before I was scheduled to speak, Trudy called my room to say that my appearance had been moved from the Lake Erie Room to Lake Superior Ballroom. There were tons of alumni, she said—and some reporters too. There'd been some late long-distance debate about whether an alumni gathering should be open to the press. Clearly, it had never come up before. After a good deal of chat, the why-get-into-a-pissing-contest-with-a-skunk school of thought prevailed and freedom of the press was served. When I arrived, I was greeted by the college damage control team, Jeremy Collinsworth and—I had to laugh—Willard Thrush. "Are you the truth squad that follows me on the campaign trail?" I asked Thrush. "Pissing contest with a skunk" had to be from him.

"We just wanted to see for ourselves," Collinsworth volunteered. "Not trust the newspapers."

"They were accurate," I assured him. "I was not misquoted.

"Our concerns go a little deeper than that," said Collinsworth.

"I suppose they do. So do mine."

▲

At first, I spoke as I had in New York, about books, writing and the college. This time I omitted clues that my departure had been at the administration's request. They knew that already. The speech I gave had nothing in it to offend the college, now or later. The college had sent the audio-visual department's Herb Urlaub to tape proceedings. Whether this was to have a record of a cherished professor's farewell or to prepare for litigation, who knew?

After applause subsided, I indicated that I'd be willing to answer questions, react to comments or—if more than a few seconds of silence elapsed—adjourn to the bar to drink in the company of friends. The evening was young and my bed was just an elevator away. Salud! But no.

"How do you feel about leaving?" someone asked.

"Leaving?" I was puzzled. Maybe I shouldn't have been, but I was.

"The college . . ."

"I didn't leave the college," I said. "The college left me. Let's be clear about that. My resignation was at the college's request."

"Why didn't you fight it?"

"I'll tell you what I told them. I'm the son of a German father and a Jewish mother. These are two races, more alike than is commonly acknowledged. History has taught both Germans and Jews a pair of priceless lessons. Not to go where we're not wanted. And not to stay there."

"How about John Henry Mallon? What do you think of him?"

"I wish him well. I would have enjoyed being his colleague and not his predecessor. Still, I'm sure our paths will cross."

"Mr. Canaris!" I knew this speaker, a trustee, a gung-ho loyalist. Never friendly, even in better days. He always called me Mister. "Do you worry that the publicity attending your departure will hurt the college you claim you're so fond of . . ."

"More than fond, Mr. McCormack. Way more. As to the college, it will not be harmed one bit."

"You can't be serious! You read the newspapers?"

"The college is not the administration of the moment. Executive discomfort is one thing. The character of the college where I've taught for thirty years is something else."

"Is it true, as some have suggested, that you're doing this to resurrect a career that's on the back burner? Trying to hype a novel that, without all this controversy, might be a non-event?"

"Mr. McCormack, hype won't save this book from failure, if it fails. Or promote it to success, if it succeeds. I've been working on the book a long time. But I've never spent a minute worrying about promotion. Neither should the college . . . or those claiming to act in its interests."

That got a round of applause.

"In some ways the goals of teaching and of writing are the same. You hope to connect to someone else, to make them care about what you care about. So that the things which matter, the things that matter to you, matter to them. So . . . here are my last words. Thank you for caring . . ."

I made my way out of the room quickly, shaking hands but not lingering, excusing myself as I went. I begged off at the bar. All this talk about caring resulted in a sudden surge of not caring, indifference to my fate. It's the way I felt after a three-hour evening seminar, stepping out of a room of overheated undergraduates, craving beer and naugahyde and cocktail waitresses. I turned at the ballroom door to wave, mimicking of the way Nixon waved as he stepped off the helicopter that hoisted him off the White House Lawn.

I got my coat. It was late and it was chilly, but I needed the cold winds, the stars and the distance between the stars. I crossed over Lakeshore Drive—jaywalked actually—and walked along the beach. It was a good idea, but I could tell that I wasn't going to be out here long. I could also tell, after a while, that I wasn't alone. Someone was behind me, headed in the same direction I was. And this person was closing the distance between us.

Was this the someone I'd feared? Who else could it be, on such a bitter night? Why would anyone else be here, now? It wasn't a bad idea, I had to admit, catching what would turn out to be my farewell address and finding me on the beach afterwards. Hadn't I invited him to seek me out? Advertised that I was ready? Dared him to reveal himself?

He walked behind me with that confidence that killers always have, at least in movies, striding nonchalantly, no rush at all, as though it didn't matter what I did. Cocky. I'd always thought of those slow, stalking footsteps as a film cliche. Yet life imitates bad art. A rub-out on a beach, with the dark waves on one side and a glittering skyline on the other. Sand whipping across my face. Closing credits in a minute. Or wait. Another cliche. I might speed up a little, the person behind me would speed up also. Slow down when I slowed down. Stop when I stopped. Cat and mouse. I'd seen that before. I decided on a different ending. Not that it would make any serious difference, it would just fast forward things. I turned and walked back the way I had come, the wind in my face now, night traffic on

Lakeshore Drive a world away, all those lights and horns.

Whoever it was stood there, watching me come. And then, abruptly, he—or she—about-faced and started to walk away. Away from me. But only for a moment. The person turned and faced me: the turn, I supposed, was to pull out a concealed weapon, a knife from a sheath, a pistol from a coat pocket.

At ten feet, I halted. It was almost certainly a male, though the size of the silhouette, back lit was all I had to go by. A man in an overcoat. We stood a short distance apart, like duelists at a can't-miss range.

"Nice evening," I said.

"Nice speech," he—I could be sure it was a he—responded.

"Ah, so you were there."

"Way in back. They wanted me to be up front. I thought that might be dangerous. For both of us I mean."

Right then, out of nowhere, a convoy of honking fire trucks roared north along the Drive, basses followed by an ambulance tenor. There was nothing to do about it. He stopped talking. Good cover for the noise of a gunshot, but it didn't come. We were meant to have a final chat, as I'd always thought we would. I guessed the ambulance would come screaming back this way. But not until dawn, when joggers came out.

"I've always wondered who it was," I said, "what clever man arranged to have the AMBULANCE letters printed backward so drivers could read them in a rear-view mirror. It took years for me to figure that out. Imagine thinking it up for the first time."

"Ezra Sanderson. Rochester, New York. Nineteen twenty . . . three."

He took his hand out of his pocket and advanced towards me. I looked for a pistol, saw only a hand. Then saw that John Henry Mallon had followed me onto the beach.

I should have been relieved. Now I felt foolish though. And angry.

"So what do you want with me? Out here?"

He had something to say, I could see it, but it didn't come out.

"Is this the part where rivals become buddies?" I asked. "I'm not your rival. Or your buddy."

"Shit . . ."

"You just said . . . that they asked you to come . . ."

"Yes."

"Who asked? I thought you were a killer. You came to the lecture. You considered shooting me there. Malcom X in the Audubon Ballroom . . ."

"Oh, wow . . ." he laughed and I had to admit it was funny. Now. "Shoot you? Hey, I don't even hunt. I'm a vegetarian."

"So was Hitler," I responded. "So you decided it was too dangerous and trailed me across Lakeshore Drive, onto a deserted strand. What was I to think? And who *did* ask you to show up tonight?"

"The college. That guy. Collinwood?"

"Collinsworth."

"He said he thought it would be 'helpful.'" Mallon wiggled his fingers when he quoted. "If I showed up it would show that the college was headed in the right direction."

"Thanks."

"And Charles Stuckey said we should talk. He called too. I'd've found you. But I wasn't going to play Baby New Year upstaging Father Time. To hell with that."

"How did you hear about the college? Who recommended you apply? The position wasn't advertised anywhere, that I know of. There wasn't a vacancy."

"*They* came after me . . . that's what I wanted you to know . . . they came after me."

"Who came after you?"

"First call was from that provost guy. Out of the blue, believe me. I know it looks bad. I didn't even ask whether anybody was sitting in that chair they offered me."

"So the college appealed to you," I said. In a way, it was

touching, impressive even, that the college would make the same commitment, or mistake, again.

"But listen," he said. "There was something fishy I smelled when I got introduced on campus, the way they trotted me right out after they saluted you. And then what happened in New York. And they call me in tonight."

"And you came, when you were called."

"I didn't come up front," he said, "I didn't perform. I didn't do what they wanted me to do."

"No, you didn't. You did what you wanted to do." There was guilt and vulnerability in Mallon and an invitation to friendship which I could not bring myself to accept. He had a writer's conviction that his talent, his work, mattered more than mine. And it did, these days, to him and to people who counted. Not to me. So we walked back along the beach in silence. And parted with a nod.

X. THEN: SUMMER, 1976

▲

IT'S EASY TO FAST FORWARD FROM MY FIRST YEAR AT THE college to my sixth. There's a pleasant ritual sameness about college life. It's like farming, with no worry about commodities exchanges or the weather. And the calendar is different. Our new students arrive in autumn, when farmers are harvesting; our graduates depart in May, when farmers are plowing and planting. The college years pleased me, and the patterns of the day pleased me: the thoughtful coffee-drinking mornings, the preparation for class, re-reading notes and papers, tension building. Soon I learned that I would never be able to walk into classrooms without feeling nervous, or leave without feeling spent. There were meeting days, grading days, ceremony days and always, like nature abhorring a vacuum, students flowing into my life and time. I realized, after a while, that if I were to have room in my mind for anything else at all—The Beast, say—I could never remember all those students, though there were some I'd remember forever. I was destined to forget names and that meant I was bound to disappoint someone down the line, at some reunion or other. Again, farmers had it right: never name an animal you ship to market.

In a half dozen years, interest in my next novel had surged and receded. People wondered when—and if—it would come.

The campus graveyard was full of brilliant professors who came, saw, and stopped; stopped research, writing, travel and, in some cases, reading. Would I join the list? I didn't think so. But one chore remained and I saw no way of accomplishing it. It came to this: I was writing about a place—my birthplace—that I'd never seen. Others had gotten away with this: Karl May had written famous westerns without leaving Germany. But I wasn't Karl May. And, when I pictured Karlsbad, I saw my parents' photographs, I heard my parents' stories. But the place escaped me. So I stalled, fiddled, waited. Then, one night, Erwin called.

"Are you still there?" That's the first thing he said. "Still alive? Still living in Ohio?"

"Obviously."

"Are you sitting down, my friend?"

"Wait . . . .yes."

"You're going home."

"Los Angeles?" *Please*, Erwin, *I thought. Not another wedding*. Twice, already, I'd been his best man. He was old fashioned: he married everyone he slept with.

"Karlsbad. Karlovy-Vary, they call it now," he said. "Now, my dear George, you will have no excuse."

▲

What were we called? Writers for Peace? Understanding? Friendship? We met, a dozen of us, at the Amsterdam airport, waiting for the short flight to Prague. Two Cubans, a Mexican, a Canadian couple, a Native American, Jamaican, a Palestinian, and the . . . evidently . . . national poet of Malta. Others I've forgotten. I'll put it this way, at the risk of sounding like an ass: mine was the only name I recognized. I never knew who organized the trip, what was its mission, and whether it accomplished what it was planned to do. In Prague, we were herded on and off busses, into meetings, onto panels. Our group divided between the diligent, the earnest—the words I use in describing mediocre students—and the opportunists, junketers, freeloaders. My group. We knew each other instantly. Nothing had to be said; it was in our eyes. And in the eyes of some of our hosts. They were Czechs after all, masters—and victims—of irony. As for Prague, the darling of today's travel magazines, back then it was a gray place, dilapidated and dissembling. Once you penetrated the Communist housing developments that besieged the old city, you could find the past. Prague was a city that surrendered and survived, though with ineffable sadness. So we visitors talked, shook hands, posed for pictures, agreed on and signed a declaration of solidarity. We ate as little, drank as much as possible.

These were the longest five days of my life. Under other circumstances it might have been possible to break out of the scheduled script, break through to some of our host country counterparts. Sometimes you'd see an involuntary grin, a narrowing of the eyes, a hint that someone was home and hoping for company. But it never lasted. What you got was irony and undue references to our importance, our accomplishments, half-mocking introductions, insincere formality. Irony, I became more convinced, was the resort of losers, the ones who surrender and live to not fight another day.

Karlovy-Vary was scheduled as a day-long trip from Prague, out in the morning, back at night. But Erwin, bless him, had negotiated a longer stay for me, an extra day. Time for me to see my birthplace, my father's city. All I wanted—let me be clear—was the stamp of authenticity you get from being in a place, touching the soil, breathing the air, a few telling details that would authenticate my tale: the puddles in the streets, the last flicker of sunlight on rooftops, the wreaths left behind in front of the monument to Karl Marx—only provided it had been erected at the time described in my book.

▲

"Good morning, friends from overseas!" someone shouted from the front of the bus. We'd been on the road for an hour already, sleeping happily. "Good morning and welcome!" the voice repeated. Amplified by a microphone, it would not be denied. I roused myself, leaned over into the aisle and spotted a balding, elfin man in a beret and an army-surplus looking parka. A few inches less than five feet, he instantly became The Gnome to me.

"Ernst is my name," he announced, "and I will be your guide to Karlovy Vary, also Karlsbad." He made it sound like we were visiting two towns. "I was born in Karlsbad—a Karlsbader you could call me—and now I will give you something of history. I begin in the fourteenth century when the Emperor Karl, out hunting in the valley of the Tepla River, pursued a deer and was led to one of sixty hot springs . . ."

In no time, everybody slouched back in their seats, closed their eyes and attempted to sleep off last night's beer and pork and dumplings. I closed my eyes. But I couldn't shut out the Gnome's voice, going on about the curing power of the springs, the science of balneology, the great hotels, promenades, music—Mozart, Beethoven, Goethe, Peter the Great, King Edward VII, Mark Pickford, Douglas Fairbanks, Marx and Freud. Vacations were longer then, three months the recommended stay, long enough to develop a therapeutic routine . . . the morning walks to the fountain . . . strolls in the mountains, promenades through town . . . concerts in front of the foundations . . . health and pleasure converging, virtue and indulgence.

I heard him out. He was working hard, too hard, on a bunch of hung-over hacks. I felt sorry for him. What he said was nothing I hadn't heard before and that pleased me, that there were no surprises. The Gnome looked to be about seventy but it was hard to be sure. A robust manner, a full-voice, a bald head and face that conduced to caricature. He might have known my parents. But the odds were against it.

"I come now to World War II, what was the end of Karlsbad and the birth of today's Karlovy Vary," he said. He described—pretty neutrally, I thought—the Sudetenland, the

Germans who lived there. Karlsbad was their town and so was Marienbad, half an hour down the road. Was there ever a place, anyplace, any time—where so many many great people visited? All at the same fountains? The list was endless, endlessly various. This was the party that everyone came to. Until Hitler. When he took power across the border, the Sudeten Germans grew restless. They were a minority misplaced in Czechoslovakia. They'd always had complaints: their estates were expropriated, their language frowned upon, their theaters and schools at the mercy of the Czechs. Hitler emboldened them. His agent was Konrad Henlein, a half-Czech, half-German bank teller. The Germans organized, skirmished, were suppressed and rose again. Ernst moved quickly through this material. This was sad, with everyone sleeping. He was speaking only to me. I thought it was odd, at the time. He came to Munich. The collapse of Czechoslovakia, the incorporation of Sudentenland into the Third Reich, Konrad Henlein its leader.

Then he rested. Maybe he was finished, though it was an odd place to stop. I glanced at the window. We were winding downhill through a forest of birch and pine. A sign announced Karlovy Vary. I was coming home.

"After the war, the Germans left," Ernst said, "and settled elsewhere, mostly in Bavaria. Karlovy Vary was born. Under a new government, committed to social justice and public health, the fountains and spas and hotels were now the property of all the people. The benefits of this famous place, the water, the air, the river and forest—belong to all citizens of Czechoslovakia, all citizens of the world. In that spirit, I welcome you here."

After a while, we came into the city itself, the old part of it. Like Prague, it hadn't been bombed or fought over, only surrendered a couple of times. So I saw row upon row of older apartment buildings, built grandly, with gables and balconies, slate roofs, angels and cherubs above doorways and below the eaves. But the buildings were in desperate shape, sagging, peeling, blotchy, moribund. Then the bus stopped outside a nondescript hotel and we shuffled down the aisle. I stopped on the top step, took a slow look around. Hammy moment. I recognized the river—it had to be the Tepla—and a line of small rococo hotels along either side and a pillared colonnade where I knew I'd find mineral water fountains. I thought of my father then. No escaping it. I felt close to him just then. That was the important thing, that contact with the dead.

"Are you alright?" asked my guide, The Gnome.

"Certainly," I said. "Thank you." I wondered if he were waiting for a tip. It wasn't a tipping country we'd been told, but Prague proved otherwise.

"Welcome to Karlsbad," he said. "Mr. Canaris."

He had a list, I was sure, but he hadn't addressed any of the others by name. "You're spending the day after tomorrow here, I understand. After the others go back? You requested an extra day?"

"Yes," I answered.

"I'll be your guide," he said. "I've been assigned. You can wander all you like, of course. But you cannot wander alone. If you wish another guide, that can be arranged . . ."

"That's alright," I said. "I'm sure you'll do."

"Things have changed," he added. "Since Kurt Gerron took his walk."

I froze. Had this . . . government employee . . . person read my book? My least well-known book? Had someone tucked it into my dossier? Was he signaling friendship or warning me to be careful?

"You've read my book?"

"All of them. All three. That's all there are, no? Three? Nothing I've missed? Nothing lately?"

Hah! It followed me across the Iron Curtain, that curiosity about my non-delivery of another novel.

"You read it in English?" I asked. "I'm not sure it appeared in Czech."

"In German," he replied. More questions came to me. What was he doing here? How had he managed to stay? And to work for the Communist government? And what was I walking into?

"Tomorrow is the full-day tour of Karlovy Vary," he resumed, back on automatic pilot. "Many interesting things are here to see, followed by a special dinner for our guests. After that we have another day to explore. Just we two. To talk or not. As you like."

▲

MacArthur Park! All the next day, I kept humming Richard Harris' kitschy song, while The Gnome force-marched us from Old Post Office to Sprudel Fountain, from Market Colonnade to Mill Colonnade, past the Hotel Pupp, Richmond, Imperial, past the Goethe and Marx, Schiller and Beethoven statues, up the cable railway to a scenic viewpoint, down the river along the Goethe Path. Karlsbad was a cake, my birthday cake, left out as long as Miss Havisham's cake in *Great Expectations*, a cake turned moldy with war and communism, spastic renovation and promiscuous decay. The Czechs ran hotels like Greeks ran freighters, like Indians ran motels, on a policy of deferred maintenance, or no maintenance at all. We walked the walk, we tasted the water, we splashed around in an old bath-house where you wished the walls would speak. The attendants didn't. They might have been running a methadone clinic.

My father's streets were beautiful. And mostly dead. Everything new was functional, only the old had elegance. If you looked, you could see the grand houses, barely tinted pink and yellow, white and blue, with dark smudges where water had gotten into the walls. You could imagine parties and gardens in better days. The town seemed deserted. There were people in it alright, but they felt like tenants, not residents. They knew it was famous, they supposed it was worth something but they didn't quite know how to cash in. The party had stopped when ownership changed and they felt abashed, even insulted, that no one grand came anymore. The rooms and pools and tables were filled by people too like themselves, vacationing workers and goof-off government functionaries, plus Tanzanian and Vietnamese delegations.

Dinner that night was the last time our patched-together group would be together. The others were headed straight to the airport the next day. By now, they'd had enough Czech food to last for the rest of their lives, baked meat —- spiceless pork and chicken—dumplings the size of tennis balls, boiled-to-death vegetables and thank God for the beer. At last they brought out the whiskey, plum brandy, clear and lethal, that led to a round of toasts from the sub-mayor and the head of the local literary club to us, and from us to them. I feigned a need to use the bathroom—I wasn't the first—and went up to my room. No one would miss me and so what, if they did? It was night in Karlsbad and I wanted to repeat Kurt Gerron's long-ago walk through town. But, unlike him, I had a destination, an address that I carried in my wallet, 131 Franz Josef Strasse. It was in my father's handwriting, that careful German penmanship, spikey, fancy letters, that he'd written on what turned out to be his death bed.

After waiting a decent interval, I walked down to the lobby, headed to the doorway. But it was pouring. Not the melancholy rain that invites trench-coated figures to walk down cobblestoned streets, not that at all. It was more like the inside of a drive-in carwash. There was nothing to be done but stand there. I'd waited all day. I felt excitement in the calves of my legs, the palms of my hands, that need to move, to be out there at night, headed to the home I'd never seen.

"You'll never find it," someone said from right behind me. It was The Gnome, wrapping himself in his parka, grasping an umbrella.

"Find what?" I asked.

"Not in this weather. And besides, the names of the streets have changed. More than once, already . . ."

"Who are you?" I asked. He was getting to me, this secret sharer type.

"Your guide, Mr. Canaris. And your guide advises you to go upstairs and sleep. Everything that is here tonight will be here tomorrow."

So, back upstairs. I listened to the rain that washed over Karlsbad, rain on the river, rain on the hot springs. The Gnome annoyed me. A little man with a secret, a bit player, Peter Lorre in a movie. Guard or guardian?

▲

After the night's hard rain, Karlsbad took my breath away. The streets were clean and sun-splashed, the gardens watered, the slate roofs shining, the statues new-born, the very air renewed. A morning to walk. Stepping out ahead of me, The Gnome led me along the river, past steaming vents of mineral water—it was as though a hot water pipe had broken somewhere deep underground. We passed the drinking colonnades, the Sprudel fountain, surrounded by the faithful drinkers, dipping ceramic cups into the water. The Gnome snorted as he passed: not a believer, I guessed. Not much of a talker yet. But to be out there in the morning, that was fine. That sufficed. He led me past the Pupp Hotel, across a bridge, and onto a switchback trail that zig-zagged up into the forest. The Gnome set a fast pace, like a tour guide who wanted to complete the day's circuit as quickly as possible. Halfway up the hill, I was panting. I stopped, turned, faked a fascination with the scene below. I was stalling. He kept right on walking and I remained standing. Fair enough. This wasn't about him, whoever he was. It was about me. For me. The spa city was spread out in the valley far below, a valley in the mountains and a crevice in time, toy-like and magical at this distance, but close enough so that I could pick out some of the buildings we passed. I knew there were trails all over the hills—a hundred miles of trails—yet this might be where my father had taken me, that last morning.

The Gnome and I proceeded uphill. This was a European forest, a forest perfected, with paths that turned one way and another, the way a woman turns in front of a mirror, changing her view and the view of her, the angle, the light, the shape. And it was as my father had told me, there was no underbrush, no brambles, thorns or fallen branches only ferns in the shade, flowers in sunny patches. I would have recognized this place, I told myself. Did the place recognize me? Or was that writer's silliness? At last we stopped, just where the hill was at its steepest, where you'd roll a half mile downhill if you stepped off the trail. He found a bench, sat and beckoned for me to join him. Was this where he would ask me for money? Something about a ticket, a relative in America?

"So," he said. "I am Ernst and you are Canaris. And here we sit where no one can hear us. In the hotel and the town, you never know. Even in the baths. *Especially* in the baths. But not here." He gestured at the woods, above and below. Then he did an odd thing. He reached over and patted my hand.

"Welcome back . . ." he said. It sounded fine, but I still wondered.

"Who are you, Mr. Ernst?" I asked.

"Who am I?"

"And spare me the . . . wisdom . . . about how hard a question that is. I want a simple answer. If that makes me a simple man, I'll live with it . . ."

"Well, I don't know how to . . ."

"Another thing," I interrupted. "None of that European talk about how complicated everything is, how we naive Americans can't grasp all of your subtle messages. I've read those books. I teach those books. So please . . . could we just talk."

"The question . . . could you repeat it?"

"Okay, just tell me this. You're a German. German name, German manners, if you don't mind my saying so. And you advertised you were born here, a 'Karlsbader.' But the Germans left after the war. You stayed and now you work for the government. What kind of work do you do? And what's it got to do with me?"

He nodded when I was done. He enjoyed my irritation. He sat there, smiling.

"It's a good thing they cannot wire a forest," he commented. And fell silent again. "I'm taking a chance on you." He resumed. "Not on you as a person. That too, of course. But not only that. On you as a writer."

"You mean you don't want me to use what you say."

"I mean just the opposite, Mr. Canaris."

▲

He survived two Holocausts he said. And still counting. Ernst was an ethnic German, a secular Jew, and . . . years before . . . a communist. That meant—he reflected—that he could have been killed many times, *anytime*, for all sorts of reasons. He saw his life, what was left of it, as a movement from endangered to extinct. He even called himself—it sounded funny coming from him—"The Last of the Mohicans."

His parents, like mine, had seen trouble coming. His father had died in 1936—"just in time," he said, straight faced. His mother left in 1938. She'd wanted him to accompany her. And so he had. They left town together, giving their home to a Gentile neighbor. ("Why pretend to bargain," his mother said. "Why haggle and shake hands?") They paraded out the door and down the street, suitcases in hand. They took the train to Prague. There his mother continued to Bucharest, to Istanbul, to Cairo and to Argentina. But Ernst stayed behind. The Prague Station was the last she saw of him. He took a local train to Marienbad, walked the remaining distance to the edges of Karlsbad, to the surrounding forest, his new home. He did this, he said, "out of love, out of stubbornness, out of stupidity." As if that trio—love, stubbornness, stupidity—all came to the same thing.

It wasn't so hard at first. He'd prepared hiding places and caches throughout the forest. He knew of cabins and sheds and neglected farms. He knew the forest stations, the summer cottages, the comings and goings at the great estates. He knew who lived where and in what months. Backdoors, cellar windows, root cellars, larders, pantries. But what helped most was that no one was looking for him. They'd watched him go, his schoolmates and neighbors, from up and down the street. What an education, those last days! Lesson after lesson. You never knew what people felt, how to read tears, commiseration, sympathy, distance, silence. You couldn't take anyone for granted anymore. You saw people in a new way, looked deeper into them, as truths declared themselves each day. The Gnome developed an instinct for these things—a gefühl—but, as good as you got at it, you could never be sure, because what was true yesterday might be otherwise tomorrow. Better, he thought, not to trust anyone.

Already, he and his mother were of the past. They were ghosts. They were the people who used to live here, used to own this or that. And the role of a ghost was to haunt. Where we sat now, he told me, was where he sat on October 4, 1938, when Hitler visited Karlsbad, soon after the Sudetenland was returned to the Reich. The Gnome could hear the cheering, the anthems down below. The Horst Wessel Lied. Once it had been waltzes, now it was marches and Sieg Heils. And full-throated joy, from the town he loved. And a month later the pine scented air above Karlsbad was joined by black smoke drifting up from the synagogue burning down below on Kristallnacht.

"Does this interest you at all, Mr. Canaris?" he asked me.

I nodded, almost against my will. New material, good material, more than I wanted. Back in Ohio, The Beast was smiling. Another meaning for my novel, another ending, if it ever ended. What would I tell Erwin this time? How many more years of work awaited me?" Then again, what did a few more years matter. I'd long since come to see my writing and professing as coterminous.

"All those years here," I said. I gestured at the woods. "Who did you talk to? And . . . what about the winters?"

"I talked to a schoolboy named Rolf Strauss," he said. "A sunny, lively fellow—fat from his mother's stollen, which I often shared. I could show you his grave . . ."

He turned towards me, met my eyes.

"The grave I put him in . . . He surprised me in a stable behind one of the great houses. I was sleeping when he found me. 'It's you!' he exclaimed. 'You're still here!' I heard him say that again and again. I listened carefully. I could hear no duplicity in what he said. Only excitement. I told him of my life in the woods. He was fascinated, as though I were describing the rules of a new game. Call it keep-away or hide-and-go-seek. He wanted to play too, he said, he could bring me food and all the news of the town. And I half believed him. Half. But only half. Could I trust him? Such an eager-to-please, easily swayed boy? Could I count on his heart? His brain? I needed both. I'd helped him on school assignments, I remembered: he was hopeless. He was working class. His mother was a chambermaid, his father a waiter at the Grand Hotel Pupp. And he was an only child, adored by parents who were eager to please, just as much as he was eager to please, in his awkward way. 'I'll come back tomorrow,' he said. 'I'll bring . . . what do you want . . . bread? Cheese?' Five seconds after he turned away, smiling and promising more fun tomorrow, I took a pitchfork off a stable wall, ran at him and plunged it into the middle of his back. He fell forward, not quite impaled but unable to turn and in great pain. I wished that he had cursed me, called me a Jew, betrayed himself in his last seconds of life, betrayed the hate I guessed was in him. Or the stupidity. I wanted both, though just one would have sufficed. I imagined him returning with the police. Or maybe he'd have come—picnic basket and all—with a group of friends he couldn't help confiding in. How long before his parents, his loving parents knew? And the parents of his friends?

"He didn't curse me. He died crying out for his mother. Stabbed in the back. By . . . let's not close our eyes to this . . . by a Jew . . ."

The Gnome was weeping, the way old men do, not with theatrical tears but with a sort of overall leakage from his watery eyes, his nose, even his throat.

"I'll never know about him," he said. "To this day." After a while, the Gnome turned and asked me if I'd had enough. Politely, like a waiter asking about a diner's meal, whether there was an interest in dessert or, perhaps, it was time to push away from the table and pay the bill.

"If you want," he said, "I can take you right to the house you were born in. I can leave you there outside and you can have your reverent moment. I'm sorry I didn't bring my camera. I see you travel without one. I can probably arrange to have you invited inside, if you wish. I don't know the people but I have government identification."

"I'd like it," I said, "if you finished your story first."

"It won't take so long," he said. "Long to live, but not so long to tell." After a few years, he took chances in town. He felt safer. The forests were still his refuge. He was safe there, safe from discovery, though the winters almost killed him. Yet the whole point of staying was to witness the fate of a place he almost equally loved and hated, the spa town down below.

"I went at night, remained until dawn," he said. "Like a ghost I walked the lawns at the Richmond Hotel, sat on a bench outside the Pupp. I did what I'd never done before: I took water from the mineral fountains. And shat like a goose as soon as I got back to the woods. No one recognized me, not even people I knew. I was older, not taller but more worn out. And bearded. A gypsy perhaps. Or a refugee from the east. The town was filling with them. I heard people call me 'Der Zwerge,' the dwarf. One time, I heard them joke, half-joke, about how long it would be before the likes of me would be called to arms. That was when I knew that the end was coming. Bit by bit. The sound of the announcer's voice on the radio, announcing strategic withdrawals that came closer and closer. The hospital trains that pulled into town, with cargoes that our magic waters could do nothing to heal. The stubble on arrogant faces, nicks and cuts from worn-out razors. Shops closed and hotels turned into military hospitals. What began with a sense of dismay, grew slowly into a sense of doom. And when 1944 turned into 1945, I overheard two men at one of the fountain agreeing that it would be better if the Americans came before the Russians.

"The Americans came to Marienbad. The Russians came here. Maybe it was Germany, maybe it wasn't, but it was close enough for them. The first troops were disciplined. They came and moved on. The ones that followed were barbarians. Looting, burning, raping . . .

He said the words quickly, saying but not seeing, stipulating but not remembering. He loved the place, he hated it. His town, his neighbors. Revenge and justice, joy and obscenity were all tangled together. Be careful what you wish for. Even your enemy's defeat. And then the Czechs arrived. The word was out. It was a land grab, a gold rush, a free-for-all in the Sudetenland, land, houses, hotels, restaurants up for grabs. So they came, paramilitary groups, gangs, posses. The 'wild expulsion' it was later called. Easy pickings, spoils of war. A knock on the door, an hour to leave, a day at most. The Germans ran for their lives, most of them. The ones who stood their ground died where they stood.

Now the trail took us out of the forest, onto a street of houses. German houses: wrought iron fences, fussed-over gardens, leaded windows, pointed gables, slate roofs, all of them run-down, lived in but not loved. The Gnome pointed to one of them.

"That's your home," he said. "What you came for."

The place was lived in, probably by someone important: a black sedan was parked at the side of the house and the place itself seemed in better condition than most. There was glass, clean and unbroken, in every window, this in a town where boards and duct tape ruled. It was a stucco house with brown painted timbers and a flagstone walk leading up to the front steps. I guessed I recognized that walk, from photos. Only from photos. The place felt familiar. *It* felt familiar. But I felt nothing. Absence. Emptiness. Distance.

"Would you like to knock on the door?" asked the Gnome. "Or me to knock on your behalf?"

"No."

"Shall I leave you alone? For your private moment?"

"No."

"Are you sure?"

"Let's go," I said.

"Fine . . ." So we walked, side by side this time downhill, into town, towards the hotel. And, all the time, the Gnome was whistling a tune that I recognized, a Lehar tune, "Vilya's Song" from The Merry Widow. Was it because his work was done? Was it to forestall any more questions from me? He only stopped when we were standing in front of the hotel.

"Tomorrow," he said, "a driver will find you here after breakfast. He will wait until you have finished your meal. I hope you have enjoyed your time in Karlovy Vary." It was so perfunctory, as if someone might be listening, though the streets were empty.

"Mr. Ernst," I said. It took an effort to summon up The Gnome's last name. "Why did you do all this for me?"

"I thought you would be interested. And . . ."

"Yes?"

"Write."

"Write what . . ."

"What you wish. What else?"

"It was a good story," I said. Now I was the one who sounded flat, a tourist thanking a guide for going out of his way a little, wondering if he'd be insulted by a tip. But he wasn't asking for a tip. He was asking for a book. I saw that now.

"Have I been helpful?" he asked. "I haven't minded this. You take me back. To my boyhood. 'Der Kleine Ernst.'"

"I was searching for an ending. Maybe you know that."

"The hardest things. Endings. Books have them . . ."

"Not mine . . ."

I shook his hand and walked towards the hotel. My hand was on the door. Then it came to me. Der Kleine Ernst.

"Ernst," I said. "Is that your first name or your last."

"Both," he said. Smiling. Bemused. "Always my first name. Later, it became my last name too. Ernst Ernst. I changed the last name. But, Mr. Canaris . . . I kept the letters, the five letters . . . that make a star . . ."

It didn't take me long. It wouldn't have taken anybody long. The letters only came out one way.

"Stern?" I asked. "My mother's name."

"We're cousins," he said. "My mother and your mother were sisters . . ."

"Your mother was . . . she lived in . . . was it Mexico?" It came to me, just barely. A relative in Latin America. An occasional letter, a stamp I saved. A distant relative. Like a passing cloud, a wisp of smoke.

"Argentina. Tante Rachel, to you . . ." he answered. "If your parents saved any photos, family photos, you might find me. But maybe not. I never liked to be photographed. And cameras easily missed me. I liked that . . ."

I grabbed his hand and pulled him towards me. "Is there anything you need? Anything I can do? Something I could send after I get home? I could stay a little longer." I stepped back and regarded him. I saw nothing of myself in him. And yet. "I don't know where to begin with you."

"Thank you. But you'd better go. I arranged for this time together to make connections. What you do with the connections . . . up to you. If you stayed longer . . . the authorities would make connections too. They'd ask questions." He approached me and we hugged, awkwardly, since he only came up to my chest. His bald head, topped by a beret, was just below my chin.

A minute later, I watched as the car they sent carried me drove away. I turned around in my seat, the way I used to turn on trips with my parents because, though it was uncomfortable and I could never do it for long, it was important for me to look back on where I'd been.

XI. NOW: NOVEMBER–DECEMBER, 2005

▲

WHEN I RETURN FROM CHICAGO I AM ONCE AGAIN SUMmoned to a session with Provost John Alfano. This time, I walk across campus with no concern at all. They have done their worst already, I think.

"Professor," he says without arising to greet me, only gesturing towards a seat, while remaining behind a formidable desk. Looking at him, I realize how much a desk means: it's a wall, a throne, a treasure-chest all in one. It separates and hides.

"I saw your father in New York, John," I begin.

"You had a couple of good nights in Chicago and New York," he says. So there will be no easy talk about his redoubtable dad. Not today. "A bully pulpit for you. I can't pretend that people here weren't concerned . . ."

"I'm sorry to hear that," I say. "But I retract nothing. Yet I can make your life easier. I've said my piece. Twice. No need for more. You can have back those appearances in Los Angeles and Honolulu."

"You're willing to cancel?"

"No need to repeat myself . . . at your expense."

"Professor . . ." He shakes his head. It was as though I'd

restored his faith in people. Or maybe his faith in me. "I was going to ask just that . . . Thank you."

"So, that's that. Was there something else, John?"

"Well, actually there is . . . are . . . two things." He stops then, knowing we're crossing a border from congenial to painful. "Commencement. The commencement address. Professor, wouldn't you just settle for the baccalaureate speech?"

Now I know that Trudy's mistake in New York was more than a slip of the tongue. They don't want a couple of thousand parents to hear my swan song. They don't want to see it excerpted on CNN and in the New York Times.

"Might as well get it *all* out, John. What was the second thing?"

"It's the symposium on your work that we talked about. We want to cancel that, too."

"Why?"

"Lack of interest, you might say."

"Lack of interest? On whose part?"

"Lack of interest from the College sponsoring the event. We don't want to invite a round-robin denunciation. An agony exercise. Which is what it would be. There are limits. Give us a break, Professor! We don't want you grandstanding at the college's expense."

"I think that all the grandstanding so far has been at my expense. Who are the people who resent my . . . grandstanding?"

He doesn't respond.

"They have names, no?"

"One of them does, George" he says. "Alfano."

Now it's my time to be quiet. I knew that all along, that the college could be generous and good, also touchy and vindictive. No, not the college. The college is something else. Always remember that, I tell myself. The college is not the people who run it.

"You never called me George before," I say, almost to myself. Bidding goodbye to a little formality and courtesy that's going out of my life. "Do you want an answer now?"

"If you're ready. If you want some time to think about it, though . . ."

"You've changed on my contract," I say, "my teaching, my salary. And I let you do it. Now you renege on your promise that I will be commencement speaker and also on your plan to honor me with a symposium on my work. And I, once again, agree. But on one condition . . ."

"What's that?"

"That you announce it."

"What?"

"Please. You know what an announcement is. I want it in a press release, on the college website, and in the alumni magazine."

"What do you want us to say?"

"No more or less than you've said to me. Or would you prefer that I make the announcement? Surely, it's better coming from you than from me."

"I suppose you're right," he says.

▲

"Do you think biscuits and gravy ever tasted any good?" I ask Willard Thrush. We're having an early morning breakfast at a country restaurant a dozen miles from campus. It's one of the places I discovered in my early years, when I wrote or read all night and raced down obscure roads in the last hour before dawn, burning off the anger or passion that were in me, back then. I got out of the habit after that first year, but now I'm back where I started, in potholed parking lots and dining rooms that smell of cigarettes and bacon. "It must have been good . . . once . . . somewhere. How else would it live on as library paste and crumbled meat?"

"I gave up on it years ago."

Just then, the waitress comes over, offering more coffee. After she refills our cups, she removes our plates. My biscuits and gravy are slowly congealing. On the world's list of endangered things, recipes rank high. The difference is that the game was over when the last carrier pigeon died. When true biscuits and gravy perished, the fakes and knockoffs took over.

"One question, Willard," I say. "I suspect you know the answer. But you might not be willing to tell me. If so . . . I understand. But who would you say . . . how would you say . . . the decision to get rid of me was made? How did it happen?"

"I don't know," Willard says. "That's the short answer. Want more?"

"Yes."

"How does a professor get shit-canned? It happens so rarely. So it's not easy, that's the first thing, not unless you make a pass at a student or knock over a 7-11. And it's getting harder all the time. Back in the day, you had department chairs who represented the administration, shaped up new hires, ran things for years and years. Mentored and disciplined. Now the department heads rotate in and out of the ranks. They're shop stewards, is all. They represent the employees, cover for them. They're the ones who hire, right? So to fire someone is like saying they made . . . ah, shucks . . . a mistake! Still, if they've got someone who's blowing off classes, not keeping office hours, taking months to return papers . . . and if the students complain . . . something has to be done. We can't have too many unhappy students, not at these prices. So . . . from students . . . to departments . . . to provost. Something like that. Your case, obviously, is different . . ."

"I should hope so. Tell me, do the trustees come into it at all?"

"Doubt it. They do what the administration recommends. They don't intervene, unless things have gotten desperate. I mean, like twice in a century they might have to tell a president it's time to go. That's the point. When they intervene, somebody big is on the way out. In your case, I'd guess some of your pals in the department took a shot at you. But maybe it started with Alfano. And, at some point, the president got into it. Know her very well?"

"Not much."

"President and provost are indispensable. Who started it, whether the president curtseyed and the provost bowed . . . who knows?"

"But why? I have my books. For thirty-five years they bragged about me. I'm a celebrated professor."

"Not really. You're a writer-in-residence. That's different. And I think you know it. You professed alright. But the writing stopped. At least the publishing . . ."

"*What have you done for me lately*?"

"What have you done for me in the last thirty years? Listen, I hate to say it, but you might want to consider that they're onto something. They wanted a new star. To dazzle, not just impress, the kids and the parents. And besides, what goes around comes around . . ."

"What does that mean?"

"Someone else was teaching writing when you came. He didn't have an endowed chair. But he had some talent, I guess, and some hope. It never occurred to you to ask?"

"No."

"His name was Trowbridge. Elbert Trowbridge. He was long gone when I came. But for years he sent in fifty bucks a year . . ."

"So . . . no hard feelings?"

"I didn't say that. Point is, I don't know what he felt. Neither do you . . ."

▲

The first session of my final seminar awaits me and, in the preceding afternoon I do what I have always done. I walk along a trail, the same pre-class walk I took thirty-five years ago, before confronting a seminar in which Natalie Taylor's death was announced to me. Now I wonder what's left of the splendid woman who'd sat with me near here, planning a Thanksgiving in California and a springtime here hunting for a house that we might share. Smart and lovely and gone so long. Now she is an entertainment trivia question. Test your movie lore.

"On your right!" someone shouts from behind me. It's a bicyclist. I know that without looking and move to the side without looking back, waiting for a cyclist, a group of them to judge from the noise, to pass. It takes longer than usual. I glance back. They're performing stunts, lifting their front wheels off the ground, doing wheelies, laughing and cursing. Now they're upon me, three heavy, porky kids with tractor hats and sagging pants and hooded sweatshirts led by a sly, skinny kid who's the leader of the pack. He cuts as close to me as he can without hitting me.

"Fuck you, grandpa!" he shouts. Then they're past me, not looking back. What they said wasn't conversation. It's garbage, like what gets tossed out of a car, making the world a little more ugly.

"Same to you, jailbait!" I shout, trembling with rage. It's not that they insult me, violate my pensive stroll. They profane a place I love, this river and forest, this bank of memories. And now they halt and turn and wait for me.

"Hey, what'd you say to me?" the leader asks. It's easy to know him. The others are welfare-fat, headed no place. Followers, dead-eyed. But the leader is clever, probably crueller. Trouble. This is when I notice they are not children. Far from it. They're teenagers, old enough to drive cars, so their behavior on bicycles is exaggerated, their stunts and obscene shouts, their way of mocking the things they used to do. They're punks.

"I said, 'the same to you,' I respond, "after what you said to me."

"That ain't all you said."

"Jailbait, because that's where you're headed."

"That's not what jailbait means," he corrects me, his face lit up. "Jailbait means underage . . . a girl who's too young to screw. That what you mean?"

"I meant what I said," I answer. And resume my walk, with the air of a man who's wasting his time. The kid's smarter than I guessed.

"Who are you, grandpa?" he says, pedaling along beside me.

"What does it matter to you?" I ask, feigning a weariness I do not feel. "You'll insult anybody."

"You're the one I'm insulting now. Just you."

"Alright. My name is George Canaris. I'm a professor at that college . . ." I pointed to the hill, the spire, the outlined dormitories that are easy to see, now that the leaves are down. Just now, it feels far away. Another world.

"Professor Canary!" He's amused. So are his companion oafs.

"What's your name?"

"Call me jailbait."

Now I've had enough. I start walking again and no one follows. It pleases me, every step that separates me from them. Then I hear something coming up from behind me, coming fast, and I turned, just in time to be clipped across the face, slapped, by the leader of the pack.

"Canary!" he shouts, as he and his friends pedal off.

I walk home, shaking, humiliated. Like a hurt kid, I plot revenge. I imagine all the bad ways their lives might turn out, without my having to do anything: the trailer camps and bad food and unloved children and dead-end jobs that would be their fate. Emergency rooms and divorce courts, no insurance on their bodies, their teeth, their automobiles. I hate them and I despise myself as well, for what I am doing. That college on the hill swallows more than careers, it swallows perspective. You could live here a long time, you could go from visiting professor to hoary emeritus, you could take summers in Maine or Hilton Head, sabbaticals in Europe or India. You could shop carefully, order cheese and coffee over the web, grow your own herbs, home-school your kids and never acknowledge that the college was surrounded—make that besieged—by kids like the ones I'd just met. Oh, we granted that there were fine local people, sturdy farmers and dedicated school teachers, able veterinarians and lawyers. That's what we said, and we meant it . . . when we said it. And yet, all around the land was streaked by dead-end viciousness, ugliness that was implacable and complacent.

▲

She sits at the table, while more talkative students dominate proceedings. She speaks when I call upon her, but not for long, and she never volunteers. But then, she amazes me. The first assignment is a dialogue exercise, getting students to offer a conversation that a reader can follow, that advances a story and establishes characters, attends to atmosphere, thoughts, hesitations, that is more than a transcript of talking heads and finally—the hardest thing of all—that uses quotation marks, double and single, appropriately.

She does all this and more. Simply put, she offers a complete story, three times the suggested length, well-observed, immaculately written. Well, here's another one shot-wonder, a one-trick pony, I tell myself. But even then, I suspect something more because her story does not involve someone a lot like her, it is not set on a campus like this, or in a suburb—outside of Philadelphia, in her case—where the college directory tells me she comes from. So, in class, I compliment her, while straining to find a few small faults. And wait for the next assignment, which is an exercise in sense of place.

She does it again: a fully wrought well-observed account of a rough-and-ready construction camp on the Alaskan oil pipeline. It's all there, long summer nights, mosquitoes, mud, wildflowers, plywood barracks filled with drifters and misfits, cut-throat card games on payday Fridays. Once again, it's more than a scene, it's a vision of Alaska as the last redoubt of the American dream, a refuge for dreamers and mercenaries. An annoyed class sits back and hears me praise a student in a way that I never have before. "Some of the best work I've seen in this class . . ." They have to listen to that, these good kids who are struggling, advancing and relapsing and advancing a little more, mindful of my warning that in writing you never have it made, the chance of failure is always there. Except for this one student.

Here's a confession: I've been looking for her all my life. I've had hundreds of students in my writing seminars and, of those, a dozen, maybe two dozen who I guessed had a chance of making if, if they worked at it, if they were lucky. But I've always been looking for someone who might be great. A natural. I guess I was looking for a younger version of myself, someone who was as good as I used to be. Or better.

But she hasn't come to me. That's odd. Usually a student, especially a talented writer, wants to get to know me. They show up in my office, with one of my books in hand. They camp outside my door. They want to know about publishers and what's the deal with agents and should they go to Iowa or Breadloaf or get a job on a newspaper or be a soldier of fortune. They want to know me. Not this one.

Finally, I cannot resist. At the start of the fifteen minute break that we take, midway through the seminar, I look at her sternly, in the presence of others, and tell her that I would like to have a word with her. In my office. Now. She accompanies me out of the room and across the grass, up the steps of my office, as if to a place of execution. I suggest she take a seat and she obliges. I make her wait: the red light on my phone is inflamed with someone's message. Actually, I called myself from home, before class. Now I pretend to attend to the message while she fidgets. Then I study her, stare at her. She has a pleasing face and troubled eyes. It's hard to assess her otherwise, especially now that autumn has gone and with it the season of bare midriffs and stapled navels. Everything about her is hidden.

"I've been wanting to talk to you about your writing," I begin. "I've been expecting you'd drop by during office hours."

She doesn't respond, just nods a little, signaling understanding, not agreement.

"Sorry to hijack you like this," I continue, "but there's something I need to know."

She nods and now I notice that her sweater—her baggy,

gnarly, shape-smothering sweater—is in danger. She's pulling a loose thread at the cuff, yanking and unraveling.

"Forgive me. I can't help wondering . . ." I watch her tense, freeze almost. So frightened! "Why are you torturing that sweater to death?"

"Oh . . . sorry," she says, placing her hands on her lap, one hand over the other, like a kid in the backseat of a car, warned not to fidget.

"Listen. Your writing is unbelievable. It's as good as anything I've seen over the years. Quite a lot of years . . ." I accompany that last line with a gentle smile, an acknowledgment of time. I'm hoping for a smile in return. But her hand is back on the sweater. And her eyes are on the clock. I've rarely felt that my company was so onerous.

"I've been wondering where it all comes from," I say.

She tenses up. Where am I going, she surely wonders. And, for my part I fear I may be invading her secret place. Disturbing her way of working, like those louts on the trail had savaged my walk.

"You're from someplace in Pennsylvania, yes?"

She nods. A rousing response, coming from her.

"But your stories are elsewhere. Alaska! And so vivid. Have you been there?"

"No."

"Then how do you get it . . . those vivid descriptions?"

"I like to research things," she says. That last word—research—takes its time coming out, as if she didn't want to risk telling me too much.

"I want you to know that if you have any questions about writing . . . about where you go from here . . . I'd like to help. I'd be more than happy . . ."

"Thanks."

I'm leaning forward now and I hold that position, even as the silence between us returns. She sits there. Our eyes don't meet.

"Okay then, go back over," I say. "I'll be there in a minute."

That night, back at home, I think about her. I sit out on the porch, possibly for the last time this year. Tonight is warm, almost humid, and out of nowhere a thunderstorm comes along with rain that you can smell coming and wind that you can hear rolling across the fields. Lovely, too. And lovely, to have come across a good writer, right at the end. A parting gift. Why was she so scared of me? It was as though she feared I'd make a pass at her! But there was an inner world she didn't want to share, perhaps, and I had to respect that. If so, her very enrollment in the seminar had been an act of courage. That was it, I suppose. She didn't have to get to know me, I guess.

But it would have been nice.

▲

Something is different. I notice it as soon as I came through the door. My friends are surprised to see me. Everybody is surprised. Conversation dies, then slowly resumes, but now—call me paranoid—I sense they are talking about me. I walk to the counter as usual, then join Derrick Madison.

"Where's Harvey?" I ask.

"Massage."

"Ah hah." We live in an austere place but it has its sybaritic side. An hour of kneading for forty dollars makes my friend Harvey a new man. It eases the paper grading and department meetings out of your system, the tenure and promotion committee, the letters of recommendation. He writes it off as a professional expense and has never been audited. So our trio is a duo. That changes things.

"Is it just me?" I ask, "or is there something strange this morning?"

"Yes and yes," Derrick responds. He likes answers like that, that invite more questions.

"Meaning what?" I oblige him by asking.

"It is you . . . and there is something going on. The college released an announcement. You're not speaking at commencement. And they've cancelled the symposium on the Canaris ouevre. For lack of interest."

"Where'd you hear that?"

"On the morning news."

"The radio?"

"Oh Christ, George. The television. The network news. Okay. What I'm trying to figure out is why they announced it."

"Excuse me," I reply, "but if an event that's been scheduled is canceled, shouldn't people be told? A matter of courtesy, no?"

"You asked them to announce it?"

"Well, somebody had to. It was their decision so . . . their announcement."

"George," said Derrick. "You're the shrewdest man on campus. Or the most naive."

I sit there, flabbergasted. It happens. I grant, especially at a college: something you say by accident, not thinking, is considered witty, deep, biting. For no reason. And you nod and take credit, though you're dumbfounded.

"Neither one, I think," I said. "Not so naive. Not so shrewd."

Derrick mulled that over. We'd had years of talk about everything, sex, death, deans and presidents, students of all sorts, news and weather. Food and far places. Now the two of us were on terra incognita.

"How long did you think it could last, George?" he asked. "Really. How many years of silence?" I didn't respond. "We've enjoyed ourselves forever around here and we never got into this. Harvey thinks you have something great tucked away someplace . . ."

"And you . . ."

"When you came here you were a writer who taught. Now you're a teacher who used to write."

"So that's a no?" You don't agree with Harvey?"

"Did once. Don't now. Sorry . . ."

▲

The phrase "tempest in a teapot" needs reconsideration. It's supposed to suggest an inconsequential upset, something trivial that's been blown out of shape. But have you ever attended to a teapot? Stood by while the water went from cold to warm, to hot to scalding? An instrument of pain and death? Have you listened . . . as I cannot bear to listen . . . to a quiet hiss that escalates into a howl of unbearable pain? Make no mistake a tempest in a teapot is hell in a small place. And that is what we have here, after the announcement.

There are articles, interviews, petitions. Reporters return to town, e-mail wars are waged. Sunday pundits get into the act, because a professor is destroying a college or a college is destroying itself. There's something for everyone in all this, for left-wingers, libertarians, neo-conservatives. Everybody comes in for it. The president, the provost and I have one thing in common: we all land on somebody's enemies list at the same time we are adopted by new best friends, enlisted in causes and camps we had never heard of.

It lasts a couple weeks and then, calmer heads prevail. The problem solvers, the truth-is-somewhere-in-between types, the compromisers. The dullards. People of goodwill and mediocre intellect step up and remind us that we are all on the same team, we all love the college. Reasonable men drop by my home and advise me it is time to put the past behind us and move forward. In the end, the commencement address is restored to me. And this is announced. As for the symposium, the issue of college sponsorship is moot because some of my former students ask . . . insist . . . on volunteering to sponsor the event themselves, a week after commencement, during reunion weekend. Charles Stuckey is among the ring-leaders. And, like that, the tempest in a teapot subsides, with no one so churlish as to claim victory. Tempest over. Boiling water now tepid, drinkable.

▲

My last seminar, my very last minute as a professor arrives early in December, two weeks after students return from Thanksgiving and a few days before they leave again for Christmas. *This is the end of the road*, I tell myself as soon as I awaken. I always knew this day would come. *Last class. Never again. Last class. Never again.* I glance around my house. There, in a closet that's half open, are all the clothes I'll ever need, enough to last me out, I calculate. What I'll wear in my coffin is hanging in there, someplace, the socks and the underwear, the pants and the shirt. I cannot know the last day of my life, but I know my last day as a professor. And that's a kind of death for me.

How to end? Anything special? In an old-fashioned movie, there'd be a moving but self-deprecating valedictory, a parting blessing for all my students, tonight's writers and all the ones before them. In the closing shot, the camera backs off and ascends so that a single table in a single seminar enlarges to encompass tables, classrooms, colleges everywhere. Enough! In a skewed, dark film, I'd walk into a seminar room and confront all the student fiction that was ever turned in to me, all the corrections I'd made, gallons of red-ink that coursed, like blood through my marking pen, pleading for accurate speech tags, appropriate quotation, spelling, punctuation, warning against passive voice, showy description, self-serving narrators, all my counsel and worrying and wisdom, all of it cutting off light and air and room to move, turning the workshop into a place of confinement, a paper-crowded tomb over which hovered a gaggle of birds, ravens maybe, squawking "awkward" "awkward" "awkward . . ."

My last seminar. I take the papers I'll be returning, covered with comments. If I ever mark up another page, it will be my own. I glance over my comments. My greatly talented girl sailed through, writing splendidly and saying little. Her reticence would bring her down to an A-minus. The others have been serviceable. Some struggled and progressed. B plus. Or struggled a little. B. Or shrugged it all off. B-minus.

And then it is over, and over with no particular sense of occasion that I can see or feel. What I had expected? It was my last seminar, granted. But also theirs, which meant something altogether different. The end of a career for me is the end of a course for them and courses end all the time, not a moment too soon. I wish them luck, I promise that I'll help them out, whenever and wherever they find me. Still, at the very end, even as we get out of our chairs, I hear someone say "thank you." Some others do too. But not, so far as I can tell, my Emily Dickinson.

XII. THEN: 1978

▲

I WONDERED IF I WERE DOING ANY GOOD AT ALL. A STUDENT had come in with the first pages of a story in which a female narrator discovers that the love of her college life, charming and attractive, has been called before campus authorities on a charge of date rape. The result was youthful disillusionment, a world turned upside down. And she'd worked hard on it, you bet, the effort was all over the page and it was on her face as well. If this were therapy, she'd get high marks, along with a "thank you" for sharing that." But writing played by different rules. Most classes, you read, you took notes, you learned lessons that you remembered for a little while, maybe longer. Maybe. That was the goal, anyway, that after you could no longer be called upon, after you were out of reach of pop quizzes and final examinations, something was in you. In writing classes it was different: you had to apply that writing lesson right away. You got it or you didn't.

"You have to consider all your characters," I advised her. "Not just your narrator. The boyfriend. His friends, the other woman . . ."

"But I don't know . . ."

"That's when you start to imagine. You have to write what you know. But you have to write . . . discover . . . what you don't know about what you know."

I sounded like a charlatan, though every word was true. It was all such frustrating stuff. Why did writing have to be so hard?

"And, you have to ask yourself something else. It's a first person narrative. So why is the narrator telling the story? And when? How many years after all this happened? How have things changed? What about her memories?"

She'd started out taking notes. A few moments ago, though, she gave up. It was all too much for her. Maybe I was too much. She'd worked so hard but she was in the only class at college where trying harder didn't always work. I'm sure that seemed unfair to her. It *was* unfair. She was on the edge of tears.

"Listen," I said. I leaned forward; if it wouldn't have been taken wrongly, I'd have touched her knees, taken her hands. "Try this. It might help. Your first person narrative may be constraining you. Try shifting into third person. That way you can attend to your other characters. You'll get distance and perspective. They'll come alive, maybe . . ." Or be hopelessly disembodied, I thought. "Let your imagination be an equal opportunity employer!"

"Okay,' she said. "You have office hours later this week?"

"Of course," I responded, shuddering. "And you can make an appointment any old time. Just call or e-mail . . ."

"Okay," she repeated, though she sounded far from convinced. "I really worked hard on this, professor," she added. This was a threat, make no mistake. This was a warning, I realized, watching her walk away, weighed down like a beast of burden by a knapsack of books, papers, water bottles.

"Next!" I shouted. I'd been busy as a union dentist and though it was past closing time, I suspected someone more was out there, waiting for me. And, as long as the customers kept coming, I stayed open.

"I liked that, about letting your imagination being an equal opportunity employer . . ."

I looked up and saw a woman who was not a student. She

was older and she dressed stylishly and there was something about her self-presentation that separated her from the kids in class. An adult gamesmanship. She wore a dress and stockings, a blouse and a suede jacket. She cared how she looked . . . to me. And how she looked was . . . let me be careful here . . . handsome? Beautiful? Some of those, but the word that came to me then, returns now, is fine. And she knew she was fine and that I thought she was fine, because women always know.

"Do I know you?" I asked. It was the most pointless question of my life. If I'd met her, I'd remember. She was like Natalie Taylor, that dark beauty, that look of adventure in her eyes, that sense of engagement, of possibility.

"No, you don't know me, Professor."

"Well, that can change. Have a seat."

She took a chair. I mean that. She didn't have a seat, as per my instructions. She possessed it. That chair of mine—an old, soft thing I'd bought at a yard sale—had been waiting all its life for her.

"My name's Stephanie Knox," she said. "And I'm from here."

"The campus . . ."

"No sir. The town. My father was fire chief for a while. My mom works at the hospice . . ." Her voice trailed off. "Do you want the rest of the story now. I don't want to bore you."

"I'll try not to be bored," I said. She was easy on the eyes. How rare, in academe, where people made a point of pride about not caring, where *I am what I am* and *I'll wear what I want* and *what you see is what you get* were the rules. I couldn't count the times I'd sat in faculty meetings and, letting my eyes wander around the room, asking myself what would happen if I were stranded on a desert island with one—almost any one—of these women.

"You've heard it before," my visitor said. "Local cheerleader and prom queen starts college, gets pregnant, marries high school sweetheart and you take it from there . . ."

"And now . . ."

"I'm twenty-five, I've got a seven-year old son and I work at the Chamber of Commerce."

"Your husband, your ex-husband that is, is still around town?"

"Of course," she said. "He wasn't supposed to go anywhere, was he? I wasn't supposed to either."

"Have you traveled?"

'Not like I want to, professor, so I read. That's traveling, isn't it? I take courses. I'm about to get my bachelor's degree. I read a lot, professor . . ."

"And . . ." I prayed she didn't have a manuscript for me to look over. Please, god, no bodice ripper, no fantasy-pornography, no perky feminist comedy, just right for Dolly Parton. "I just wonder if I can stay here five more minutes without seeing you yawn and look at your watch."

"Let's see what happens in the next five minutes," I replied. I was rooting for her. Dreiser got it wrong. You could have *An American Tragedy* with nobody drowning. Just make them stick around at the scene of a crime, a life sentence, reproached by dreams.

"Why I came to you," she said. "I know you've been wondering." She reached into her pocket and pulled out a clipping that she offered to me.

"I know about that," I said. A New York magazine had just published a list of the hundred best novels. Well, maybe it was more narrowly defined than that, the hundred best American novels. Maybe. No, it had *Ulysses* at the at the top. Modern novels, I suppose that was it.

"I heard you wrote books," she said. "And I was wondering if you could tell me how to begin."

"Where to begin?" Did it matter? And then I realized that it did. If she started at the top, with James Joyce, surely that would be the end of it.

"If I were you," I said, "I'd start at the bottom."

"Oh . . . why?"

"Well, I've always believed that it was better to start at the bottom and work your way up, rather than the other way around."

"I see . . ."

"The other thing is, if you start at the bottom . . . that means, all the sooner, you'll find your way to me."

"I beg your . . ."

"You mean you didn't know?"

"Know what?"

"I'm on the list."

"You are?"

"Number 88, I believe. *Out On The Coast*, by George Canaris . . ."

"Oh my god!" She blushed, she flushed, she covered her face with her hands. And then . . . a saving moment . . . she laughed. "Swear to god, professor . . . I never knew!'

▲

She worked her way up the list, starting with *The Magnificent Ambersons*, *The Forsyth Saga*, *Barchester Towers*, *Man's Fate*, *Steppenwolf*, *The Age of Innocence*. She climbed the rungs of the ladder that led to me. Our arrangement, was that she come to my office near the end of student hours, wait until my last paying customer had left. She did the reading. She came prepared with questions, she'd marked passages, she was interested—but intelligently—in the authors' lives. She had a quality that was rare among students then and, in intervening years, has only gotten rarer: hunger. No wonder she responded so to loss and longing in *Jude the Obscure*: that sense of regarding, from a far distance, the life she wanted to live. Based on her performance in our tutorial, she could have come to me any time and I'd have obliged her. Even if sex, or the chance of it, weren't in the neighborhood.

It was fun resisting it. Eleven books had been thoroughly

read, thoughtfully examined in meetings that began at ten and ended around midnight. She brought me cider and apples, maple syrup, small gifts and wondered aloud how she could ever thank me for the time I was giving her. And I answered that it was a pleasure having her in my office once a week, a pleasure dealing with someone who wasn't out for a grade. She left the office ahead of me; I always claimed to have a few errands left to do. And then I'd stand in the window, watching her walk across the parking lot, a single, solitary woman, driving back to the rest of her life. I wondered what she was thinking, as she followed her headlights back to town. She hadn't offered much of herself: no invitations to family outings, no little hints about going out for lunch or coffee, no eagerness to show me a side of Ohio that the college folks never saw. She withheld herself, in a way that went from impressive to exasperating.

▲

Our book was *Winesburg, Ohio*. It was hard to be in this part of the country and not respond to it, that dated, clunky, bittersweet elegy for lives left behind in small places. Even today, you couldn't drive through these Ohio towns, many of them diminished now from what they were when Sherwood Anderson had written, without wondering about the people who left, the ones who never left, about the fertile richness of the days, the isolating darkness of the nights, and all the secrets kept behind those white clapboard bungalows, those solitary farm houses. And Stephanie got it, on the level of instinct and intellect she got it, she knew she lived in Winesburg.

"And I want to leave it," she said. "I don't hate it. It is what it is. And what it isn't. And what it isn't is . . ."

She hesitated, for a long minute, and just then I didn't want to hear a litany of complaints about all the things that were missing in her life. I didn't want a shopping list.

"What it isn't . . ." she began again, "is enough. Maybe it's the place. Maybe it's me. No hard feelings. No blame. My being here . . . it's a no-fault accident. I'm like . . . the fellow in Winesburg . . . waiting for the train to take him away."

"So there," I said. "I think you've got it. You know what's next on the list?"

"*Out On The Coast*," she said. "By George Canaris."

"I hope you like it," I said. "But . . . please . . . it's not required." She had good critical instincts. It wasn't what you got from students. "I liked it, I didn't like it, it sucked." She had a suspicion of writing that was pure style, of characters too simply drawn, of plots that relied on coincidence, on endings that pandered to the taste for happiness. "Have you looked at it yet?"

"No . . . not even a peek."

"Well, I'm taking a chance on something then. It might backfire. What I suggest is that we move our next discussion to my house. And that we meet at an earlier hour. I'll cancel office hours. So I can prepare a meal for you."

"Are you sure?" she asked. There was something in her voice, a kind of directness that signaled we were stepping into new territory. Hers. Did I really want to go there?

"Yes," I answered, without quite knowing what she wanted me to be sure about. Taking a chance? Making a mistake?

▲

"So," I said, stirring the goulash. "This is what I made for you." She leaned over, inhaled, liked the smell. "My mother's recipe. It needs a while more. And I need a drink. In winter, I like a Manhattan."

"I like the sound of that," she said.

"I thought you would." I reached for the whiskey, the bitters, the vermouth and the ice and the maraschino cherries. "If it were called a Sandusky . . ."

"Don't even go there, professor."

"If you don't like the taste . . . not to worry. I'll drink it. I'm good for more than one. And I'm not driving home."

I saw it then, my first intimation. She wondered, whether

she'd be driving home. And maybe she thought of all the nights we'd parted, driving away while I stood at the window, watching her go. Had she seen me there?

"When I was a kid . . ." she said, nodding at the maraschino cherry bottle. I was pouring a few drops of the sweet red syrup into the drinks. "I used to think that there was such a thing as a maraschino cherry tree . . ."

"Here," I said, giving her a glass and raising my own, "is to whatever possessed you to come knocking on my office door . . ."

We touched glasses and she drank, nodded approval. I gestured towards the center of the room, where she sat on the couch and I in my easy chair. We began talking about *Out On The Coast*. My first book, my best known, and number eighty-something on someone's top one hundred. I reached across and took her copy of my novel. I hadn't touched it for a while.

"You know," I said, "you could pass a quiz on this book with higher grades than I could." I flipped through the pages I'd written a lifetime ago. I noticed that she'd marked up some pages, that there were exclamation points and question marks in the margins. "What I mean to say is, I'm not the same fellow who wrote the book. I remember the man, I admit, and I kind of liked him. But when I think back, he's like a close friend that I've lost touch with over the years . . ."

"Alright then, that's a good place to start," she said. And then she did two things, two different things that worked together wonderfully. The first was what she said.

"Here's my first question, professor." She was brisk, all business, like a cutting-edge honors student laser-locked on graduate school. "How would you rate that man . . . I mean that writer . . . that you used to be. His strength and weaknesses as a writer.

I closed my eyes, leaned back, wondered where to begin, and when I lowered my head and opened my eyes, I saw that she had kicked off her shoes and lifted her legs onto the sofa, folded them underneath her, as if she were on a beach or a bed. That was the second wonderful thing.

"The strengths of youth," I said. "A wilder sense of humor than I have now. That's for sure. Back then, it was hysterical, delirious. All of which fit a Hollywood novel that goes from the 30's to the 50's. More my father's world than mine. But it wasn't so long gone. There were people and places still around. In decline, maybe, but hanging on. I began with a bunch of old-timers, wise-guy screenwriters and camera men and a couple of actors sitting out at the Motion Picture Retirement Home in Woodland Hills during the Eisenhower years. They watched new films, commenting on them, the past holding court on the present. I kept using that device all through the novel. A kind of chorus. And my father took me out there to visit, to sit through screenings. 'A bunch of Jews in the orange groves,' he said. About my sense of humor. It wasn't so attached to a view of life. It was more full of surprise and discovery. Now, my writing has darker tones. There's no getting away from that. Also, with the story set in the recent past it wasn't as historical . . . or as personal . . . as my . . ." I stopped short. I didn't want to talk about The Beast. ". . . as my writing is now."

"Your cast of characters. Harry . . . is it? . . . Cohn. George Raft and Bertolt Brecht . . ."

"I knew them all. The way a kid does, I mean. Saw them at the house, or when my father took me on location. Summer jobs on the lot."

"Actresses?"

"Then . . . and later . . . some." From somewhere far away, Natalie Taylor touched me. That stopped me. Never say never, never say always. A businessman's slogan. But I said both, to myself, to Natalie, just then. Never. Always. Stephanie pressed on, noticing the right things, the complexity of characters, the tangle of motives, from gangsters to stunt men, screen-writers to flacks. And the underlying sense that this was a story set in a time and place that was over, that could never be revisited, except in story. All along, our discussion was like an exam she'd been preparing for, a final or at least mid-term. And, she made the grade.

"Alright," I said. "Soup's on."

"Can I help?" she asked.

"You can watch," I said. "Up close." But I changed my mind, when I saw her, curled up so comfortably on my couch. "Just stay there. Like you are. It won't take a minute."

She waited while I set the table, which was my working desk, with the typewriter moved to the floor. I brought bread and cheese, ladled the goulash into bowls, carried a bottle of wine to the table. She watched me, closely, sharply, measuring something. And when I walked over to invite her to join me, I saw what she hadn't noticed yet: that our monotonous, month-old gray sky was shedding snow. The driveway, the lawn, the car were already under a couple of inches.

"Come here," I said. I was standing at the front window.

"Oh my gosh," she said, with something of a shudder. "It's really coming down."

"Let's worry about that later," I suggested.

"I've got an idea."

"Yes?"

"Let's not worry about it at all . . ." She'd come up behind me when I invited her to see the snow. Now she moved towards me, circling her arms around me, clenching her hands over my stomach and then slowly turning me towards her, so now I was holding her, regarding her face, feeling her press against me. She was there for me, right there, eyes wide-open and the only word that came to me—it became a talisman for all our best moments—was what I'd thought the first time I saw her.

"Fine," I said. Then, a kiss, that began with a brush of lips, then was an opening onto warmth, wetness, tongues and absolute desire.

"The goulash, will it wait?" she asked. "Because I can't."

"It'll be okay."

"Fine," she said. So we left the food and progressed to another kind of feast. She whispered into my ear, in a way that was both innocent and wanton, if that can be. It was a line she'd been saving for months, that she'd heard me use on another woman.

"Professor," she said. "Let your imagination be an equal opportunity employer." And after that an invitation no one could decline. "Everything is on the table."

▲

It was still snowing, when we made our way to the goulash. I have a weakness for bathrobes, light ones in summer, terrycloth in winter, so that's what we were wearing when we sat down to eat, like a pair of athletes who had worked out strenuously, yes, and showered together, and now had time to satisfy an appetite, well-earned.

"Don't you think we got the order right?" she asked, raising a glass to me. "I didn't want to rush things but I didn't want to sit here eating, while all the time something else was in my mind."

"A good idea . . ."

"This is wonderful."

"Don't be shy. Or fussy. I've always believed in crumbs and gravy stains and wine . . ."

"I'm happy." She gestured outside. The early snow, with wet, large, leisurely flakes had yielded to something smaller and denser, that meant we were really in for it. "I love being here with you, watching outside. We're all warm and snug and outside . . . cold. Beautiful. But you wouldn't want to be out there for twenty minutes."

And, like that, it came to me, the memory of Ernst Ernst in the forest around Karlsbad, almost forty years before. How a kind of winter sport, hiding out from his killers, began as a game. How he ducked from barn to basement to hut to cave, raiding storerooms, pantries, apple cellars, food closets and liquor cabinets, mischief and fun combining. Until winter asserted itself. How the cold found him, the tips of his fingers and ears and toes, then his nose, throat, lungs. It was odd to think of him just then, with a beautiful and smart woman across a food-covered table, contemplating more love before long. Odd memory. But that's what being a writer was. Part of you, loyal and disloyal, was always someplace else.

"Hey, professor . . ." she looked a little worried. "Have I lost you already? You were off someplace."

It was her worst fear, I supposed. After sex and food—the satisfaction of appetites—she would have no way of holding on, of hanging in. Here I was, drifting off, and I could see concern on her face.

"I'll tell you what I was thinking," I said. "Wait." I poured us some wine. "It's about sharing with you. And, to tell the truth, it makes me nervous."

"Oh. Sorry."

"We've shared a lot," I said. "And I don't mean . . . just now. We've talked about books for a couple of months. A great way to connect. The way you came through that door, no way of knowing what would happen."

"I was so worried. No way looks would save me. Am I right?"

"But there was something in your eyes that was . . . alive. Intelligence? Depth? Hunger? Something there. Salad, now?"

A spinach salad with a warm bacon dressing: I'd saved bringing it out earlier, so we wouldn't have to discuss the Ohio custom of eating salad while the teenager in the kitchen deep-fried some chicken and melted cheese over everything else.

"Okay . . ." She was back on point. "What was it you were thinking about telling me?"

"I want us to be together," I said. "Would that interest you?"

"I'm sure. Yes."

"I want you to be here for me and me for you. Here. And other places. We can travel. I haven't done much of that lately . . . But . . . now . . . not alone . . . yes . . . It appeals."

"Can I just say this? I wanted to be with you from the moment I left your office that first time . . ."

"But you have a son," I said.

"Dillon. Yes." A shadow fell between us then. It was my fault and I'm not sure it ever quite cleared up. She'd been reminded of a marriage that was a mistake, that devalued her in my eyes and her own. And there was a son she cared about, whom I didn't have time for.

"Well, I don't know how to put this without sounding selfish . . ."

I hesitated, knowing that I wasn't sounding selfish, I was *being* selfish. And she watched me, knowing all this, her first hopes yielding to disappointment and then to a decision.

"He's my kid, not yours, George," she said. "You'll never have to meet him."

She'd said exactly what I wanted, but with a decisiveness that startled me. Just for a moment, I felt shame and loss. Whatever else we'd be, we'd never be a family. I was being selfish, alright. Maybe she was being selfish too.

"God, look at you. You're relieved. It's written all over you. I'm just chattel . . ."

Chattel! I wouldn't have guessed she knew that word. I had looked it up more than once myself, re-learning and again forgetting the meaning.

"There's something you need to know. I have a child too. There's someone else who lives here. Someone who's been here a long time and cannot be evicted. Or hidden from you."

With that, I thought I'd have her interest. How mysterious I sounded, introducing her to the book I'd been working on for years. By this time, I should note, ten years had passed since my arrival. *It's worth the wait* was yielding to *what are we waiting for*?

"Oh," she said. "This must be get-to-know-The-Beast."

"You've heard about it?"

"Who hasn't?"

"What do they say?"

"You've got believers and you've got doubters."

"The doubters are winning."

"Well, I guess I'll put up with The Beast. Did you say something about cognac."

"Why yes . . ." I started to get up. It surprised me that she hadn't pressed me about The Beast. Her questions about *Out On the Coast* had been searching. Was her reticence about The Beast a display of faith? Or its absence? She was as distant from my "child" as I was from hers. And so available, now, to me. I watched her stand on tip toes to reach for the cognac glasses. I liked the shape of her ass, covered—as by snow—by white terrycloth. She was smart and sensitive and how I loved looking at her pour the cognac into glasses, turn and walk back towards me! Fine.

She sat down and handed me my cognac. "Just two things, professor. Could you start a fire?"

"Sure . . ." I headed towards the fireplace, knelt to arrange some newspapers, kindling, logs. I concentrated on what I was doing. It was one of the things that I was proud of doing well. Writers need a few things like that, that don't involve words. Starting fires was one of mine. And every time I did it, Ernst Ernst was with me, wondering whether he dared a fire, whether smoke would draw killers to his hiding place.

"Now," she told me when I had the fire lit and glowing, "could you turn out the lights in here, professor? And turn on the outside light?"

I stepped over to the switch and turned off the living room light. Outside, the porch light revealed whiteness on the ground, swirling whiteness in the air. Inside, were firelight, crackling wood, flickering shadows.

"You don't mind if I keep calling you professor, do you? Because I want you to keep being my professor. And could we please keep meeting to talk about books? In your office, like before? And no funny business, I mean it . . ."

"'Gladly would he learn and gladly teach,'" I answered.

"What's that?"

"Chaucer. The Clerk in *The Canterbury Tales.*" I sat beside her on the couch.

"Say it again."

"'Gladly would he learn and gladly teach.' See? It goes both ways."

We touched glasses, watched the fire inside, the snow. The cognac. Already we'd learned to enjoy relaxed silence.

"I love this," she said after a while, snuggling against me.

"I'm glad you found your way to me."

Outside the snow storm was peaking, whipped by wind that made white twisters and cyclones right outside. And here we were, warm and luxuriant. What kind of luck was that? How long could it last? And if you admitted that it might not last—that it couldn't last—did that make it, make her—less worth having? Or more?

"Is it time for bed now?" I asked.

"Let me think it over." Her hand moved up and down, slowly, thoughtfully, inside my bathrobe. After a while she opened her bathrobe and mine, and moved onto me. Cognac still in hand.

"Not yet," she said, sipping slowly, moving slowly, too.

▲

Stephanie and I lasted for almost ten years. In offering this now, I realize that I delete customary suspense. We did not live happily ever after. Come to think about it, no one does. The issue isn't whether we made it, she and I. My answer would be we made it for a long, good time. And the happiness was in spite of the fact that I knew from the beginning that she would leave me. So, yes, here's an author who claims he saw an ending coming. But that didn't make the pages of the book any less worth turning.

No secrets in this town: by dawn the next morning, when Stephanie and I were still sleeping, a maintenance man, driving to work, noticed her car outside my house. When we were showering together—a situation that got out of hand, when I saw her soaped up—as though swathed in cotton candy—the news made its way to the bookstore, where Harvey Leichter picked up the New York Times and, with him, it traveled to the coffee shop where he crossed paths with Louise Becker, on her way to visit Jefferson Overstreet out at the nursing home. By noontime, we were in the public domain.

"You're finished," Derrick Madison announced at the coffee shop the next day. "You know the old story about Balzac . . ."

"Yes," I said. But that didn't stop him. He proceeded for Harvey's benefit.

"Well, Balzac was a tremendous womanizer. And after one room-rattling climax, he looks down and says 'There goes a novel I won't write.'"

"He wrote more than his share anyway," I responded.

"Yeah, but Balzac had more than a couple novels in the tank. *He* could afford to lose a few in bed."

▲

We discovered a way of living that suited us. I retained my house, she kept hers. Once or twice a week, she spent the night with me. We resumed our slow climb up the 100-best-novels list. Now, all of them were more highly regarded than mine. I wondered, though never aloud, where The Beast would land on such a list. I looked up, way up, at *The Great Gatsby* and *Moby Dick*, and *Huckleberry Finn.* Would The Beast find its place among them? Or hurtle downward, rung by rung, crashing and onto remainder tables and mulch piles, like Harold Brodkey's *Party of Animals*, Ellison's *Juneteenth*, Marguerite Young's *Miss MacIntosh, My Darling*? Works of a lifetime with the span of a mayfly.

During the week, Stephanie sometimes called me at midmorning to offer lunch. She had an hour, forty-five minutes after the drive from town, and that led to a hurried breathless lovemaking which she quite liked. And that was part of our . . . I hate to call it routine, for it was anything but . . . our pattern. But there was more. We walked a lot. For her, walking was an addiction. An appetite. Europeans were like this, one sees it all the time, after-dinner strolls, widows with canes on hiking trails. One did not expect to find this in America, least of all in the Midwest. And she drove the way she walked, the way I had driven during my first year at the college. She drove well and very fast, down unmarked roads I never guessed at, that ended at abandoned farms or mills, covered bridges, pathetic hamlets that used to be real towns. She drove all hours. Sometimes she'd awaken me in the wee hours, especially on a moonlit night. She hated wasting moonlight. I remember one such night especially. We drove into her past. Her grammar school, her high school. The homes of childhood friends and dead grandparents, ex-in-laws and ex-husband. We came at last to the house she grew up in, in a tidy bungalow, long and narrow, with a rickety garage in back.

"It's what it is," she said. "Nothing special."

"Were you happy?"

"Aren't you the professor who told me that happiness isn't a steady state? Now you see it, now you don't?"

I nodded. On that gray empty street, no cars coming or going, no lights on in the houses, nothing stirring, we whispered like spies.

"Sometimes I was happy," she said. "Most of the time, come to think of it. I guess the problems came later. When I turned pretty. Happened overnight almost. Suddenly boys are stopping by. And men! Sheriff's deputies see me walking home from school, they offer me lifts. Want to protect me, you know? The phone's ringing all the time. My father looks at me. 'What's going on?' he asks. 'Are you in heat or something?'"

We drove out, past homes that were at last coming to life, men and women with mugs of coffee, piling into cars and heading for donut shops. We drove to the edge of town, where subdivisions were cutting into farmland. It was sad to see what used to be a farm reduced to a house and a falling-down barn, sitting on one last acre of land, surrounded by ranch houses. In one such development Stephanie paused in front of a new house, brick veneer, aluminum siding, two car garage, a clump of shrubs on either side of the front doorstep.

"That's where I sleep when I'm not sleeping with you," she said. "Right now, Mom's in the kitchen, making Dillon breakfast. My room's next to his, around back."

"Your mother knows about us?"

"Sure. And she'll be there for me, no matter what. But she still likes Mike. Always did, always will. He still looks in on her. Odd jobs, cup of coffee, checking on Dillon."

"Holding a torch for you?"

"Yes," she said. "It's sad . . . He's got someone living with him now . . . but I can tell . . ." She turned to me and I saw, for the first time, tears. "That's something I can't figure out. Someone hurts you. And sometimes, you hurt someone else. And I can't decide which is worse. Giving or receiving pain. It's like Christmas, backwards . . ."

That morning, she returned me to the house, kissed me in the driveway and drove off to work, without coming inside. And it frightened me, the way she did that, not looking back. Granted, I knew she'd be with me again—that same night, in fact, and that, as usual, everything was on the table. I knew she'd drive away from me a thousand times like that and she'd come back, until that one last time, when she would drive away and not return.

I learned a lot from Stephanie. She'd already made clear that you don't grow up as a small town beauty without getting noticed and marked. What I had left to learn was that when you stayed in the same place along with most of your high school friends, you were bonded for life. No store, no gas station, no landscaping or construction crew lacked an admirer. A shout, a joke, a signaled availability. Those were the men. The women—called "girls"—went much deeper. These were war veterans, purple hearts and all, survivors of their hook-ups, estrangements, marriages. They drank and laughed a lot, got loud and coarse sometimes, and divided into two teams. Team A: all the good men are taken. Team B: there are no good men. I never was invited to one of their parties but I met them individually; they all wanted to check me out. Some of them are still around, one at the Motor Vehicles Bureau, another in real estate, a third a health club receptionist. They're older now, and sadder than when we met. I suppose they consider Stephanie the one who got away. So do I.

▲

I returned from the Post Office with her first passport. And, because I had renewed my passport so my dates would match hers, there were two new passports. We were starting at the same point, traveling together. Now she held her passport, which was a ticket to ride, a diploma, she opened it to make sure her picture was inside. There she was, wide-eyed and innocent. A deer in headlights, I said.

"I've been reading *Travels With My Aunt*," I said. We'd stopped three quarters up the best 100 list, after reading *The Heart of The Matter*, and decided to go further into Greene. "There's a line, the best line so far, that life is all about the accumulation of memories. And that is what we are going to do."

"Where are we going?" she asked, sounding like a kid. She wanted to travel—that was clear from the start—but had no idea where. What she wanted was **out**. That was as specific as it got. Perhaps she was uncertain about making a suggestion, fearing I'd pronounce it cliche.

"Wait," I said. "You hold a passport that is good for ten years." I took her passport and riffled through the pages, about two dozen of them. An unwritten book, *tabula rasa*. "There's room for lots and lots of stamps. Entry, exit. And sometimes visas. They can take up a full page. Go back and forth between, say, Hong Kong and Macao and the book fills up. Still, there's lots of room. But suppose you fill up the passport, before it's expired? What then?"

"Get a new one?"

"No. You . . . we . . . go to a U.S. Embassy, the consular section. And they'll sew in an additional bunch of pages. There's no charge. And that's my promise to you. Extra pages."

She turned away from me, overcome. Unusual, in someone who was always in command. She walked out to the porch, into a May morning, and sat on a step. The fields, just plowed, were brown and glistening and there were all sorts of blossoming trees I never learned the names of, ornamental pears, apples, cherries, pink and white and sweet smelling.

"Why me, George?" she asked. "That's what I ask myself. You've got talent and you don't worry about money and I guess you could have found a woman to live with here. Or city women. You could have had regular deliveries . . . You've met my girlfriends. Quite a bunch. Pretty as I am. Hard working. Great, great lays, to hear them talk about it. Always a sense of humor. 'A good man is hard to find, a hard man is good to find.' They say I should go for it. But my mother thinks I'm on the way to being a kept woman, living off a man from the college. And around here the college means snootiness and attitude. She'd want me to keep my job. And give back this passport . . ."

She held it out to me.

"Enough," I said. "None of your friends came to me, Stephanie. You did. And, yes, you looked wonderful and you knew it. And you were scared. You wanted to talk about books. I took you at your word, that it wasn't a clever pass. And we began. You worked. You read. You thought about what you read. You had questions and answers. There were things you missed that annoyed you. Shrewd moments too and funny ones and then . . ."

"Would I get an A?" she asked in a little girl voice.

"I'll never tell. But listen. I found myself wondering about you. What your life was like. Who was in it. Things that don't occur to me with students. With them, I know more than I want to know. You were a mystery to me. And, after a while, I'd stand in the office and watch you leave, watch you walk across the parking lot, get into your car and drive away and . . ."

Odd. At the very end I faltered. ". . . and I didn't like that. Listen, we've both had bad luck. Divorce for you. For me . . . I don't know if you know . . . someone I care for died . . ."

"The actress?"

"Yes. And let me say this. I'm speaking about myself now. I don't know if it makes sense. But I believe that once you love someone, you always do. Always. The phrase 'falling out of love' doesn't make sense to me. If you lose love, you never had it. That goes for . . . the actress."

She nodded. Whether it was to signal agreement or only understanding, I didn't know and didn't ask.

"That goes for the actress. And . . . for you."

That surprised her. She just looked at me, as if waiting for a qualifier, a footnote, a correction. And none came.

"Now," I said, "we've got these passports to fill. Starting in June. We've got memories to accumulate . . ."

She studied me, still. She considered something—I could see her making up her mind. She glanced at her watch. She was due back at work.

"Could we accumulate a memory now?"

XIII. NOW: FEBRUARY, 2006

▲

JOHN HENRY MALLON CALLED ME, A FEW DAYS AFTER HE arrived and we agreed to get together. When it didn't happen, I let it go. It was nice enough, I thought, that he'd expressed an intention to become friends. Perhaps it was best to leave it at that. No loss.

Then, on a Tuesday night, a car rolls into my driveway and he comes clumping up my front steps, announcing that he needs a drink.

"A post-seminar drink?" I ask.

"What else?"

"I'll bring you some cognac," I say. I go to the kitchen, grab a bottle of Hennessey's and a few beers besides. The beers are for thirst, the cognac for heartbreak. And I realize that all my nights of coming home, feeling the way Mallon feels now, are over.

"I can say—and I'm one of the few people around here who are entitled to say it—that I know just how you feel," I tell him. Though he'd been scheduled to teach a literature course—"Geddis, Barth, DeLillo, Pynchon"—he'd talked the College into letting him do a writing seminar. Now, he regretted it.

"They tired me out," Mallon says. "No. I was tired before I began. I read their stuff, I read it twice. Oh my god . . ."

"They're beginners," I say.

"They're beginners?" Mallon asks. "No. I'm the beginner." He continues, sounding like I once did. He mentions the way they turn you into a copy editor, a line-editing schoolmarm. How they assume that geniuses don't have to know about indenting paragraphs, about quotation marks and speaker identifications, and if a character changes name in mid-story, hey, that's for some editor to catch. Before long he talks about the nearly good papers, the tangled imperfect, the simply hopeless. Shuddering one moment, chuckling the next, he tells me I can have my job back. I tell him it's not his to give. Or mine to take. Besides, he's only joking.

"Some camp out in my office every day," Mallon goes on. "They want me to look over a first paragraph, a first sentence, even, and pronounce it great. Did Melville walk around publishers' offices, pulling 'Call me Ishmael' out of his pocket, for Christ's sake? Kid shows me a few lines, Asking if this is the real thing . . . I tell him it's like he showed up with a handful of jism, asks me what it's going to be. Could be a boy, I tell him, could be a girl. Could be nothing, could be he was just jerking off. Now he hates me . . ."

"Fine," I say. "But you can't . . . you shouldn't make a career out of putting them down. Because sooner or later someone . . . one or two of them . . . will rescue you. I mean it. Save you. Amaze you." Then I told him about Mary Cantonelli. My angel, rated X, my career savior! How often had I wondered about her? I shared that with Mallon, I describe the pass she'd made. Having saved my career, she could just as easily have ended it. The power of life and death. Why did I tell Mallon? I wanted him to know I was young and published once, like him; I had been powerfully attractive. I was a bit proud of that. Where was Mary, I wondered. There was no mention of her in the class notes section of the alumni magazine, where her graduation year slid further back into history with every issue. No sight of her at reunions either, yet I could not believe that we would not meet again. I speculated that she wanted to have accomplished something she was proud of, before she showed her face again. That might take a while, Mallon rejoindered. Then I told him about what that first Cantonelli-Stuckey seminar felt like, what they all felt like, some students who came in writing well, others were rough but talented, and some pancake flat. And they had come alive in front of me, solved problems, filled silence, and gotten better. Maybe they'd have gotten better without me, but it happened in front of me and that made me feel lucky. Blessed, even. And, for Mallon, I save the best for last. The quiet miracle of last semester, the ultimate service ace. Like a sommelier blowing the dust off my finest vintage, I poured John Henry Mallon a glass of my Emily Dickinson.

▲

Derrick Madden walks into the coffee shop, proud as a peacock. It's hard for outsiders to understand how the possession of news—something that isn't out yet—can affect a person at a small college. It puts a grin on your face, a spring in your step, a spin on your prose. It's as if you've just hit the jackpot, the g-spot, the mother lode.

"Gentlemen," he says. Harvey and I look up from the obituary section of the New York Times, where we'd been checking to see who hadn't made it through the night. We'd been debating whether the people who ran the agate-type classified obituaries would accept an advertisement relating to the death of a flagrantly non-Jewish mobster, John Gotti, say?

"Losers," Derrick says. Then he sniffs the air, wrinkles his nose as if trying to identify a particular scent. "Do I smell . . ."

He milks his moment shamelessly, expertly.

"Do I smell . . . could it be . . . wait a minute . . . *Alfano* burgers?" He produces a sheet of paper which I recognize as a college press release. Those are famously disingenuous documents, written in assiduously spin-doctored lawsuit-avoiding language. "Anybody want me to read this?"

"God no," Harvey answers. "Just summarize."

"Okay," he agrees, scanning the release, holding it at a distance between two fingers, as if he might catch something off of it. "A true friend of the college . . . a loyal servant . . . student, professor, provost . . . a decade of faithful stewardship . . . presiding over a time of enrichment and growth . . . leaving . . . oh my . . . leaving at the end of the month . . ." He feigns studying the release more closely, truth-seeking. Might as well look for lips on a chicken. "Is it an award? A new job? No . . . wait . . . something about pursuing new opportunities. 'Personal reasons.'"

"Poor John,"I say.

"Poor John?" asks Derrick. "Why do you think he got fired?"

"Because of me?" I ask. "Does it look that way?"

"I'd have to say it is that way," Derrick says. And Derrick has a way of knowing these things. "It's been a series of embarrassments lately. Something happens and the trustees don't hear about it, it doesn't matter. It happens in public, in print, on T.V., that's something else. It happens in public once, maybe it's forgiven. Not forgotten. Forgiven. This happened twice, this Alfano-Canaris duel. It happened when they told you you were finished. Bad enough. Then it happened again, when he falls for that please-tell-the-world-you're-not-letting-me-speak ploy of yours. Suddenly, we're the enemy of free speech."

"Poor John," I repeat.

"Not so poor. Pathetic, yes. Poor, no. I hear they gave him five years at half salary. And he agreed not to complain."

"Who's replacing him here?" Harvey asked.

"I can't say," Derrick replied. And that gave the game away.

"I'll be damned," Harvey said. "You!"

"Don't blame me, guys. I just answered the phone."

▲

It takes winter to make me wonder if Jefferson Overstreet wasn't right. If you aren't teaching here, if you have no students in front of you, your life thins out. I can't bear to sit in my office.

It's like an abandoned bird's nest, a few twigs and feathers waiting for a strong wind. It's a wrist-slicing season, unrelievedly bleak. Here, February brings no winter pleasures. No Alps arise in front of us, no daunting slopes and glaciers, only gray skies and slush, threadbare houses and cars corroded by salt. The walking trail is denied me, glazed by ice. It's a wretched time and place. One morning, coming down from the post office steps, I fall, spectacularly, publically, at the busiest time of day. My legs go out from under me and I land hard, in a puddle of icy water, stunned and embarrassed. A group of students surrounds me, urging me to stay down. I lurch to my feet and thank them. Someone walks me to my car, asks me if I'm alright. He defers to me, youth to age, he condescends. He calls me *mister*. Was I able to drive? "Sure," I snap. "You can fall on your ass at any age." "I'll remember that," he says

▲

And now the worst. Louise Becker calls. She's heard about my post office fall. She wonders how long I can live alone. She's kidding, but she isn't kidding one hundred percent. I then ask if she wants me to keep Jeff Overstreet company at the home. And there's silence on the line.

"Hello . . ." I ask after a moment. "You still there Louise?"

More silence.

"Louise?"

"He died last night."

Odd, the thoughts that came to me just then, not the thoughts themselves, but the order of their arrival. My first is that for once the college will be able to turn out a straightforward press release about someone's departure. The second is that it has been several weeks—maybe a couple of months—since I'd dropped in on someone I considered a close friend. The third is that someday I will die and it will be announced like this and people will react the way that I am reacting now, just as selfish and self-centered.

"Are we still having breakfast?" Louise asks.

"If you're up to it."

"What's the alternative? Sit home and cry? On an empty stomach? You've got to eat, you know . . ."

"Eat and die," I say. "Okay. I'll be watching for you . . ."

A few minutes later she pulls into my driveway, gets out and watches me as I walk towards her.

"You hurt yourself."

"Wrong. The sidewalk hurt me. Gave me a bruise that looks like a thunderstorm *and* a sunset."

"Where is it?"

"Where I fell. Where I sit. And, no, you can't look."

She walks around and opens the door for me, pushes the seat way back to make room. With small favors like this, a dollar off a haircut, a discounted movie ticket, old age insinuates itself.

"Who called you?" I ask.

"The nursing home," she said. "Actually, I was the first one on the list of people to call."

"Were there others?"

"Let's just say it was a short list."

"Will you do the same for me?"

"God, professor, you know how to flatter a girl."

"How'd he . . . go?"

"In his sleep. At least, in his bed. At night. Who knows whether he was sleeping? They just say that."

We parked in the old country square and go to a place that used to be Greek and used to be open twenty four hours. It's not Greek anymore, but a spinach and feta cheese omelet lingers on the menu.

"You old guys," Louise says. "Mean and stubborn. You think Jeff was ever young? Dreamy?"

"I'm sure he was," I said. "I know I was."

"You got it out of your system young," she said. Then she touched my hand. "Sorry, sweetie." She'd been around at the time of Natalie Taylor's visit and sat, tight-lipped through my years with Stephanie Knox. She was protective, like a mother. Well, not quite like a mother, not always. Sometimes she felt jealous, acted neglected. To this day. There was something in our friendship, a possibility, a turn or a stop, way back down the road.

"Did you hear what happened to John Alfano?" I ask.

"Please, George. Of course I know."

"Kind of harsh. And swift. They didn't even let him finish out the year."

"He'll live," Louise snaps. Anyone who attacks me is her enemy.

"I'm associated with his undoing," I say.

"He undid himself," she responds.

"You're so tough."

"Somebody around here has to be," she says. She hands me a piece of paper, then takes it back. "Before you read it, I want to tell you that it's all over campus. Faculty mailboxes, under the doors of administration offices. I suppose newspapers will get it, and trustees."

OPEN LETTER

> Ex-writer-in-residence George Canaris has turned the last year of his overlong, over-paid stay at this college into a carnival act, self-promoting and self-serving. After years—decades—of silence, he turned his justified replacement by a younger, better-known, better writer, John Henry Mallon, into a cause celebre. He took his pitiful act on the road, at college expense, pleading with graduates and journalists to come to his rescue. Then, when his five seconds of notoriety faded, he cleverly induced the college to announce its understandable withdrawal of an invitation to speak at commencement. When a symposium on his novels sank like a stone, he persuaded the college to announce this as well. Once again, he conjured a bogus freedom of speech issue and discredited his employer of 35 years. He also arranged

> for the firing of its competent provost, John Alfano, the first and as yet only member of this college's administration to call Canaris on his life-long bluff. It cost Alfano his job. But the point Alfano made should be considered. Missing in all this melodrama is an honest acknowledgment that George Canaris is a fraud. His long-awaited masterwork, the so-called "Beast" is a hoax, perpetrated upon a trusting and supportive college. If these words seem harsh, let Canaris refute them. Until then, the only Beast in town is not the invisible book, but its all too visible non-author, Canaris himself, and if there is a victim of an assault against free speech in the vicinity, it is John Alfano.

"Any ideas?" Louise asked.

"This is not the person we've been hearing from," I told her. "This is over-determined, self-righteous, erudite and prickly. A faculty member for sure."

"A faculty member?" Louise asks.

"Or a provost."

▲

I sit in my office, at my computer, deleting dozens of messages related to the anonymous letter. Before now the press has been sympathetic. I was one man against an institution, a writer against a bureaucracy. Now, they correct for previous generosity. My name is considered for inclusion on a long list of frauds and plagiarists, from Chatterton to Clifford Irving. And—in some people's opinions—my fraud is worse. Other people included what they stole in their work. I never worked at all, at least after arriving at this college, which coddled me for years. So there is punditry, editorial and op-ed, there are round-robin discussions in The Chronicle of Higher Education. There are funny bits by humorists and—so I hear—a wisecrack on late night talk shows, something about how "the dog ate my homework" has been replaced by "the college ate my masterpiece."

▲

"Hi, Professor Canaris," says Millie Gottwald, from last semester's writing seminar. She'd started at the middle of the pack, awkward and scared, turning out sentimental stuff about a visit to grandmother's house, right after the old lady died. She came in for criticism that she deserved and fledgling fellow-writers can be brutal. She listened, though, she sorted it out. She didn't get defensive. And her work got better, surprisingly so. She was no Emily Dickinson but she was very good and, I have to admit, she contributed much more to class discussion than Emily ever volunteered.

"I'm not bothering you?" she asks. Was it just good manners or was it faux naivete, pretending that I wasn't in the eye of a shit storm.

"Not a bit. I was just checking my e-mail. I love deleting it. It's like weeding."

"You can go through it and delete it all at once," she says. "I can show you. It's easy!" This is how computers subvert colleges. The students are more at ease with them than their professors, especially the older ones. We stumble into cyberspace, they glide and soar. They can't believe our clumsiness.

"I'll stick to killing them one at a time," I decide. "Call me old-fashioned. How are you, Millie?"

"Nervous," she says. "I need to talk to somebody about plagiarism."

"Well, you know there's a committee. Academic Infractions, I think it's called. I'm not sure about their procedures. I've never done any business with them . . ."

"You'll be doing business now," she says.

"Pardon me?"

"This is about plagiarism in your class. Our class . . ."

I was dumbfounded. I'd gathered that plagiarism was a problem, getting worse. Computers again. Surfing instead of thinking. Why come up with an answer when you could download it? We only caught a fraction of the cheaters, I heard. But plagiarism in a creative writing class was grotesque.

"I hate to do this," Millie says, handing me a manila folder.

I recognize the title instantly. I recognize the opening paragraph and, as I scan the remaining two dozen pages, I don't see anything that I did not remember in what I had called—oh, my God!—"about the best work I've ever seen from a student." The only two words that are new are the author's first and last names, for which my Emily Dickinson substituted her own.

"Where . . . how . . . did you find this?" I ask.

"There's a new search engine—not so new, actually—that let's you type in words from a story." She adopts the pedantic voice that even nice students assume when computers let them turn the tables on someone older and in this particular case, not wiser. "Obviously, it can't be an ordinary phrase. 'He opened the door,' say. But there were all sorts of special things in this story. You loved them."

"And this appeared in what?"

"A web literary magazine. You go to their home page, you'll find that it won a prize from them. Best short story. "So . . ." She smiled at me, and there was adult, female pity in that smile. "You picked a winner. A lot of us put good work on the table. But she got the A."

"A minus, actually,"

"And we got B pluses and B's. And we think that kind of sucks."

"I agree," I said, wincing at the word *sucks*: a porn film word successfully infiltrating campus language. "It sucks. Big time."

▲

Jefferson Overstreet spent forty years teaching here and survived his retirement by fifteen more years. His name had been installed on an office building and attached to a scholarship. But the college he'd served had "moved on." Even the history department had turned over utterly, not only in name but in style. So his memorial service attracted a mere handful of local people, three professors and perhaps a dozen middle-aged academics who were his former students.

"People who die in the gas chamber draw bigger crowds," Louise whispers while we sit waiting for more organ music to end.

"He hadn't had a class for fifteen years," I remind her.

"He *did* have classes for forty years," she counters. "Have they all forgotten him?"

"Not showing up at a memorial service isn't the same thing as forgetting," I suggests.

"Well, I think it's lousy," she persists. And so do I. It was sad how life shrank, once you stopped teaching. For a while, you showed up in college fund raising efforts and publicity. They used your name, when they wanted to honor the past. But this usually entailed juxtaposing a dour black-and-white photo of some war-horse like Jeff Overstreet, a thou-shalt-not-screw-up expression on his face, with a smiling technicolor of a current favorite, every students' new best friend. Time wasn't on the side of the old professor, that was the unintended message. But Jeff knew better. A historian, he knew that time wasn't on anybody's side.

Two days before, I'd seen my Emily Dickinson, sitting at the same seminar table where she'd shone so brightly. Now, it was the location of the college's Academic Infractions board. Present besides the accused and the accuser were five board members, three faculty and two students. Also, one counselor, someone from the Dean of Students' office whom Emily had selected in her hour of peril.

She was guilty as hell. That she'd committed flagrant plagiarism was beyond dispute. What more was there to say? She was a liar, a cheat, a thief, and my only regret was that the writer she'd stolen from would never know that his or her story had indeed changed someone's life. And it was too bad that the seminar students who'd sat around this very table with her could not attend. Now I wanted it over. Give the accused a cigarette, a moment of prayer and put her up against the wall. Or on the bus to the airport.

Ah, but wait a minute! She had been distressed she said, deeply troubled and though the whole semester was "kind of a blur," she granted that "it was possible" that she "might have" done "something like" plagiarism in my course. But she'd been in counseling since then and she was better now and she hoped, with time, to serve as a role model for other troubled students. With that, her sidekick counselor pulled out notes from a phone conversation she'd had with Emily's psychiatrist, verifying that she had been under treatment and that her confusion, her memory loss were "not inconsistent" with . . .

"Excuse me," I said. "Everyone in this room has to be here. Except me. I've heard about all I can bear of this. May I leave?"

"Certainly, Professor," the board chair—a likeable woman from chemistry—said. "We're about to begin our deliberations anyway. Was there anything you wanted to add before you go?"

As I arose, my intention was to leave without further comment. But I saw her there, picking at the same sleeve she'd been working over when I called her in to my office, wondering where her unprecedented talent had come from.

"I thought of you as a student that I'd never forget," I said to her. This was a hambone scene, the inner critic in me howled. But I was determined to play it. Her eyes were turned away from me, her expression was fixed. Was she in inner agony? Or turning cartwheels somewhere? "'My 'Emily Dickinson.' That's what I called you. In private, until now. Deep and secret and brilliant. I tried to get to know you. As professor to student, or writer to writer. You did not respond. Do you have anything to say to me now, at the end of your short, bright career and . . . come to think of it . . . at the end of my career as well?"

She sat motionless for a while, then leaned towards her counselor. "Do I have to talk to him?"

"No, you certainly don't," came the reply. The counselor looked up at me. "This isn't helping anyone, professor."

"Oh. Then . . . by all means . . . be helpful." And I departed. And now I sit with Louise waiting for someone to say a few words about an honorable, scholarly grouch. The officiating priest—he'd arrived a few years ago, handles ritual and scripture nicely, the way Episcopalians do. But then he appeals to anyone present to say a few words. He's too honest to fabricate a eulogy for someone he'd never met. He waits for someone else to care.

"I came here too late to know Jefferson Overstreet," President Tracy begins. "I waited in line with him at the Post Office and we talked about the weather. And I was aware of him at reunion weekends, of all the people who wanted to see him. And that's about all, I'm afraid to say. But I was aware of him from the day I came here. From the day *before* I came. Because Professor Overstreet was one of those grand old names that are connected with this place. You couldn't know the place and not know him. I always wanted to sit down and have a good, long talk with him."

"Yeah, right," Louise mutters. "One phone call away, for years. This is Jeff Overstreet!"

"Is there anyone else?" the chaplain asks. And then I sense Louise Becker standing up next to me.

"What I want to say is a little bit different," she begins. "And maybe it doesn't belong. You've talked about how scary he was. I don't doubt that. But I know that you know that behind that scariness there was a kind of love. Love for his work, writing and teaching, like you've all said. Love for students. Not every student, not every day. Still . . . But there was another kind of love. Love for this place, this college. Now lots of people who show up around here say they love this college. They love it . . . say they love it . . . in the line of duty. Then they leave and I guess, move on to some other place which they also love a lot. That's the style now. Come and go. Move up and on and out. Jeff Overstreet never left. Never. And, from where I stand, that looks very impressive. This place belonged to him. Completely. Always. And for as close to forever as anybody can come. Thanks."

XIV. THEN: 1975–1990

▲

MEMORIES. THAT WAS WHAT I PROMISED STEPHANIE Knox. The accumulation of memories. And now I wonder, the way old lovers do, how her memories compare to mine. Memories. In the film that will never be made of these pages, this section would conduce to montage. That first summer we went to Southeast Asia, Thailand, Laos, Vietnam, Cambodia, and Burma, the following to Singapore, Malaysia, Australia and New Zealand. Heat and dust behind us, we then headed for Hapsburg Europe—but not Czechoslovakia—and then the Mediterranean, after that the Scandinavian countries. I had been to many of these places before, in the lush years between my first and second novels. I'd traveled and I'd read a lot, I had names and addresses and I suppose that I was the very definition of what the New York Times refers to—obnoxiously—as a sophisticated traveler. I knew where to stay and what to avoid, I sniffed discovery, avoided cliche. And, in no time, Stephanie matched me, step by step. By the end of the first year, we planned together, by the end of the second, she took care of all the logistics, reservations, itinerary. We consulted, I sometimes corrected. My contribution was to teach pace, to slow her down, the way one slowed down love, teasing and prolonging, resting and renewing. Any place that was worth visiting rewarded lingering. By the third year, we were in perfect rhythm: she was driver and navigator. Yet even as we went about the business of accumulating memories, I wondered if we weren't at cross purposes. I kept my doubts to myself. But that didn't erase them, erase this question: whether I was adding to a list, while she was crossing things off.

Lists. We'd begun with a list of books, those hundred famous novels. Now it was a list of places, of memories. The difference was I resided among those memories, I carried them with me. I incorporated them. Stephanie worked through them and looked beyond. So I wondered—wonder, today—whether she has gone back to any of the places that I thought we loved, to a garden compound in Bali, the lake country of Austria. Does she remember our spring walk in Berlin, Unter den Linden? that hawker stall that made oyster omelets for us in Singapore? or how find it felt to sit in a rickety pavilion in Luang Prabang, watching the sinking sun set the Mekong on fire? I'm ambushed by memories all the time, an angle of light, a gust of breeze, a scent of something in the air, and I am there. And what about you, Stephanie, I wonder. Did you—do you—ever go back? Only forward? Was once good enough? Been there, seen it, done it? Do you never re-read a book, revisit old places? Or does it still please you to move into the future even as I, more and more, revisit the past?

▲

We're in New York, May, 1982. This is by no means our first visit to the city. We've paused there any number of times, on the way out or back from Europe. But though she was diligent and considerate in her attention to foreign places, New York cowed her. The pace, the edge, the anger. Along with giddy success, violence and ugliness could never be discounted. You walked back from a $200 dinner, back to a boutique hotel and you encountered a homeless wino taking a watery shit between two parked cars. You strolled around Central Park reservoir at dusk, while the sun crashed in New Jersey, gilding the apartments along Fifth Avenue with its expiring rays and then the skyline bristled with lights and the sky was dotted with stars and a shady figure standing by the pumping station at the north end of the reservoir whispered obscene proposals as you passed. Or you crossed from one side of Madison Avenue to the other, segueing from a new suede coat to a perfect Linzer torte, and a spandex-clad messenger on a bicycle ran a light and clipped you as you stepped off the curb.

No, she insisted, this was one place she would never live. It brought out the Midwest and small town in her. But never say never, I told her. The city was full of people like her. She laughed at that: I can still see her sitting on the deck of a Dayline Cruise around the island, sitting as though she were in a lounge at Newark airport, waiting for a delayed flight to Columbus. It took five years for the one place she would never live to become the only place she'd ever want to live. I watched it happen, saw the confidence and shrewdness grow. And something else: the love of money. New York is honest that way. You get what you pay for and with money, all things are possible. She began to lobby for trips to New York and sometimes she spent a week at a hotel, on her own, while I flew back and forth on weekends, and every time I joined her she was noticeably less curious about how things were on an obscure campus back in Ohio.

So it's a fine spring morning. After a breakfast of bagel and sable—she prefers sable to lox—we turn into the park. It's a part of New York that never changes, I tell her. Around us, buildings elbow each other along the street, then reach for the sky. But the park remains. Cherry blossoms are not quite gone and the leaves have that first flush of timid green. There's no other place she wants to be, she tells me. Really, where else but here? She jogs in the park these days, even around the reservoir at dusk. I'm the visitor in from Ohio, she's the native. And now, in the west 70's, we find a block between Amsterdam and Columbus that's been used a lot in movies, thanks to a line of identical front stoops that empty out of brownstone apartments onto a treelined sidewalk. More like Neil Simon's New York than Edith Wharton's but classy and, as I have recently learned, expensive. We sit on a stoop at my suggestion and watch joggers and dogwalkers headed for the park. We camp out with the New York Times and coffee in paper cups.

"Excuse me" says someone coming out of the entrance behind us. We scoot to a side and she—and her golden retriever—have no trouble passing. But passing by isn't the point.

"I'm so sorry," she says, "but this is private property. You can't just stay here. It's not you but . . . there are derelicts . . ."

"I'm sorry, " I said. I reach in my pocket and pull out a set of keys that I dangle in front of her before passing them over to Stephanie.

"Apartment Five-A," I say. "We were just going in."

"Oh . . . well . . . welcome to the neighborhood," she says. I nod and turn to Stephanie.

"What's up?" she asks, in a wide-eyed way I haven't seen much lately. Sometimes, I miss the earlier Stephanie. But innocence dies along with ignorance.

"Remember when we talked about memories? That morning when I gave you your first passport. Remember what I promised?"

"That we'd have to sew in extra pages?" It's an answer couched in the form of a question. The early Stephanie. We'd accomplished that goal: a triumphant morning in the U.S. consulate in Bordeaux, the morning after some students had conjectured we might be American spies. "Spying on just *what*?" my sassy companion responded. "The grapes?"

"There was another promise. Beyond the passport stamps. Beyond all the hotel rooms we'd check into . . ."

"A lot of hotel rooms," she says. The way other guests investigate mini-bars, closets and room-service menus, Stephanie insisted on making love, as promptly as possible after checking in. A hotel room that we didn't use that way was a hotel room gone to waste.

"I promised something else," I say. "I didn't tell you what it was . . ."

By now we're on the fifth floor. There's some awkwardness with the keys, top lock, bottom lock, left or right turn and while I'm fumbling, Stephanie is like a kid, jumping up and down. Our hearts, I'm thinking, are young and gay. And then we're inside.

"This was what I had in mind," I announce. I stand in the doorway, watching her take the measure of the place: a living room, a dining room, a bedroom and kitchen, a view of the street, down to the front stoops we'd claimed. And then she comes back to me.

"George? The rent?"

"No rent."

"How's that?"

"We own it . . ."

"Oh my God. How much . . ."

"Don't ask . . ." I say. "Listen. We were spending all that money on hotels . . . and it wasn't nearly as much time as you want to have here . . ." I sounded braver than I felt. I'd behaved rashly, calling Erwin, arranging for a $200,000 advance. The Beast was my master now. I convinced Erwin—I half convinced myself—that the obligation would make me write.

There's something intimidating about an empty apartment. The dusty floors and sills, picture hangers still in the wall, the empty refrigerator. The place reminds you that this void you fill has had tenants before you and will have more after you're gone, all your possessions, your chairs, pillows, books, and paintings, your first love and final illness are there for a while and then they are not there.

"You'll have to furnish this place," I say. "You or a decorator."

"I'll take care of it," she says. "You watch. I'll make you proud."

"This will help," I say. I hand her a bank book, a joint account that I established the day before.

"Oh my God," she says a second time. She leans into my

embrace, where she stays. Then I sense her stirring in a way that I recognize, moving against me in a pattern that only has one outcome.

"Oh, George," she said. "You've saved my life."

"Really?"

She kept moving against me, even as I sensed her scrutinizing an apartment that had no furniture, no carpet, no mattress. The floor had been swept but not cleaned. She was an ingenious woman, but this might test her.

"We may have to celebrate later on," I offered, but half heartedly, for her predicament excited me.

"No," she said, surveying the streaky windows, morning sun reaching out to dust balls that had lodged under the radiator. "No siree," she said. "Right here. Right now."

▲

New York claimed her and she claimed New York. After a few years of redecorating, of courses at the New School, she wanted a job because she was tired of being a visitor in the city. She wanted, she said, to be a player. But she had no idea how to proceed: a forty-something woman who had taken fifteen years to obtain a college degree and whose most recent employment had been as an office manager in an Ohio town's Chamber of Commerce.

"Just get me an interview," she said. "You must know someone."

"What kind of a job do you want? What field?"

"It doesn't matter. Just get me in the door someplace. Once I get the interview, there won't be any problem."

Indeed not, I thought. I walked toward the window of our apartment, hers really. I studied the street, the image of the pensive professor, hands clasped behind my back, pondering incalculable possibilities. But it wasn't that hard. I already knew I would call Erwin. What I was wondering was whether she had thought—and calculated—all this from the beginning, whether she aimed at me as she now targeted her unknown future employer. Had it been like that? "Get me in the door someplace." Now I faced her, smiling the smile of someone who'd come up with a bright idea. She sat on a couch, her shoes on the floor, her legs nicely folded underneath her, as she had sat that first night at my house, when she told me that everything was on the table, all things were possible, no hang-ups or inhibitions.

"How does publishing sound?" I asked her.

▲

Erwin was sensitive. He knew better than to install his client's mistress in an office down the hall. Stephanie worked a few floors down, for another imprint in a house that had collected a number of them. She started in publicity. It suited her. Watching from a distance, Erwin had good things to say of her.

"She's remarkable," he told me. "She works like a demon, has good instincts, learns fast. This isn't just another English major who loves books and wants to be around writers. I mean she has an instinct for the business. Just the other day when someone was being scathing about a dreadful new novelist we're fussing over, she said something to the effect that bad novelists who sell pay for good novelists who don't. Tell me, is that something she learned from you? Have you coached her?"

"Less and less all the time," I answered.

▲

"You're wondering why I came," she said. A surprise visit. In winter. This was as we walked along the river, that second-string tributary which flows so prominently through these pages. This was a few years before today's paved running trail was built. We walked along railroad tracks, like country children dreaming of the far-away places. And we had stopped at a rusted trestle that had seen its last train twenty years before. It was one of those March days when winter starts to lose its grip, when the sun warms and thaws and when you can sit outside, in a sheltered corner, and soak up the rays.

"Yes," I answered. "I've wondered."

"Any ideas?"

"Yes," I said. "I think you've come to say goodbye. I think you've come to thank me for all sorts of things. The books, the trips, the apartment, the phone calls on your behalf . . . you've always been grateful. Always will be. And . . . if I need you, ever need you . . . you'll be there for me. But now it's time . . . it's past time . . . for you to move on with your life. Something like that."

"Oh, Christ, George . . ." she said. "I shouldn't have asked . . ."

"So . . . I was right?" I asked. I knew I was right, it was the surest thing I knew, but that didn't stop me from praying that I was wrong, ass-backward wrong. She was pregnant, she hated New York, she wanted to spend more time with me.

"You said it," she said, softly. "You said it for me, damn you, like you always knew . . . I wish I didn't feel you were so in charge. It's like you've seen all this coming, from years away." Now she leaned into me and—it surprised me—she was crying. "You started this," she said. "You get the credit. Or the blame. Whatever."

"You came to me, Stephanie. It started then. That first knock. 'Let your imagination be an equal-opportunity employer.' Remember?"

She laughed at that, wiped her eyes, gave me an impulsive kiss. Maybe we had not made love for the very last time. Only the second-to-last, or the fifth to last. This was something that it was better not to know.

"Have you found someone?" I asked.

"They find me, George. But I haven't done anything yet. I mean anything. I'm funny that way . . ."

"That's nice . . ."

"But there's interest aplenty. Even . . . I don't know if I should tell you this . . . someone you know who's been mighty attentive."

"Not . . ."

"Bingo . . . He wants to take me under his wings."

"That rascal." Of all the feelings that might have surfaced—anger, betrayal—laughter prevailed. Erwin had been married twice already and he did not have it in him to be alone, my awkward life-long friend.

"He's the marrying kind," I said.

"No way, George. That dog won't hunt."

"But there are other dogs?"

"Other lives," she said. "Maybe for both of us."

"Oh, not for me . . . I doubt it. I'll keep doing what I do here. And traveling with Erwin. I'm glad he doesn't attract you . . ."

"I'll buy the apartment from you . . ."

"No, you won't."

"What?"

"That was a gift . . ."

She took my arm and we walked along the river, then uphill to the campus, where her visits, as they grew rarer, became more prized. I had a feeling that the scene had played about as she'd expected. It couldn't have gone better. And yet there was also a whiff of disappointment, that it had gone so smoothly: a sense of something else, waiting to be said. I guessed she had already found a man. A few weeks later, it turned out I was right. A young publisher—Sherman Cutter—was that year's wunderkind. He was starting his own imprint and had chosen Stephanie as his aide. They had moved in together, they were an item, literally, in newspapers and magazines, which sometimes mentioned me as her discoverer, her long-time companion, left-behind now.

We could have parted right then; we'd had our last talk. But her plane wasn't until the following morning and she saw no reason not to spend the night with me. So we prepared a meal, took our time about it, chatting like old friends. We talked about the publisher's new list and her mother's unexpected affection for Manhattan. She was wondering about getting a dog. She liked picturing herself walking a dog around the Central Park reservoir, the Great Lawn, the softball fields in the shadow of the 59th Street skyline. She liked the idea of being up at dawn in the park, out in the dusk. So that was us, the last night in the house. Talking about dogs. Breeds of dogs, big versus little, long haired versus short, pure versus mix. Her last request that night returned me to our very beginning, the snowy evening, the fireplace, the terry cloth robes, the clink of cognac glasses. Not that she mentioned our first lovemaking. It was something else, something she almost forgot, which she said with a snap of the fingers. Now she remembered. Could I please e-mail her my—actually my mother's—recipe for goulash?

▲

"Well, I'm out of here," she began. The next morning I awoke and found her standing over me, fully dressed, ready to leave. But there was an expression on her face that scared me. "I've got a one o'clock in the city, would you believe?" It wasn't what she said; it was the briskness of it, the way she stood over me as I lay in bed. "We did this pretty well," she said. "I'm kind of proud of both of us, no kidding. Very grown up, very European, I'm tempted to say, but what would I know? That's more your department. But it's all kind of low on emotional wallop, I have to say. A girl could ask . . . do you feel bad at my leaving you, George? Do you feel anything?"

"Yes," I said. "I feel something. And it's bad. But . . ."

"Well? Come on?"

"I always knew that you would leave. And that I would stay . . ."

"So bittersweet! Why stay? Why stay here?"

"I came here to accomplish something . . . a grand thing that would take a lifetime and that required me to be in a place like this . . . which gives me time. And asks no questions . . . not many, anyway, and not directly . . ."

"The Beast? That old thing?"

"Yes."

"You never talked about it to me. Never showed it to me. Oh, you told me you were working on it. A couple of weeks during the school year. Summers, too. But you put it away whenever I came into the room . . ."

"It can't be shared," I said. "Until it's done. And there are things that have to happen before I can finish it. It's not entirely up to me. I'm sorry. And I'm not the kind of writer who announces I had a good day, 'listen to this' . . ."

"I know. That's what you told me. And it didn't bother me at first. Too much else was happening that was good. But after a while . . . Oh, George, you should hear them talk about you. If you only knew . . ."

"Has-been. Fraud. Con-man. That sort of thing?"

"They came at me. They figured I must know what you were up to. Since we were living together, traveling together. Loving each other. They kind of thought—can you blame them?—that I might be in your confidence. I never was . . ."

"I'm sorry," I said. "I told you at the start. I warned you . . ."

"You could take me into the world. But not into your confidence. Know something, George? There are some people out there—your friend, Erwin, tops the list—who think I . . . what's his word . . . 'diverted' you from your great mission . . ."

"Is that why he wanted to take you off my hands?"

She ignored that. She just stood over me, looking down. In hope. Or pity.

"I hope you do whatever you've been trying to do," she said. And had to add: "And I hope you keep getting away with whatever it is you're getting away with. I don't know." She bent down and kissed me, not on the lips but on the forehead, the way you say goodbye to someone in a hospital bed, not sure whether you'll be seeing them again.

"Right now you look like the loneliest man in the world to me," she said. And then she rushed out the door, maybe because she was overcome by tears. Or behind schedule. I jumped out of bed and ran to the window, in time to see her climb into the car and drive away, without a wave goodbye or a backward look. Just as I had always pictured.

▲

A month after Stephanie said goodbye, I was in my office, confronting The Beast. During the Stephanie years, I hadn't ignored the project. There was work to do and now and then I did it. The book hadn't been written in sequence. The first and most finished part was the middle, dealing with my parents' time, the inter-war years. That was nearly complete. I might have published it years ago, a small, resonant Hitler-shadowed novel of Europe-on-the-edge. A little Alan Furst and Eric Ambler and Aharon Appelfeld and Joseph Roth, bless them all. But that's what it would have been, another book on that honorable shelf. By now, I wanted more. I wanted the glory days, going back to Goethe. I wanted the post World War II period, America and Russia in the neighborhood. And the Communist years, which were no kind of an ending.

Now I reached out for The Beast, found a scene in which Goethe, well into his seventies, proposes marriage to a much younger woman and is rejected. He writes a poignant elegy in nearby Marienbad. Age and death declare themselves. This was meant to be an important moment, for The Beast was all about recognitions and discoveries, character and fate. They were in the water and the air. But this Goethe business eluded me now; it felt preposterous to even consider it in a professor's office in Ohio. Where, I wondered, were interruptions when I needed them? No incoming e-mail, no requests for a letter of recommendation, no phone call from the department secretary who was sending over a prospective student who might want to be a great writer! Had it come to this? So I closed my eyes again, leaned forward and wondered what would become of me. That was when I felt—no, sensed—someone behind me, someone who had come into my office while my back was turned. I felt hands on my shoulders, someone leaning down to me, the scent and sense of a woman, a voice from out of the past.

"Hello, sweetie . . ."

I swiveled around in my chair and saw—more than ten years after I'd held her in my arms in this very office—Mary Cantonelli.

"My God!" I said. "Look at you."

"Look all you want," she replied, flashing the sly, rebellious smile I remembered. She was in her thirties now, and unchanged: she was grown up back in college.

"What are you doing here?" I asked.

"Reunion planning weekend," she answered. "And also . . . it's a big secret . . . they want to make me a trustee."

"You must have made a pile, Mary. Or married someone wealthy."

"Both. But I lost my husband last year. A great guy. In a dumb hang gliding accident off Molokai. Wind slammed him against a cliff like a bug against a windshield." Her words were irreverent but her eyes had tears which she didn't mind my seeing.

"So you lost someone," I said. "I know how you feel."

"I know you know . . . I was here that seminar we heard she was dead . . . I remember . . . And after my guy died . . . I thought about you and your Natalie. Natalie Taylor."

Hearing Natalie's name, her full name, pleased me. It was just a name coming up in conversation between people who hadn't seen each other for years. But it was more than that. It was two people connecting with a third and it was the power of words and voice and memory against death and forgetting. Quite a power, I thought. I should make use of it more often, I thought.

"Anyway," Mary Cantonelli said. "Anyway . . ."

"Anyway . . . would you like to sit down?"

"No. As a matter of fact, I'd like you to stand up."

I did as she asked. She was standing just where she had stood, that afternoon years before. I was close to her, but not touching.

"After Jim died, I thought about you, Professor Canaris. I thought about you before then, from time to time, sure. What you said about writing. It helped me in my own writing. All those aphorisms and taboos. 'Don't wait for inspiration.' 'Avoid dream sequences and, at all costs, flashbacks.' That stuff . . ."

"I didn't know you still write," I said. Impossible to ask the next question without sounding like a twit: have you written anything I might have read?

"Ten," she said, holding out the fingers on both hands. "Books."

"Published?" God, what a fool I sounded like.

"Random House. In the United States that is. The foreign rights . . . I can't keep track."

"Mary Cantonelli . . . have I been on another planet?"

"I use a pseudonym."

"Which is . . ."

"That's for later," she said. She stepped into me. "Careers and stuff. What a crock, professor."

"Not such a crock," I said. "I was leading three books to zero when I last saw you. Now it's ten to three."

"I remember us holding each other right here, locked and loaded. Ever so ready. I had you, didn't I? Right at the edge . . ."

"Yes . . . yes, you had me . . ."

"One little move, one more wiggle . . . we'd've been on the floor . . ."

"Definitely. I've thought about it often. The things we don't do. They stick around."

"You bet they do. Come here." Mary laughed out loud. "They're not putting me on the Faculty Affairs committee for nothing!" She leaned against the wall, put her arms around me and pulled me towards her, kissed me as she had before, moved against me all the time we kissed and then . . . what a misfortune! . . . there was the sound of footsteps, of knocking on the door, more knocking. At last we saw a paper slipped under the door. Mary pushed me away, gently, and stooped to retrieve the paper. She held it against a last ray of sunlight, reading aloud. "I Know Why The Caged Bird Goes Ka-Ching: Art and Marketing in the Poems of Maya Angelou. I love it. Wise-ass students!"

"I have a weakness for them," I said. "You were the first."

"How have you been?" she asked. She'd calmed down now the moment had passed.

"An affair ended recently."

"I heard," she said.

"Oh . . ."

"People talk."

"And you? Your writing name is . . ."

"Sara Bright."

And I knew it. Sara Bright was the author of a series of well-regarded mysteries involving a woman who worked as a State Department official, a cultural officer who doubled as a CIA agent, generating adventures all over the world. She was on a par with Tony Hillerman and Sue Grafton and when someone had mentioned her just lately, Derrick Madison opined that she was "too good for her own good."

"I've got an idea about us," she said. "This is serious."

"Alright . . ." I couldn't wait.

"And don't respond until you've heard me out. Alright? I want to be your guardian angel."

"Do I need one?"

"Your book does. I want to help you get it out. And I think I can help you. I'm a total pro in this. Trust me. I'd like to read it. Whatever you have. Go over it. Not as an editor. I wouldn't presume that. But as a reader. See what's done and what needs doing. Make a plan and a schedule. I don't want people to laugh at you. And that's what they're starting to do . . ."

"They've been doing it a while," I admitted.

"You got me out the gate, professor. I want to return the favor. Get you to the finish line. My guess is, you're all over the place with this thing. Going backwards, forwards, sideways. I'm not sure you'd even recognize the finish line when you crossed it. It could be you've crossed it a few times already."

"I've wondered about that myself."

"Now . . . this part is hard. Ask yourself, how many of the working rules you gave us in seminar you've broken? Write daily. Outline as much as you can but don't be surprised when something unexpected happens. Never lose touch with the manuscript. Satisfy yourself but remember . . . always the audience. What matters to you matters to them . . . See how much I remember?"

"I cannot let you read it," I said. I couldn't help it. Her offer was generous and this might be the end of it, but I couldn't let her see it. Something in me seized up at the thought of putting The Beast in someone else's hands.

"Never mind that," she said. "We'll talk it through. The plan of it, the trajectory, scenes and characters. All that. What you used to call the narrative arc. Or was it arch?"

"Arc. I hope. Arch is fine as well . . ."

"There you go," she said. "Professor, you're going to finish that book."

▲

It's too bad the college alumni magazine never found out about my arrangement with Mary Cantonelli. There we sat in a terraced garden in Kahala, Diamond Head in back of us, the Pacific spread out in front, and we were discussing Gogol's madness, Turgenev's melancholy, Beethoven's mysterious "immortal beloved," Hitler's paintings. I had a huge cast of characters and she researched them all. My homework had been sporadic, hers was systematic. We discovered new characters: a German-Jewish author, Theodor Lessing, murdered in Marienbad in 1933. We created fictional characters—the policeman who was detailed to follow "Charles" Marx's movements around Karlsbad. We conjured courtesans, usurers, gamblers, quacks, obscure painters, legendary pastry chefs. All this, with the scent of plumeria and the blaze of bougainvillea all around, with morning walks in Ala Moana, breakfasts at the Chinatown market, and, afternoon naps when rains came over the mountains. Naps in separate rooms, alas, for Mary withheld herself from me until the completion of my book. No sex, she said, and no sulking about it.

By 1988 our job was done. Eighty percent of the novel was finished. Our collaboration was over. Except for the ending. There were times I thought that maybe I should let go of it, unfinished. Didn't Musil's "Man Without Qualities" stop well short of a conclusion? As did Hasek's almost unfinishable "Good Soldier Sveik." "War and Peace," for that matter, trailed off into tedious philosophizing. Who needed an ending?

That would be an option, Mary and I agreed. No disgrace at all. And, if something happened, I urged her to arrange for publication of what we had worked on together. She gave me a look I loved. "You mean I get to read it?" Still, I was looking for something that would carry my magic place, my Hapsburg Brigadoon, beyond the Communist vacationland it had become. It had to emerge from that. The world had to turn a few more times.

▲

There it was, among a pile of mail that included a Walmart advertisement and a Sprint bill and a parcel containing a vintage copy of *Out On The Coast* that a book collector wanted me to sign. An envelope from the Czech Republic, which had undergone its "Velvet Revolution" the year before, I saw the initials "E.E." on the left corner, above an address in Karlovy Vary. A message across the miles and years.

The printed card came out of the envelope first, the sort of thing that invites you to a wedding or a graduation, only the print was darker and there was no request for an r.s.v.p. He was already dead and the funeral was over. There was an embossed Jewish star at the top, appropriate for a Jew and a Stern. There were no names other than his own, no grieving family in need of condolence, no signature of any kind. He must have set it up in advance, arranged to have this sent to me. And for a letter to be enclosed.

Dear cousin:
When you read this, I will be dead. It's coming soon. Not tomorrow or the next day, but soon. And I do not want to wait for the last minute to write to you. I write on a good morning for me and for Karlsbad, warm and sunny, the streets crowded, people strolling along the Tepla, stopping for coffee and cake at the Elefant, crowding the cable car that goes up into the mountains behind the Grand Hotel Pupp. Was it working when you were here? I sit on a bench this morning, clasping a cane that is pointed into the ground between my knees, regarding the hills where I took refuge during the war. They are out of range for me now.

I know more about you than you realize. When I saw your name on that list of left-wing writers, I knew that some purpose had brought you back here. Since you were a writer, I guessed that this place was part of your writing. So I told you my story. Maybe, as your long-lost cousin, I would figure in a book.

I have waited for the book. Please understand: it is not as if I expect that I will figure in your story. Not that. It is because you and I have a feeling about this place. What kept me here in that freezing forest is what brought you to a birth-house you had never seen. We both believe that there is a story here. We both know it. In this place, the story of your times can be told. All the great ones came here and commoners, dictators, musicians and writers. They haunted Karlsbad. They haunt you. Soon, I may haunt you. Perhaps I already do. Please. Save a dead man's life. Keep something alive. To be in between the lines of a story is the only after-life I hope for.

You must finish. Do you need a beginning? An ending? Come back one last time. A week is enough. Two weeks are generous. Come in summer. Leave your pen at home. Take the bath, drink the waters, walk the forest. Remember me.

Time for me to go. Time for you, Mr. Canaris-Stern to say "Genug" and "schluss." Finish your work. History is endless. Our lives are not. You must let go, you must stand back, make and finish a story. For your sake, cousin, and a little bit for mine.

▲

"No soap, sweetie," Mary Cantonelli had said, when I called Honolulu. "This one's for you. Just you. I'll fly to Ohio to take you to the airport. I'll meet you at the airport when you come back . . . But that's it."

"Is this because of your new husband?"

"Well, I know he'd think it was odd," she granted. "But no. I could get it past him, easy."

"Then . . . what?"

"This is something you have to do without me. You're the writer. You come back with that last chapter, I'll be there in a wink. Go get it, professor . . ."

My next call was to Erwin. It was the first time I had proposed a trip and I was sure he'd be delighted especially when I hinted that it might lead to The Beast's completion. I was startled when he declined. His first excuse was health: impending prostate surgery. I proposed a postponement, from June of one year to June of another. Delay wasn't acceptable; it was welcome. My old friend could not deny me, in this moment of need. But he did.

"What is it?" I asked. "What's the matter?"

"I can't. I won't."

"Why?"

"Listen, my friend. I've been awaiting this book for years, like I've waited for no other. Sometimes I've probed, sometimes I've hinted. I've been patient and demanding, long-suffering and urgent. All to no avail. Now comes this invitation. And it is tempting. But I am the editor and you are the writer. I will wait for your manuscript . . . Forgive me."

"Alright then . . . but I'm disappointed."

"There's a lot of disappointment going around, my friend. I've been fending off your creditors too long . . ."

"Creditors?"

"Oh, please, George. The ones down the hall who advanced you $200,000 for a book that was due years ago. The money that enabled you to set up your girlfriend in a Manhattan apartment. I must tell you, they contemplate a law suit . . ."

"I see . . ." I said.

"I doubt it."

"Doubt they'll do it?" I asked hopefully.

"Doubt you see."

After Erwin, other possibilities came to my mind. Derrick or Harvey or maybe both. But their presence would change things. Stephanie Knox was booked, I knew without asking. I even wondered about Louise Becker. I knew she would come. But that would make me into a tour guide. In the end, I guessed, I would have to walk this last walk alone.

▲

Arriving in Prague in the late afternoon, jet-lagged, I forced myself to remain awake for a while, walked the Charles Bridge, which was full of Dixieland bands, water colorists, mimes. The sullen city I remembered from my first trip had melted away, like so much ice and slush, and now it was the Paris of the nineties, low prices, good living in an unbombed

European city, backpackers and expatriates welcome. All around town costumed bewigged youths hawked tickets for concerts in cathedrals. At all hours, every day, someone in Prague was playing Vivaldi.

▲

By the time I got to Karlovy Vary, the whole enterprise seemed pathetic, an aging writer acting like a cub reporter. Did I really have to be here? Couldn't I have invented something? Wasn't that what fiction was about? Here, strolling along the river, I wasn't a writer, just another tourist. There were hordes of us, Germans, Russians, Americans, sitting in cafes, pricing crystal, were sipping mineral water, drowning in Czech beer. There were knick-knack shops, up and down the street, all new, and once-dour buildings were splashed in new coats of yellow and pink. Even the unrenovated places showed signs of life: sand, cement, tiles. What had happened in Prague—the discovery that the rest of the world might find you charming—was happening here.

And I was the loneliest man in the world. How unlike my long-ago Manila debauch, all sex and songs! Another man, another world. Here the prostitutes and I just shrugged each other off. And yet—as the Beast will demonstrate, I found an ending for the book. I found Russian mobsters, elderly Israelis, British soccer fans, Sudentenland Germans, American military shopping for crystal, spandex-clad kayakers racing in the Tepla. I drank, I gambled, I attended a Hawaiian Tan beauty contest at the Grand Hotel Pupp. There were characters and endings all around me. An ending for The Beast. And an ending just for me.

One night I found my way to a concert in Bathhouse Number Four, along the Tepla River, just beyond the Grand Hotel Pupp. Like most old buildings, it was imperial and decrepit. I sat in a folding chair in a mirrored, high-ceilinged gilt-edged hall that had seen better days. Sooner or later, it occurred to me, the whole point of life, or living to a certain age, is to have seen better days. And remember them. I watched the place fill with a crowd that made me feel like the youngest man in the room: they closed their eyes when the music played, let it carry them back. The music obliged: Franz Lehar and Emmerich Kalman, waltzes, polkas, comic routines, love songs, a transmission out of the past. I walked out humming the slowly final waltz of "The Merry Widow," sexy and wise, wishing I had danced it with someone I loved. I'd settle for this, settle for The Beast to come to this: a melody in the air. History went on. Lives ended. And stories were somewhere in between. They stuck around a while, if you were lucky. It was dark when I stepped outside, watching the concert goers head for their hotels. They moved slowly. I was full of energy. I started walking briskly, away from the town, towards the edge of the forest, to the Dvorak statue, the monument to Beethoven. Then I found the river—monuments to Schiller and Goethe—and walked into the spa district, past the fountains and bath houses. My burst of speed settled into a more measured and pensive stroll. I took things in as though I would never see them again, which seemed like a safe bet. Then I realized that what I was doing in my last night was what Kurt Gerron had done on his last night here. The slow walk, the silent appraisal of a place where the best and worst converged. A goodbye.

XV. NOW: MAY, 2006

▲

IN APRIL OF THEIR SENIOR YEAR, OUR STUDENTS REALIZE that slow, meandering time has brought them to the edge of a cliff. They shudder at a world of low wages, sketchy jobs, unpaid internships, abusive bosses, tiny apartments, maxed out credit cards, no respect. They look back fondly at the world they're about to leave: approachable teachers, understanding counselors, malleable rules and a campus which is never so blossoming and beautiful as in the weeks before they're required to go. This is what I call the zone of last things. Last night of drinking, last road trip, last walk on a trail. Seniors itemize things—and people—to do before they leave: "senior lists." It's like the last night on a ship, before it comes to port, a party that is both melancholy and frantic. And now I realize that I am on such a ship myself. This year, I am in the zone of last things.

▲

"*Kickoff* ten-k race, *kick off* for the college campaign," Willard Thrush exclaims. In a season of endings, of anger and whining, I rely on Willard to cheer me up. A warrior but a happy one.

"On reunion weekend?"

"Yes! And what a course! It ends up going up the hill, finish line right at the top. That's brutal. I couldn't even walk it."

"And you're inviting even the old timers? Here for their fiftieth?"

"No age-ism from me. Everybody can enter. The older the better. A whole field of realizable bequests. And don't you get it—kick off for the college!"

"Lovely," I respond. "No way the president'll go for it. Marvelous idea, though. And, come to think of it, not a bad way to crump out. On the lower slopes of your alma mater. You're too good for this place, Willard. You need a larger canvas."

Willard and I step out into a pot-holed gravel parking lot and the air is sweet, the trees are blossoming. And, as we approach the restaurant, which adjoins a service station, the smell of coffee and bacon come out to greet us.

"Where else but here?" Willard asks as he reaches for the door.

"Paris?" I ask. "As in 'Springtime in Paris'?" Willard shakes his head, as if I've disappointed him.

"You've got to be kidding," he says.

Inside, everyone is in a good mood. It's that kind of a morning. Pancakes for Willard, cheese omelet for me. Perfect except for the weak coffee and cottony bread. For the thousandth time, I complain.

"Fussy, fussy," Willard says. "You sound like Mallon."

"Mallon?"

"Name ring a bell? The big book writer they dumped you for? Seen him at all?"

"Yes, I answer. "But . . . come to think of it, not much. He called me a few weeks after he arrived. Right after seminar. He badly needed a drink. And I supplied it."

"Your successor is in deep yogurt."

"About what?"

"A woman student," Thrush says.

"Oh, my God," I respond. "After all the trouble they went through to get him."

"Yeah. Right."

▲

As usual, I go to morning coffee with Harvey and Derrick. This morning, they wanted to know what I had in mind for my commencement address. People are wondering, they told me. Will I go gently and wisely? Or will I deliver a last angry blast. Will I use commencement to—as Derrick said—"drop a turd in a punch bowl."

"It's a hard audience," I said. "No matter what I do, someone will be disappointed. In fact, I'm not sure who the audience is. Is it the kids and parents in front of me? The administration and faculty? The people who'll read excerpts in newspapers? I just heard C–Span will have a crew here."

"You should check with John Alfano," Derrick said.

"Is he back in town?"

"He's doing the baccalaureate speech the day before you. I guess they thought one thing would balance out the other."

"He has good reason for anger," I said.

"And better reason to sit on his anger," Derrick said. "When they gave him a settlement—generous, you'd better believe—it included a clause that he not discuss his dismissal. Those things are all the rage around here these days . . ."

"Amazing."

"I don't know what they're thinking," Derrick said, in the voice of an acting provost whose point of view has not prevailed. He soon left us. A faculty member—he could not give us a name, a department, or gender—had odged a grievance about non-promotion from assistant to associate professor. That was all he could tell us.

"I have a feeling our trio is fading," Harvey said.

"I'll be around," I said, half-heartedly.

"I hope so," he said. "I'm not sitting here by myself!" He smiled a moment, a sad smile. The inevitable downsizing that accompanies age, all its subtractions, we knew where it ended, but was this where it began?

"Could I just say something?" Harvey asked. "I wish you all

the best. I hope you're still . . . a contender. Not only for your sake. It's for me too. It's about how I feel when I look at myself in the mirror in the morning."

"I hear you," I acknowledged.

▲

At lunchtime, Louise Becker comes by with an update on plans for reunion weekend. She's come out of retirement to organize the Canaris carnival. She's on the phone with Charles Stuckey every day; he's already flown her to New York. "He put me up in a hotel!" she marvels. As if he might have left her on a park bench. Stuckey is her new sweetheart.

"He really cares about you," she tells me. "He can't manage to say it directly. But I can tell."

"Well then . . ."

"And his partner . . . the newspaper man . . ."

"Alva Morse."

"They're so nice together. He's coming too. Alva, I mean."

We're sitting on the front porch, at a card table: salad, omelette, white wine. "You know something, George?" she asks.

"I do. But not what's on your mind this minute. I can't begin to guess."

"You're so lucky. Remember poor Jeff, shuffling off the way he did. That little memorial service?"

I nodded. It was sad, how infrequently I'd thought about Jeff Overstreet since he died. And if I let him down so badly, what about everyone else? What about the college itself? Could we even speak of such a thing? A college that remembered?

"So . . . what is my good fortune? That I shuffle off more promptly? In front of a larger crowd?"

"Stop it! You can be such a downer." She looked at me as if I were a mopey, morbid kid. "Sometimes I just want to shake you." She fished around in a manila folder that had plans for the reunion weekend. We'd gone through it already. Initially the dinner—now it was called a banquet—had been consigned to the college catering service. They handled most such functions, operating out of vans which had "Heartland" lettered on the side. An oxymoron. And they professed excitement over "local food." Stuckey had vetoed them and was bringing in a crew from New York. So there'd be no freezer-burned broccoli and gray-brown beef for me and my friends.

"I'm just going to list the names of the people who'll be here," Louise said. "These aren't 'maybes.' These are the definitely coming. I'll read the name and I want you to react. Okay. Say something. Just a line."

"Louise, I give pop quizzes. I do not take them."

"You need practice, George. They're coming a long way and they're paying real money. And most of them are not the usual suspects. This is the first time back for a lot of them. This is about you. For you. Okay?"

"Starting at the top. Charles Stuckey."

"Ambitious. Intense. Lot of talent. Lot more ambition."

"Alva Morse."

"I hardly know the man. I suppose he'll write a follow-up story. Clever fellow."

"Stephanie Knox," Louise said. "I guess we can skip her. I kind of wish you skipped her. Moving right along . . ."

Moving right along. Half an hour later we were done. I suppose it came to about two names per minute, moving briskly as we did. Louise gave me just enough time to say whatever came to me, a fragment of a story, a turn of phrase, a way of laughing, something in their eyes. Nice kids, talented and troubled or placid normal kids who wondered about writing and decided to give it a whirl. Sometimes it was a solemn undertaking—first step of a thousand-mile journey, so they told themselves. Sometimes it was a pure lark, one step up from pottery or guitar. Yet they were coming back to me, not just the ones I would have guessed but others I was surprised remembered me at all. At the end—but not before Louise warned that reservations were still coming in—at the end I was in tears. It was more than I expected. More than I deserved. There was an audience of readers around the world that I would never meet. That had been literature's appeal—reaching out across miles and time, from beyond the grave even. But then there was this audience of insistent students—aging students—coming back to say goodbye. Which audience mattered more? I wondered. But I didn't wonder for long.

▲

"I guess you heard about what happened to me," John Henry Mallon said. "Some version of it."

"I heard that something happened. With a student. But that's all."

"You want to hear it? Would you mind listening? To the whole story?"

I hadn't seen Mallon since the semester began and I hadn't missed him either. Willard Thrush had rattled me. To learn that I had replaced someone, just as Mallon replaced me. There was a difference, I told myself. Mallon fully knew what he was doing. I was oblivious of my impact on one Elbert Trowbridge. Did that make a difference, my ignorance? He wasn't in the yearbook department photo for either of the two years he'd been here. "Not pictured." A name in a caption. After that, I found his name attached to a few teaching positions—bowling Green, Ohio State-Wooster, Baldwin Wallace. By the early 1980's the trail evaporated. Was he still in the profession? On the planet?

Mallon had come by unannounced, early in the evening, inviting me out for a ride. Now we were parked outside a tavern in a small, sad town a dozen miles from campus. He produced a six pack and a small bottle of Canadian whiskey: we were having boilermakers. The white clapboard building we were about to enter—once a country store, now a strip club—served no alcohol. So, like others around the parking lot, we were having a pre-performance cocktail.

"How can we all fit in there?" I wondered, glancing at the narrow structure before us.

"That's what she said," Mallon joked but then—suddenly embarrassed by his own vulgarity—he looked out the window, shaking his head. Outside, we saw couples leaving the club, stepping into their vehicles, others getting out and entering the building. There was an interesting symbiosis, I guessed: inside you had porn-film fantasy queens and after you saw them you and your date repaired to your truck to emulate what was happening inside. I was curious about what was going on inside. More curious than I was about Mallon's misfortune.

"There was this one girl in my seminar, didn't say much in class," he said. "Started coming by the office, just to talk, the way we encourage them to do. When the class went out for drinks afterward, she came. She was twenty-one, so we had drinks, the rest settled for soda. Or sneaked the alcohol. She comes to my house one night, halfway through the course. I'd had a few drinks, already. Do I have to tell you, Canaris, that around here the evenings get long?"

"Did she . . ." I sounded old-fashioned. ". . . offer herself?"

"Offer herself? If you call reaching inside my pants and pulling me towards her offering herself, by golly, I guess she did!"

"Did you talk about her grades? Quid pro quo?"

"No. That's what kills me. Never happened. That's untouchable. You can tumble around in bed till dawn but it doesn't change your writing."

"So . . . no grade."

"An A for foreplay and a B for the main event and a C plus for the post-partum wrap up and an incomplete for the second round. Those are the only grades she got that night." Mallon swallowed a shot of VO, flushed it down with half a can of Gennessee Ale. "Time we went in, Professor. You can hear the rest of the story inside. It kind of fits . . ."

The former country store was long and narrow, with a rickety wooden floor and a stamped tin-ceiling. It was windowless and dark, especially after you first entered. The stage—more accommodating to a slide show or lecture than a striptease—barely accommodated two dancers who performed in front of perhaps twenty tables, card tables, cocktail tables, picnic tables, all jammed with customers. The waitresses were dancers between shifts. They gave Mallon a hug and led us to a cocktail table against the wall. Eventually, I adjusted to the light. I might have had breakfast with some of these farmers. There were some high school kids and even a bearded Amish fellow in a corner. One table was all women, one of whom I recognized as a friend of Stephanie's.

"What do you think?" asked Mallon, gesturing towards the tiny stage. Now my habit with women—and I believe women do the same with men—is to instantly say yes, or maybe, or no. One dancer was a solid yes and the other a strong maybe. Both of them were writhing along to a Lionel Richie song about easy as Sunday morning and they had it down, slow sexiness and languor seasoned with a certain boredom and the faint hope of having, doing, being something else, somewhere else.

"Better than expected," I said. "Much better."

"There's two others come on later. This is the junior varsity."

"Just fine," I said. "But what about . . . that student?"

"That student. That heat-seeking missile!" he burst out. And then he told the story which he had chosen to tell me in the place where he had chosen to tell it. It was the oddest mix: an account of campus downfall while frisky dancers, topless, got into "What's Love Got To Do With It" and "Uptown Girl" and "These Boots Are Made For Walking" and . . . my personal favorite, always a slow song . . ."Do It To Me One More Time." That was the soundtrack accompanying the cautionary tale that the author of GAMESHOW and now Stribling Professor of English was telling.

"She didn't even wait for final grades," Mallon said. "Soon as she saw my comments on her next submission, she decided she'd been raped. Filed a complaint. So Derrick Madison gets into the act. And this kind of committee they have. Turns out her father's a lawyer. It's a shit storm. I'm resigning."

Things on stage were getting artsy. To the off-the-scale notes of Minnie Riperton's "Loving You" the girls joined in a vaguely lesbian number, glancing off each other, snuggling, fondling; the sort of intramural foreplay that made the men in the place squirm in their chairs because they sensed an appeal to them, the plea for a lover, a real man to come out of the audience and rescue one or both of these women so sadly left to their own devices.

"You had some problems with her too," Mallon said. It came from a distance: I was lost in the on-stage cuddling, comforting, consoling. Did they prefer each other, these two, or were they just pretending?

"With who?"

"That same student. Plagiarism, I hear. Derrick Madison told me."

He said her name. The real name. She of the unraveling sweater and downloaded fiction. My Emily Dickinson. For a stunned moment, I kept my mouth shut and my eyes on the stage, wondering if there were anything I could do for Mallon, a favor from one writer to another. I might appeal to the president, perhaps point out that Emily Dickinson was a serial predator.

"It's alright," Mallon said. "I don't want what happened to you to happen to me."

"Getting replaced?" I was confused.

"Hell, no, that's already in the works. No. I mean I haven't written squat since I've been here. Like you." He was a little drunk, or acting like it, but his meaning was clear. So much for my thought of helping him.

"Well, then," I said. "Off you go."

After that, we watched a few more dances; we were just part of the crowd. I was Mallon getting restless. I suggested we go. But we had to wait. It was rude, I thought, for us to leave in mid-song. It interrupted a performance. I'd spent too many years glaring at students tumbling into class ten minutes late. So we let the girls' enactment of "Emotional Rescue" conclude before we began weaving among tables, saying "excuse me" as we passed and that is when I felt someone's hand on my arm. It was the hard-eyed kid who'd assaulted me on the running trail, abused me in front of my house. Now he stared at me, gave me a mean little grin. "Yo, Canary," he said. And let me by.

▲

Back at my house, I considered The Beast. I was confident that I had the ending in view when I returned from Karlsbad in 1992. But I did not have it written. It amounted to about a fifth of the book, covering the end of the war, the turmoil in Karlsbad, the fate of the Germans, the long years of Communism, the emergence of a town that was touristic and thuggish but still endearing. I had a whole new cast of characters to introduce. It took six years. Then, even I had to admit the writing was done. What followed was editing. Not revising so much as cutting some things, moving others. I went through the novel from beginning to end, making changes as I went. I did that twice a year for three years. Then, I dove into it at random, seeing whether something bothered me. At last, I gave Louise the manuscript, to type onto discs. The Beast had metamorphosed. It was all in my mind now; a memory and idea. And for a whole year, I didn't write or read a word of it. I merely tried to remember what I had done. And then, I'd had enough. It was done. Period. Over. My life's work. Would I let go of it? Or it of me? In either case, a fate—a matter of life and death—was waiting for us both. So I stalled.

▲

I saw two men get out of a car that pulled in at the end of my driveway and proceeded no further. I thought they might be lost, looking for directions. Few of the houses along the river had numbers on the doors or mailboxes with names. Then I recognized John Alfano. And, alongside of him, his father.

"He made me do this," the younger Alfano said as he stood at the bottom of the porch. He wasn't happy to see me. "It wasn't my idea."

"How you doing, Professor?" Charlie Alfano asked.

"Fine. Come on up here you two."

"You got it." Charlie Alfano saw only two chairs. He gestured for his son to go inside and bring out another. And the former provost obliged him.

"This could be the last time I ask him to do something and he does it," Alfano said. "Next week he dumps me at an assisted-living community in south Jersey. And I have to go. He's already got power of attorney, in case my mind goes before my legs."

"I know how you feel. Only I don't have any children to tell me when it's time to move on."

"Sounds like my son tried to play that part for you," Charlie countered. He sounded good-natured enough. "Us old farts are stubborn." Now, John Alfano came out with a third chair that he sat in. His father was already relaxing and I was in a rocker that once belonged to Hiram Wright. It would last me out.

"You know what I miss?" I asked. This just came to me. Charlie Alfano brought it out. "For half my life, there were older people watching me. First it was my parents and their friends, even the people up and down the street. These fussy, accomplished over-critical refugees. And later, when I came here, there were senior professors who were truly frightening. Jeff Overstreet, Hiram Wright . . ."

"Harry Stribling?" John Alfano asked.

"He was a little beyond it, I think. I'll never know what he thought of me. Or if he thought of me at all. Those others were more than enough. And they treated me like my parents had. 'George, that was good.' 'George, you should always do a little bit extra.' 'George, you went too far there . . . Or not far enough.' A pat on the head, a slap on the wrist, a stroking or a spanking. But they were always watching. You could count on it. And all of a sudden, they were gone . . ."

"They say you become a man when your father dies," Charlie sympathized. He studied his son as he said it. "I'm still here. Which brings me to this visit we're making. You two had a beef."

"It's over now," I said. "From where I sit . . ."

"Hey, George. Let an old man finish."

"Sorry."

"I thought we should talk about it. I know what happened. You had this duel and you both got winged. And now they pat the both of you on the back and ship you out. End of story. But you need to talk. Right? John? Right?"

"Okay," John Alfano said, on cue from his father. Then he stopped, the way he used to stop in his provost role, deciding what . . . or how much . . . to say. But, with his father presiding, it was as though we'd gone back in time, to grammar school, one of those conferences that involved a parent, a teacher and a troubled student.

"It wasn't just me, professor," he began. "And it wasn't me first. But without me, it wouldn't have happened. You were here thirty years, in a chair, with a high salary and a low teaching load and a book you talked about that nobody ever saw. They heard about it, they wondered about it, they joked about it. After a while we wondered if the joke was on us. I'd go to conferences and people would ask if Canaris had finished that big book. I defended you for a while. What a fine teacher you were, what a good man. But there were a lot of other fine teachers around here. Fine people too . . ."

"A moment, please," I interrupted. I went to the kitchen and returned with three beers. Charlie Alfano reached into his shirt pocket.

"Okay if I smoke a cigar, professor?"

"Is that what I think it is?"

"It's a White Owl."

"That's not a cigar. That's what comes out of a cigar factory when they sweep up at the end of a shift." I got up and returned with a pair of Hoyo de Monterreys and a cutter. I snipped off the end of a cigar and handed it to him. The old man started to put his White Owl back in his pocket. I gestured for him to turn it over to me and when he obeyed I flipped it towards, but not into, the river.

"Jeez," Charlie said. "What a waste."

"John . . ." I said. "Continue."

"So a new president arrives and, yes, I know you think presidents are kind of irrelevant. 'Like ornaments on the hood of a car.' Your saying. But this one was anxious to make a mark . . . and to be seen making a mark. And there you were, Professor, so vulnerable, so ripe—past ripe—for the picking. You have no idea. No one in your department was going to stand up for you. Only me. Believe it or not, I was your last line of defense. Meanwhile, some trustees got intrigued by the possibility of replacing you. And I intervened, again and again. Until. . . ."

I waited while he shook his head, composed himself. What he'd given me so far was news. But what was coming next, I suspected, would be a confession. For that, I waited.

"Until it came to me . . . this idea that what you needed was exactly what happened. You needed to resign. You needed to be shaken up, to be challenged to finish that book. The first time I thought of it, it scared me. I thought I was rationalizing. Maybe you think that's what I'm doing now. I resisted it. I worried what you'd think of me. But at the end, I was convinced. You needed this. Maybe I was right. Maybe not."

"Maybe you were right," I agreed. "Maybe not."

"I'll give you this," Alfano continued. "You fought back. You danced rings around me. Those speeches to the alumni. The way you got the press involved. And, just when things had quieted down, just when we thought we could back off on the commencement speech and the reunion celebration, you say, okay, just announce it . . . and we do, because it was a reasonable request . . . and it's worse than before. And I'm out of a job . . ."

"Listen," I protested. "I'm not that smart. I didn't plan it out . . ."

"So you did it without thinking. That's smart. You had the instincts . . ."

"John," I said. "What are you going to do?"

"I'm leaving. That's for sure. But I've gotten feelers. I'll be okay. Maybe better than okay. When you think about it, it turns out we have something important in common. This place. Which we thought was the only place. The loving of it and the leaving of it . . ."

"Guys, I'm choking up," Charlie Alfano said. In fact, he was the one who wasn't choking up. "Professor, you should think about South Jersey. They got all planned down there. So long as you can still wash and wipe, you get an apartment and a little kitchen and bus trips to Atlantic City. You're in a wheel chair, it's meals on wheels. After that . . . God's waiting room. I'll need company."

"I can think of a worse fate."

"I can't," Charlie snapped. "Come on, son. We gotta go. It's time for my nap."

John left without a handshake, only a nod, and—watching father and son depart, I realized that the old man had imposed his will on his son. What was intended as a reconciliation felt like a humiliation. There was more that he'd wanted to say. We hadn't discussed—I hadn't asked him to confirm—that nasty letter that had shown up all over campus. His work, I was sure. And now I saw him walking his father around to the passenger side of the car, opening the door for him, standing back and staring at me with no expression on his face at all, as though he were seeing me for the last time. Was he the one who'd planted that for sale sign? Or someone else? Someone like that jailbait kid? Someone in my department, could it be? I'd never know. That was alright. I accepted the presence of enemies in principle; that didn't mean I wanted to engage them personally.

▲

After the Alfanos leave, I miss them. I envy John, having his father in his life for so long. My parents would be over one hundred now and it's unrealistic, picturing them alive and missing them. But I do, more and more, especially my father, in his last days, remembering Karlsbad, commissioning my life's work, that he would never live to see, to comment or reproach. Now, when I let the manuscript go, it will be in the hands of strangers. It is a process I have no confidence in. And no wish to witness. I am as pure in my disinterest as my dying father had been.

▲

"I've got some news for you," Louise Becker said. She hadn't asked me to breakfast. She ordered me. And now she sat across from me at a restaurant in town, a place she could smoke without fear of reprimand. I braced myself for more details of reunion weekend and another urgent plea to free The Beast.

"It's my thoughtful moment, first thing in the morning," she said, gesturing at her cigarette. "Mantra, rosary, worry beads. That stuff, Last thing I do before closing my eyes at night. I never did try having a cigarette after sex, like in the movies. I guess I'll have to save that for my next go-round."

"It's over-rated," I said. "As for me, I'll take my morning coffee and the Times crossword."

"Remember they accidentally-on-purpose said you were giving the baccalaureate speech? And you said, no, no, you promised me commencement?"

"Of course I remember," I said.

"Well, you could have both speeches now. Alfano took off, last night, I guess. One less baccalaureate speaker. His wife's in town, his father, but not Alfano. He left behind a note. 'There is some shit I will not eat.'"

"A line by e.e. cummings," I said. "He had it from me. Words to live by . . ."

"'Personal reasons,' the college is calling it. Speaking of that . . . of personal reasons . . ."

"Yes?"

"How do I look to you this morning, George?" she asked. "I'm just wondering. Same old Louise? No-nonsense secretary? Loyal typist, not-so-merry widow, grumpy grandma? That's my repertoire."

"You don't look different. You are . . . Louise." I was dissembling. She had lost weight and seemed more drawn and tired. I blamed the upcoming Canaris-fest.

"So I went to the doctor about this cough." On cue, she coughed. "That cough. And it was x-rays and tests and want to know what he says to me today, when I ask if I have cancer? He says, 'I'm not even using that word yet.' Would you believe it? That *yet*. Three letter word tagged on at the end. Like he's breaking it to me gently. *Yet*. The termites are in me, George. It won't take long."

"I'm sorry, Louise." I reached out for her hand, reached gently and she grasped me, as if I had the power to save her, healing power.

"I've got the kids and a sister I get along with. And friends. But you know who was the first person I thought of telling? I'm looking at that person right now. I'm holding his hand."

"Thanks, Louise," I said. I couldn't help wondering who was the first person I would tell, if it happened to me. Not if. When. Willard Thrush?

"I wanted you to know. Those others, I'll get hugs and tears and shrewd glances. How long have I got? They'll start looking over the house, deciding what they want and what goes into the yard sale."

"They're better than that, surely."

"Maybe. But it's not what they want, I'm thinking about. It's what I want . . ."

My heart sank. It was emotional blackmail, coming right at me. But blackmail from someone I cared about, someone I owed, blackmail for an unselfish purpose, from someone dying. Odd, now that she told me, I wondered how I'd missed it. The thinning hair, the bones coming out of her arms and in her face. The way she picked at her food.

"I want that book out, George. Don't want flowers, don't want grandchildren in my bedroom. Don't want to be selected for a new experimental medicine. No miracle for me, thanks. I just want that book out. In my hands."

Another fit of coughing saved me from answering. You couldn't even call it coughing; it was as if she were trying to clear her throat. It was nothing, really, in itself. You'd think twice before going to the doctor, just for that. An annoying little cough. Painless. But it was the beginning of the end.

"I always thought that I'd go first," I said. "Age before beauty."

"You got it wrong, George. Age . . . you keep getting more of it. You pile it up, year by year. And beauty . . . it gets less and less . . ."

"But I am older than you. Five years, no?"

"Yes. Remember, you used to say that when you were a senior in high school, I was in eighth grade. Like you'd be robbing the cradle if you went out with me . . ." She rubbed her cigarette in the ash tray. "Looks like I'll beat you to the finish line."

"Maybe not. I want you to fight this thing."

"Sure, George. Whatever." She glanced down at her uneaten breakfast. Is there anything less appealing than eggs, bacon, and home fries turned cold? Maybe that's how all food looked, when you were sick, maybe that's what life itself was like, when you got as sick as Louise was going to get. We stepped outside, onto the town's public square, that had a civil war memorial and benches and gardens and, because this was yet another American town gutted and hollowed out by strip malls, not a soul in sight. I doubted Louise would fight, if it were a fight she couldn't win.

▲

Dressed, for the last time, in academic regalia, I stand at the commencement podium and wait for a nicely prolonged round of applause to taper off. Derrick introduces me decently: I am a legend, a writer-professor-critic, I am a sun that rose and set, I am the waxing and waning of the moon, I am the distant stars and—humor here—I am the lightning that shot out of the sky, splintering trees and charging the air with electricity. He pumps it up; now I am applauded before I open my mouth. But there's something more: three cameras pointed my way. Reporters are seated to the side of the stage. And, while marching in, I noticed an unusual number of local people. The word is out that an unpredictable character is on stage, someone the college had attempted to suppress. People have come to see if the college will take a tongue-lashing in the name of free speech. But even if that is so, it does not describe the majority of the audience, four hundred graduates and a thousand parents, grandparents, brothers and sisters who wouldn't care if I soaked myself in kerosene and lit a match, so long as I finish quickly.

"You will notice," I begin, "that I did not carry a written speech with me to the podium. This was not my original plan. I contemplated a formal speech in which good and bad things were richly mingled, scathing comments about this place, drift, dilution and compromise, pandering and self promotion on one hand, thoughtfulness, dedication, intelligence, commitment and enduring decency on the other. All those things are here, trust me, all of them are on display, every day, every year, well represented this minute, in the crowd before me and the people on stage behind me, and in me. Enough of that. Something else came to me. Something better. Also, you'll be pleased to hear, shorter."

That earns a round of laughter and a ripple of applause. I even hear the popping of a champagne cork from among the students. As I pause—conveying the impression of deep thought—I meet the president's eyes. She nods at me, as if to say thanks, thanks for not making trouble today and I nod back, as if to say you're welcome. I wouldn't say that's the beginning of a friendship. But it is something. Perhaps it is the most we are capable of.

"More than thirty years ago, I sat with my editor at a boxing match in Los Angeles watching a Cuban lightweight engage a Chicano lightweight—both former champions—in one of the greatest, bravest performances I have ever seen. The world has forgotten them, I'm sure, but I still get excited when I remember that night. And that was when my editor thought it would amuse me to learn that a college I'd not heard of, located in a place I'd never heard of, had inquired about employing me. It was preposterous, he said, they couldn't be serious, they couldn't expect to be taken seriously. He thought I'd be amused. And I was. I laughed. We both did. And then I realized I wanted to make a change in my life, I wanted to leave Los Angeles. I wanted to be in a place where I could work on a book that was going to take me a long time. And I said yes. I came here for just a while, a semester or a year at most. And now, amazingly, I stand in front of you, more than three decades later, to say thank you and goodbye."

Another rest. My voice falters in those last words and it isn't stagecraft. Something has happened an upswelling of emotion. Get a grip, I tell myself. Tears aren't in the program.

"So I have been asking myself—as you who sit in front of me ask—how it happened, what it means when your life coincides with the life of a place you would never have guessed at and in ways you might never have imagined. With all the world and many colleges from which to choose . . ." I let my voice trail off again. I think I have them and would have them for a few more minutes, which is all I can bear.

"Do you know how it is when you hear a song somewhere and for some reason it captures you? You can't shake it. You hear it again and again, it stays in mind, you're humming it, you're hearing it all the time. That is what happened to me last week. A song came to me that connected with what I want to say today. I cannot sing this song. Neither could Rex Harrison. He performed it in 'My Fair Lady.'"

Now I wonder, as all professors wonder—and the wonders increase with age—whether I have made a reference that my listeners wouldn't catch. Rex Harrison is dead. Broadway musicals are dead. Never mind.

"It's a love song, of a kind. A love song that includes anger, exasperation and distance. Defiance even. Bittersweet love. It's called 'I've Grown Accustomed To Her Face.' Permit me . . . You see, I brought just one small piece of paper after all." I read the lyrics slowly, in a style that suggests Harrison's rendition, shouting at one moment, sharply erudite at the next, then whispering as though in a confessional. "'I've grown accustomed to her face. She almost makes the day begin . . ." I tell them how I had come to know this place. Its semesters, its seasons of bleakness and of blossoming, its moods and weather. 'Her smiles, her frowns, her ups and downs . . ." Up and downs all right. I conjure some of both. Students who discovered themselves in front of me, learned to read critically, write imaginatively. The love of language. The connection with other times and places, a connection forged in front of me, at this small place in the middle of nowhere. Memory, always the power of memory, the freemasonry of it, the ones you remember, the ones who remember you. The ups and downs. Loss of focus, loss of purpose, faddishness and opportunism, in professors, manipulation in students, and insolence. Initiatives that were market-inspired, big buildings and soft programs, focus-group propelled, that added nothing to what matters most, the transaction between students and professors.

"'. . . are second nature to me now'." After a while, the rhythms of the place are like tides, you move with them, you incorporate them. They are you. Those moments of teaching that exhilarate and surprise. And—it's like love—you can be so surprised. One day when you're prepared and primed to the nth degree . . . and nothing happens. You convey information and opinions, they take notes. It might as well be a class in dictation. On other days, you're harassed, tired, slightly hung over. And something unexpected happens, something combusts. A discovery in the text, a new reaction, a new issue. You come across a question . . . that you . . . the professor . . . have not asked before.

These are interesting questions . . . the ones that you're not sure about. And from somewhere in class, you get an answer. And as you have rescued students, because that is the professor's profession, they rescue you. That is wonderful. And it happens . . . sometimes.

"'I'm glad that she's a woman and so easy to forget'." Easy to forget. Wishful thinking. And we all think wishfully. Have any of the professors and administrators on this stage not contemplated leaving? Have we not been tempted by life in a different place, bigger, better, richer, warmer, more sophisticated? Have any of today's graduates not climbed the walls of their room, paced those prison-like dormitory halls, smelling of wax and disinfectant, hoping for a different life? I have left here many times, in my mind. But I have stayed. I came to realize that this was home to me. Often as I left it, often as I was more than ready to go, I could not wait for my return. I needed this place and could not picture myself apart from it for very long. What happened elsewhere—whatever recognition or accomplishment, triumph or failure—would not matter would not really have occurred, until it was known here. I measured my life from here.

"And now we go. I yield this podium and make way for you. We finish together. 'Accustomed to her face.' It is her face, isn't it? For 150 years, this was an all-male school yet, even then, it was alma mater. Not pater. A woman. Despite those thrusting phallic spires, those orderly row of maples, those towering oaks, those redoubtable pillars and fence posts, those hoary fraternity lodges secreted in adjoining woods . . . it's still a woman and it's the love of a woman that we're talking about. Not the only woman in the world, not your last, but a lover nonetheless.

"'Accustomed to her face.' This is what I want to say at the end. Epitaph, credo, salutation, valedictory, all rolled up in one. Remember her. That's my only advice to you. Remember her and your younger selves, as the years carry you away. Remember. To remember something is to keep it alive and to keep yourself alive as well. To forget or to be forgotten is to die. Remember. And

Remember. And remember a little bit, a writer who decided to close things out not with a sermon or an editorial but a lyric, a few words from a song. 'I've grown accustomed to her face . . .' Thank you . . ."

The applause begins as soon as I step away from the podium. It lasts a while. I bow at the students, who were on their feet, as were their parents behind them. I turn to face the faculty, nod at them, then face forward, hand over my heart. What am I hearing? A bit of relief? A little respect? Appreciation that I had finished ahead of time? Llistening to me has been these students' last assignment. But before the applause slackens I wave goodbye and go to my seat.

▲

I soldiered through the post-commencement reception. It was easy; it wasn't about me. It was for the graduates and their families, animated conversations yielding to polite regards when I passed through. I posed for a few pictures, thanked Derrick for his introduction, and left as soon as possible. Carrying my academic garb and my new sash—it came with my honorary doctorate—I wondered if I would ever wear these things again. The sense of endings was all around me. The campus was emptying out in a way that never failed to amaze me, kids tearfully embracing in front of the bookstore and the post office, saying goodbye to friends, roommates, rivals, lovers whom they knew better than they knew the waiting parents to whose custody they would—only briefly—be restored. This was the last of the zone of last things. They were done and so was I. Their future was before them and mine was in front of me. Their futures seemed almost endless. They'd be going everywhere, anywhere. The rest of my life was waiting, just down the hill. When I looked back, it would be with loyalty and love and only a little anger. I hoped that I had made the most of the talent I had in the time I was given.

AFTERWORD
by
MARK MAY

▲

"... THE TALENT I HAD AND THE TIME I WAS GIVEN." THOSE are the last words in the manuscript Billy Hoover retrieved from George Canaris' refrigerator. He wrote them shortly after his graduation address and a few days before the following weekend, a college reunion which included a celebration of his life and work. A few days later, he was dead.

I witnessed Canaris' speech, from a few rows behind him. We were seated in order of seniority and I was well to the back, barely ahead of newly-hired instructors and counselors, many of whom had slipped newspapers or crossword puzzles under their regalia. It was something to do while 400 students got their diplomas, one by one. But no one read or worked a puzzle while Canaris spoke. I was there and his account of his performance is one of those too-few things in *Gone Tomorrow* I can verify. His account is accurate and errs, if anything, on the side of modesty. George Canaris had the administration scared shitless. He turned the year into a public relations nightmare. Maybe the college benefitted in the long run—any ink is better than no ink, they say. But they wasted a lot of time and billable hours, trying to figure out how to handle him. It's not that Canaris was a troublemaker, it's that he was an unknown quantity; in his case, he carried "unknown quantity" to new heights. So there was tension and discomfort when he got up to speak in a place that had gotten soft and touchy and—though it still brags of its uniqueness—a lot more like dozens of other places than it cares to admit. People listened to him, watched him. It's as if they were seeing the last of a kind of professor that everybody used to have but no one, these days, wants to be.

What would Canaris do with himself? That's what I was asking. You work in a factory for forty years, you aren't expected to miss the place. You've put in your time and you're a retired machinist. It's different if you're a retired professor. You've lost what you were, you don't speak with that same authority, you don't get listened to the same way. You've lost that captive audience. Canaris said it himself: "to forget . . . or to be forgotten . . . is to die." Granted, that book that people talked about was supposed to be out there, somewhere, maybe. About that, I had no opinion. If it existed, or if it were any good, we'd be seeing it. If not . . . well, we'd never know what we missed, which is another way of saying we wouldn't miss it at all. And Canaris would be forgotten a little faster, but maybe that's an idea we have to face up to, all of us, when we grow up. This leaving-a-book-behind-to-keep-your-name-alive thing has gotten old. We have plenty books to remember already. What's one book more or less?

▲

It made sense that they honor Canaris on reunion weekend because it's a weekend that's all about memory and this year was about remembering Canaris, who was himself a player in the game of memories, being a writer. But I need to put some things in perspective. Canaris was one professor, English was one department. And reunion weekends attracted a ton of people who didn't care much about writing and reading. They were in other disciplines maybe or they came back to drink and bullshit, to show off the person they married to the person they hadn't, to display their children, to speculate about which one of a dwindling group might wind up as the last surviving classmate. You sensed the college moving through time, or something that time itself moved through. All of that happens every reunion weekend and, I confess, I'm a sucker for it. But Canaris' farewell happened only once. And I was invited, whether it was because I was a fellow writer or a future literary executor, I can't say. Maybe he just liked me and wanted me to be there. That's a possibility.

The opening reception, on Friday night, was at Canaris' place, down on the river. He insisted on it and since there was so little parking there, you had the choice of taking a college shuttle from up on the hill or walking. I hopped in the van and that was a mistake, because what I saw was a parade of people—solitary people, couples, groups of three or four walking through late afternoon lights which turned things golden and made it feel like a bit of pilgrimage, a kind of tribute.

There were hors d'oeuvres and drinks on the front porch and on the lawn, a caterer's kitchen and dining tables. One look at the offerings—sashimi, grilled mushrooms, satay chicken and steak tartar, curried shrimp—told me that Charles Stuckey was doing right by the old professor. And there was Canaris, in his glory, greeting people as they came down the driveway. With all that attention, I didn't want him wasting time on me, so I joined two or three locals, Billy and Lisa, his wife, and Louise Becker inside the house, making sure the caterers found what they were looking for. We were joined by Trudy Kent from alumni relations.

"So . . ." I said, "who are all those people. Can anybody tell me?"

"I was wondering the same thing," Lisa said.

"We can do this," Trudy said. We were like the crowds behind the ropes on Oscar night. "Louise . . . help me out."

"Sure . . . you start."

"Okay. That tall guy in the white suit is Charles Stuckey, the publisher, and that other one is Alva Morse, the reporter. He's Stuckey's special friend."

"And see that woman over near the river," Louise added. I saw a dark-haired woman in a kind of flower-print dress that made me happy summer was rolling in. "That," Louise continued, "is Ms. Stephanie Knox."

"She's from here," Trudy contributed.

"Not anymore," Louise said. "Not hardly."

"Is that the one George was with?" I asked. "Back in the day?"

"That's her, alright."

"Wow," Billy said. "There's a car that takes unleaded premium."

We stayed on the porch. It was fun, just watching, more fun that diving into that thickening crowd. People ate and laughed. While we were watching, Knox was joined by another dark beauty.

"I'm starting to see a pattern here," I told Billy. "Who is that one?"

"That's Mary Cantonelli," Trudy said. "Student of his. A trustee. Lives in Hawaii."

"And a close friend of the professor's," added Louise. "And . . . while we're seeing patterns . . . you all know about the actress, right? Natalie Taylor? Take a look at a picture of her sometime . . ."

With that, Louise bowed out, headed home. She said she was exhausted. Outside, Trudy made a welcoming speech on behalf of the college and of the president, whom other reunion events had prevented from attending but she sent along her best. I barely listened. I was laser-locked on those two women, Knox and Cantonelli, who'd been connected to Canaris. They weren't young, but they had style, they drew looks. They expected to be listened to and, when they didn't want to be heard, they withdrew. That's what they did now, turned their backs to the crowd and stood by the river, talking like old friends, sharing intimate knowledge.

What happened next happened fast. All at once. Trudy had just introduced Charles Stuckey, who would review tomorrow's schedule. Canaris was out on the lawn now. And, from on the road, a truck, high off the ground on oversize tires raced by, slammed on the brakes. We could hear music pounding from inside, waves of bass notes that made the truck thump and shudder, transmitting concentric circles of noise in all directions, a noise against which nothing could stand. We were stunned. Then the music stopped, and the driver leaned out from inside the cab, surveyed the scene, the catered picnic, the friends of literature, the good professor.

"Hey, the library ain't open today," he shouted. "Pisses me off."

This was humor, coming from him, this was irony being born.

"So I was looking for a good book," he continued. "Anybody help me?"

No one responded but Billy had left the porch and was walking towards him. He was walking slowly—this wasn't pursuit—but he had almost reached the road.

"Fuck you, Canary!" the kid said. This wasn't funny and it wasn't nice. It was from the heart. He flipped a finger at all of us, as if proudly gainsaying a rumor that he was missing a middle digit. The music resumed—as though the truck could not be driven without it—and the road warrior raced away. Billy turned to where his college car was parked; he was one of the few who had driven. Billy slid behind the wheel and radioed a call to security, to the sheriff.

"Suppose he lives along the road?" I asked, when he returned.

"I know the people who live along the road," Billy said. "He's not one of them."

"Do you know him?" I asked. It seemed like an honest question but Billy bristled.

"No, Mark. I don't know him. I don't know all the screw ups in the county . . ."

Outside, Charles Stuckey finished outlining tomorrow's program, which would consist of two panels, one on "Canaris:

The Writer" and the other on "Canaris: The Professor." That night there'd be a special banquet and maybe a few words from the man himself.

"Got a few words for us right now, Professor?" someone shouted out.

I expected Canaris to wave him off. But maybe the punk's party-crashing inducted him to change his mind. He stood a moment, thinking; the crowd was still recovering from the ugliness that had been directed towards him.

"We live in a fallen world," Canaris said. "You didn't have to come back to Ohio to be reminded of that, though Ohio can be relied upon to remind you. Perhaps we need to be reminded. Of waste, vulgarity, noise and anger, in our neighborhood. Yet, this is a good place. And never better than today. The idea that you have all come here means a great deal to me. You honor me. My idea of heaven—heaven on earth or elsewhere—is continuous, unexpected encounters with old friends. This evening has been a kind of heaven for me. Thank you."

▲

Appearing a few days after Canaris' death, "Canaris Last Weekend," The Sunday New York Times article by Alva Morse offers a lively and detailed account of what happened the next day. Morse's article is available, as are the college videotapes of the two panels and the closing dinner. For that reason and because I want to get things that Alva Morse was in no position to report, I'll be brief. The first session—"Canaris: The Writer" —involved three former students—two professors and a book review editor, discussing his three published works, which they agreed had a lasting claim on American readers. The problem, if there was a problem, was that these books were known quantities; everyone had read at least one of them. But The Beast was the book that no one had read. The Beast was in the air, between the lines of every speech, even—make that especially—when people loyally insisted that if Canaris never wrote another word, the three books were sufficient to guarantee his standing in the first rank of American authors. When things like that came out, I watched him, sitting there smiling, nodding non-commitally. I sensed a trace of disappointment in the audience, polite as it was. People who believed in Canaris had come a long way, hoping to be in at the beginning, not the end of something.

The afternoon session—"Canaris: the professor"—was altogether more congenial. Instead of commenting on what was published and what was not, people talked about a man who had been their teacher. The writers' testimonials had been heartfelt and a little self-serving. Witty and funny as they were, it felt like a daisy chain. The unpublished people in the audience were much more fun. One after another they arose to remember authors he'd introduced them to, not just the usual suspects but off-beat picks, Evan Connell, Kem Nunn, Katherine Dunn, Edward Allen.

"I hated him for what he said on my papers," said a stock broker up from Nashville. "My high school teachers told me I was an A student. He told me they were wrong. And that they had 'much to answer for.' After that, he showed me how to read and write."

"Boy, did I hate Rabbit Angstrom," a woman recalled. "A sexist rat and heel and loser, that was Updike's hero. By the time we finished he was like an older brother, a wacky uncle. I cried when he died. I may never get over it."

The dinner raised the bar for Ohio entertainment: goulash soup, roast duck, creamed spinach, dumplings and gravy, linzer tarts, and coffee, cognac and chocolates. Charles Stuckey had put together a meal that Canaris would relish. When dessert was served, Stuckey got up to speak. The word was out that Stuckey was anxious to obtain the so-called Beast: it was the sort of thing he could turn into a "publishing event." It had the mystery of B. Traven, of a new Salinger novel, a lost Hemingway manuscript. It would be a big deal. A bigger deal, if it were any good.

"I was your student, Professor Canaris," he said. "An arrogant little twit, dead-certain I was going to be a great writer. Greater than you, greater sooner, greater longer. Could I just say it embarrasses me . . . to remember the way I was . . ."

"We remember," Mary Cantonelli shouted out. "We're embarrassed too!"

"Hey," Stuckey fired back. "It embarrasses me to remember the way you were . . ." More laughter. And then, a shift in tone. "My memories of you are good, Professor. I'm glad I was your student. And I would love—this comes as no surprise—to be your publisher and I swear in front of this audience, in front of people I ask to hold me accountable—that when the manuscript you've been working on all these years lands on my desk it will get the recognition that it deserves and, moreover, whatever royalties you earn will be matched by my company's contribution to a scholarship fund at this college in your name. Have I made myself clear, sir? I want to publish your book and everyone who is in this room tonight wants to read it!"

It worked far better than he planned. He might have had more to say but when he stopped for breath, applause broke out . . . Mary Cantonelli was the first to stand . . . and it caught on, right away, and it went on because this was the moment everyone had been waiting for, a way of saying what they wanted, that they believed a book was there, they believed it was good, they believed in Canaris. No, they didn't want to pry, they respected his privacy and his sense of timing, the thirty years of work, if that's what it was, though anyone would have to wonder what took so long. Now they didn't have to say any of that. They just stood up and put their hands together and kept on doing it.

The look on Canaris' face! You could see it change He'd gotten a round of applause, and he'd been hearing applause all year long. He was nodding appreciatively, moved and touched, thank you very much. But this turned into something else. An insistence. A demand. A non-negotiable requirement. It wasn't a thank-you round of applause anymore. They wanted more. And everybody knew what more they wanted an encore: I saw Canaris' pleasure and approval give way to concern and then—for just a second—panic. That roomful of clapping admirers imprisoned him. He'd set a few traps lately, for the college. For John Alfano. Now he'd stepped into one himself. He nodded, acknowledging he was caught. Then, thanking Charles Stuckey, he headed towards the lectern.

"This year has turned into a series of goodbyes and this evening is the last of them and the best," he said. "You cannot spend year after year in a small college in Ohio and not have doubts about all sorts of things. But at the end I'm convinced that my choice was right and my life was good. I only need to look at you to feel assured of that. Endings are hard. One searches for the final note. Finding it and striking it. That last second of personal sound, before eons of silence. Does one wind down? Or up?"

"Up!" someone shouted. I was tempted to see who it was but I kept my eyes on Canaris.

"About my book . . . my famous book . . . My choice would have been not to part with it, not to let go of it until I am . . . oh, what is the word I'm looking for? Dead? Yes, that's it. Because I have no confidence in how books are judged or ignored."

Now he was sounding old and a little pathetic. Letting fear run the show. He must have sensed the same thing.

"Enough of this," he said. "The case you make is overwhelming . . . ." He turned to Stuckey . . ."You shall have the book."

▲

"Well," Billy said. "You've read what was in the refrigerator. So have I. What do you think?" It was a week after Billy found Canaris' account of his last year. I'd read it and liked it. But it wasn't what we were looking for.

"It's not The Beast," I said. "That's for sure. He mentions The Beast often enough but it's not The Beast."

"What would you call it?"

"The more important question is what would I call him?"

"Meaning what?"

"He could have been lying, Billy. Lying a lot and lying for a long time."

"That's what writers do."

"It's not like that," I said. "I need a beer."

I walked into Canaris' house, which had turned into my workplace. Canaris, I thought, I've grown accustomed to your house. Great place for writing. Or not writing.

"There's a ton of questions," I resumed. "Ugly questions, some of them. Does The Beast exist? Or was George Canaris a talented, pathetic, life-long fake? Was someone after him—the way he claimed . . . or was it all about publicity? If so, for what? This book we found . . . is that what we get instead of The Beast?"

"Jesus, Mark," calm down," Billy said. I'd gotten loud, sounding like a prosecutor. "There's people, real people, we can contact, check out what he says."

"Okay. I'll do that. It shouldn't take long, win or lose. Don't get me wrong, I hope we find that book. But you'd better get used to the chance that our friend was a Guiness Book of Records liar. One of the saddest cases in the history of American literature. And that he got away with a hell of a lot around here for a long time . . ."

"Professor, I saw the look on those faces when they talked about him. How they applauded him."

"Maybe that just shows how good he was at lying. Besides it's not the look on his students' faces when they wouldn't stop clapping . . ."

"No?"

"It was the look on *his* face. At the time, it puzzled me. Now I've read this thing . . . I understand it. He fell for 'the college that swallows careers.' Swallowed the Beast, too. And there he stands in front of all these years of students. And they're the ones are clamoring for the book . . ."

"I hope to hell you're wrong."

"So do I," I said. "But I don't think so. That hit and run? It's like what they said when Elvis died . . . Good career move."

▲

"Is Louise Becker in?" I asked the woman who opened the door to a brick cottage, one of a row of cottages that curved around the edge of a golf course, just behind the strip of franchise food restaurants and discount stores on the edge of town.

"Well, yes," she answered. It was a dumb question, I realized. She was a hospice worker and that meant that Louise would be at home for the rest of her life.

"I'm Mark May. I work at the college and I need to talk to her. It's important. Can she see me? Today?"

"I'll ask," she said. She came back quickly, leading me to a sunroom in the back, where Louise reposed on a chaise lounge, a tray of food at her side, undisturbed, and a cigarette in her hand.

"Hello, professor," she said, waving her cigarette my way. "She makes me smoke out here. Silly, huh? It's my house. And the damage is done."

"Would you give it up? If you had it to do over?"

"For what?" she asked. "Golf?" And sat there, not changing her mind, until she turned to me. "I've been expecting you. You're George's literary executor, right?"

"Right."

"Executed much?"

"That's why I came to you," I said. I considered telling her about the manuscript we found. But for now I wanted to concentrate on the missing Beast. So I didn't exactly lie. I dissembled.

"I didn't know Professor Canaris very well," I began. "But I liked him. He mentioned that you worked on The Beast with him, worked on it for years."

"He told you that, huh?" Louise said. "I thought it was supposed to be our little secret."

"Well, he's gone now. I suppose it doesn't matter. And all

secrets are made to be told to someone eventually. Not kept forever. Don't you think so?"

"I guess so," she nodded. "I guess it's time for telling secrets. Can't hurt him, can it?"

"No."

"Here's a secret for you, then," she said. And fell silent, as if savoring the last moment of solitary possession of what she was going to tell me now. And I was willing to wait. When I thought of all the waiting that had been done on behalf of this manuscript, it seemed bearable. How long had his friend Erwin waited? Or that audience on reunion weekend? Or the thousands, maybe hundreds of thousands who'd loved his first two novels and taken "Gerron in Karlsbad" as the promise of something great to come?

"Here's a secret for you," she repeated. "I knew George Canaris from the first day he worked here. I adored the man. Maybe it showed, maybe not. Maybe it still shows . . ."

"That's the secret?"

"No secret . . ."

"Then . . ."

"I never typed a word for him."

"What?"

"Well, I did letters of recommendation for students by the dozens, sure. Professional achievement reports for the provost, sabbatical leave reports, sure. But not fiction. Not one word of fiction."

"The Beast?" I asked. A chasm was opening beneath me. If this were true, it meant that the Beast was a lie. And not the last. It also meant that the book we had found was itself a mass of lies as well.

"The Beast. I'm telling you I never typed a word of it."

"He never asked you to . . ."

"Never."

"You never pleaded with him to release it? You didn't beg him, just lately, to let go of it?"

"Professor May, is this so hard to get? Nothing. Ever. Not one word. Ever. Got it?"

"Okay, Louise. But it turns out Professor Canaris did leave a book behind. But not the one we were all waiting for. It's the story of his last year at the college. The first scene is when the provost called him in to tell him it was over for him here. The last scene . . . the last thing he wrote . . . is graduation . . ."

"He typed it himself? That little sneak!" She wondered about that. That got me wondering too. About her. Was she . . . what she denied . . . his customary typist? For books?

"So it's the story of his last year, Louise. And you're in it. A lot. As a loyal friend and fan . . . and typist . . . anxious to see the book she'd worked on for so long in print . . . You keep coming at him . . ."

She took it well. She didn't blink or flush or waver. She reacted to my story the way she treated that uneaten, still covered delivery from Meals on Wheels on the tray next to her chair.

"Well, it's a novel then."

"You're certain?"

"Novel means it's a made-up story, right? People who never lived, things that never happened? Story that sounds true but isn't?"

"Want to read it? See how you come off?"

"No thanks," she said. "I'm not into fiction."

▲

"It's a George kind of place," Mary Cantonelli said. She walked around the room, scanned the books, the bed, the kitchen table, the view of the river.

"I like it here," I said. She nodded. I had called Mary Cantonelli in Honolulu, found she was in New York. She readily agreed to stop in Ohio on her way back to Hawaii. Now she took in the place like someone who'd come in with a realtor, someone who liked what they saw but knew it wouldn't work out for them.

"You like it a lot?" she asked me.

"Yes."

"You're single?"

"Lately."

"Then I ought to tell you what his house says. It says I want to be alone. I'll welcome visitors. I've got a porch for that. And there's room in the bed for company, now and then. But no one . . . no one . . . moves in here with me."

"I still like it," I said. "But I go back and forth. Sometimes it feels like a gift from one writer to another. Passing it on, you know? But then—when I consider the other side of things—the worst possibilities about Canaris, it feels tawdry. Here's the package: the house, the college and a career of talk about a book that no one can find. Then I'm not so sure I want to live here."

"Let's sit on the porch," Mary said. "This'll take a while." She was a brisk, confident, sexy woman. Work hard, play hard, I guessed, but good humored and gutsy either way. We stepped out into a July morning, sun lapping over the porch railing. But she turned and glanced at the room we'd just left—room-for-one, as she'd described it.

"My old professor," she said. "Okay, I think I know what's coming here. So you ask and I'll answer."

I told her how I hadn't found The Beast but that Canaris had left behind another manuscript which was full of references to The Beast and his struggles with it. And her work on it with him.

"He says you came to his rescue," I told her.

"Uh huh. Does he talk about a meeting in his office when I was a student and we were about a nano-second from getting it on?"

"He does. Are you going to sue me?"

"Hell, no!" A raucous laugh, a light in her eyes. "Wonder if they'll use it in the alumni magazine. 'Mary's Near Miss . . .'"

"About The Beast," I said. "Yes or no. Was it all a lie?"

"Not all a lie. I wouldn't say that. But I wouldn't bet there's a manuscript either. Look, it was in his head, I'm sure of that. We talked it through for years. I could give you a cast of characters, a list of locations, an outline of the plot. I could name the characters we researched, the ones we invented . . ."

"But you never saw a line of writing? That's what he claims. Those were the rules."

"Right, those were the rules. He didn't offer, I didn't ask."

"So take a guess."

"Okay, my guess is that the book doesn't exist. It did, in his mind. He was thinking about it, doing the research. That's work. He wasn't lying . . . Listen . . . uh . . . is it Mark? It got difficult. I really wanted to help him get this book out. But after a while, I wondered if he just wasn't lonely for the company of someone who still believed in him. Trouble is, after a while I didn't. It got sad . . . and a little creepy . . ."

"Then why didn't he move on to another book?"

"Excuse me? It sounds like he did."

"I mean over all the years . . ."

"Listen, Mr. May. Maybe I'm not supposed to say this. I'm a writer. But can you name any author worth reading who didn't write a bad book along the way? Take F. Scott. Is it really important that we have The Beautiful and The Damned? It could be Canaris was saving us from something. Saving himself from something too."

▲

"I've been wondering for years," Stephanie Knox said. "From the day I met him to the day I left him. And since then."

"I'm glad you agreed to see me," I told Stephanie Knox. And it was no lie. It was easy to see why Canaris was attracted: she was special. She was meant for other places. And now that she'd escaped, her early yearning for adventure was combined with a sharp sense of self, something like the sign that you see in front of for-sale houses: serious offers only. She felt like something of a player. But not with me. She checked me out and dismissed me, in a wink. I dismissed something too: the idea of telling her about the book we'd found. She didn't need to know that.

"Any friend of George's is a friend of mine," she said. "Ask anything."

"I only knew him near the end."

"He must have seen something, to make you his executor," she countered. "Does that amount to much?"

"It amounts to searching for the book he said he was working on for thirty years."

"I guess if you'd found it, you wouldn't have called me."

"I suppose not."

"Charles Stuckey is dying to have it. You must know that."

"I wish I could give it to him."

"You don't think I know where it is, do you?"

"No. But you were with him for years. So I want your opinion. On whether I'm looking for something that exists."

"I knew about the project. I knew about it before I met him. He told me just enough about it so that I'd respect his wishes. And keep my distance. He'd say he was working on it . . ."

"At home?"

"Yes. I never moved in with him. I visited lots. And we traveled a ton."

"You never snooped?"

"No. When we were there, we were together. And we were plenty busy . . ." She smiled at the memory. "Very busy."

Yes, I know. Everything was on the table: I almost said it, what I remembered from the book. What Canaris had told me. Let your imagination be an equal opportunity employer.

"We wore each other out, those early years. I think The Beast took a back seat for a while. But it was always there. Look, you're with a writer, you expect a writer will always be somewhere else in his head. And he was. Always drifting off. That's evidence of something, isn't it? But that's all I know. I don't know what was written down."

"No one does."

"It got to be a joke around town. He got to be a joke too. I couldn't stand that. So I left. I began to think maybe he wasn't a winner, not in the long run. And I play to win . . ."

"None of my business. But would you have married him?"

"Oh, sure," she said, snapping her fingers. "Like that. Divorced him, too, eventually. He knew that we were headed in different directions. He was tied into this place and I was outward bound. We had our fun though, for a while. No regrets."

"If the book were . . . a phantom, would you regret that?"

"Yes. He took such shit. More of it each year. Turned him into a sad case. I'd like those people to know they were wrong. That's if they were."

"Were they right?"

"I hope not . . . but . . . That damn book. Listen Mark. I had a bad marriage. And a troubled kid. He might have done better if George had let him in. *We* could have made it. But there was no room for him. And no room for me, not beyond a certain point. And now, if it turns out that it was all . . . talk . . . it was all for nothing . . . one big nothing . . . the selfishness of it is staggering."

▲

"You celebrating something?" Billy Hoover shouted from the doorway.

"The end of my literary executorship. Piss on the fire, call in the dogs, the hunt is over." I waved at the house that I could no longer picture living in. A womb of fraud. And I couldn't picture returning to the sad little bungalow where Willard Thrush had found the two of us happily watching the shopping channel a few weeks before. "I'm out of here."

"This house?"

"This college."

"Okay," Billy said. I thought we were friends but, I had to admit, he took the news of my going very much in stride. He sat at the desk where Canaris didn't write and just looked at me, as if it were my turn to say something. I waited him out.

"Let's take a break," he said. "You and me."

▲

We joined a long line of cars and trucks waiting to pay five dollars to park in a cow pasture. Down below, I saw a clutch of hard-used trailers, a nomad camp of a tribe that grilled Italian sausages, hamburgers, onions, doughnuts, french fries in hot tubs of grease at one county fair after another.

"You've got to be kidding," I said. Already the whiff of midway came to me, fat and grease and sugar. "This," I said, "is hell. And you know it."

"You do me a favor, I do you one. Snob."

We passed a parking lot that was a staging area for a parade of old-time tractors and I had to admit it was something, these contraptions out of The Grapes of Wrath and the ancients on top of them, who were either thin and wizened, all bones and veins, or sumo wrestlers in dungarees. Billy knew a lot of them and paused to talk. This wasn't the kind of place you breezed through. Or he wasn't a breeze-through kind of guy. It was impressive, those farmers and tractors, as long as they stuck together, neither one of them would die. Some of the farmers even knew me. They worked in maintenance. "How you doin', Professor?" They shook my hand. Then we were on the midway, a binge-eating fast food orgy. We hastened to the livestock barns, where poultry, pigs, goats, sheep, rabbit were being judged and auctioned: the smell of grease gave way to that of manure. It was an improvement. Aromatherapy. With evening rolling in, we found seats in the grandstand, among people inhaling cotton candy and corn dogs. Down in front, a dirt track curled around inside a stockade, where I saw mounds of dirt, mud puddles and a finish line. From a booth near the finish line, a hearty fellow who represented a local car dealer welcomed us to the county fair's "tough truck" contest. And so it began. One by one, trucks and jeeps and vans careened around the track, powering up the hills, crashing down into puddles. They lost hubcaps and bumpers and sometimes a door, they billowed smoke, they choked to death in troughs of mud, they died on the course or collapsed across the finish line and the worse the disaster, the louder the cheers. The gathering of aging farmers and tractors inspired respect: reverence for tradition, equipment carefully maintained decades of harvest and husbandry on farms that passed from generation to generation. That was one version of Ohio country living. And this was its opposite: reckless, random I-don't-give-a-shit destruction, stupidity incarnate. I'd hate myself in the morning, but I sat there fascinated. That was when Billy leaned over, during a brief lull when they were pulling a disabled pick up out of the mud.

"Louise Becker died yesterday," he said. "Service is the day after tomorrow."

"I'm sorry," I said. "But she was in bad shape. I think she was ready."

"She was ready alright," he said. "I think you should go to the service. The viewing."

"The viewing."

"You mean . . ."

"Open casket. I'll pick you up."

"I hate funerals."

"You're not supposed to like them. But you go."

He studied the race track and, seeing what he'd been waiting for, pointed to a contestant revving up for a run. So far, the other vehicles had been junkers, more or less. This was a black truck, high off the ground, that I knew. I'd seen it at Canaris' place, out on the road, revving and blaring music, while some delinquent mocked the "Canary."

"You knew the driver?" I asked.

"Sure. I lied to you," Billy admitted. "He's a mean little shit and a natural born liar. I wouldn't trust him to give an ambulance driver directions to a hospital. But his father got fired from a maintenance job at the college. His mother worked in the college kitchen. He hated the place and that 'jailbait' line Canaris flipped him off with really festered."

The race started and I'll say this much: Jailbait could drive. Yes, the whole thing was stupid, destructive, etc., no doubt about it: an American Studies seminar could churn out a shelf of papers about how it epitomized a failed culture, a super-power in decline. But God, he was good! The way he took on those humps, hurtled water barriers, cut curves, always close to being out of control, but not quite, and he blew through the course, aced it, ate it up and when he finished with a first place time and a free set of tires or something, he jumped out of his truck, hauled himself up on the roof and executed a low, mocking bow in the direction of a pumped-up, I'll-be-damned Buckeyes.

"I told Canaris I knew him," Billy said. "You . . . sorry, Mark . . . but you didn't need to know. Canaris said he wanted to meet the kid. They'd gotten off on the wrong foot, et. cetera."

"Did it ever happen . . ."

"No. Canaris died. Anyway, next week he's joining the Army . . . That make sense to you?"

The kid was down off the hood, his great moment ebbing away. Now it was other racers surrounding him, high-fives and hot damns, beer and pizza to follow.

"Yeah sure," I answered. "I'm all for getting out . . ."

▲

I followed Billy down the line that had come to pay its respects and I wondered what the no-nonsense Louise Becker would have thought of her own funeral. The mourners were like the customers at one of those eat-all-you-can smorgasbord operations that had come to town lately: "carving three meats nightly," they advertised. Tonight they were serving Louise. She lay there, eyes closed, hair nicely done, an annoyed expression on her face, as though death, or life, had ticked her off. I assumed that once we'd nodded and moved on, we'd be out of there. But Billy pointed me to a seat in the last row of folding chairs.

"I keep telling you," he whispered, "around here you don't just pass through. You stick around."

"Like the county fair," I said.

"Right."

After all comers had a peek at Louise, a minister arose. I'd expected that. Louise was surely skeptical, but this wasn't her show. Her daughters called the shots. The man who spoke was here at their request and what he said was consoling to them. He described Louise affectionately, her cigarettes, her sarcasm, her straightforward approach to life. He quoted her admonition to sniffling daughters and whiny grandchildren. "If you want to cry, I'll give you something to cry about." Smiles and chuckles. Louise had been a friend to impoverished neighbors and famous—unnamed—professors "out at the college." So far, so good. But then he assured us she was in heaven now and the heaven he described was no misty enterprise, it wasn't essences and auras, it wasn't some kind of ineffable spiritual aftermath. It was life in Ohio: the sequel. It was instant replay, it was Louise in a heaven just like home, only with no need to water the plants, no line at Walmart checkout, and gasoline back down to a dollar a gallon. Louise had kept her part of the deal with God and now God would deliver on his end in heaven. So why cry? Louise was as happy as a clam; it was as if Publishers Sweepstakes van, not a hearse, had pulled up her driveway.

"Poor Louise," I said, once we were back in Billy's truck.

"There she goes . . ." Billy confirmed.

"I was really hoping . . . though I know better . . ."

"I know. Can't blame you."

"It's about all of us . . . about who we are. What we can do. What kind of place this is."

"I guess . . ." he said. He wasn't headed to campus, but I didn't care where we were going. "You got involved, didn't you?"

"It was as though he were meant to send me a message. Whether I should go or stay."

"And the message is . . ."

"Go . . ." I conceded. "Or stay and spend the rest of my life wondering what might have been. Or spend the rest of my life promising to devise something that never comes. Leaving a 250-page apology behind."

▲

That night was going to be my last in the professor's house. I put things in order, left behind notes for the crew that would come to pack things up. I cleaned house and assembled all of my own things that I'd brought down from campus during my weeks as George Canaris' literary executor. There was quite a lot: bit by bit, I'd been moving in. My last night. There was no way I could live in that house or stay on that campus.

"All set?" Billy asked when he pulled in the next morning.

"Absolutely."

"Got any coffee inside?" he said. "Man needs coffee before he does some heavy lifting."

"There's not much to lift," I said. "I'm so out of here . . ."

"I still need coffee," Billy said. I went inside to start the coffee, wishing I had instant. But I found ground coffee and filter and went back outside to find Billy relaxing in my rocker, stretching luxuriously.

"Anyone would miss this porch," he said. "Keep your eyes on the road and the river and the college . . ."

I didn't answer. Everything he said was true.

"I'll get the coffee," I said. No milk, but Billy liked it black and so did I.

"Literary executor," he said when I handed him his cup. "One syllable away from executioner. That's what Louise said you felt like."

"When?"

"When I dropped by the day before she passed. But I looked

in on her every week at least. She said you were all business. A representative of the college. And you were in such a rush. There's a difference, Mark, between people and homework."

"Sorry."

"She talked. I listened and learned. You don't show up with a list of questions that you cross off after you've asked them. She wanted that book out, professor."

"Are you kidding? She told me she never typed a word on it. It didn't exist."

"She gave me the book. Hard copy and discs. Hey, could I have some more coffee . . ."

"Where is it? Give it to me! You should have given it to me right away! How long have you had it? Where do you have it?"

"Could I have some more coffee? I'm asking nice."

"I want that manuscript now."

"Stop rushing."

"No kidding, Billy. I insist."

"What you going to do? Call security?"

"I'm literary executor. You're not."

"Up yours, professor," Billy said, rising out of his chair. "I'll get coffee someplace else. And you'll get the book when I'm finished reading. If I like it . . ."

▲

When Billy left, I sat on the porch and calmed down. And laughed at myself, eventually. I drank the coffee I couldn't drink while he was here. He'd be back, when he finished reading. I never got around to moving out of the house, by the way. It's my house now, the whole package, the smell of wood, the sound of rain on the roof, the ups and downs of the river, the coming of the seasons, the passage of the years. If it comes to living with someone else, I may need another house. But I'll never let go of this. It's hard to say when it began, my possession of this house or its possession of me, but I suppose it happened that first morning, searching through Canaris' desk and book shelves and it extended to the moment that Willard Thrush sold the place to me for half its market value. But I will always date my ownership to the morning Billy returned, a few days after our argument, stepping across the dewy grass, saying something about what a hot day it was going to be, "a real steamer." He climbed the steps and placed Canaris' manuscript in my hands. I felt better about everything. And I was glad that Billy Hoover had gotten to read the manuscript before me.